Evie Blake is a pen name for the author Noelle Harrison. Noelle was born in England, moved to Ireland in 1991, and now lives in Norway. She has written several plays and four novels.

VALENTINA

Evie Blake

headline

First published in Great Britain in 2012 by HEADLINE REVIEW
An imprint of HEADLINE PUBLISHING GROUP

1

Cataloguing in Publication Data is available from the British Library

ISBN 978 0 7553 9887 4

Typeset in Sabon by Avon DataSet Ltd, Bidford-on-Avon, Warwickshire

Printed and bound in Great Britain by
Clays Ltd, St Ives plc

HEADLINE PUBLISHING GROUP
An Hachette UK Company
338 Euston Road
London NW1 3BH
www.headline.co.uk
www.hachette.co.uk

For Barry, you are my all.
And for the Valentina inside every one of us.

$\mathcal{B}$elle

THEY CARRIED HER NAKED DOWN TO THE WATER'S EDGE. They laid her down upon the still warm sand, her feet facing the sea. She could feel it lapping against her ankles as if it was another lover leaving icy kisses upon her toes.

The night was moonless, but a few stars gleamed, tiny pins of hope, tears within her heart. It was so dark she couldn't see their faces any more. She felt as if she were spinning out of the real world and into another cosmos. A place inhabited by her fantasies. Her companions had become something other than mere men. They were shadow creatures pulsing with their need, their desire. Although she was out in the open, by the sea, she could just as easily be inside a dark cave or a blacked-out room. She was a little frightened, but not enough to want to stop. She was becoming like them: her other self.

*V*alentina

VALENTINA PUSHES HERSELF UP ON TO HER ELBOWS AND gazes at her lover. Six months they have been living together. She leans over and carefully arranges her arm across Theo's back. She loves to do this while he is sleeping, when he doesn't know how she likes to imagine the two of them together, and all that could be possible. Tenderly she strokes his flawless skin, letting herself express a rare moment of affection. It is a gesture she is careful never to make when Theo is actually awake.

Valentina examines her flaxen whiteness against the sallow colouring of Theo Steen, and considers what a perfect contrast the two of them are. She is as pale and fine boned as her beloved twenties icon Louise Brooks. He is dark skinned, more sultry than any Latin lover she has ever known, yet with disturbingly bright blue eyes. It would make more sense if it were she who was dark. She is after all the Italian, while Theo is from New York, his parents Dutch immigrants. She doesn't know much about his background, but it appears very different from hers. He is close to his parents, both of them, and to Valentina's eyes his childhood was charmed. So much attention and expense lavished upon him. Theo is an accomplished cellist, equestrian and fencer, as well as speaking a myriad of languages. He could have gone into any profession he chose. He is one of those men she thought would irritate her. A privileged high-achiever who doesn't need to worry about making a living, and can indulge full-time in his passion – the study and analysis of modern art. Yet she did not dump him at the first opportunity, as she thought she might; instead here he is in her bed, lost in the innocence of sleep right beside her. He is *living* with her.

Valentina looks down at her sleeping lover. Theo is lying on his stomach, his head turned away from her. She wonders where his dreams take him. She wonders if he will wake with the memory of her touch upon his skin. Last night she wanted to make him come so much, and yet strangely she had no desire to have an orgasm herself. This is not usual for her, not very Valentina, she thinks. Even now she is not demanding morning sex. At some point does the passion fade? If you took away the sexual desire between her and Theo, would there be nothing left? Strangers before their union; and strangers again afterwards. Is it time to end it? *No, not yet*, a voice begs inside her head, and she tries to swallow her anxiety. She is panicking unnecessarily. This is just all so new to her, to be cohabiting.

She has never shared her apartment with anyone else, not

since her mother left. It still startles her how easily it all fell into place, the fact of Theo moving in. She knows why she asked him. It was a knee-jerk reaction to her mother's warning. Is he using her? Instinctively she rejects the suggestion. He was so hesitant about accepting her offer. Asked her several times if she was sure. There *is* something different about him. Already he has seen her at her lowest, and he didn't leave.

Valentina knots the end of the sheet around her finger, pulls it tight. A ring of white cotton pinching her flesh, making her bite her lip. It's because he doesn't take anything for granted, she thinks; despite his easy life, he never stops trying to please her.

She lies back down on the bed and smiles up at the ceiling, studying each glinting crystal of the chandelier as she dwells on last night. She tentatively runs her tongue over her lips. She can still taste him. She savours the saltiness of her lover as she recalls how she caressed him with her mouth, pushing him as far as he could go, not stopping despite his plea to be inside her. She would not allow it. She wanted everything to be focused on him. And so she kept on going: licking, teasing with her teeth, flicking her tongue around his length and squeezing his velvet hardness tight between her lips. She needed to feel his abandon inside her mouth. His vulnerability, and her power. She had taken him over the edge. And when Theo cried out her name, it was like a flare to her heart. Burning her and yet warming her at the same time, filling her with the dual sensations of fear and satisfaction. How could that be? Normally she doesn't like her lovers to speak, let alone cry out. She always insists on making love in silence. She hates false proclamations of love, uttered in the heat of passion. Yet Theo called to her, and deep down inside her there was an answering echo, despite her conscious denial. Now the salty flavour of him lingers still upon her lips. No wonder she dreamt of the sea. She closes her eyes and pushes away unwanted images, her smile fading. But they resurface, these disjointed sensations from her dream. Sinking under water, unable to swim up to the light; darkness, suffocation.

'Hey, what's wrong?'

She opens her eyes. Theo is lying on his side, his head resting on his hand, his clear blue eyes studying her.

'I had a bad dream last night.'

He pulls her towards him, and she lets him fold his arms around her. She closes her eyes and feels his chin as he rests it on the top of her head.

'Do you want to tell me about it?' he asks, his voice muffled against her hair, but she doesn't reply, not immediately, and he doesn't push her. It feels so good to be held in her lover's arms; she doesn't want to take them back to her nightmares, ruin a fresh new day with her baggage.

'No,' she says.

'Okay, darling.' He kisses the top of her head. The endearment trips off his lips so easily. Can he really mean it? She finds it hard to do the same, the words sticking in her throat. *Darling.* She stiffens in his arms, wanting now to push away from him. Theo gently unravels his body from around her, as if sensing her need for distance.

'I'll make some tea,' he says, getting out of bed, studiously avoiding eye contact. She watches him in all his glorious nakedness as he strides across the room. He wraps her silk dressing gown around himself, but it only adds to his manliness, emphasising the masculine contours of his body. She feels a stirring below her navel, deeper, deeper, as she watches him walk out the door. Why did she chill in his arms? Now she would like to make love.

She glances at the clock. It's already after seven. She should be getting up; she has a busy day ahead, yet still she cannot stir from the sanctuary of their bed. She yawns and stretches, awaiting Theo's return with the tea. She is glad she didn't blot this morning with her narcissist fears.

Valentina isn't fond of the past. She has never understood the obsession amongst her contemporaries with relationship transparency, the need to dredge up your personal history and expect your lover to share it. It bemuses her how so many young women want to manipulate their boyfriends through pity. The last thing she wants is to be a victim. No, it is better to never look back, always maintain a little mystery. She believes you should keep your secrets to yourself. That has always been her motto. And yet . . .

She can't get Gina Faladi's words out of her head. Said in all innocence, of course. Gina is a sweet person, if a bit too submissive in Valentina's opinion. She has seen the way she lets her boyfriend, Gregorio, boss her around. God knows what he is like under the covers. Yet despite this, Gina is one of the best make-up artists Valentina has ever worked with. Last week they flew to Prague together to do a fashion shoot for *Marie Claire*. It was on the way home, after a couple of glasses of wine on board the flight, that Gina asked her the question that now keeps circling inside her head like a big black cat.

Where does he go?

That was what Gina said. Valentina was about to reply that she had no idea, and so what, she and Theo didn't do jealousy, but when she saw Gina's eyebrows beginning to arch, she changed her mind.

Work. She took a sip of her red wine. *Going to exhibitions. Meeting artists. Buying art*, she expanded vaguely. A good excuse, and who knows, possibly true. But the fact of the matter is that Valentina has absolutely no idea where her lover disappears to once a month and for several days at a time. Yes, there have been articles and reviews, and before he met her, two books had been published, one on German expressionism and one on futurism in Italy in the twenties, but there is not nearly the volume of work one would expect from such a globetrotting art critic. And what is he doing in Milan? His part-time lecturing at the university hardly provides a good income. Surely he could get a better position in a university back in America? Yet when she asked Theo why he was in Italy, he avoided answering her, waving his arms around like a true Italian and stating vaguely that it was where he needed to be right now. Every day she expects him to tell her he is going home. And yet here he is, still based in Milan nearly a year after she met him.

In the beginning, Valentina didn't care where Theo went. In fact during the first couple of months of living together she looked forward to his little disappearances. She couldn't help doubting her rash offer, and blamed her mother's words for pushing her into making it.

'Don't let him possess you; that's what they all want to do. And for God's sake don't move in together.'

As usual her mother had taken the wind out of her sails. What had induced Valentina to call her anyway? She had been on some kind of a high, after the first few exciting weeks with Theo, and she had had this foolish urge to share it with her mother. She had even sat up half the night to wait for a good time to call her in the States. Yet of course she should have known better. Instead of being happy for her, all her mother could see were the negatives.

'Valentina,' she warned, 'you and I, we're not able to give ourselves up totally to just one man. We need space. I learnt that the hard way, honey. Don't rush into anything.'

Her advice made Valentina furious. She was *not* like her mother, who was vain and self-centred, an attention-seeker and unable to share, even with her own children. She had to prove her wrong. So that very evening, much to Theo's astonishment, she invited him to move in with her. Why not?

His landlord had just given him notice, and he needed to find a place to live anyway. Her apartment was huge and cost her nothing, since it belonged to her mother. They were to be flatmates, she told him, who happened to have sex together. The incongruity of her proposition made him laugh and call her a crazy woman. Even so, he accepted.

Yet if she is honest with herself, Valentina has to admit that she is afraid her mother could be right. She finds it hard getting used to compromising. She and Theo rarely argue, and they have similar tastes in music, food and art, yet it is the little things that get to her. She likes the bedroom door open at night, and a light on in the hall, whereas Theo prefers complete darkness and a closed door. She likes silence when she works, and he plays music. Usually it is something they both like, but occasionally he puts on music from the eighties that her mother loved – Joy Division, The Cure – way too loud so that she can hear it even when she is in her studio or in her darkroom developing pictures. It always makes her grit her teeth. And sometimes he talks too much. He is careful not to talk about himself, or push for too many questions about her mother (something other lovers all end up doing, which puts her off them instantly), but he is obsessed with discussions. It could of course be on art, or a film they might have just seen, and that is fine. But Theo also loves to get stuck into talking about current affairs, economics or history. He is constantly quizzing her on Italian politics. What do people think of Mussolini now? What happened to her family during the Second World

War? Valentina has no interest. She had a stomach full of politics when she was a child. Her mother's bedtime stories of what had happened to her father's family during the war were enough to put her off for life, as well as her mother arguing over the rights and wrongs of communism with her brother Mattia, on the rare occasions she saw him. Somehow she equates the clash of her parents' ideologies with the reason why her own father left all those years ago. Valentina doesn't like idealists. Those who neglect their own families for the sake of the common good. Theo seems more pragmatic; how can he not be with his upbringing? And yet when he starts talking about the world and hope for change, it makes her edgy. Does he notice the tightness around her mouth as she sets it in an uncommunicative line, the clench of her jaw as he pushes her to give an opinion? It is no coincidence that usually the very next day Theo will announce that he is heading off on a work trip, as if he knows she needs to be on her own.

Valentina has always been used to solitude. She grew up as if she was an only child, since Mattia was thirteen and away at school by the time she was born. Her father left before she was old enough to remember him. Even Mattia claims he doesn't know where he is. So it was just her and her mother, who taught her from an early age to be self-sufficient. When she was very young, Valentina's mother took her with her on her photographic assignments, and the long hours spent waiting turned her into an avid reader.

Once Valentina was thirteen, her mother left her behind in

Milan, claiming she didn't want to disrupt her education, but Valentina suspected that it was because she didn't want her teenage daughter cramping her style. All the men loved Tina Rosselli. She was an icon in her world of glamour and style. To her credit, she never hid her age, but to be accompanied by a glaringly younger version of herself was a little too much for her vanity to bear. Thus Valentina would spend whole weeks at a time on her own in the apartment, her only company her mother's sulky cat, Tash. She remembered bringing Gaby back with her one Friday after school, and her friend's complete astonishment when she realised that Valentina had been alone all week. It was a fact she was careful not to broadcast when she was in school.

'But who looks after you?' Gaby asked her, wide eyed with pity.

'I don't need anyone to look after me,' Valentina replied haughtily.

'Do you do everything yourself?' Gaby asked her. 'Your clothes?'

Valentina couldn't help but notice her friend looking down at her crumpled school skirt and blouse. The nuns were always telling her off for her messy uniform, a criticism she was careful never to relay to her mother, who was fiercely proud of her appearance and always left Valentina strict instructions to be neatly turned out.

'I don't care about how I look,' she said nonchalantly. 'It's only school.'

Gaby gingerly hung her satchel on the back of a kitchen chair. The table was littered with unwashed cups and a couple of sticky plates.

'So do you cook for yourself?' she asked Valentina.

'Sort of.' Valentina sashayed over to the fridge, feeling very grown-up. 'Are you hungry?'

'Always!' Gaby grinned at her. 'Hey, let's eat everything we're not supposed to. I'll go to the bakery while you cook.'

Valentina limply hung over the fridge door, and stared inside. There was a jar of pesto, a block of Parmesan and a container of rigatoni. That was it. Gaby joined her by the fridge. She put her arm around her friend's waist when she saw its paltry contents.

'Is that it?' she whispered in horror.

Valentina couldn't reply. She was seeing the inside of her fridge with her friend's eyes. She felt so ashamed of her mother.

'Mama's not that into food . . .'

Gaby squeezed her waist.

'I can cook something nice for you. My mother taught me how.'

Valentina bit her lip. She loved Gaby, but sometimes she couldn't help feeling a little jealous. Gaby's mother was one of those traditional Italian mamas. Plump, doting, always feeding you. It was why, Gaby complained, she was twice the size of Valentina. Yet Valentina admired Gaby's budding curves. She herself was still tall and narrow, with no shape at all. Her mother had never taught her to cook.

'Okay, I'll go to the bakery and buy us some little cakes,' Valentina offered.

'Get a selection, four different ones each!' Gaby called as Valentina went out the door.

Not only did Gaby cook for her, a sumptuous meal of pesto and rigatoni, with a rich tomato sauce (where did she find the ingredients in the chaos of the kitchen cupboards?), but by the time Valentina returned with the cakes, she had also swept the floor, washed the dishes and wiped the kitchen table. Her friend's desire to care for her filled Valentina with awe, for she knew she would not think of doing the same for her.

'Aren't you lonely?' Gaby asked her as she polished off the tomato sauce, licking the spoon hungrily.

'Never,' Valentina said, sitting back and feeling the rare satisfaction of a full belly. 'I like being on my own. Although I wouldn't mind having you as my cook.'

This love of being in her own company has never gone away. So until Gina's fateful words, Valentina had actually looked forward to Theo's short absences. Only two, at the most three, days away. Long enough to relish her solitude and to miss him, but not too long to worry about where he is or what he is doing. The fact that he has never offered an explanation demonstrates that he believes they are above the possessiveness others can get bogged down by. They really are flatmates first, lovers second. He never asks her what she has been up to.

Valentina gets out of bed and draws back the curtains, opening the French window slightly. She is cooled by the autumnal breeze, yet even though her skin is prickling from the chill, she likes to remain naked. She closes her eyes and the wind feels like a hand stroking her, all the way from her forehead, down her cheeks and neck to her throat and chest. She feels her nipples harden as the temperature drops inside the room, and wind licks between her legs. She can hear the constant stream of traffic through Milan, the heartbeat of the city, and yet she catches what peace there is as well. She visualises random images of tranquillity: a pigeon taking flight in the cloisters of Sant'Ambrogio, a boat drifting down the Naviglio canal, an empty swing in Parco Sempione rocking in the breeze. She smells the dying leaves, imagines them spinning off the trees on Via De Amicis. She likes this time of year in Milan. The city has finally cooled after the heavy, humid summer. August can be a nightmare, forty degrees and yet skies as grey as lead. Everyone tries to get away. This year she and Theo escaped to Sardinia for three weeks. Just as hot, yet the sea breezes lifted the oppressiveness of it.

She opens her eyes and feels such a longing to be back in Sardinia, outside in nature, naked on the warm sand, smelling the salty tang of the sea washing over her. As she walks across the bedroom, she imagines wading through the balmy sea. She feels the weight of her nakedness and catches a glimpse of her bottom as she passes the mirror. Men have always admired her behind. She has to admit she is rather proud of it. After being such a skinny teenager, she was pleased when her curves finally developed. She hates to see other women ashamed of their bodies. Struggling into swimming costumes behind towels at the beach; self-conscious and eyes averted when trying on clothes in changing rooms. Can they not see how beautiful they are, in all their diversity, within their curved contours: the creamy velvet of their skin, breasts of all shapes and sizes, soft stomachs, broad hips, voluptuous thighs? The only other women she knows who are as open as she is about nudity are the models she photographs. Those stick-thin girls are past any kind of self-consciousness. Sometimes when she sees models who are obviously anorexic it makes her tense, almost angry. She is, as all her friends will tell you, one of the most non-judgemental people you will ever meet. Yet anorexia brings back ghosts for Valentina. Images of her mother she would like to forget.

By the time Theo returns to the bedroom with a tray laden with teapot, cups and saucers, Valentina is back in bed, sitting up expectantly, a pillow stuffed behind her back against the iron bedstead. This is one of the advantages of living with someone. Just by making her a pot of tea, Theo makes her feel cherished.

Her lover carefully places the tray in the middle of the bed, and climbs back into bed beside her.

'Will you be mother?' he asks her.

The English phrase amuses her. The last thing she could

imagine her mother ever doing is pouring tea out of a teapot like a duchess.

'Of course,' she says, looking at Theo from under her lashes. 'As you know, I like to be in charge sometimes.'

He grins back at her as she picks up the teapot and begins to pour tea into his cup. As she does so, Theo leans forward and cups her breasts, one in each of his hands.

'Don't want my property getting splashed by hot tea,' he explains, winking at her.

She swats him off nonchalantly, yet a part of her likes this. She leans back against the pillow, nursing her hot tea between her hands, and wonders if they are the image of an old married couple, sitting side by side in bed drinking Earl Grey tea for breakfast. Well at least we're naked, she thinks comfortingly.

'Are you okay now?' Theo asks her.

She nods, sipping the tea. The warm liquid comforts her, and yes, she can honestly say that her night-time fears are banished for today. Theo puts his cup of tea down on the bedside table, leans over towards her and kisses her on the neck, just under her ear. It tickles, but also sets her heart racing a little.

'I have something to ask you,' he whispers, his breath lifting her hair.

Involuntarily she stiffens with unease. No, not now; she doesn't want to talk about it this morning.

'I have to get up. I want to develop some pictures before I go on the shoot,' she says, placing her cup back down on the tray.

'It's just a little question, Valentina, don't worry.' She looks at him, and he is smiling at her, his eyes brimming with bemusement. Is he mocking her?

'Well, go on then,' she commands.

'My parents are coming to Europe,' Theo says. 'They are going to Amsterdam first to visit my grandparents but then they thought they would come and see me, us, here in Milan.'

'They know about *me*?'

'Of course they know about you!' he laughs. 'We've been living together for six months, Valentina. They are dying to meet you.'

She looks at him in horror. He is completely relaxed, as if this is something of small consequence. The fact that his parents are coming to Milan. That he wants her to meet them. Her mouth dries up for a minute and she is unable to speak.

'They're not coming until the end of November,' he continues. 'I know it's ages away, but I wanted to give you fair warning.' He hesitates, beginning to notice the expression on her face. 'I know you're not keen on family stuff.'

She shakes her head vehemently.

'No, Theo, I'm sorry. I can't meet your parents.'

'What?' He looks astounded. His mouth drops open in shock.

'I told you this before. This is how I am,' she says stiffly, pulling back the covers, straining to get out of bed. Theo catches her arm, restraining her.

'Valentina,' he says softly. 'Really, it's nothing to be worried about. They are nice people. I've told them so much about you. They just want to meet you.'

She whips her head around.

'You told them all about me!' she spits.

'Of course I did. You're my girlfriend.' Theo looks wounded.

'That's the first I knew about it,' she says cruelly.

Theo's forehead creases in confusion.

'Well what are you then, if you're not my girlfriend? We're living together, Valentina. We've already been through—'

'Don't say it . . . I told you not to mention it again . . .'

'But Valentina . . .'

She holds her hand up, stops him before he starts to speak.

'I am your lover, Theo. And that role is something very different from a girlfriend. The term "girlfriend" implies that we have some kind of vested relationship, a possible future. "Lover" is a more transitory term. It is a temporary condition.'

'Christ, Valentina!' Theo exclaims. 'You are an infuriating woman.'

'Remember, Theo,' she says calmly, and it is a good feeling, this sensation of being in control, 'when you moved into this apartment, I told you it was convenient. It suited us both. But I also told you that it wasn't going to be for ever, remember?'

She listens to her voice. It is outside of herself, and she is unpleasantly reminded of her own mother speaking. *Don't let him possess you.*

18

'Valentina, I am not asking you to make any big commitment. It's just my parents. I'd like you to meet them, that's all.'

'I'm sorry, Theo,' she says, climbing out of bed and looking down at him. 'I don't want to. They can stay here, but I'll go away. You'll have the place to yourselves. It's much better that way.'

Theo looks her up and down in disbelief. Just his gaze causes her nipples to harden, and she can't help noticing his reaction to her naked body in return.

'It's not better that way,' he says softly, entreating her with his rich blue gaze. A part of her wants to give in, to fall back into the bed, sink into his arms and comply. Yet her terror dominates. She can't bear the thought of meeting Theo's parents. It brings her too close to him, too much into his world. And if that happens, how will she find her way out again when it ends, because surely one day they will tire of each other? Nothing lasts for ever. She sighs deeply and turns away from him, picks up her dressing gown from where he discarded it on the floor and puts it on, tying it tightly around her waist.

'I can't talk about this right now. I have to get ready. I've a lot to do today.' She wanders over to the dressing table and picks up her hairbrush, pulling it listlessly through her hair. She watches Theo getting out of bed, defeat still clear in his features, and she feels guilty. It's time to change the subject.

'Do you want to go to Antonella's opening tonight?' she asks, trying to sound more upbeat. Theo pauses in the doorway of the bedroom, towel in hand.

'Sorry, I can't. I have to go away. I've another job.'

'Again?'

The word slips out. Deadly. Valentina wishes she could snatch it back. She turns away quickly, yet she can still see his face in the mirror. His expression is impassive now.

'Do you not want me to go away?' he asks.

She backtracks furiously.

'No, of course I don't mind. It's just a surprise. I didn't know you were going away *today* . . .' Her voice trails off and suddenly she feels foolish, exposed.

'Would you like me to cancel?' he asks, leaning against the doorway and looking at her with interest.

'No, of course not,' she snaps crossly. 'I was just wondering where you're going. It's not that big a deal.' She tries to sound indifferent, focuses on arranging her hair.

'Are you sure you don't want me to stay?' he asks. She can feel the heat of his gaze, although she still refuses to catch his eye.

'No, I told you, I don't care,' she says harshly. 'I was just curious, that's all.' She softens her voice.

Theo drops his towel and walks over to stand behind her. As he leans over her and strokes her hand, she can feel his erection pushing against her silk-clad back. She knows he is trying to entice her to turn around and touch him. Yet she resists.

'I always thought you weren't that interested in where I go or what I do,' he says quietly.

'You're right. I don't know why I asked you really. I like mysteries,' she explains, trying to keep her voice light. 'They keep things from getting boring.'

'I see.'

He spins her around on her stool and he is smiling at her as if he knows something she doesn't.

'What is it?' She pushes her finger into his belly, which is so firm it almost springs back. What art critic has a stomach like that?

'I have a present for you,' Theo says. 'I believe it will stop you from being bored while I am away.'

'Oh really?' she says huskily, reaching towards him now. Maybe she does have time to make love before she has to go to work. She is aching to feel him inside her. The morning's conversation has made her feel unsettled. She knows that if they make love it will calm her down. Yet just as she is about to touch him, Theo steps back and shakes his head, looking at her flirtatiously.

'Now, now, Valentina,' he says, walking across the room towards the wardrobe. 'Patience.'

He opens the wardrobe and takes out a large package, placing it on the dressing table in front of her.

'But why have you got me a present?' she asks, and their eyes lock in the mirror. He hesitates for a minute, holding her with his gaze that seems to say so much. Words she doesn't

21

want to acknowledge. She casts her eyes down.

'Because I believe it's time for you to have this,' he tells her.

So it's not something she might want, or like; it's something she should have. Why is he being so obtuse? She leans over to unwrap the package, but Theo puts his hand over hers and pushes her fist into his palm. She looks back up at his reflection in the mirror. She feels as if time has stopped as she looks into Theo's glacial blue eyes, the only northern part of him, and for once she is inquisitive for his secrets. She sees herself reflected: tiny and naked. A little butterfly of flesh imprinted upon his iris.

'Later,' he says, pulling her up from the dressing-table stool. 'Open it when I am gone.'

He kisses her, and she lets herself succumb to his touch. His hands work at the knot at her waist, and when he has undone it, he slips the dressing gown off her shoulders so it drops to the ground. His erect penis pushes against her pelvis and she is craving him, aching to feel him within her. She stands on tiptoes and wraps one leg around the back of his. He is almost breathless as he lifts her up and pushes into her.

'Valentina,' he gasps. 'Oh my Valentina . . .'

'Shush,' she says, putting her finger to his lips to silence him. He carries her over to the bed. She is twisted around him, feeling his length going deeper and deeper inside her. They fall together as one on to the covers, and she squeezes him tight, urging him to push faster, harder into her. He raises himself above her, taking both her hands in one of his, and lifting them above her head. She is lost in the power of his passion. He pulls back ever so slowly, and as he suddenly rams back into her, she can't help gasping slightly. She joins him in force, thrusting back with all her might, and they become one throbbing entity. She closes her eyes, relaxing at last. This is what she needs. Complete abandonment. She is all sensation, her body leading her, no thoughts involved. He touches her deep within, as only Theo can, and she begins to pulse around him. She has an image of ripples in water, ever increasing, ever decreasing, to the swirling whirlpool at its very centre. They climax together and she is dragged down, as if the bed itself is the bottom of the ocean drowning them. The water is black.

Afterwards, he cradles her in his arms. She knows she needs to get up, that she is going to be late for work, and yet she is paralysed, held tight within her lover's embrace.

'Valentina?' he whispers into her ear.

'Don't talk,' she entreats him. Don't ruin our peace. He ignores her.

'Valentina, please be my girlfriend.'

She doesn't reply.

'Valentina, I want us to be more than casual lovers. Flatmates.'

She turns to face him.

'No, Theo. I don't want that.'

'Are you sure?'

She nods, and he looks so sad she almost agrees to his

request. But what's the point? She is not girlfriend material.

She tries to console him with her body. She places her hands on his chest, pushes her fingers through the twirls of hair and tugs them, before raising her fingers to her lips and licking them, pinching his nipples tight. All the while he stares at her, speechless, yet his body doesn't respond. Eventually he takes her hands in his, and lifts them up and away from his body.

'Why not?' he asks. 'I don't want to change who you are. I just want to be able to call you my girlfriend.'

'Theo . . . I can't . . . you know that . . . I told you before . . .'

Her inadequate words stumble over each other. She pulls her hands away from his grasp.

'Can you not just think about it? Please try, Valentina.'

She wants to scream at him that it is no good. She can't let herself fall in love with him. And yet she finds herself agreeing to think about it. Even though she knows it isn't fair, she lets him walk away hopeful.

It is too late now. He has gone. Where, she has no idea, apart from the fact that it will be cold, since he took his down jacket and snow boots. She is glad he didn't push her further. *Will you be my girlfriend?* No, she could never do it. Why can't he let things just stay as they are? Casual. Fun. Sexy. But living with someone is hardly casual, she suspects. Has she been a fool to let a man move in with her? And why does he need some sort of commitment from her? She doesn't want him to leave . . . and yet she can't give him what he wants. Maybe her mother is right after all, she thinks sourly. Maybe she and her mother are the same. Inconstant butterflies, flitting from one man to the next.

Valentina shakes the thought from her head, and picks up the package on the dressing table. It is surprisingly heavy and she places it back down again. It is a plain brown-paper parcel tied with string. No label on it. No card. She is full of anticipation. What could it be? She hopes it isn't a grand romantic gesture. My God, what if he is building up to a proposal? The idea horrifies Valentina. She has no intention of ever getting married.

She steps back and stares at it. She is not sure she is ready to face what lies inside that brown paper. She has a feeling it is something important. She walks into the bathroom and turns on the shower full blast. As the steaming water cascades over her shoulders, down her back, stomach and thighs, she opens her mouth and lets it run through her. She tries to wash away her anxiety, forget the look in Theo's eyes just before he left. Why is it that all her lovers want to cage her? She hoped Theo was different. She gives him so much space, and yet even he isn't satisfied. What annoys her most is how his excursions are beginning to bother her. Sometimes she finds herself waking up in the middle of the night when he is away and wondering if he is okay. She will be on the verge of sending a text when she manages to stop herself. Their rule is never to contact each other when either of them is abroad. She hates the pestering nature of texting. The last thing in the world she wants to be is needy.

She is pulling on her stockings when she can bear it no longer. She has to know. Wearing nothing but her G-string, suspender belt and one sheer stocking, she squeezes the package and tries to weigh it in her hands. It could be a picture, or a book. It's too big to be a ring, anyway, thank goodness. She unties the string, which is knotted tightly and takes ages. Typical Theo. Then she slowly rips off the paper until it is shredded at her feet.

She is holding a black book. On second thoughts, it is an album, but old, made from some kind of black velvet that is so worn it is no longer plush, but bare cloth. As she opens the book, she is hit by a strong scent of old roses, sweet and decaying. She looks at the open book and sits down on the bed in surprise. How strange. Her present is a riddle. Attached to the first page is a negative. She can tell immediately that it is old, because it is bigger than modern-day negatives. It also has a yellowish tinge. It is attached to the thick, card-like paper by a tiny sliver of tape that she can easily remove. She takes out the negative and holds it up to the light, but it is impossible to make out the image. She flicks the page and finds another negative. She turns the next page, and the next. All of them contain negatives. Nothing else. No words. No pictures. No explanation. She feels inexplicably annoyed, and tosses the book behind her on to the bed. What kind of a present is this?

No ordinary present, that's what, Valentina.

She can hear Theo's voice inside her head. She cannot help but be reassured. She picks up the negative she peeled from the album. This is more than a gift, she thinks. This is a game. A thrill of excitement stirs inside her belly. Theo is playing with her. Giving her little fragments of . . . what? Him, her, the mystery that surrounds him? This is fun, and certainly not a marriage proposal or anything too romantic. She carefully places the negative on her bedroom bureau and pulls on her other stocking. She cannot wait to get into her darkroom to make a print and uncover the first clue in her lover's puzzle.

$\mathscr{B}$elle

SHE RETURNS AT DAWN, TO ENTER HER OWN DEEP LAGOON of dreaming. She stretches on her back, her arms flung upwards and grasping her bedstead, her toes pointed, the sheets entwined around her naked body. Through a chink in the curtains she can see the pink blush of day. She hears a blackbird call to her and she imagines it sitting on her balcony, its oily feathers sleek in the morning light, singing as freely as her spirit feels. She closes her eyes and remembers the sensations of the night, a stranger's skin against her skin, and the musky scent of shared desire.

She doesn't feel wicked, nor does she feel good. She is detached from these emotions. She listens to the church bells of Venice, in time with the beat of her heart and the measured lap of the canal outside her window. She pushes her hand across her brow, lifting her hair as if to feel for fever, but in reality remembering the heat of his hand upon her forehead, less than two hours ago.

It is 1929. Picture her now, Signora Louise Brzezinska as Miss Louise Brooks. They are kindred spirits, she and the actress. Women who wish to share their sexuality, their eroticism and their affection. Despite her husband's possession, Louise cannot live just one life with him. She is impelled to take risks because she needs to be another Louise. The Louise who plays the part of Belle, starring in her own private drama.

It happened quite by accident the first time. She was on her way to a costume party. Her husband was abroad and she had decided to be brave and attend on her own. She had been looking forward to it for so long. Her life had become unbearably dull, every day filled with running the household and looking after her husband's needs. The only time they seemed to go out was to Mass. The party offered her some small escape, especially since she was required to dress up. She liked dressing up. She liked being another woman.

She decided to be daring, since her husband was not at home to be disapproving, and copied the image on a postcard from an arcade machine in America which one of her husband's associates had given her, of a young woman dressed in Egyptian costume. Since the discovery of Tutankhamun's tomb a few years ago, she had been fascinated by Egyptian imagery. She had found some books in her husband's library on the ancient gods of Egypt, and had spent hours studying Horus and Thoth, with their bird heads, and sinister Anubis, half man, half jackal, guardian of the dead and yet potent with sexuality. Sometimes during the solitary days when she seemed to spend every hour poring over these books, she would dream of Anubis, his splendid dog face snarling, licking, biting, while his human half was inside her, satisfying her in a way her husband never could.

This particular night Louise wanted to be Egyptian precisely because it gave her these sensations, the mixture of seduction and the macabre. She had her seamstress make her a shimmering outfit: a long transparent gown of black chiffon decorated with gold beading worn underneath a cream silk skirt that parted at the centre. This was held in place by a sheath of rich gold damask tied around her waist and curving beneath her behind, emphasising its outline. On her top half she wore dark silk, sleeveless, split down either side right to the waist. Over this was an embroidered garment that was little more than a brassiere encrusted with thick gold beading. On her head she wore a gold band neatly clipped around her black bob. The outfit was more than daring and Louise loved it.

It had been her intention to take a gondola down the canal to the party, but at the last minute she decided against it. Although it was a warm night, her maid, Pina, insisted she wear a light woollen stole draped around her shoulders, fearful that her mistress was a little too under-dressed for propriety. She had begged her to wear one of her furs, but Louise claimed it was too hot.

Louise listened to the sound of her heels ringing out on the cobbles of Venice. She loved to walk in this city. Sometimes she would let herself get lost and disappear for hours, much to the annoyance of her husband. This night she chose a circuitous route to the party, since she didn't want to arrive too early. It was a quiet, empty trail through the city, and she was sure her husband would disapprove of her reckless behaviour, but there was a part of Louise that could not help but disobey him. It gave her satisfaction even though he would never know.

She had just passed Campo San Polo when she paused on one of the little bridges. Putting her hands on the balustrade, she looked out at a corner of Canal Grande which she could see from where she stood. Here in Venice the streets were like a network of narrow branches stretching and reaching across a great sky of water. Sometimes she felt marooned. It could be a haven, or it could be a kind of jail. She reached into her bag, took out her cigarette case and snapped it open. The walking had made her hot, and she hoped her cheeks were not too red from the exertion. She would have one cigarette before she moved on so that she could compose herself. She wanted to look cool and aloof when she arrived, just like a dark Egyptian soul. She pulled her stole from her shoulders and looked at it in disgust. Louise Brooks would not be seen dead in such a mediocre garment. In a moment of abandon, she dropped it into the canal. She hated that stole. She shook her head and adjusted the gold band around her head.

'Shall I rescue that for you?' A man had appeared by her side. She started in surprise.

31

'No thank you,' she said, turning to look at him.

He was not a tall man, but he had a beautiful face. Dark honey eyes, and a soft curly moustache. He looked young. Maybe the same age as her. Perhaps younger. She took a drag of her cigarette and stared at him. She saw the surprise in his eyes at her audacity.

'Are you going to a costume party?' he asked, indicating her attire.

'No, sometimes I dress like this because I want to,' she lied, enjoying the suggestion in her answer. She put her head on one side and smiled at him. He smiled back, and she noticed that he had a little chip in one of his front teeth. A thought came unbidden into her head. How it would feel for him to tease her nipple between his teeth; how would it feel for the sharp broken edge of his front tooth to catch on her skin? She looked into his eyes and his pupils had dilated so that they were almost black. He took a tentative step towards her, and she didn't move.

'Are you working?' he asked, so quietly it was as if the water beneath the bridge spoke.

Working? What could he mean?

He stepped forward again. From the glint in his eye, and his hand in his breast pocket, fingering some notes that he had begun to remove, she now understood what he meant.

He was up close. She could feel his excitement through his trousers as he pressed against the light layers of her skirt, which shifted easily as soon as he touched them to reveal her bare leg. For one so young, how bold he was to approach a woman he thought was a prostitute. Surely he had a beau? He was handsome, looked respectable, and yet she smelt it on him, his potent sexuality, just like her.

'How much?' he whispered.

She shivered with fear and excitement. She should have slapped him and walked away, but she didn't. Her lips went dry, but she tried to keep up her sanguine façade. She named a figure, not knowing if it was the going rate, as she stabbed her cigarette out on the parapet of the bridge. She could see her hand shaking uncontrollably as if in shock at her own words. She grasped it tightly with her other hand, stilling her astonishment. *What exactly was she doing?*

He counted out the notes, looking around him to make sure no one was watching, and handed them to her. She didn't even glance at them as she stuffed them into her bag.

'Where?' he asked urgently, his hand around her wrist as if he was worried that she might flee now that she had his money.

Where? She hadn't thought of that. She could hardly take this stranger home. And even if she could, she knew that if she didn't follow her instinct right this very moment, she never would. She would give him back his money. She might still walk away.

Yet at the same time as her doubt, another emotion emerged: a sense of power she hadn't felt since before she got married. Louise was in control again.

'Over there,' she said, her voice low and husky, indicating a tiny alcove on the other side of the bridge, barely visible from the street.

He expected her to do it. This was the thrill. After thirteen years of her husband deciding when they would have sex, and being in charge – she was never allowed to actually touch his penis; just had to lie back and let him do his business – this young man wanted her to touch him. She reached out, her hands shaking with anticipation. It felt different from how she had expected. Softer, yet stronger. She squeezed hard and then relaxed her grip. She felt his penis nuzzled into her palm as if it was a being in its own right. Her back was against the old Venetian wall as he pulled aside her skirt, as simply as if he were opening a curtain. He fingered her for a few moments, and it was a delicious sensation. Her husband had never touched her here before. She pulled her silk underwear down and opened her legs wide. With his penis between her hands, she pushed him into her.

She was in Ancient Egypt now, in a dark tomb of desire. She was Anubis's love slave. The young man growled into her neck, and together they rocked backwards. He lifted one of her legs so that it hooked around his back. Oh, this young one has done this before, she thought. It excited her to imagine that he believed she was experienced too. All he wanted from her was sex. He licked her neck hungrily, pushing up into her. She pulled her silk top back from her chest, and yanked down the brassiere. She put her hand behind his neck, forcing his head down to her breast. Oh yes, she could feel him sucking, and that broken tooth dragging on her nipple. He pushed in and out of her, faster and faster, and she was moving with him, not lying like a dead woman as she did for her husband. She was making love with her Egyptian jackal god. She desired him, and yet she feared him. He was burying her under layers of his touch. The deep earth of her longing was reaching into her and extracting her passion. Ah, she thought, sex is not death like it is with my husband. It is the life in death.

And now Louise was so deep inside her jackal god that she was no longer flesh and blood, no longer a woman, but gold dust dancing in the night air, a tiny part of Ancient Egypt brought alive in Venice. It had been so long, so, *so* long since she had felt these sensations. She was full of this young man's penis. She sensed her vibrations exciting him, and he sped up, biting her nipple as he came, and jolting her up towards him so that he was deep inside her, deeper than her husband had ever been.

A moment's breath and the young man pulled out. He was grinning with delight but she refused to smile, although she was proud of the effect she had had on him. It had made her happier than she had been in a long time.

'Good night, madam,' he said, lifting her hand to his lips and kissing it delicately like a true gallant before disappearing across the bridge.

Louise was left shaking. She was shocked. Not at what she had done, no, she did not feel ashamed or disgusted with herself. Her shock was at the discovery of who she was. A vessel for lovemaking. She knew it in her heart, just as anyone who has a calling does. She had never felt so alive, so whole, so elated. What was love without sex? It couldn't be real love. Yet what her husband classed as sex she would call procreation. The only reason he touched her was because he wanted a child. What had happened just now was sexual liberty in all its glory. Louise and this boy sharing their desires in a dark alcove in the backwaters of Venice. This was her freedom.

She rearranged her clothing. Took out another cigarette and smoked it, looking at the moon reflected in the canal. Her discarded shawl lay upon its surface like a gaping wound within its silver orb. An omen of pain to come, she feared, and yet she wondered if she would ever be brave enough to do again what she had just done. She tossed her half-smoked cigarette into the canal and set off towards the party.

As she walked briskly through the Venetian night, Saint-Saëns' 'Danse Macabre' played inside her head as if it were the musical accompaniment to her night walk, enticing the dissolute ghosts of Venice to join her in a dance of liberty. If she could have passion and love, would that make her happy? she wondered. Or would it destroy her? She wasn't sure. All she knew was that it would never be a possibility with her husband. If she were to have any hope of finding this kind of love, she would have to separate herself into two: Louise, the wife of the respectable Polish businessman in

Venice; and Belle, her hidden self, the whore. She made a promise as she walked. She would find this kind of love despite the consequences. If Anubis himself came to take her away, she would follow him gladly. For Louise, life without love was death.

$\mathcal{V}$alentina

HOW WILL VALENTINA TELL HIM WHEN HE GETS BACK? That she can't be what he wants: that *girlfriend* is the first step to . . . what? Love . . . engagement . . . marriage? After she tells him, things will deteriorate no matter how she tries to divert him. It's such a shame. She doesn't really want him to move out. It is good he is away for a few days. It gives her a chance to prolong the illusion that everything is okay. Maybe if she plays his game, with the photo album and the negatives, it might be enough.

She closes her eyes for a moment and tries to stifle familiar memories. Those few weeks before letting a lover go. How a touch that could turn her on one day leaves her cold the next. What happens to her? Why is it that as soon as a man tells her he loves her, she switches off? I am just more like them, she thinks crossly. They flit from break-up to break-up all the time, and never get called unfeeling, heartless or shallow. And yet underneath her anger, Valentina feels the edge of another emotion. It is a feeling she doesn't want to admit to.

Valentina drops the enlargement into the stop bath and waits. She looks at her watch and counts. She is in the crimson confines of her darkroom inside the apartment. It was always her mother's hiding place, away from her and Mattia, and probably their father. Now it is Valentina's. Although she only uses it for work, not liking the memories the space evokes.

Valentina often uses film and enjoys developing photographs the old-fashioned way, yet she has never been fond of her darkroom. She has never liked small, dark spaces. She clicks her fingers. Another twenty seconds before she can fix it and turn on the lights.

She leaves the print in the fixer for five minutes, trying not to peek. She doesn't want to look at it until it is fully developed. She starts rearranging the row of prints hanging above her. Taking them down and examining them. Wondering if they are good enough to exhibit. Theo said they were, but she's not sure herself.

For as long as she can remember, Valentina has taken pictures. Her mother was a fashion photographer, just like she is now. Valentina was given her first camera when she was eight years old. It was a Kodak Duaflex II from the sixties, which her mother used in her work. It can still take pictures and Valentina has kept it all these years. Although she grew up in the digital age, her mother insisted on teaching her how to use film cameras and develop pictures. She is primarily self-taught (well, mother-taught). Despite going to college to improve her skills, she has never been one to follow the crowd. She experiments constantly. Theo says that's why she is so good. She shoots from the heart as well as the head. When she sets up a shot, even for a professional shoot, it is primarily instinctive yet at the same time meticulously orchestrated.

Valentina has a passion for the details in life. She notices small things that most people would not even acknowledge: the texture of a lip, a wisp of loose hair, the angle of an eyebrow arch, the length of an eyelash, the apple roundness of a cheek or the slenderness of an ankle. She finds these details, or close-ups, extremely evocative. Often she will create a frame with her fingers and choose a spot on her lover's body – the stubble on Theo's chin, for example – leaning down close and examining its exact pattern until he prises her fingers off him, teasing her for her obsession.

Valentina examines her latest work. After several years of shooting women for fashion magazines and looking at female bodies, sometimes so scantily clad they are practically naked, she has begun to feel the urge to make a more creative study. She loves the beauty of the female form, and even though she is not gay, she still finds looking at women erotic and stimulating, pushing her to try to create sensual images.

Using the medium of film, and shooting in black and white, she has so far only taken pictures of herself. She intentionally steers away from models, and has been too shy to ask any other women she knows. Up until this last batch of photographs she has remained clothed, dressing up in some of her mother's old outfits from the sixties. She knows she looks just like her, and the images are unnerving. Valentina's aim is to create a world of fantasy images where women become unreal, juxtaposing innocence and lust and seducing the viewer so that no matter how prudish they are they cannot deny the beauty in desire.

This new series of photographs was taken in Venice. She has always felt drawn to this city. Its poetic and sensual overtones constantly bewitch her. In fact it feels more like home to her than Milan. She shot her pictures in the early morning. She found an abandoned palazzo and began by taking pictures of the morning light streaming through the gaps in the boarded shutters. She moved outside then, squeezing through a narrow doorway that led to the canal. It had been raining the previous day in Venice and the water level was high. She crouched down by the edge of the canal and began to take pictures of the murky water. Despite the sunlight illuminating the surface, it was impossible to see to the bottom it was so dirty. So full of secrets, Valentina thought. She could smell the decadent scent of Venice, putrefied salt water. The thick opaqueness reflected back her face. She looked so serious.

She shifted position and a tiny part of Venice crumbled into the water, peppering its surface. Through the ripples she could see her legs, and she took pictures of their reflection. She began to make out other parts of her body. She took off her jacket and took a picture of one of her bare arms. It seemed as though it did not belong to her any more, this pale, slender waving line, beckoning to her. The girl in the green water was no longer Valentina, but another girl, who looked the same but unlike Valentina wanted to be seen. Look at me, she appealed. Her pale face, dark eyes beseeched her. Valentina took another picture, and another. She closed in and her watery self undressed for her. Here was a shot of the inside of a bent knee and upper thigh, teasingly cut off. Another of her stomach, creased from crouching, her belly button like a black seed floating on the water's surface. She zoomed in on one breast as it floated upon the water like a white bloom. How long she was taking pictures of the naked girl in the water she didn't know. She was completely focused on her work. It made her breathless and excited to be doing this. She never felt this way when she was doing a fashion shoot.

Gradually the sounds of the day around her began to re-emerge. A vaporetto passed by at the top of the tiny canal, causing the water to lap and break up her imagery. Valentina's erotic girl disappeared and suddenly she saw herself again, crouching by the canal, her eyes wild and her body naked. Hastily she put down her camera and retrieved the clothes that were strewn all around her.

Now she leafs through the prints. They look even more erotic in the red light of the darkroom. She has no memory of taking her clothes off that morning, and yet of course she did. How else would she have been able to create these watery images of her fantasy woman of Venice? She picks up the last image. It is a close-up of her bottom half crouching, from her waist to her knees. Her stomach is rippled by watery reflections of light and dark, and below, between her legs, is a dark, dark shadow of suggestion. The viewer senses she is naked, yet they cannot see her private parts clearly. The water keeps them hidden. Valentina can't help feeling turned on as she looks at this image. She wishes that Theo were with her in the darkroom so they could make love.

She puts the pictures aside, begins to rub herself gently, fingering her nipples, and then stops suddenly. The negative. She is too curious about Theo's gift to continue. She takes the print out of the last tray of water and blots it with a towel, taking it with her out of the darkroom and into the bathroom. She plugs in the hairdryer, puts it on low and air-dries the print. Gradually an image emerges. It is frustratingly hazy and at first it seems to be of nothing at all, just shadow and light. She turns off the dryer and walks back into her bedroom. She is still wearing only her dressing gown over her stockings. She places the picture on her bureau and stares at it as she throws off her dressing gown and puts on her bra, lifting and tucking her breasts inside its lacy underwire.

Well, what is this, Theo?

She can't work it out at all. Is it some kind of landscape? She sees an outline that looks like the curve of a valley between two hills, but that is all she can make out. There is something about the texture of the landscape, though, despite the obvious age of the picture, which makes her think that in fact it is not what it seems. She can't bear it. She has to know.

She picks up her phone and considers calling Theo, but that would be breaking her rule, and only a few hours after he left. Besides, she doesn't like telephone conversations. For her the phone is purely functional, for work and the organisation of her schedule. She stares at the screen of her phone for a minute, thinking. She leans the photograph up against the lamp on the bureau and steps back. And something hits her. Something about the curve of that landscape. Of course, it's not a long shot at all, but a close-up. She should know that after all the hours she has spent looking at women's bodies. This is the outline of a naked back. But whose?

Now she really is curious. In fact she is so intrigued that she does something she has not done since the day Theo moved in, despite all his mysterious disappearances. She decides to have a little look in his desk, just in case there is some kind of paperwork explaining where he got this album, or explaining who the model is. He need never know. There has to be a point to this present, and she can't bear to wait until he gets back to find out. What was it he said? *I believe it's time for you to have this.*

Although the study is supposed to be a shared room – this is her apartment, after all – it has in fact become Theo's domain, just as the darkroom is hers. It is at the back of the apartment, and overlooks a small communal garden belonging to the whole building, as well as providing a glimpse of the red tower of old Sant'Ambrogio, whose cloisters are Valentina's favourite place of refuge when she wants an hour on her own to think.

She opens the door and switches on the light. She is surprised to see that Theo has some new art on the walls. Pictures he hasn't shown her. The last time she was in here, there were only a couple of paintings up. Now there are about five, hanging this way and that, looking as though they have been thrown up there with no thought whatsoever. Given Theo's curatorial background, Valentina is perplexed. She looks at the art and feels even more confused. She knows Theo's taste. Modern, either German expressionism or minimalist abstract, yet two of the pictures are the opposite of this, and they are copies. There is for instance a copy of a Watteau painting, and she knows for a fact that Theo dislikes rococo. Well, it is none of her business in any case. She really isn't that interested in Theo's art collection. She makes her way to the desk, which in contrast to the haphazard walls is neat and ordered. The bulb in the desk lamp is gone and the overhead light is inadequate, so Valentina pulls the cord by the window to raise the blinds. As daylight floods the room, she notices a small toolbox under the desk. She opens it, but there is nothing inside it to help with her investigation concerning the photographs; just a pair of pliers, wire, glass cutters, and a small hammer for hanging pictures.

As she stands with her back to the window, leaning over the desk, Valentina feels a prickle on the back of her neck. She swings around and sees a man in the communal garden. Could he be a new neighbour? Somehow she thinks not. He is staring up at her blatantly. She drops the blind quickly, aware of her near nakedness, and looks through the slats at the man. She notices he has a camera in his hand, and that he hasn't moved. He is tall, with a shock of thick blond hair, and instinctively she knows he isn't Italian. Why has he got a camera? It's a grey, rainy day, hardly the weather for taking pictures. It feels as if he is waiting for her to come out to him. Was he taking pictures of her?

To her surprise, Valentina isn't angry. In fact she feels a little aroused by the idea of the man in the garden watching her walking around semi-naked. Unwillingly, yet again she wishes Theo were here. What has her lover done to her? He has turned her into a sex addict. The thought amuses her. Really, she doesn't need that much encouragement.

She sits down in Theo's chair, drums the top of his desk with her fingers and stares at the jumble of art on the walls. She really does want Theo here, so that they can make love on the desk again. That was what they did within the first hour of him moving in. She had offered him the use of the study, since he had to do so much writing, and brought him in here to show him the space again. Yet after weeks of living in each other's pockets, the day Theo officially moved in she became bashful and nervous. Her rational mind was aghast. *You have asked a man to live with you. You are giving up all your privacy!* Yet she couldn't stop herself from doing it. The chemistry between them was so intense, it literally felt like sparks were flying in that dusty, dim room. She remembers she was wearing one of her mother's sixties outfits, in preparation for a party they had been invited to. It was a little navy mini dress, with a slit from where it fastened at her neck, all the way down to the small of her back. They were standing right next to each other as she showed him the bookshelves stuffed with art books her father had left behind. Her skin was prickling with anticipation. He slipped his hand inside the back of her dress, and leant down and kissed her on the lips. She will never forget the sensation of his hand on her skin that day; something snapped inside her as if her whole body was opening up like an offering.

Valentina sighs and closes her eyes, replaying the scene in the study. It was so spontaneous and enticing, the way he picked her up and sat her on this very desk. With consummate skill he continued to kiss her, while carefully removing all the items from the top of the desk. Then he pushed her gently on to her back on the leather-topped table, and devoured her until she was singing inside with ecstasy and desire. How long will she have to wait now until he is back? And even then will he want to touch her after he hears her answer to his request?

She pushes her fingers inside her G-string. She sees Theo in her head, and imagines it is his finger touching her. As she takes herself further and further, she imagines that the blond man in the garden is in fact Theo, returned, watching her from afar. He loves her so much he needs to take pictures of her. She hears him calling to her, his voice in harmony with the birdsong rising from the garden. She sees herself opening the blinds, and the window. She imagines Theo climbing in, placing the camera on top of the desk before kneeling down in front of her. He spreads her legs wide apart and buries himself between them, and she is pulling on his black hair, gasping in abandon. She is letting Theo do something to her that she has never let him do before. She is opening up to him, trusting him. And then she is coming, and her imagined lover lifts her up and pushes himself inside her. They are on the desk, just like they were before, reliving their old passion, making love like two people possessed.

Afterwards Valentina sits in the dusky room, hugging her knees and revolving around and around on Theo's desk chair. The art on the walls becomes a carousel of colour and energy. She thinks about the stranger in the garden, and wonders why she imagined he was Theo back again, in fact not gone at all.

She grasps the edge of the desk with one hand, stops spinning, her eyes alighting upon one of Theo's newly acquired paintings, a copy of a Dutch Master. Another strange choice for him. It is a painting of a woman in a Dutch interior, black and white tiled floor and panelled walls. She is standing at an open window, holding a letter up to the light, her head turned away from the viewer as if she is aware of their prying gaze. She is like me, Valentina admits to herself; she is trying to hide her feelings. No other lover has ever had such an effect upon her as Theo. To be able to make her come just at the thought of his touch.

Could she do it? Is it possible that she could welcome Theo's parents into their apartment in the role of his girlfriend? The idea of it makes her chest tight with dread. She stands up suddenly, pushing the chair back from the desk so that it makes a hideous scraping sound on the marble floor. She is pathetic. All he wants is to call her his girlfriend. He is hardly asking her to marry him. It's a normal enough request after living with someone for six months. Antonella calls herself someone's new girlfriend almost every couple of weeks. Like Theo said to her earlier, it's no big deal. And yet to Valentina it is. If she is Theo's girlfriend, then she is his. She can't let that happen, ever again, for Valentina belongs to no one.

$\mathcal{B}$elle

SHE RECLINES ON HER BED LIKE AN ARTIST'S MODEL. SHE is naked apart from her black stockings and lace garters. She puts her hand on the dip of her waist and trails her finger up the hill of her behind, down again and up the slope of the side of her chest. She is in profile like a valley landscape. She can sense him behind her, taking off his clothes. Gazing at her back. She doesn't need to look to know that he is folding each item neatly, one by one, before putting them on the seat of the armchair. The Doctor is precise in every way, particularly in his lovemaking. She closes her eyes and imagines she is in a movie. No need to talk. All she needs to say is in her body.

A warm hand is placed upon her shoulder and she knows that the Doctor is ready. She turns around and he is facing her, glorious in his nakedness. She takes pleasure in really looking at him. Her husband has never allowed her to do this; since she became Belle, she wouldn't want to. Always they undress in the dark, and she believes that she now knows the Doctor's body better than her own husband's.

'Are you sick, Belle?' the Doctor asks her.

She nods.

'Would you like me to make you feel better?'

She nods again.

The Doctor smiles and opens his big black bag. Belle moistens her dry lips with her tongue. What is he going to take out? She is a little frightened, although she knows in her heart the Doctor would never hurt her. Despite the fact that they never acknowledge it, Belle and the Doctor have moved in the same social circles for years. He calls her Belle, not Louise, and never hints that he might know her true identity, which of course he does. What other woman in Venice sports such a stylish black bob as Signora Louise Brzezinska?

The Doctor starts to take instruments out of his bag. Each one gleams hard, cold and metal.

'Do you want me to make you better, Belle?' he asks again.

She nods and the Doctor smiles at her benevolently. He picks up a severe-looking type of forceps and examines it before putting it back down again.

'Well turn around now, like a good girl, and I will see what I can do for you.'

She turns her back to him again, the image of his medical instruments, shiny and bright, still in her head. He has never done it before, but maybe this time he will touch her with one of those things. The thought is frightening and thrilling at the same time.

She feels the silk band going around her eyes and being tied at the back of her head, gently and with respect. She looks into the black cloth and she can see nothing. Her breath quickens. Now she knows exactly what the Doctor wants to do, and yet each time he comes to visit her she cannot help this expectation that overwhelms her as soon as he places the blindfold over her eyes. Such a considerate man. He allows her to enter her fantasies as he enacts his own.

The Doctor gently pulls her back down on to the bed. He picks up her right ankle and moves her leg to the side. He pulls her garter off and slowly peels off her stocking. She feels it being wrapped around her ankle, binding it to the bedstead. It is not so tight that it will leave a mark, and yet it is tight enough to make her feel tension. He moves her other leg now, takes off the stocking and ties this foot to the other side of the bed. She is lying on her back, her legs wide open in a provocative V. He leaves her arms free. The Doctor likes her to dig her nails into his back. She wonders how he explains these marks to his wife, but maybe the reason he is here right now with her is because his wife never sees his naked body any more.

She hears the Doctor moving around the room. She knows he is looking at her exposed, wide open for him, and picking up his instruments one by one, thinking about it. She should be frightened, but she isn't. Her arms are free and she can easily untie herself if she wants to. Yet she has no desire to pull off the blindfold or undo the stockings tied around her ankles.

She feels the Doctor's weight as he gets on to the bed and leans over her.

'I think I have just the thing to make you feel better,' he whispers.

'Please, Doctor,' she says.

'Where does it hurt?' he asks.

She lifts her arm and places her hand on her belly.

'Here, Doctor.'

He takes his time, and the anticipation makes her stomach clench. Will he touch her with one of his cold instruments? Eventually she feels his warm lips on her skin, and the tension is replaced by relief. He massages her belly with his hands.

'Where else does it hurt, Belle?'

She brings her hand up to her breast, touches her nipple.

'Here, Doctor.'

He lifts her hand away and begins to kiss her nipple very gently, fondling her other breast at the same time, and Belle feels herself melting beneath the healing hands of her doctor. She cannot see him through the blindfold and this makes the experience even more erotic for her. She is imagining a man doing this to her not just because he desires it, but because he loves her and wants to pleasure her. She knows the Doctor doesn't love her, but that doesn't matter now. He has become her dream man, the ultimate lover she hopes to find one day.

'Where else does it hurt, Belle?' the kind voice of the Doctor asks her.

She brings her hand down between her open legs.

'Here, Doctor, it hurts so much right here.'

'I'm going to make you all better now, Belle,' the Doctor says.

He slowly kisses her all the way from the tip of her nipples, down the centre of her chest and stomach. He kisses across her pelvis until he comes to where her hand is placed. He picks up her hand, kisses it gently and removes it. Now he is kissing her below. Making her better, as he calls it. Such a lover this man is. She feels like congratulating his wife every time she sees her. The Doctor kisses her deeper and deeper, gently using his fingers to help him go further. Even though she is blindfolded, Belle still closes her eyes. She is tied to the bed, and yet she feels as free as a bird. A blackbird. She hears its song inside her head, and it trills with pleasure as the Doctor caresses her with his tongue.

In this moment of ecstasy I am all spirit, Belle thinks.

This spirit, this energy of who she is feels like fire in her blood. It fuels her as the Doctor brings her closer and closer to the edge. She imagines that another man is here with her making love. She doesn't know him yet. He is a projection, but she feels he will come soon. This man who can do everything for her.

The Doctor pulls away from her.

'How are you feeling now, Belle?' he asks her.

'A little better, but Doctor, I need you to make sure I don't get sick again.'

'Of course, my dear,' the Doctor says politely. A second

later she feels him push inside her, and it makes her sigh with pleasure.

'Is that better?' he asks.

'Oh yes,' she breathes.

'Good girl,' he says, beginning to pick up rhythm. Now she knows that the Doctor is going into his own fantasy world. And she too is gone, far away from this room in Venice. She is in her special place, somewhere beyond the dimensions of the real world, in the heavens and at the bottom of the sea. At the same time she is in a small room, a tiny dark cupboard of desire. She locks the door, leaving her thoughts outside and letting her physical sensations take her beyond her body, so that she is right on the very edge, the tiny sliver of a fine line between calm and storm. She holds it for as long as she can, but it is only a matter of seconds before she succumbs to the Doctor's relentless rhythm and she is climaxing. He doesn't stop, not for a second, but keeps on as she cascades around him, thrusting into her deeper and deeper. She knows he is lost in the ending of his own private game, and she can feel him growing more urgent, hot, fast jabs. Although her legs are rigid, her feet bound to the bed, she raises her chest towards him and digs her nails into his back. He groans with pleasure and she pushes her fingers deeper into his flesh as he comes with a loud cry.

Belle stands by the open French window, the curtains fluttering inside and draping her naked body. She watches the Doctor rowing briskly away, his black bag stowed beside him in the boat. He is all business once again. Who would have thought what the good doctor likes to get up to when he is not saving lives? She considers that maybe she is a kind of doctor as well. Helping her clients find release, and the satisfaction that they can't seem to achieve in their marriages or relationships with other women. She compares herself to one of Venice's most famous courtesans, Veronica Franco. She was a *cortigiana onesta*, an intellectual prostitute, admired by men not just for her erotic skills, but for her mind as well. Veronica Franco equated virtue with intellectual integrity. Belle would like to write poetry too. She tries to compose something in her head. Instinctively the words are Polish, not Italian, and the vista of the narrow canal in front of her is replaced by a fleeting image of the woods back home. Tall evergreen trees, stretching on and on, swaying in a soft breeze, whispering to her . . . re-creating these new sensations her body is feeling.

I am moving. The branches, the leaves that shade my heart begin to stir.

During Veronica Franco's time, in the sixteenth century, there was no shame attached to being a prostitute. So, Belle reasons, she is not being immoral. She is stimulating her clients' imaginations and ultimately helping her men to treat their wives better. Isn't it preferable that they come to her, a willing participant in the act of sex, rather than force themselves on reluctant wives and fiancées? This is what she is good at, so why not share herself if she so chooses? She wishes that there was a man out there who could understand this. To love Belle you have to let her be free.

She turns to look at the bed, the sheets still crumpled from their game. The Doctor has left a generous pile of notes on the pillow. It is more than enough to cover the rent on her apartment for the next month. It is hard to believe that it is just over a year since her first astonishing encounter as Belle on the night of the costume party. For the few weeks after it happened she tried unsuccessfully to forget about it. Yet those sensations were there with her all the time. Imaginary fingers touching her, the feel of him within her grasp, making her on edge as if she had an itch she was unable to scratch. When she couldn't remove the image of herself and the young man from her mind, she tried to relive it and bring it into the bedchamber with her husband. That was a disaster. Signor Brzezinski told her she looked depraved in her Egyptian outfit, and after he had stripped her of her finery and washed the make-up off her face, ignoring her tears of disappointment, she felt empty of any kind of desire. Of course it was what he called her apathy that seemed to give her cruel husband pleasure, and he had sex with her then, her passiveness driving him on so that it was clear he did not care whether she was enjoying herself or not. All those old emotions returned: her humiliation and her powerlessness, smothering the part of her she had unearthed the night she was an Egyptian. And so it was with a sort of desperation that she tentatively began her career as a prostitute. As soon as her husband left for business again, she disguised herself as best she could and went exploring. The first few times she found clients around Ponte di Rialto, but as the weather turned colder, she soon realised that she would be more comfortable, and more respected, if she were to rent an apartment somewhere in the city, a good distance from her home ground.

How fast things have changed since then. Now she truly is living a double life: sometimes the demure Polish wife of Signor Brzezinski, at other times the exotic courtesan Belle, with her entourage of special clients. She knows that it isn't an ideal life, and yet it is what she needs right now. She isn't hurting anyone. Not even Signor Brzezinski if he finds out, for he cannot love her. So where is the badness in being Belle?

Since she is a prostitute out of choice, rather than need, Belle never sleeps with anyone she doesn't want to. She has a golden rule about Blackshirts and refuses to have sex with them. She cannot abide Mussolini's fascists, although her husband openly admires the dictator. There are other monsters as well who prowl the streets of Venice, and she is always very careful not to be tempted. She has heard of sick beasts who take pleasure from hurting prostitutes. She never wants to risk that.

She crosses her apartment, and goes into the front room, where she looks out of the window, turning her gaze towards the lagoon. There is a misty haze hanging over the green water, and an aureole glow behind it as the sun tries to break through. The overall effect is ethereal and dreamlike. She feels as though she is living in a mystical city, a place of dreams and fantasies. Could she live this life in any place other than Venice? She doesn't think so. This city, founded by Venus rising from the sea, lends itself to sexual intrigue. It is part of its history.

She surveys the boats nearby, watches the sailors and the dockers busy unloading their exotic wares. She thinks of all the distant lands these boats have been to. How many women just like her, living in other towns and ports, might be looking at them and longing to be aboard too? Her attention is drawn to one boat in particular, a smart white schooner, and the figure of a man walking down the gangway. She cannot make out his face, but she can admire his body even from here. He is tall, and walks with a languid grace, a sexual confidence she recognises. She wonders if he has heard of her, and finds herself hoping he will be a sailor who comes looking for Belle.

ᚱalentina

VALENTINA IS LATE AGAIN. SHE WALKS AS FAST AS POSSIBLE in her heels. She is wearing one of her mother's mini dresses from the sixties, a Bridget Riley dress, all black and white stripes, making her feel strident, not shy like usual. It is a feeling she likes.

She steps out into the evening rush hour of Milan, confident that cars will stop for her now she is wearing her mother's dress. Maybe she should take a taxi? But the gallery isn't far, just off Corso Magenta. It is Theo's fault she is late, she thinks churlishly. If he hadn't given her the black book this morning, she wouldn't have spent the time between arriving back from her shoot today and getting ready for the opening frantically trying to print as many of the old negatives as possible. She is disappointed. They are all close-ups of different parts of a woman's naked body. Some kind of twenties erotica, she supposes, although they are inconclusive, as if they are a tiny part of a bigger picture. What do they mean? Why has Theo given her a bunch of old negatives? Is it just because she is a photographer interested in erotica and he came across them on his travels? That conclusion is a little lacking. She expects more from him. And his behaviour this morning gave her the feeling that this present has some kind of message. After all, he told her it was time for her to have this gift.

Well, Valentina thinks crossly, he has either over- or underestimated me.

She tries to forget about Theo and the negatives for the moment. He is a problem she will have to deal with when he gets back. Tonight she is on a mission. In the large black portfolio she is carrying is a presentation of the erotic pictures she took in Venice. She has finally built up the courage to approach the gallery owner Stephano Linardi. She wants a show in Milan. For one second she thinks of Theo again, of his belief in her talents, and a part of her wishes he was with her. She hates going to these events alone. She finds it hard to play the game and talk niceties to fashionable acquaintances. Yet Theo is so at home in this world, charming all and sundry with his soft American drawl and his easy anecdotes about prima donna artists and groundbreaking exhibitions. She has got used to his company, although she is always very careful not to be too demonstrative in public. Behind the scenes is fine. Unbridled passion in a lift, or in the ladies', but no holding hands in front of friends and colleagues; that is pushing her limits.

The Linardi Gallery is packed to the gills. She is pleased for

Antonella. She hopes she sells out. She grabs a glass of prosecco from a passing waiter as she weaves through the crowd, most of whom greet her as she walks through. She nods in acknow-ledgement but avoids conversation.

'Ciao, Valentina!' She is engulfed in a big hug. She teeters back on her heels as Antonella releases her.

'Well?' she asks, getting straight to the point.

'Ten. I've sold ten paintings already!'

'Brava! That's fantastic.' Valentina squeezes Antonella's arm. She is not as tactile as her friend.

'Yes,' Antonella replies enthusiastically. 'And I have already mentioned you to Stephano. Did you bring some pictures with you?'

Valentina indicates her portfolio, her mouth suddenly dry with unwelcome nerves.

'Excellent. Let's go and find him.' Antonella whips her arm under Valentina's elbow and propels her through the crowd. 'Stephano! Stephano!' she shouts over the hubbub.

Valentina winces. This is far too blatant for her liking, but it obviously works, since Antonella got a show here more quickly than any other artist she knows.

At the sound of his name, a tall, thin man with curly blond hair, wearing a pair of Armani glasses, turns round and looks at them. Antonella shoves on through the crowd and deposits Valentina in front of him, making a hasty introduction before disappearing again to mingle. Why oh why does Antonella always do this to her? Sometimes her friend exasperates her by her expectation that everyone is as forthright as herself.

'So you are Valentina Rosselli, the fashion photographer?' Stephano asks her, looking at her curiously through his spectacles.

Valentina has always found glasses on a man sexy. She really doesn't know why. She loves it when Theo puts his on to read. It turns her on no end, and usually she pulls the book out of his hand and has her way with him.

'Yes,' she replies, her face stiffening into impassiveness, which always happens when she becomes shy.

'And of course you are the daughter of Tina Rosselli. Following in her footsteps.'

Valentina tenses further. The last thing she wants to do is talk about her mother and her photographic oeuvre.

'Yes, but I am an artist in my own right,' she says tersely. 'I brought my portfolio to show you.'

'Well, it is a little noisy in here,' he replies, looking at her curiously. 'Let's talk in my office.'

He leads the way up a spiral staircase and along a corridor of red-brick walls, oddly bare for an art gallery. His office is a white box with one enormous graphic print by Vignelli on the wall behind his desk.

'I must say,' says Stephano, sitting down at his desk, 'you look just like her.'

Valentina nods in acknowledgement, but she is irritated. When will the Milanese forget her mother? She has obviously long forgotten them. Tina Rosselli hasn't set foot in Milan for more than seven years.

'Here.' Valentina brusquely shoves her portfolio at him to shut him up. Stephano opens it and pores over it, saying nothing for a few minutes. He spends rather too long looking at the last picture, the one of the reflection of her private parts in the Venetian canal. She knows they are not actually visible, but still, it makes her slightly uncomfortable to think he is looking at her completely exposed.

At last he shuts the portfolio with a snap.

'These are good,' he says, blinking at her behind his glasses, 'but I am afraid not appropriate for the Linardi Gallery.'

'What do you mean?' Valentina realises she is surprised. Deep down she knew they were good too.

'This is a fine art gallery, principally paintings, a little photography, but what we do exhibit in terms of photography is not pornographic.'

'This is not porn,' she counters icily.

Stephano Linardi shrinks from her glare and flings open the portfolio again at the last image.

'And how would you describe this photograph, for instance, Signorina Rosselli?' He peeks at her from over his glasses.

'It's erotic photography. It's art.'

He huffs, closing the portfolio.

'Maybe in your opinion. Don't misunderstand me, it is beautiful, and your technique is interesting, but we have a certain kind of client here in Milan. I am not sure this is the right place for your work. I am sorry.'

Valentina snatches back the portfolio. This man is an art snob, and she already dislikes him.

'It's fine. I'll find another venue.' She is not going to persuade him. She has never begged for anything in her life, and she can see his mind is made up.

'But look,' he says, putting his hands together and knotting his fingers. 'Why don't you leave the memory stick of your images with me? I do think you are very talented and I will ask around to see if there are any galleries of a more avant-garde nature who might be interested. How about that? I really am sorry. This *is* Milan. Maybe if you were trying to put it on in New York or London, it might be easier.'

Valentina forgets about Stephano Linardi and his gallery. She refuses to be disappointed and decides that in fact this gallery is way too conservative for her libertine sensibilities. She thinks of going home, but she doesn't want to have to sit in on her own, so she hangs around the gallery, waiting until Antonella and a gang of her friends decide to continue the night out dancing.

Valentina has been friends with Antonella since art college. The two of them naturally gravitated towards each other through their mutual disregard for following the crowd. Both of them focused, passionate and ambitious. Antonella special-ised in fine art, whereas Valentina of course had gone for photography. Antonella was different when they were at college. Quieter, most certainly, and more serious. She is still obviously very ambitious, but the last year or so she has come out of her shell. She is a tiny woman with a zesty smile, brilliant brown eyes and the most disproportionately large chest for such a small frame. Men cannot help but be drawn towards her, so that she is never without some new beau on her arm. Yet despite all her many affairs, she claims she is searching for true love, a Mr Right to come into her life. A mythical figure Valentina has great fun teasing her over. Still, Antonella always has the effect of making Valentina feel lighter of load, as if there is hope for a Hollywood ending one day.

Tonight Antonella is elated from her exhibition success, almost unbearable company. Yet still Valentina trails along, unsure whether she has actually met any of the other people with her friend. They go to a promotional night at a new club. It is packed with the young and beautiful, the air thick with cigarette smoke despite the ban. Within ten minutes Antonella is being chatted up by a muscle-bound Spaniard, and not long afterwards she disappears with her prize, blowing Valentina a drunken kiss as she departs. Now that her friend is gone Valentina really should go home. She hardly knows the other people in the club, yet every time she thinks about leaving, she remembers that Theo isn't back at the flat. Tonight she doesn't want to get into her empty bed all alone.

She should find someone in the club and take him home.

Despite the fact that she and Theo are not officially in a relationship, as she keeps telling him, somehow she has found that she hasn't been tempted to sleep with anyone else since she met him. She is not so sure about Theo. I mean, *where* does he go? she asks herself again. So what has happened to her? She was such a different creature when she met Theo. She was a free spirit. That was what he called her. He loved her contradictions. He said that on the surface she was the picture of demure, but behind that front was another Valentina, open, brimming with abandon. He didn't think she was a slut for sleeping with him the first time they met. He called her a goddess. Yet now it seems he wants her to change. *Girlfriend.*

That's it. She's going to pick some guy up tonight and take him home with her. There is no shortage of choice. The table she is sitting at, with the dregs of Antonella's friends, is surrounded by young men. She orders another glass of red wine and eyes up the talent. She likes the look of one particular guy. He seems a little older than the others, and has floppy blond hair. She gives him a little half-smile and hooks him, before turning away to sip her wine. Within a few seconds he is standing beside her. The music is pounding through her body, making her heart race, as she looks into his eyes, her message clear.

'Hi,' he shouts down at her. 'I love your hair.'

She cradles the back of her bob with her hand.

'Thanks. I've always had it like this.'

'Really?'

'Yes, since I was a little girl.' She opens her eyes wide and childlike, and he grins at her.

An hour later, Valentina and Alexandro, the floppy blond, are stumbling out of the club into the tart autumn night. Valentina flags down a taxi, and the two of them scramble inside. As soon as the taxi takes off, they fall into each other's arms.

Alexandro is on top of her in the corner of the taxi, pushing his tongue into her mouth, and suddenly it really isn't as pleasant as Valentina thought it would be. She pushes him away from her.

'What's wrong?' he asks, sweeping his floppy fringe away from his face with a sweaty palm. She can see a few pimples on his forehead. Just how young is this guy?

'I need some air,' she says, winding down the window on her side of the car.

He lunges in again, and she tries to reciprocate. She really does. Yet Theo is inside her head, and this guy smells all wrong. He feels wrong. She slides out from under him, shifts to the other side of the cab.

'I'm really sorry, Alexandro, I can't do this.'

The poor fellow looks crushed.

'Why? What's wrong?'

'Nothing. I just feel sick. Sorry.'

The rest of the journey is spent in hostile silence. When they pull up outside her apartment building, she can't get out of the taxi quick enough. She throws twenty euros through the open door, and Alexandro accepts the money without even looking at her. What on earth was she thinking of? He must be a student. She is probably nearly ten years older than him. She rushes up the steps to the front door of the building, suddenly sober despite all the wine she has drunk. She feels foolish, and something else, a kind of yearning. She wishes that Theo were here so they could laugh about how silly she has been.

She is just unlocking the door to her flat when her phone begins to ring. Who on earth could be calling her at four in the morning? Theo? She rummages in her bag and pulls out her phone, but when she looks at the screen it is a number she doesn't recognise. She didn't give Alexandro her number, she is sure. She thinks briefly of the stranger in her garden. Could he have got hold of it somehow?

'Yes?'

'Signorina Rosselli?'

'Yes, who is this?'

'Excuse me for calling at such an unsocial hour . . .'

'And who am I talking to?' Curiosity overwhelms her instinct to cut off the call.

'My name is Leonardo Sorrentino. I was hoping that you might be interested in doing some photographic work for me.'

'You'll have to go through my agency,' she answers abruptly.

'No, I don't mean fashion photography. I am talking about your other kind of work.'

Valentina is silent for a moment. Very few people know about her erotic photography. She hasn't even got it up on her website. How did this man get her number?

'Who told you about my other work?'

'I am afraid I can't say, as the party wishes to remain anonymous. They are sponsoring a visual project I have initiated, and seem to think that you would be the ideal person to document it, especially since you are a woman.'

'I am not a documentary-style photographer,' Valentina protests.

'I know that.' He pauses. 'That's precisely why we want you. We'd like you to approach the project from an artistic angle. We need you to show another viewpoint, break down stereotypes . . .'

'I really don't know what you are talking about.'

'Let me explain, Signorina Rosselli. I run a club. It is a special place, for those of us who desire a particular way of expressing our sexuality.'

'What kind of way?' asks Valentina, dark visions of terrible things in her head.

'I guess you would know it by the name of sadomaschoism, but I do feel that is a rather unfortunate name for what we do. It is more sex games . . . or sex with stories, I call it.'

S&M. Valentina's interest is piqued. She has always been fascinated by this, although she has never indulged in it and never thought she would want to. Isn't it demeaning for women to be tied up and have things done to them? Yet she has to admit that sometimes when she and Theo make love, she has an urge to ask him to tie her up. She doesn't know why. Does that show that there is a part of her that is weak and submissive?

'So,' Leonardo continues, 'are you curious enough to call by tomorrow evening and have a discussion with me?'

'Okay,' she says slowly, not sure how she will feel in the morning. Well, she can always cancel. 'Can I ask why you've called me at such an hour?'

'I saw you earlier tonight at the exhibition but I didn't manage to catch you before you left. And then I had to work . . . so I have only just knocked off now. I assumed you would still be up; Stephano told me you went off clubbing with your friends.'

So it was Stephano Linardi who recommended her to this man. He must have showed him her memory stick of images. That was quick work. She should be grateful to the gallery owner, but she still can't help resenting his rejection of her photographs.

Valentina can't sleep. She opens up her iMac and logs on. Types in *S&M*. Several disturbing images come up immediately. A woman trussed up with a thick, coarse rope, her wrists and ankles tied together. A girl hanging from some kind of hammock made of lengths of rope that twist around her body so that her breasts poke out and her private parts are exposed and vulnerable. Do these women actually enjoy this? She shuts down her computer and snaps the lid closed. She wishes she had someone to talk to. But there's no one close enough apart from Theo, and he is unavailable of course. What would Theo think of this 'project'? Somehow she knows that he would be all for it. He often calls her his intrepid Valentina. He used to like her adventurousness. Has she become boring lately? Is that why he keeps going away? She thinks again of that pimply student, Alexandro, and winces.

She wanders into her bedroom, unzips her dress and lets it slide off her tired body. She unclips her stockings and they slither off her. She is so exhausted she leaves them discarded on the floor. She lies on her bed in her bra and G-string and reaches over to the bedside table for the last print she developed. She stares at it for a long time, until her eyes begin to droop. The picture is a close-up of an ankle. A tiny ankle with something tied around it, like one of her stockings maybe? She shivers at the thought of what might have been done to the owner of this ankle. Tied up and helpless. Yet at the same time she feels unexpectedly turned on. She wonders if the stranger in the garden is still outside, watching the apartment. Does he want to break in and tie her up? Do unspeakable things to her? It is a nasty, dirty thought, but it is also a private one. Valentina closes her eyes, pushing her fingers under the string of her panties. She imagines her ankles being tied to the bedstead, and her arms as well. The hands touching her are not her own, but someone else's. Now she is blindfolded and in the dark, and all her terror and desire combine as one. What will happen next? These erotic images Theo has given her are pushing her towards some kind of cliff edge. She is not certain whether he wants her to step over it or not. Does he *want* her to have a double life?

Belle

THE DOCTOR IS VISITING AGAIN. TODAY BELLE IS KNEELING on her bed, facing the window, as he stands behind her. He ties the blindfold around her head and the familiar racing of her heart starts up. What is he going to do to her today? She licks her lips in anticipation. She really does enjoy her sessions with the Doctor.

He lays her down on the bed and ties her ankles to the bedstead.

'I believe you are feeling poorly, Belle,' he says.

'Yes, Doctor. Please can you make me better?'

'Let's see what I can do for you today,' he replies.

She hears the bag unclip and the jangle of metal as the Doctor rummages through it. He is playing with his instruments again. Teasing her. In her head she sees all the things he showed her last time. Maybe today he will use one of them on her? Her breathing becomes short and shallow in her chest.

'Now don't be frightened, Belle,' says the Doctor, as if

reading her mind. 'I have something here that is going to make you feel so much better.'

To her surprise, the first sensation on her skin is not that of his soft lips, but something liquid. He is trailing some kind of oil down the centre of her stomach. He rubs it in, kneading her belly in slow, rhythmic circles. She can smell its fresh, sweet herbal scent as it sinks into her skin. The Doctor pours more oil on to her, over her breasts, down her stomach again and along her thighs. His strong, kind hands work away, his fingers pushing into her flesh, and she is lost in the divine sensation of the scent of the oil merging with his slow, measured touch.

The Doctor takes his time, massaging every part of her, from the tip of her chin to her arms, hands and fingers, to her breasts and stomach, the tops of her legs, her calves, feet and toes. He unties her ankles from the bedstead and flips her over. He pours oil down her back and works it in, gradually moving from the back of her neck down her spine, lower and lower to the top of her bottom.

'Are you feeling better, Belle?'

She moans into her pillow, unable to speak. She is as liquid as the aromatic oil that is seeping into her skin. She feels like silk, and she wants to wrap herself around this man and take him into her. She feels the Doctor moving over her, and the next minute he is lying on her back, pressing the front of his naked body into her oily skin. It feels wonderful to be so close. It is as if the oil is binding them together, its aroma weaving a spell so that Belle is no longer in the Venice of today, but in a Venice from long ago, a city of dark Moors and mystic Christians.

The Doctor pushes inside her, and gently they rock together. They are spinning in their sensual abandon, and to Belle it is as if they are creating something beautiful together for all to see. A painting of such detail; an imprint of their passion.

'Darling,' he calls gently, picking up speed and pushing his arms beneath her so that he can cup her breasts. He pounds into her, and she rides with him on an Arabian stallion across the dunes of the Sahara. She is dancing for him under the desert sky, shooting stars mirroring the elation flaring through her, tiny bells shimmying around her belly. They are kissing each other, mouths filled with honey, feeding each other sweet sticky dates and lying on cushions in their tent as it billows in the hot wind. And she is lost in a sandstorm of her sexual abandon, climaxing as the Doctor, her Arabian prince, buries himself deep inside her.

Today the Doctor doesn't rise immediately. She can feel the aromatic oil and his seed running down her thighs, and instinctively she reaches down with her finger and touches it. She wishes she could take this feeling of freedom she has here in her apartment back with her to her house, and her marriage. She has tried to arouse her husband, but to no avail. Her motive is not pleasure, but peace. If he were satisfied, then maybe he might be less angry with her all the time.

When Belle was first married, she believed it her duty to try to please him in bed, for if it hadn't been for Signor Brzezinski, she and her mother would surely have been left destitute. Stranded in war-torn Warsaw, with no one to protect them, she had made her father a promise on his deathbed that she would accept Signor Brzezinski's marriage proposal so that they would be safe. He had been a means for their escape, and Belle had never stopped feeling as if she owed him.

She did not love her husband, and it seemed clear to her that neither did he love her. She had never understood why he chose to marry her of his own free will. She had had no choice. And yet Signor Brzezinski had been gallant once. She remembered his kindness to her and her mother in the early years of her marriage, when they first lived in Venice. It was only after her mother had become sick that his attitude had changed towards her. And once her mother was no longer living with them, Signor Brzezinski became a different man, as if a dark soul had been hiding behind his polite exterior all the while. He became rough in the bedroom. He raped her several times in her sleep. During the day he was constantly berating her. Nothing she did was good enough. Her marriage had become a nightmare. Every breath she took annoyed her husband.

The Doctor leaves, as stealthily as he came. Belle pulls off her blindfold and gets off the oily bed. Her sheets are ruined, but she doesn't care. She walks over to her full-length mirror and gives herself a hard stare. She likes what she sees. A woman in her prime, flushed with her recent satisfaction. Her eyes wide and dark from her Arabian adventure with the Doctor. She smoothes down her dark bob, a few loose strands bothering her. Her hair seems even shinier tonight, as if there are desert stars hidden beneath its black sheen, as if she is glowing from the inside out. How different she is here to the woman she is in Signor Brzezinski's house.

She draws a bath, carefully washing away all the oil so that she is lying in a spicy, steaming pool. She dresses hastily, knowing that her husband is due home today and expecting her at the dinner table. She needs to be back at the house before him so she can change out of her Belle clothes and become Louise again.

She hurries home, across Ponte di Rialto, past the market, and across Campo Rialto Novo, her boots clicking on the cobbles. A pigeon takes flight, causing her to look up, and at that exact moment she catches the eye of a man passing by. Rather than looking away, she holds his gaze. There is something about him she recognises. He has a face like a wolf's, with burnt almond eyes, and a gold ring in his ear. He looks like a pirate, an adventurer from the past. The man smiles at her, and she knows she could have him if she wanted. But she is on her way home and she doesn't have time. She walks on, trying to ignore the pulsing sensation inside her breast. She can feel his eyes upon her back. She knows he is looking at her, but she doesn't turn around. After all, he is just another sailor.

Valentina

THE STORY OF HOW SHE AND THEO MET STILL ASTONISHES Valentina. She has never believed in love at first sight. Of course not. So it was desire at first sight, or something like that. She still can't understand her behaviour that night. She wasn't drunk, and although she knows she can be spontaneous, it is hard for her to understand how she could have brought a complete stranger home with her. Yet Theo has never been a stranger. Enigmatic, a mystery, yes, but she has always felt she knows him, right from the moment they looked at each other on the metro.

It was around ten at night last spring, and she was on her way home from seeing the movie *Midnight in Paris* with Gaby. She said goodbye to her friend outside the cinema as Gaby had made arrangements to meet her new lover later. A fact Valentina refused to comment on, despite her friend's entreaties for her opinion. What could she say? Gaby's new man was married. Deep down Valentina was worried for her friend, but she refused to tell her what to do. She had no right to judge.

And so she banished thoughts of Gaby's endangered heart, and marched down the street to take the metro home. The carriage was half full and she was minding her own business, staring up at the advertisements on the other side of the train but not really looking at them. She was thinking about the film, and the possibilities of moving through time like Owen Wilson's character had done. What period of time was a golden era to her? If she could go back, to when and where would she go? She knew instantly, of course. It would be the twenties in Hollywood, the silent movie era. The jazz, the flappers, the hedonism! She smiled inside herself at the thought of it. She would get to actually meet Louise Brooks. If they could have a conversation, what would she ask her?

Do you believe in love, Louise? Is it possible to be a free spirit, and be loved for it?

At the thought of her icon's responses, Valentina felt momentarily sad. Louise Brooks had paid dearly for being a forthright young woman before her time. Hollywood had turned its back on her, and her talent had been unacknowledged. She believed that if Louise Brooks were a young actress now, she would most certainly have played Marion Cotillard's character in Woody Allen's film.

Valentina cast her eyes around the carriage and imagined herself in a movie, travelling back into the past. The other passengers become unfocused shadows, superfluous extras, as she smoothed down her pencil skirt, crossed her stockinged legs and clasped her gloved hands in her lap. She was Miss Valentina Rosselli, acclaimed starlet of the silent movies, on her way to a day's filming. This was not the metro in Milan but a streetcar in Los Angeles in 1926. And as she was having this rather delicious fantasy, she found herself staring straight into the curious eyes of Theo Steen. Within the haze of her dream he stood in front of her, more real than any man she had laid eyes on before. She could not help but admire him. Smartly dressed in a pinstriped suit and tie, his dark hair groomed, he could have stepped right out of an old movie. He had the features of a screen idol. And he was looking right at her. Blatantly.

It was impossible to look away. His eyes, such a deep blue, seemed to belong to a magician. It passed through her mind that she was being bewitched, because she could sense her own eyes widening, her lashes fluttering involuntarily, and she knew her pupils were dilating. The train stopped at Duomo and a group of teenagers got on, filling the space between her and the stranger. Yet still their eyes found each other. In fact the jostling bodies between them added to the eroticism of their optical connection. He could reach her only with his gaze. She tried to pull away from those hypnotic eyes, yet all she could manage was to take in his face. Dark hair, as jet black as hers, tanned skin, a square jaw with dark stubble. She imagined the feel of that stubble on her naked skin, and it made her shiver involuntarily. He was staring at her hungrily, and she wondered for a moment whether he was dangerous. She tried to look away, down, anywhere but at him. She considered getting off at Cordusio and walking the rest of the way home. Yet just at the moment she was about to get up, he smiled at her, and that changed everything. Valentina rarely smiles, and yet she is drawn to those who do. Theo's smile was engaging, open, teasing. This man was no danger to her. She tipped her head to one side and gave him a little Louise Brooks half-smile in return, one of her eyebrows raised, a question in her gaze. It was the most she could manage, but it was enough. The gang of youths got off at Cairoli, and then it was just the two of them left, a fire building between them in the empty carriage. Yet neither of them spoke. It was as if words would break the erotic spell between them.

They both stood up at exactly the same time to get off. How did he know this was her stop? She walked towards the doors, sensing that he was standing right behind her. Just before the train trundled into Cadorna, he picked up her gloved hand in his and swung her around to face him. His lips found hers in a perfect screen kiss. As the train stopped, she fell against his chest. He smelt of Bulgari, strong, true and enticing. The doors slid open and they stepped out on to the platform together hand in hand. No words passed between them. There was no need, because their eyes had already made an agreement on that bewitching train ride. They walked hand in hand down the platform and up the escalator, through the barrier and out into the stormy March night. It was raining torrentially, but this added to the eroticism of the moment. He put his arm around her shoulders in an effort to protect her from the rain, and ran with her down the street, letting her lead him to wherever she wanted to take him.

Once inside her apartment, they kissed again. Deeper this time. They clung together, feeling the shape of each other's body through their wet clothes. He took a breath and stepped back as she ripped her wet gloves off, dropped her coat to the floor and began to undo the buttons on her blouse one by one. She waited for him to speak, but it was as if he knew what she wanted. No words. Nothing false, just the blind truth of desire. Instead he arched one of his eyebrows and spoke with his expression. He slipped out of his jacket. She noticed, despite his ardour, that he was careful to hang it on the back of a chair before he began to unbutton his own shirt. Ah, she thought, pleased, this man has high standards. White heat was rising between them like a summer haze as they watched each other undress, not yet touching, taunting each other with the promise of their bodies.

They took their time, a bold, languorous dance of foreplay. He yanked his shirt out of the waistband of his trousers and took it off. She slipped her own blouse off in return. Slowly she unclasped her bra, and let it drop from her breasts. She watched his chest tighten, heard his shallow breath as he looked at her. She could see his erection in his trousers, and it was answered by an ache below her pelvis. She shouldn't be doing this. Stripping for a stranger in her apartment, promising him sex. They had not even introduced themselves to each other. And yet the pure abandon of it drove her on. She could really lose herself tonight in this man. She slid her hands around to the back of her skirt and unzipped it, wiggling out of it so that she stood before him, wanton in her G-string, stockings and suspenders. His lips curled up into a smile, his eyes warmed with appraisal as he took her in. He unzipped his trousers and let them fall from his waist. She could see him pushing against the soft fabric of his boxer shorts and she longed to touch him. Smell him. Feel him in her. A dream man from the twenties, alive and breathing in her own real-life silent movie. She could see the dampness of rain glistening on his chest and she stepped forward boldly, leaning down and licking the raindrop off his skin. He held her shoulder with one of his hands and brought her closer to him, so that she could feel his length brushing against her stomach. He was so much taller than her, and his height made her feel even more aroused. She wanted to climb him, so he could bring them both down and pin her to the ground with his long, muscular legs.

They rubbed against each other, warming their damp, chill skin. His silence was intoxicating, as if he knew that to speak would destroy the passion between them. She felt like a different woman, all normality abandoned, just sheer delight and desire fuelling her. What was making her behave in such a way? Was it the whole romantic notion of it, as if she really were living a scene in a film, or was it her carnal need pulsing through her, the badness of what she was doing urging her on. She didn't know. She didn't care.

She took his hand and pulled him towards her bedroom, walking backwards through the debris of their clothes. He followed her lead, and once inside the room he took her up in his arms and carried her to the bed. The romance of it took her breath away. No man had ever carried her like that before.

He placed her carefully on the bed, and knelt next to her, hovering over her. He stroked her body with his fingertips, and she found herself exhaling a deep, guttural breath that made her feel as if she had never really exhaled properly before. He unclipped her stockings from the suspender belt and rolled them down her legs. She could tell he was enjoying this rare ritual. Not many girls wore stockings any more. He hooked her G-string around his index finger, and pulled it suddenly with tremendous force, so that it ripped in two. The energy shifted between them as he gathered her up, and they began kissing again. Her heart began to race as their now warmed bodies merged together. This man was a panther beneath his civilised exterior. Her skin was singing with delight at his touch, as if they had been meant to meet, as if there was some other power at play this night that had led them both to be on that metro in Milan at exactly the same time. A ridiculous idea, and yet a wonderful fantasy.

His mouth on hers, his taste so sweet and right, she reached down with her hands and tugged at his boxer shorts, cradling his penis in one of her hands. She wanted him right now, before the magic disappeared between them. Still kissing him, with her other arm she reached over to her bedside table and opened the drawer, pulling out a condom packet. She drew back from him slightly, found his hand and gave him the packet. She wanted to make sure it was what he wanted as well. He smiled at her in appreciation. A gentleman, of course, no question of not using a condom. He sat back on his heels while he put it on, and she watched him, her insides melting with anticipation. Then he picked her up and rolled them, so that she was now on top. She took him in her hands, and as she leant down, pressing her lips to his, she pushed him up inside her.

It had been a couple of months since she had had sex, and yet she knew already that this was like no sex she had had before. Was it their anonymity that made it so incredibly intimate? How much this human being trusted her. How much she trusted him. It was heady. She lifted her body, and balanced above him before pushing down again. He reached up and cradled her breasts in his hands, his mouth a little open, his tongue flicking across his teeth.

In the beginning she had thought he would come inside her, and it would be enjoyable for her but she wouldn't climax herself. She had never been able to orgasm if her partner was wearing a condom, and especially if it was the first time she slept with someone. And yet with this stranger, something new was happening to her. He didn't succumb to his own pleasure first; instead he held her arms with his hands and moved her up and down, pushing his hips up to hers and making her ride him faster and faster. Deeper and deeper he went, and on and on. She had never made love for so long. They rolled over again and he was on top of her, pushing up into her. She began to feel herself quivering. Could this be possible? She was panting, crawling up the walls on the edge of her abandon, tipping over, so nearly, so nearly. He leant down and bit her nipple, pushed up again inside her, and to her shock she was coming, throbbing around his hard length. She looked into his eyes, almost black now, and they stared right into hers, sheer as onyx with his own sensations. He gasped as he joined her in her orgasm, falling on top of her so that they were both sinking into each other.

Of the few one-night stands that Valentina had experienced up to this point in her life, she had found them all disappointing. Embarrassing almost, when the deed was done and she was trying to get rid of the guy without seeming too cold. Yet this time was different. What kind of magic was this? He seemed to find her as irresistible as she found him, for after the first time they made love, they did not fall asleep or even talk to each other, but started all over again. How was he able to do it? she wondered. Was he some kind of superman? So many times they made love that first night. It was as if they explored every inch of each other's body in the space of eight hours. Underneath him, and on top. Standing. Sitting with her back to him, and him leaning over so that he could grip her breasts from behind. Kneeling in front of him as he took her from behind. Sitting on him on a chair in the kitchen when she went to get them a glass of water and he followed her. On top of him on the hall floor on the way back. Curled around each other in the shower the next morning. All this passion felt like a kind of homecoming, and yet she didn't even know his name.

Valentina sprays some canned air on to the old negative and gently brushes it with a sable brush. She places it carefully between two pieces of clear plastic and puts it down on her dresser. She remembers those first moments when she woke up the next morning, expecting in the cold light of day to be awkward with this stranger in her bed, at the very least to want him to leave. Yet that didn't happen. She awoke to his kisses, and they made love yet again, as tenderly as if they had been lovers the whole of their adult lives.

That night was the most erotic of her life, yet she never expected anything from it. Even after they had finally made their introductions: Theo Steen, American, art historian, in Milan to work on his post-doctoral thesis, single; Valentina Rosselli, professional photographer, native of Milan and single too. Even when Theo joked over coffee and brioche the next morning that this would be a good story to tell their children, she thought he was just being funny. How could two people who had met in such a way have a chance of sustaining any kind of relationship? And yet somehow they managed to become lovers. She was so surprised when he rang her the following evening and asked her out for a drink. She had believed she would never hear from him again, and was hesitant about accepting his invitation. Now their lives are entangled, no matter how hard she tries to keep her distance. Is this what these negatives are about? A means for Theo to communicate with her?

She picks up the enlargements she has done so far and arranges them in a row on her bed. As well as the 'landscape' back and the tied ankle, there are four more images. One is clearly an ear lobe with a gold ring in it. Instinctively she feels this is a man's ear rather than a woman's. The gold ring is too plain and small to be women's jewellery. There is a picture of a gloved hand and arm, holding a long string of pearls. Valentina particularly likes this image, the contrast of the black glove and the white beads. There is a pair of lips, un-smiling and dark; she imagines them stained with red lipstick if the image were colour. Finally, most tantalisingly, there is an eye. Just one. It is so close up it took her a while to realise what it was. The eye is looking down so that in fact all that can be seen is an iridescent eyelid, framed by a straight and defined eyebrow and long black eyelashes sweeping the tip of the subject's cheek.

Who *is* this woman? Valentina is consumed by curiosity. The only person who can give her any idea is probably miles away from Milan. Is Theo trying to drive her crazy with frustration? He knows this puzzle will obsess her, and yet she has to admit it, at the same time he knows she will love it. But how can she find out the identity of the close-up woman . . . and now a man as well? She has absolutely no information about them. There was nothing in Theo's desk. She chews her lip, picking up the tied ankle image and staring at it again. These images have started to become part of her dreams now. Last night she dreamt her ankles were tied to the end of the bed, just like in this picture she was looking at before she fell asleep. She had the most erotic dream about Theo caressing her all over. She woke up wanting her lover, and disappointed to find he wasn't there. Maybe it was the phone call with Leonardo Sorrentino that made her dream about such things. Well she doesn't have time to analyse her dream psychology now. She has a meeting to get to with said Leonardo, owner of an S&M sex club.

What to wear? It's early evening, yet she doesn't want to dress up too much and attract unwanted attention at this club. At the same time she doesn't want to stand out as looking too casual or square. In the end she dresses in black trousers and singlet with a leather jacket, always a safe option, and always complementary with her black bob. She puts on some dark lipstick, the colour of oxtail, and grabs her camera bag on the way out the door. She is not sure if she will need it, but she guesses it's better to be prepared.

Just as she is about to get into her taxi, she sees a figure stepping out from behind a car on the other side of the street. He has his hands in his pockets and he is staring at her. She glances behind her as she approaches the taxi. Yes, quite definitely he is looking at her. Instinctively she knows that this is not the man from the garden. He is older, shorter and stocky, with grey hair. He looks as if he is about to say something, but she doesn't give him a chance. She jumps into the taxi. As it speeds away, she turns around and looks out the rear window. He is still standing in the middle of the road, his hands in his pockets, frowning.

Two strange men watching her within the last twenty-four hours. She can't help feeling a little unsettled, wishing Theo were here. She takes her mobile phone out of her bag, rotates it between her hands. Maybe she could call him. Ask him when he'll be back. She wonders what he would say if she told him about the watchers. Would he tell her she was being paranoid? Certainly the man in the garden could have been a figment of her imagination. Yet the man she saw just now *was* real, and he did look as if he wanted to speak to her. She chastises herself; he is just some sleazeball wanting to chat her up. That's what Theo would tell her. *Valentina, you are unaware of the impact you have on men.* She laughed when he said this. Told him he was being ridiculous. She was no Marilyn Monroe.

'Absolutely you're not, darling. But not every man wants a busty blonde, you know.'

She pops her phone back into her bag and dismisses the thought of the strange men. She has an interesting evening ahead of her. She is already jangling with nerves. What will this Leonardo Sorrentino show her tonight? She needs to be grounded and calm, not worrying about anything else right now.

The S&M club is in a part of Milan Valentina doesn't know very well, near Via Garligliano in the Isola district. The part of Milan that used to be like Venice, until Mussolini decided to block up all the canals. It used to be a very rundown, seedy area, but recently it has become quite trendy. Like S&M, she supposes, which is gradually being viewed as more acceptable as well.

Along with her nerves is excitement. Her heart is beating fast, and she can feel her stomach cramping with anticipation. After what she saw on the internet last night, she decided not to look up any more images of S&M. She doesn't want to be put off any more than she is already. It isn't that she judges these people. It's just she can't see the attraction of pain when it comes to sex. And yet she is intrigued. She wants to understand this dark side to human sexuality. Is it a perverse thing to want to do? Or is it liberating, acting out natural instincts even?

Leonardo Sorrentino is the opposite of what Valentina expected. He is young, for a start. She had this image of an older man, fat and bald and a little obscene. A stereotype, of course. Leonardo is probably only a couple of years older than her. He is dark skinned, like Theo. Even reminds her of her lover a little, with his easy smile, although Leonardo is not as tall as Theo, and his eyes are dark brown rather than blue.

He is dressed in an impeccable and expensive-looking navy suit, and a shirt the colour of violets, which despite its pretty hue looks far from feminine on him. She can smell the Armani as soon as she walks through the innocuous entrance of the private club.

'Signorina Rosselli, thank you for coming,' he greets her.

'Call me Valentina,' she says, feeling awkward at his formality.

'Leonardo,' he smiles back, squeezing her hand in his.

They walk down a long corridor of shiny black marble tiles, with dimmed lighting on the walls. Any minute Valentina is expecting to be led into a den of torture instruments, yet when he finally ushers her into a room at the end of the corridor, she can't help feeling a little disappointed by its plainness. Soft lighting, a large cream sofa and matching cream rug. Not one whip or chain in sight.

Leonardo invites her to sit. He takes off his suit jacket and drapes it on the back of his chair. His purple shirt is made of soft silky cotton, and clings to his well-defined chest. He has just two buttons undone, not too much and not too little. He takes a bottle of white wine from a fridge in the corner of the room.

'I must tell you how much I liked the series of erotic self-portraits you took in the canal in Venice,' he says as he pours out their wine.

Valentina stiffens in shock. No beating around the bush with Signor Sorrentino. She imagines him looking over the images of her exposed body. She has a feeling that he saw *all* of her even if it was in his imagination.

'How did you get to see them?' she asks him. 'They haven't been published or exhibited anywhere. Not even on the internet.'

'I am afraid I have promised I won't tell you that, Valentina.'

'Was it Stephano Linardi? Did he give you a copy of my memory stick?' she demands. She knows she is being too direct, possibly rude. She has always found social graces a challenge. Leonardo arches an eyebrow in reply.

'He said they were porn, not art,' she tells him.

'Well in my opinion they are neither,' says Leonardo. 'I would call them erotic narrative. You are telling an erotic story with your images.'

He pauses, takes a sip of his wine.

'I have seen it in your fashion photography as well, how you choreograph a scene. This is why I would like you to do this project for us. It's so important to get the right tone.'

'But why do you want pictures taken in the first place?'

'Actually it wasn't my idea,' Leonardo admits. 'I have been approached by a third party, who insists that I don't reveal his identity to anyone. He wishes to publish a book of erotic and tasteful photographs of the S and M scene. There is also the possibility of exhibiting the work.'

How can S&M be tasteful? The thought passes fleetingly through Valentina's head.

Interpreting her silence correctly, Leonardo says, 'I can

assure you that sadomasochism can be quite beautiful and graceful at times, Valentina.'

'But I have no experience of it,' Valentina admits, trying to look unembarrassed.

'That is exactly why I have asked you do it. You are an unbiased observer. Well, I hope unbiased. If you do think that sadomasochism is, well, a sick perversion, I suggest we don't pursue the project. For your own sake.'

Valentina thinks about it. She takes a sip of her wine, while peeking at Leonardo under lowered lashes. He looks the picture of wholesomeness. She can't help wondering if he is a dominant or a submissive. It is hard to imagine him doing anything too brutal. Just as with the mystery of Theo's book of old negatives, she is driven by curiosity more than anything else. She knows she will not walk away from this opportunity.

'No, of course I don't think it's sick. In fact I am fascinated,' she admits.

Leonardo smiles at her again. He has a broad smile, almost dazzling. She cannot return it, and it makes her feel as if she appears even more surly than usual. He cocks his head on its side in puzzlement at her sour expression, his smile slowly fading.

'Well, good,' he says, standing up, speaking more formally again. 'So first of all let me show you around so that you can start thinking of ideas. Really it's completely up to you what you want to do. Most of our clients have agreed to be photographed, so you can choose to be a fly on the wall and simply make a record of what is occurring, or you can construct your own scenes if you like.' He pauses, smiling at her again, this time more slyly. 'That could be quite fun for you.'

Valentina still doesn't return Leonardo's smile.

'Maybe,' she says coolly, but she can feel her body begin to heat up beneath her leather jacket. *Construct her own scenes?* The idea is enticingly erotic. She can apply all her passion for detail and theatricality in this sensual setting. The possibilities make her almost dizzy with excitement.

'Remember, Valentina,' Leonardo continues, 'I don't want pornography. Any man or woman off the street can do that. I want something artistic. That's why we've picked you. We want eroticism.'

'I understand,' Valentina says as she follows Leonardo out of the room and further down the black marble corridor. He leads her to the top of a staircase, also made of black marble, and turns to her.

'There is no one here at the moment,' he tells her. 'It is a little too early in the evening, but I will show you one of the rooms our clients might use. That is if you are ready?'

She nods, following him down the stairs. The lights grow dimmer and dimmer, and she feels a prickle of fear down her spine. She hates going into dark, confined spaces. At the bottom of the staircase is a small oval hallway with three doors leading off it. There is one light casting a murky glow around the space.

'So, Valentina.' Leonardo points at the doors one at a time. 'Behind each of these doors are different levels of experience, so to speak. The wooden door leads you into what I would call our more-pleasure-than-pain room. The leather door is more pain than pleasure.'

Valentina swallows hard. What's the difference? How much pain still allows some pleasure?

'And this room,' he walks up to a steel door, polished and shimmering in the dim hall, 'this is the Dark Room.' He presses his hand against it, turning round and staring at her with an expression of triumph. She can see it then instantly. He is a dominant; there is no doubt.

She looks away from Leonardo and stares at the metal door.

'What happens in the Dark Room?' Her voice is almost a whisper.

Leonardo takes a step towards her. He is so close, his Armani aftershave is almost overpowering.

'In the Dark Room you are scared, Valentina, because as the name implies, there is no light. You can see nothing, not even your hand in front of your face.'

'Why would anyone want to go in there?' Her voice lowers.

Leonardo flashes her a flirtatious look.

'It is precisely because of your fear that you are able to heighten your sexual experience to a degree you will never have anywhere else.'

Valentina doesn't move. She knows this man wants her to

react. To laugh, perhaps. Or exclaim. Even run away up the stairs. She won't do it.

'I see,' she says calmly. 'But I suppose it will be no use to me if it is all in the dark. I won't be taking any pictures in there.'

Leonardo nods, a lazy smile spreading across his face.

'Quite right. There is no need for you to go into the Dark Room . . . unless, of course, you want—'

Valentina cuts him short.

'Can you show me the other rooms, please. I'm afraid I have to go soon.'

Leonardo's smile widens. He knows she is lying. Already he has worked her out. She is scared of the Dark Room.

'Very well,' he says, strolling over to open the wooden door. 'This is what we call our Atlantis Room. You will see why, I hope, once you have experienced it for real.'

Valentina pauses on the threshold. She looks at Leonardo's hand, his elegantly manicured fingers, as he slowly turns the handle. Her heart begins to race. She has a feeling that once she steps into the Atlantis Room, her life will never be the same again. It is a choice she is making on her own, without the consent of her lover, and yet as she moves forward, she hears Theo's soft American accent in her head. *That's my girl, my intrepid Valentina.*

$\mathcal{B}$elle

THERE IS A KNOCK ON HER DOOR. BELLE CHECKS HERSELF in the mirror. She brushes down her dress, her hands gliding over the slinky black material. It is one of her maid's uniforms, which Belle adjusted herself. Something she enjoyed doing, sitting on her little balcony in the Venetian sunshine, sewing and listening to her neighbour playing Bach on his harpsichord. She is not allowed to do this sort of work at home, but she loves to make things and it gave her great satisfaction adjusting Pina's uniform for the needs of her client. The little black dress now hangs just below her bottom, and above the line of her black stockings, which are of course decorated with white lacy garters. She has a crisp white apron on over the dress, and a little white maid's hat crowns her black bob. The Russian knocks again. My, he is impatient today, Belle thinks, picking up her feather duster and opening the door.

'Good afternoon, sir.' She bows her head respectfully as the Russian strides purposefully into the room.

'Good afternoon, Katya,' he says, looking stern. 'And what took you so long to answer the door?'

'I am sorry, sir, I came as fast as I could.'

'Well that's not good enough, Katya,' he replies, fixing her with a steely glare, making Belle's heart race a little. 'You will have to be reprimanded.'

'Yes, sir.'

'Do you know why?'

'Because I did not do as you said.'

'That's right, Katya. Last time I told you to answer the door promptly after my first knock. Today I have had to knock *twice*.'

The Russian holds his arms out for her to take off his coat. He smells of tobacco, and sandalwood. It is an intoxicating mixture. He hands her his hat and gloves and she places them neatly on the sideboard. He has a small riding crop in his right hand, which he slaps gently against the palm of his left hand. The sight of it makes her stomach clench.

She leads him into her bedroom and he walks behind her, using the riding crop to lift the hem of her dress so that he can see her bottom.

'I am pleased to see that you have followed my directive, and dispensed with underwear.'

He speaks so formally, Belle thinks, like the bureaucrat he is. She can feel him trailing the tip of his riding crop down her bottom, and flipping it gently against her legs so that she squeals with fright and excitement.

'Contain yourself, please, Katya. You must submit to your punishment with humility.'

'Yes, sir,' she replies, casting her eyes down demurely.

He sits on her bed and puts the riding crop down beside him. Then he crooks his finger and beckons for her to come closer.

She is standing right in front of him now. She can feel her nipples pushing in anticipation against the cheap artificial silk of her maid's uniform. The Russian's voice drops an octave.

'So, Katya, tell me what you are.'

'I am subordinate, sir. I did not follow your orders.'

'And what do you want me to do?'

'I want you to spank me, please, sir.'

The Russian takes her forcefully by the hand and puts her over his knee. Belle's breath becomes short and shallow. They have done this before, and yet every time she feels a thrill. She can't think why. When her husband hits her, she certainly does not enjoy it. She feels degraded and angry. Yet when the Russian spanks her, Belle has to admit she finds it strangely erotic. It must be because she has free will. She knows that all she has to do is tell the Russian to stop and he will. She can break the spell of their little charade at any time, but she doesn't want to. Her skin is tingling with anticipation. She can feel his erection pressing into her chest.

The Russian pulls up her maid's uniform so that her backside is bare. He massages her bottom with his hands. She wonders if he will use the riding crop. It is right there next to him on the bed. All her senses are heightened, and when his bare hand slaps down on her backside, she feels it vibrate through her whole body. Its hurts, a little, but not too much. She knows it is stimulating the Russian, and that what will come after her punishment will be so very sweet. He spanks her again and again, and her flesh feels raw and alive. Five, six slaps and he stops. She hears his breath heavy with desire as he stands her up.

'Good girl,' he says, pushing his hands between her legs, and touching her. 'What do you want me to do now, Katya?' he asks, the whiskers of his little beard tickling her chin, his expression benign now that he has spanked her. Belle reaches down with her hand and touches his hard penis, which is pressing against his flannel trousers.

'I want you to show me who is master.' She gives him her sweetest smile and widens her eyes in innocence.

Belle is on her hands and knees looking at the pattern on her Persian rug. Her dress and apron are discarded beside her, but she still wears her stockings and maid's hat. The Russian pushes into her with a low moan, and holds on to her breasts. He immediately begins pounding into her with such force she almost collapses on to the carpet. She loves this primal sex with the Russian. The contrast between his cool aristocratic bearing and the wild passion once he is inside her. He holds her waist with both hands and grinds into her, going further and further. Belle closes her eyes and joins him in his wild abandon. She is

Katya, his little Russian maid, his love slave who will do anything for him, because he takes care of her and always will. It is a fantasy she likes, despite the fact she hates being bound to her husband. She can't explain this contradiction.

The Russian is crying out, 'Katya, *milaya moya*!' as he finally comes, his vibrations sending Belle into a spin so that she is climaxing as well. They collapse on to the Persian rug, both of them glowing with perspiration, and the Russian rolls off her back to lie beside her.

Belle turns to him. Now he is a different man. Tears are streaming down his face. His expression is one of utter devastation.

'Oh, dear Igor,' she says, taking him into her arms. He presses his wet cheek against her bare breasts, and she strokes his hair, letting him weep. She looks down at his scarred body, his back covered in red welts, the marks of his time in prison in Siberia. Despite his aristocratic bearing, Igor was in fact a revolutionary, a comrade of Lenin's. It might have been amusing to consider how this diehard communist liked to play the lord and master, if he wasn't such a tragic figure. He was forced to flee Russia after Lenin died and Stalin replaced him. He tried to stop Stalin's rise to power, and now he was a wanted man. Belle has made herself feel sorry for him, never asking about before the Revolution, whether he was one of those Russian soldiers who burnt their way through her homeland the year she married. That was so long ago now.

She holds Igor in her arms until he has stopped crying, the

two of them naked. She feels cleansed by his wash of emotion.

'Who is Katya?' she asks tentatively.

Igor sighs, turning to look at her with melancholy eyes.

'Despite my revolutionary background, Belle, I have to admit I am not working class. I was brought up in a wealthy bourgeois family. We had a maid. Her name was Katya.'

He sighs again, as if he has the woes of the world upon his shoulders, then moves away from her, standing up. She sits up on the rug, watches his pale back, stiff and narrow. He reminds her of a heron, a solitary, aloof figure, watching the business of life swim past him.

'I was in love with Katya,' he says, dropping his head and clutching his hands together.

'What happened, Igor?' Despite his obvious distress, she senses that her Russian needs to tell her this.

He spins around to face her. His eyes are still wet from his tears, yet lit up with passion like the blue flames at the heart of a fire.

'She died. It was my fault. I was supposed to take care of her. She was so loyal . . . so innocent . . . so sweet . . .'

Belle gets up and walks over to Igor. She puts her arms around him. Now that they are no longer in the throes of passion, their nakedness seems so trusting and pure. He bends his head and speaks into her shoulder.

'I left her behind thinking she was safer, but she wasn't . . . My family escaped, but not Katya. I had ordered her to go with them if the time came to flee, but apparently she refused.

She waited for me until everyone else had gone, and the Whites rode into town looking for me. They made Katya pay for my absence.'

'Oh, Igor.' Belle embraces him tightly. He lifts his head, looks her in the eyes. She can see the anguish in their blue waters.

'Dear Belle, thank you for understanding.'

She squeezes his hand.

'You will find love again, Igor.'

'Do you believe that, Belle?' he asks hopelessly.

She looks inside her heart. There is a perverse part of her that almost envies Igor. At least he has known what it is like to be in love. She says a silent prayer.

'Yes, I believe that within one lifetime, every single one of us will experience true love. If we lose it and our hearts are open enough despite our loss, we can find it again.'

'Everyone!' He smiles ruefully. 'Even Stalin? Or Mussolini?'

'Yes, even them.' She smiles back, gently wiping his face with her maid's hat. 'It is the human condition.'

$\mathscr{V}$alentina

WHEN VALENTINA STEPS THROUGH THE DOORWAY INTO what Leonardo calls the Atlantis Room, all appears serene, not at all the den of iniquity she imagined. The walls are painted Prussian blue and the floor is white marble. There is a sturdy black desk in the centre of the room, with a large sea-blue pile rug beneath it that takes up most of the floor space. There are no windows in the room, only one large skylight, which lets in a golden glow as if it is the middle of the day, although Valentina knows it is dark outside. There is a wrought-iron daybed, and sturdy white wooden beams support the ceiling. All in all it is bright and minimalist, like an Ikea showroom.

'So, Valentina,' Leonardo says, 'let me talk you through everything in our Atlantis Room.' He walks to the desk and sits down upon it facing her, his legs spread a little provocatively. Valentina tries her best not to look at his crotch, glancing up at the skylight.

'I thought it would be darker in here,' she comments.

'Some of our clients don't like the dark,' Leonardo says. 'They want to act out their scenes somewhere that could almost be from their ordinary lives. So this room is what we call a day room, or a light bondage room.'

He pulls out several drawers in the black desk and indicates for her to come over and have a look.

'Here, for instance, are a number of things a dominant can use with his or her submissive.'

In the first drawer Valentina looks into, she sees a whole bunch of electrical sex toys – mostly vibrators, but a breathtaking array of types: petite pink clitoral massagers, elegant medium-sized vibrators with curves in various places to provide different stimulations, and full-on dual-action vibrators. One of them is so immense it is frightening; how would it feel to have that up inside her? She quivers internally at the thought. Most of the products she recognises as part of the Swedish LELO range, sleek, stylish designs that appeal to her artistic sensibilities. They look like art objects rather than tools of passion. She imagines the squeals of delight if Antonella were here. Her friend would certainly explore the contents of this drawer. She picks up one item, intrigued by its design: a black oval pod that loops into a ring at its tip. Leonardo reaches into the drawer beside her, his hand brushing against her bare arm, making her catch her breath despite herself.

'It works with this,' he says, taking out a round golden object. 'It's a remote control.'

He presses a button, and the toy in her hand starts to vibrate. Unwillingly she feels herself blushing.

'It has several different speeds,' he says, as easily as if he is showing her how to change the channel on a television.

'Thanks,' she says, feeling the pod throbbing against her palm.

'Do you know what it is?' he asks, his lips curved into a mischievous grin.

'Well . . . it's a kind of vibrator?'

'Yes.' He nods, trying to keep a straight face. 'But one for her *and* him.' He takes it from her, and pushes the ring end around two of his fingers. 'This is a ring to go around the penis. It stimulates the man, and helps enlarge him.'

'Right,' she says, trying to look dignified, as if this is a conversation one might have with a man you have only just met.

'And this part, the pod, can be used to stimulate either her clitoris, or, if you swing it around, his balls.'

Valentina can't help it. She imagines herself and Theo playing with this toy. The thought makes her blush spread to her chest, weave into the sinews of her body, so that her heartbeat is racing. Something primal within her wants to touch Leonardo. It is absurd. She takes a step away from him, and hastily puts the sex toy back into the drawer.

Leonardo, seemingly unaware of her physical reaction to him, pulls out another drawer.

'Here are toys a dominatrix can use to pleasure her submissive . . . if he is a man.'

Valentina looks inside. She recognises an array of gentle-man's plugs and G-spot massagers. One of them looks uncomfortably large. There is also a collection of gentleman's rings, some of them quite beautiful. Sleek black onyx, burn-ished gold, silver studded with tiny diamonds. She wonders idly if Theo would like one.

Finally Leonardo pulls out the last drawer.

'In here we have some items used in light bondage scenarios,' he says, looking at her with curious eyes. She guesses he is watching her to see her reaction, and keeps a poker face plastered on her features. She feels silly after her ignorance over the vibrating toy. She doesn't want to show herself up again. However, there are no surprises when she looks inside. The usual bondage gear: several sets of silver chains, with varying thicknesses of links, silk ties, a rope, blindfolds in different materials, handcuffs, and a ball gag for the mouth.

'So for instance,' Leonardo picks up a chain and balances it on his fingertips, walking over to one of the beams, where he swings one end over it and pulls both ends together, 'one could be chained up like this.' He loops it round a vertical beam and stands with his back to it. 'Or the chains could be bound around you like so.'

He catches her eye, and she can't help imagining being chained to one of these beams. There is a loaded pause before he drops the chain on the floor and picks up the handcuffs, swinging them between his hands before throwing them at her, so that she is forced to catch them.

'One could be handcuffed to the end of the daybed . . . or to the desk . . . There are all sorts of variations.'

He walks past the black desk, stroking it with his hand as he passes. She can't help noticing how long and slender his fingers are, and wondering what he can do with them.

'This room can become an office fantasy. Or,' he says, opening up a set of doors behind him to reveal a storage space, 'it could be a doctor's or dentist's surgery.'

He wheels out an examination chair for her to see. She looks up at him in disbelief, and he is grinning at her.

'Please sit,' he commands.

She hesitates, gripping the handcuffs tightly.

'Don't worry, I won't do anything.'

She shrugs, embarrassed by her coyness, then walks over and climbs into the chair.

'Sit back,' Leonardo says. 'Relax.' And she can hear the humour in his voice as he presses a button on the side of the chair so that it tips back just like at the dentist's.

'Now you see you could be bound up on this thing and all sorts could be done to give you pleasure.' He pauses. 'And pain.'

Leonardo grins down at her, and she can see that he is actually having fun showing her all these things. She has an irresistible urge to laugh out loud, which is something she *never* does. However, she manages to maintain her sangfroid. Looking at all these instruments and gadgets in this brightly lit room makes them seem silly. They are just toys really, she thinks. All these people are doing is playing games. It's harmless enough, isn't it?

Yet when she looks up at Leonardo as he leans over her, the scent of him beginning to pervade her, she feels a tremor deep within her pelvis, a sensation halfway between fear and excitement. She is missing Theo. It's Theo she wants. So why is Leonardo having this effect on her?

'Any ideas, Valentina?'

She sits up, ignoring his gaze, and swings her legs over.

'I'll have a think.'

He takes her hand and helps her off the chair. His skin is warm and soft, yet not too hot.

'Well, let me tell you about tomorrow's protagonists,' he begins.

'Oh.' She lets go of his hand, and fumbles with her bag, looking inside for a notebook, the handcuffs still dangling from one of her wrists.

'I thought we should start gently. Just in case it's not for you. You see, we really do need you to reflect our mindset.' His earlier mischief is gone. He is all earnestness now.

'Yes, I understand,' she says, handing him back the cuffs. Their fingers brush again, and the contrast of his warm skin after the cold metal make her shiver a little.

'Okay then,' he says, putting the chains and handcuffs back in the drawers. 'I have two ladies coming here tomorrow night. Rosa and Celia. They are both dancers, and they take it in turns over who dominates and who is submissive. They are both very sensual.'

Valentina writes in her notebook: *Rosa. Celia. Dancers. Sensual.*

Leonardo opens the door for her.

'And is that it? Just the two women?' she asks him.

'Yes, I think that will be enough, for the first time. They have very beautiful bodies,' he whispers into her ear as she walks by. 'I am sure you can create something extremely erotic and visually pleasing with those two girls.'

Valentina feels a wave of relief. Women's naked bodies. That is something she is used to. She needs to build up to her first photograph of a full-frontal man, especially in a bondage scenario.

They are back out in the dim corridor now. Valentina glances at the steel door of the Dark Room. Its presence taunting her.

'Neither of those girls is interested in the Dark Room, Valentina,' Leonardo says, noticing her look in its direction. 'Although sometimes they might be tempted behind this door,' he adds, tapping the green leather door. 'Our very own Velvet Underworld. I am hoping that you will use this space as well for some of your pictures. Would you like to see?'

'Of course,' Valentina says as nonchalantly as she can, although she is dying to see behind the leather door.

The Velvet Underworld is all that Valentina expected from a bondage den. It is the opposite of the Atlantis Room, decorated like a nineteenth-century bordello with flock wallpaper and velvet couches. In the centre of the room is an enormous four-poster bed hung with purple drapes. The walls are covered with gilt-framed mirrors, as is the ceiling. Valentina can see a dozen reflections of herself as she walks into the room. She looks austere and judgemental in her sombre clothes, against this background of colour and opulence.

'I have to admit, this is the more popular of our two rooms,' says Leonardo, sitting down on the bed and fluffing up one of the pillows. 'The sadomasochists of Milan still like a little luxury,' he jokes, spreading his legs like he did in the Atlantis Room and leaning back against the pillow. Is he deliberately trying to wind her up? 'There are in fact a lot of toys and implements in this room,' he continues. 'Would you like to explore it for yourself?'

'Okay.' She turns her back on him and his provocative crotch, and circles the room. The first thing she notices is a large wooden cross attached to the far wall, with leather straps for arms and legs. There is a harness of some sort suspended from the ceiling, and a hammock like the one she saw on the internet. In the corner of the room is a selection of whips hanging off the wall. She goes over to them and fingers the leather strap of the largest one, squeezing the hard tip between her fingers.

Mio dio, *that must hurt!*

She finds it hard to get her head around the idea of being whipped. Why would any woman *want* to be beaten? Yet she forces herself not to make assumptions. She needs to understand why. That's the reason she is here, isn't it?

'I am afraid we are running a little short of time,' Leonardo says, looking at his watch. 'I have this room booked in about ten minutes and I need to make preparations.'

Valentina turns to him as he lounges on the bed. She can't help wondering if he is one of the people using this room tonight. Her lips have suddenly gone dry, and she tries to moisten them surreptitiously with her tongue.

'You can have another look in here tomorrow or some other time, okay?' he says, getting up off the bed.

She has seen enough for tonight anyway. Her head is full of images from the Atlantis Room and the Velvet Under-world. Amid all the shock, and curiosity, she is also feeling stimulated, and yes, she is getting some ideas for her shoot tomorrow. Blue. Dancers. Naked beauty. All those pretty vibrators. She can work with that. Her pictures will be explicit, of course, but it will be women, and that makes her feel a little safer.

Leonardo accompanies her up the staircase and to the front hall again.

'So you'll be back tomorrow night?' he asks, giving her a long look.

'Of course,' she says, blinking at him in the brighter light of the reception area.

'I haven't scared you off?' he asks, smiling at her almost shyly now.

'No, not at all,' she says, kissing him lightly on both cheeks in parting. His Armani pervades her senses again, and as she pulls back she notices something else. To her surprise, Leonardo is wearing a small gold earring in one of his lobes. The image doesn't seem to fit with his sleek businesslike appearance, as incongruous as a love heart tattoo on his arm would be.

'Well, thank you, Valentina,' he says as she makes her way out.

'What for? It's you who's hired me . . .'

'Yes, but you didn't have to accept.' He smiles at her as he clicks the door shut, and she is left in darkness on the doorstep, the image of his charming hazel eyes still imprinted upon her irises.

Valentina makes her way towards the metro, mulling over her encounter with Leonardo, reliving her impressions of the two bondage rooms he showed her inside his club. In one way they did not come up to her expectations, and in another way they confounded them. For some reason she actually finds the Atlantis Room the more erotic of the two spaces. And then there is the Dark Room. Would she ever have the courage to go inside?

She tries to stay focused on the job in hand. This is a big and exciting photographic assignment. Her first proper exploration into the world of erotic photography. How fitting that only yesterday, Theo should have given her that present of the book with the old pornographic negatives. It feels as if it is some kind of sign, confirming that what she has just agreed to do – creating a book of S&M photography, no less – is going to be a positive move for her career. She quickens her pace at the thought of Theo and his gift. He could be home tonight. Sometimes he only goes away overnight. She finds herself hoping he is. He can explain his present to her, and afterwards . . . Well, her tour of Leonardo's club has given her plenty of ideas for what she and Theo might do in their own bedroom. The last thing on her mind is to answer the question he left her with yesterday morning. Somehow her encounter with Leonardo has lightened her mood. Tonight, deciding whether she wants to be Theo's girlfriend is just not as important as being his lover.

$\mathscr{B}$elle

SHE WANTS DARKNESS. SO TONIGHT BELLE GOES BACK TO Ponte di Rialto, where her career as a Venetian prostitute first took off. She cannot bear to be in the light, for her clients to see the marks upon her body. This morning Signor Brzezinski did not hit her with his fists, as usual, but decided to use the back of her hairbrush instead and beat her hard upon her backside. In the same place her Russian had spanked her, and yet this time it was not fun. He hit her again and again relentlessly until she was forced to beg him to stop. And what was her offence? She laughed at him. And spoke Polish. Signor Brzezinski was standing in the centre of her bedroom, hand on his hip, declaring what a great leader Mussolini was, that finally he was bringing Italy back to her former glory as an empire. It occurred to Louise that her husband looked a little like the Italian dictator himself – short, bald, big head and thick lips, overemphatic expressions, pontificating. Too Italian to actually be Italian. He looked ridiculous: a stout Polish man in a red silk dressing gown, which was too long for him and trailed on the rug, spouting his rough Italian as if he had marbles in his mouth.

She laughed, and even spoke to him in Polish, forgetting for a moment that she should be careful.

'But we are Polish! What do you care about Mussolini and Italy?'

Signor Brzezinski moved swiftly across the bedroom and gave her a hard slap across the face.

'Don't ever talk to me in Polish again.'

She challenged him further. What did she have to lose? She recognised the narrowing of his eyes and what would come next.

'But it is where we are from. You cannot wipe out who you are.'

He grabbed her hand and yanked her up from the bed. She swallowed her screams. If she called out, it only made him worse.

'I belong to this city,' he hissed in her face. 'And you belong to me since the day your father gave you to me.'

He grabbed her hairbrush from her dressing table. She saw its silver back glinting in the morning light, making her catch her breath. So hard and cold and painful, she thought. He pushed her down on the floor, so that her mouth was filled with felt from the rug, and sat astride her, immobilising her completely. The first time he hit her across her thighs. She gritted her teeth. She would not plead with him.

'You are never to speak Polish in this house again,' he snarled, pulling up her silk nightdress and whacking her hard on her behind.

Louise squeezed her eyes shut, tried to remove herself from the brutal, stinging slaps of the hairbrush against her naked backside.

What has happened to her husband? He hasn't always been like this. As Belle walks through the dark, silent city, the canal quietly lapping at her side, she has a memory of when they first moved into their house in Venice. It would be fourteen years ago now. Her mother was with them then. Signor Brzezinski was so kind to Louise's mother. She remembers them sitting on the balcony, marvelling at the green hues of the canal, and for the first time since they had buried her father, her mother managed a wan smile. Signor Brzezinski joined them, a bottle of champagne in one hand and three flutes held by the stems in the other. He sat between the two women and made a toast.

'To our new life in Venice,' he said in Polish, turning to Louise's mother. 'May I always be able to take care of my two very special ladies as your dear husband would see fit.'

Louise remembers that her mother paled at the mention of her dead husband, yet she did not cry, but held her son-in-law's gaze with defeated eyes.

What has happened to that man? While her mother lived with them he never made demands on Louise. She was so young when she married him. And he said he would wait until she was ready. Yet underneath his courteous mask, there were

119

demons lurking. Sometimes at night she would hear him yell out from his bedroom, followed by the crashing of furniture. She would sit up in bed, afraid to go in, wondering if her mother could hear him as well. She put it down to what he had endured himself before they left Poland. Of course such events could break a man . . . to witness the murder of his entire family . . . and yet on the outside it seemed to make Signor Brzezinski stronger, more successful and determined. She never found out how he had become so rich; or how he managed to get her and her mother out of Warsaw after her father died, right under the noses of the occupying Germans. As her mother used to remind her again and again, they owed him their lives.

Louise's mother seemed to avoid Signor Brzezinski during daylight hours. She never really recovered from the death of her beloved husband. She couldn't settle in Venice, and had no comprehension of Italian. As the years passed, she receded into a fog of confusion. She was a young enough woman yet, and still very beautiful, her Slavic features drawing men to her. She could have remarried, and yet she remained with Louise and Signor Brzezinski until that terrible day eleven years ago. By then she seemed not to know where she was any more. Inside her head, she moved between Italy and Poland. She would see her dead husband in their house. And often Louise would find her standing stock still like a ghost herself, talking to the empty air around her, saying again and again, *It was wrong, Aleksy. It was wrong. Look what we have done to her.*

If she tried to ask her mother what she meant, the older woman would look straight through her and ask her who she was.

Where is Ludwika? she would say. *What happened to my little girl?*

Signor Brzezinski insisted it was for her mother's own good that she should go into the new hospital on the island of Poveglia. He told her there was a new doctor there, making incredible breakthroughs in mental disorders. If anyone could bring her mother back, it would be him. Yet every time Louise visited her mother – which she had to admit was less and less frequently, for she found the whole experience on the island disturbing – she seemed even more lost to her. She spoke no more, and wandered along the shoreline of the miserable island communing with unseen spirits rather than recognising her own daughter.

It was the night after her mother left that Signor Brzezinski changed. Louise was upset, sobbing into her pillow, for with the departure of her mother she was racked with guilt. What would her father think of her for letting her mother go to that dreadful place? Signor Brzezinski came into her bedroom, and at first Louise thought he was there to comfort her. He climbed into the bed next to her, yet instead of taking her in his arms as she expected, he pulled her hands away from her face.

'Stop crying,' he ordered her in Italian. She was so surprised that she stopped almost immediately, staring at his shadowy face in the darkness of her bedchamber.

'Now that your mother is gone, Louise, it is finally time for you to grow up.' He pulled the straps down on her nightdress so that it dropped to her waist, and pawed roughly at her breasts with his hands.

'No, not tonight,' she said to him in Polish. 'I am too upset.'

To her deep shock, her husband slapped her hard across the face. She gasped in horror, raising a hand to her stinging cheek, tears beginning to well in her eyes again.

'Don't ever resist me. You are my wife and it is time you did your duty. I want a son, Louise.'

Up until now, Louise had managed to retain her virginity, but that night Signor Brzezinski ripped it out of her.

Afterwards he was kinder, even held her in his arms as she sobbed in shock and fear. She remembers his words, and still they confuse her.

'It's your turn now, Louise,' he whispered. 'Make me love *you*.' He sounded almost desperate as he said it, a tremor in his voice, like a man who actually had a heart. Something Louise now believes he could not possibly possess.

Oh how he hurt her this morning. He seems to be getting worse and worse. And yet she can't leave him. She promised her father on his deathbed. It was an oath she swore on her mother's life, to marry Signor Brzezinski and protect her mother. She cannot break that promise. It is sacred. Her mother might be an inmate on Poveglia, but maybe one day she will come to her senses and return home. Louise has to remain in Venice, at least until the day her mother dies. If she can escape into her double life, maybe it is enough to help her survive her marriage.

Belle moves stiffly along the narrow laneways of Venice, the nightmare that is her home receding gradually. Her husband has gone out with some of his business associates, but he will be back later, drunk and more foul than he was this morning. She needs to purge herself of his smell and his touch the only way she knows how.

Down by the bridge, it doesn't take long to pick up an anonymous sailor. He is tall, and black as the night, his spicy odour so strong he banishes the scent of her husband immediately.

She leads him to an alcove, a short walk from the bridge, but he shakes his head.

'Will you come to my boat?' he asks, in a low, melodic voice. Normally she would never agree to this, but today she wants to take risks. She nods her assent, and he pulls her to him, puts his arm around her waist, almost lifting her off the ground he is so tall.

He leads her to the harbour, where all the boats are jostling together, their rigging creaking and moaning across the stillness of the lagoon. He offers his hand as he leads her up the gangway and on to the deck.

'Is this your boat?' she asks, wondering if he is some kind of exotic West Indian pirate.

'Oh no,' he says. 'I'm first mate. But would you like to meet my captain?'

He grins at her, and his teeth are so large and white in his dark face that he startles her. So this is his game. she thinks. Is she a gift for his captain? Or has she been acquired under orders?

He takes her below deck. The odour of men is powerful. Sweat, strength and sex. For a more sensitive woman an overpowering scent, probably unpleasant, yet Belle is excited by it. She is in a male den. It heightens all her senses, makes her feel even more wanton.

The First Mate leads her into the Captain's quarters, and shuts the door behind him. To her surprise, there is no one in the room. She turns to her companion, gives him a questioning look.

'Oh, he is coming,' the black man says, bringing his hand down to trail her face softly with his finger. 'But first I have my orders . . . to prepare you.'

She catches her breath as her chest tightens. What is this beautiful man going to do to her? Anticipation sweeps through her, and suddenly her body is no longer in pain. The stinging memory of the hairbrush is gone for good, and her body is softening, opening up.

'Well now,' she says coquettishly. 'Blow out the candles first, why don't you?'

The Captain, as pale as his first mate is black, holds her in place. His right hand is pushing back her fringe, his left hand cupping and lifting her chin. His breath is upon the back of her neck, and she can feel his naked body pressed into hers, the length of his penis against her back. She is aching for him to be inside her, but he is holding back, watching the First Mate kneel down in front of her. In the flickering light of a lone candle, he slowly unlaces her boots and carefully unfastens her stockings, placing them one by one on the Captain's chair. The last two precious items of clothing that remained upon her body until this point. He lifts her legs one at a time, strokes their length before kissing each of her toes. At the same time the Captain has moved his right hand and is now caressing her right breast. As her nipple hardens between his rough fingertips, she imagines herself slick and sweet as syrup.

She has never done this before. Shared her body with two men at once.

She can smell the salt of all the seven seas in the creaking wood of the Captain's cabin, hear the coaxing whisper of the lagoon palming the hull as the First Mate begins to lick her gently. She gives a tiny gasp as he pushes the tip of his tongue deep inside her. Oh where did this exotic, beautiful man learn to do that? This is so much better than one on one. She can feel the competition between captain and first mate. Who is the better lover? Who can make her climax first?

The First Mate pulls away, and upon his captain's command the two of them pick her up and carry her to the far end of the cabin, where it is darker still. She can see that they have spread some cushions upon the floor. Of course the two of them have planned this all along. They lay her down upon the cushions, placing themselves on either side of her, opposite ends to each other. The First Mate is on her right and begins to lick her again, while the Captain pushes his finger into her, exploring her wet warmth brewing, pulling his finger out and tasting her in his mouth. She rolls on to her right side, knowing instinctively what they want. This is what makes her so good. This is why they come looking for her. All the men of Venice want to know her, all the sailors, soldiers, adventurers and opportunists. All of them want her. She is one of the treasures of this city.

She lifts her hands as if in prayer and strokes the First Mate's penis before guiding it into her mouth. She hears his groan of satisfaction as she flicks her tongue around its end. At the same time the Captain thrusts hard into her and she squeezes her legs tight around him, pushing her backside into his stomach. *Oh yes*, she hears him say. And something else. Maybe another woman's name, but what does she care? All she wants is to obliterate the pain and hatred of this morning with all this loving. The Captain's powerful length is thrusting in and out, one hand holding her head back, the other squeezing tight her waist, and the primal sensation of this along with the delicacy of the First Mate licking her is sublime. She is so close, and she wants it to be perfect. She coaxes what is inside her mouth. She can taste him and she knows he is ready. Now the Captain is thrusting more urgently, and she rides with him, faster and faster, up and up inside her.

The boat rocks gently beneath them as their legs writhe in unity. The velvet of the cushions brushes against them, heating their skin, sticking them to each other, as the three of them, strangers and yet divinely connected, climax at the same time. She opens her mouth, flicks his penis into her hand with her tongue, bringing him to the edge, as the Captain flies open inside her. She shudders in response around him, again and again, so whole and yet so fractured within a second.

They are still now. Connected to each other by their limbs, their heartbeats, their fading need. She can hear the two men panting, coming down. She feels as if she is sinking through the cushions, the wooden floor of the cabin and into the deep waters of the lagoon beneath them, at one at last with everything around her. She is whole again, no longer broken.

Belle stares out at the lagoon, pausing on the quay as she passes the boats. All are in darkness, as if every sailor is abroad in Venice, drinking and carousing. She has left her Scottish captain and Jamaican first mate behind on their boat, drinking rum. Money was exchanged, a handsome sum, and they bade adieu with respect. She has no desire to ever see either of them again. The evening served a purpose, and now she must return home, most likely to be raped by her husband, but at least she has the satisfaction of knowing that she has had her pleasure first.

As she turns away from the harbour, she notices the white boat she was looking at the day the Doctor was at her apartment, and remembers the sailor she saw as she hurried home the other day. Of course it was the same sailor she had seen on the boat. One and the same. She wonders idly who he is. There was something different about him.

She shivers, despite the fact that it is far from cold. It is as if she has a premonition. She looks at the white boat again. A church bell tolls like a warning in the black night. She thinks how like a phantom vessel it looks. As if it has come out of the mists of another dimension. She thinks of the haunted island of Poveglia, somewhere out on the dark lagoon. Her mother and the other lost souls, both alive and dead, who inhabit that dreaded place. She tries to suppress the memory of the last time she set foot on Poveglia's cursed earth, which is not real soil, but the burnt bones of its victims turned to thick ash. She instinctively puts her hands over her ears to shut out the ravings of her mother as she walked away. *Who are you? Where is Ludwika? What have you done to her?* It was as if she knew that Louise was becoming Belle. A prostitute, her parents' ultimate shame.

There is a flare of light. Someone on board the phantom ship has lit a lamp. She sees a flash of a face, indistinguishable, with a golden ring about it, like a vision of the future, a circle of hope. She wonders if it is the mysterious sailor. The golden ring shrinks to a point of light within the lamp, and she can no longer see its bearer. She shakes herself as if from a deep sleep, and begins to walk away. Yet the image of the light, the face and the ghost boat remains inside her head. She feels as if the lamp was lit for her, as if *he* is searching to find her in all the dark.

$\mathcal{V}$alentina

VALENTINA READS THE EMAIL IN DISBELIEF.

Away until next week. Have fun. Love Theo x

He has never stayed away this long before. Why does he not want to spend time with her? She doesn't care if he is seeing someone else. That's not the point. It's the fact he is avoiding her that hurts. He knows how she hates to sleep alone. It is her weak spot.

Valentina was reared to be independent and emotionally self-sufficient. Her mother, in the role of professional single parent, needed no man to look after her, and this ethic was ingrained into Valentina. Although their apartment in Milan was their base, her mother ensured that Valentina got to see as much of the world as possible by the time she was an adult. She wanted her daughter to be wise beyond her years, skilled in the art of manipulating men. Yet Valentina grew up shy and antisocial, secretly craving not her mother's approval, but her affection. Maybe her difficulty with men is due to the fact that her father disappeared when she was so young. And now her lover seems have disappeared as well. Is she as unloving as her mother? Has she driven Theo away? He asked her to be his girlfriend, in other words to enter into a proper relationship with him, and she told him she would think about it. Is he just giving her a bit more time to make up her mind? Yet she doesn't need any more time. She can't do it.

She has only ever been in love once in her life. After that disaster she swore she would never let her guard down again. Her mother warned her, but Valentina disregarded her advice. Even at the age of nineteen she would do anything to prove she was different from her mother, and so she fell head over heels in love with her photography tutor at college, Francesco Merico. It didn't matter to her that he was ten years older than her and married. When she was with Francesco she had his undivided attention. It was the first time in her life that she felt she was the centre of someone else's world. He wrote her poetry, took endless photographs of her and of course initiated her in the pleasures of lovemaking. Valentina gave him everything – her thoughts, her creativity, her virginity and her heart. She cringes now when she remembers how naïve she was. She really did believe he was in love with her too. She believed him when he told her he was going to leave his wife.

She lived in this blissful escapism for seven whole months. For Valentina their secret trysts were romantic and exciting, their forbidden lovemaking erotic, and she felt worldly when she was with Francesco. At last she was a woman.

It took just one moment for her fantasy to fall apart. She was on an errand for her mother, collecting a dress she had had altered at Prada in Galleria, when she saw Francesco ahead of her, with his wife. Immediately she pulled back and concealed herself in the crowd. She watched her lover as he put his arm around his wife's shoulders, protecting her from the bustle of shoppers. They did not look like a couple on the edge of a break-up. But there was worse. As Francesco and his wife paused to look in Gucci's window, they turned slightly towards her and she could see Signora Merico more clearly. She was very pretty, with blond hair, and a cherub's face, and she was quite obviously pregnant. Valentina tore her eyes away, and looked up into the soaring iron and glass of the Galleria arcade. No, it could not be true. She lowered her eyes and looked at the Mericos again. Signora Merico was pointing at something in the window, her other hand resting possessively on the dome of her belly. Her condition was undeniable. Valentina glanced at Francesco. She couldn't resist it. He was talking to his wife animatedly, oblivious to Valentina's proximity, and she saw upon his face the expression of love she had thought belonged to *her*.

She doubled over in shock, gasping and imagining herself crashing head first into the old mosaic floor. An old lady passing by asked her if she was feeling all right. *Si, si, grazie.* She managed to pull herself upright. The last thing she wanted was Francesco seeing the nakedness of her pain and humiliation. She turned on her heel, fleeing through the packed

131

Galleria. The cruciform avenues of the shopping arcade seemed to last for ever, as her body moved as if in slow motion, her heartache dragging her down like chains around her feet. Finally she emerged on the other side, the familiar bulk of La Scala in front of her.

Valentina will never forget the pain of that heartache. It was as if she were physically sick. By the time she got home, she was hyperventilating, choked with emotion and almost unable to breathe. She was relieved that her mother wasn't there to say *I told you so*. She couldn't even make it to her bedroom. She curled up on the hall floor in a foetal position, tearless, but sobbing inside. Yet this is not the end of the story.

Valentina is still ashamed when she remembers how badly she behaved. Being in love turned her into a monster. Even though she had seen the truth of the situation with her very own eyes, she still couldn't bear to let Francesco go. A part of her wanted to make him pay for all her pain. While his wife was out of town, she insisted on going to Francesco's apartment and making love to him with all her heart, so that she could tear his out. She wanted him to think of her every time he was in bed with his wife. She plagued him with questions: did he really love her, when was he going to leave his wife? She told him she could not live without him. On and on and on she hounded him. She didn't care about his wife or his unborn child. She killed his desire for her with her need, yet he never actually tried to break up with her. He consistently professed his love for her, and at times she almost believed him. He was so convincing, so tearful when he spoke of his situation. How difficult it was to leave his wife now she was pregnant. It was a mistake. He didn't want them to have children. Yet all Valentina could hear were lies, and all she saw was that one image of Signora Merico, sweet and beguiling in her pregnant state. No man could walk out on that.

How badly it ended. She became crazy with love for him, and was on the verge of confronting his wife when her mother intervened. She forced Valentina to go on holiday with her to Greece for three weeks, making her hike across arid, parched mountainsides and soak up the history of ancient sites and ruins with her. Valentina felt half-dead, but she still followed her mother, like a thirsty kid following its nanny goat for solace. Her mother took her diving in the cerulean perfection of the Mediterranean, and slowly all the raw beauty of Greece helped Valentina to find a tiny spark of faith in life. Gradually she managed to climb back from the edge of the abyss. The black pit of her loss became smaller and smaller, and slowly she was able to step aside from it and detach from her pain. By the time she got back to Milan, she was resolved. She would never let this happen to her again. Yet she wanted to see Francesco one last time and have the satisfaction of telling him that it was over, for good. She wanted to tell him what a lowlife she thought he was.

She never got the opportunity. The night they returned to Milan, her mother informed her not to even think about seeing Francesco. She had friends in high places and had seen to it that he would never work in Milan again. He had been forced to leave Italy with his wife, and move to England, where he had managed to get a less prestigious but adequate teaching position.

'The poor fool,' her mother said, as she poured herself a big glass of red wine and slumped down territorially on the couch in the sitting room.

'Francesco?' Valentina asked in a whisper, still dazed by her mother's drastic action.

'No, his silly little wife,' her mother said nastily. 'I am sure he has done it before, plucked some virgin student before you, and I am sure he will do it again after you. What a sad life that woman has to look forward to.'

Valentina stood in stunned silence for a moment, taking in her mother's harsh words.

'Maybe you should have told her, and done her a favour,' her mother said. She took a slurp of her wine and looked up at her daughter with dancing eyes.

She thinks this is funny, Valentina thought. How can my own mother be so cruel?

'He loved me!' she shouted suddenly.

Her mother raised her eyebrows, her eyes glowing over the rim of her wine glass.

'Valentina,' she said softly, 'have you learnt nothing from me?'

Too much! she wanted to scream. Too much about what

her mother called the illusion of love. That the best way through life was to share your body, but never your heart.

'Of course he didn't love you. He doesn't love anyone, not you, not his wife, not even his pathetic self.'

'Stop it!' Valentina screamed. 'Stop interfering in my life. Telling me what to do . . .'

For once, her mother looked surprised.

'I have been trying to help you, Valentina,' she said calmly.

'Well you're not. You've turned me into a freak . . . like you. You drove my father away, you've driven away every man who loved you, you even drove your own son away. No one can stand you for long . . .'

Her voice trailed off. She was so angry, she couldn't express herself. All she knew was that it was wrong that her mother had interfered and sent Francesco packing. She had wanted to see him one last time. To tell him herself that it was over. Or was it to give him one last chance?

Her mother said nothing in response to her outburst. She stared at her daughter as if for the first time, and for a moment Valentina thought she saw her eyes watering. Was her mother going to cry? She had never seen her do that before. The thought of it was terrifying.

'I'm moving out!' she exclaimed rashly, and stormed out of the room and down the hall. She slammed her bedroom door and locked it, but there was no need, for her mother didn't come after her. She leant against the door, anger still coursing through her. And yet she felt better. No longer lovesick. It was as if a window had opened in her life again and she could breathe fresh air.

The next morning, Valentina slept in late. By the time she arose, there was no sign of her mother. She found a short note, left for her on the kitchen table.

I can see that you are a woman now. And like me, you need your space. I have to go to America on a job. I am not sure when I will be back, but I will call. Enjoy the flat. It's yours. Tina

So typical of her mother to pull the rug from underneath her feet. Valentina had been anticipating a big talk this morning. Maybe even some kind of apology from her mother for interfering in her love life. Yet all she had was this bald note, signed *Tina*. Not even *Mama*. Not even a kiss. Valentina realised she had made her mother angry. Well, she was still furious with her too. Let her go off in a huff to America on one of her fancy shoots. What did she care? She didn't need her mother any more. She was nearly twenty after all.

How was Valentina to know that in fact her mother had decided never to return to Milan? Tina Rosselli had had enough of her home city, where she couldn't go anywhere without everyone knowing who she was. Would she never live down her reputation? She had fallen in love with a country where she had the opportunity to reinvent herself. After a few weeks, she wrote to Valentina asking her to join her in the States, but her daughter resolutely refused. She tried again a couple more times, but Valentina was firm in her determination to stay in Milan. And so time rolled by, and the truth is that mother and daughter have not seen each other for more than seven years.

To this day Valentina still blames her mother for the loss of Francesco. Illogical, she knows. Yet Tina denied her a resolution to the affair. She needed to know whether Francesco actually loved her, or whether she had just been a diversion from his marriage. She needed him to answer this question, face to face.

Over the years she has never forgotten how powerless her love for Francesco made her feel. She never wants to feel like that again, and so she has managed to keep every man she meets at arm's length. That is until she met Theo. She can't deny it; since he moved in, the dynamic of their relationship has changed.

She reads his email one more time.

Have fun.

What the hell does he mean? She thinks back to the first few weeks of their affair. How exciting it all was, how different, how much *fun* they had.

The second time they met started normally enough. He had rung her and asked her to meet him for a drink at the Principe di Savoia in Milan. She thought it a rather grand location but assumed they would have one delectable *aperitivo* there, and move on to somewhere less lavish. However, when she arrived at the hotel bar at the appointed time, there was no sign of Theo. She wound her way through the armchairs and little tables, slightly daunted by the sheer luxury of this place, yet loving its opulence. It was so Milan, so *her*. She sank into one of the large wing-back armchairs and ordered a mojito. To her surprise, when the waitress returned with her drink and a selection of juicy olives and other scrumptious treats, she handed her a rather bulky envelope. On the front, in elaborate calligraphy, was written her name: *Signorina Valentina Rosselli*.

She knew instantly it was from Theo. He was the kind of man who wrote in fancy script. She tore the envelope open, and a key card fell out into her lap, along with a roll of black silk and a small white card, on which was typed in Courier font, *Room 342. Put this on before you open the door.*

He must mean the piece of silk, which she unwound to reveal a blindfold. Quickly she folded it up again, in case anyone had seen it, but the lounge was all but empty and the waitress had disappeared. She took a sip of her mojito. Part of her was incredibly annoyed. How presumptuous of him. This was only the second time they had met. In fact their first proper date. Didn't he believe in wining and dining a woman? Yet what else could she expect after their first encounter? She should finish up her *aperitivo* and march right on out of here, leave him stewing in Room 342. There was a part of her, though, that had been aroused by his little game. How very naughty this was. Hadn't she known the night was going to end this way? Why else had she put on her little black silk dress, with the zipper all the way down the back? And only a tiny black lace G-string and stockings underneath? So what if the night began how she thought it would end. She was a liberated young woman and could do exactly as she pleased.

So it was that Valentina found herself riding the elevator up to the third floor of the luxurious Principe di Savoia. She had always wanted to stay here, but never imagined it would be like this. How could he afford it? she thought as she stepped out into the corridor, her palms sticky as her hands clutched the room key, her pulse racing. What if he changed his mind when he saw her again? What if the magic between them had only been for that one night? Well, she was here now. She couldn't turn back. Outside the door she surveyed the corridor to the left and to the right. Not a soul in sight. She slipped on the blindfold, and pushed the key card into the lock. When she heard the click, she pushed the door open.

What an incredible night that was. In fact, Theo *did* wine and dine her, but in silence, no chitchat, and with her blindfold on. She can still recall that first delicious fizz of cold champagne in her mouth. He fed her, and more shocking to her than that, she let him. It was a meal she could never forget. He started with antipasti. Tiny titbits of sundried tomatoes, grilled aubergine and roasted peppers, succulent in virgin olive oil and rich with garlic. Next came spaghetti, laced with creamy pesto sauce and Parmesan.

'Suck,' he urged her, as he fed her forkfuls. She imagined him looking at her lips as she sucked on the threads of pasta. She wondered if he was as turned on as she was.

'Now, Valentina, I have some meat for you,' he said. She could hear the tease in his voice, and she found herself on the verge of giggling, an unusual sensation for her.

'Stand up, please,' he ordered. He walked around the back of her, and she could feel his fingers on her zip. 'My, what a clever dress,' he remarked as he unzipped it all the way down, right to the hem, so that it fell away from her body and slid off her arms and front.

He took her hands and guided her back into the chair. She started with fright as he placed a plate on her lap. It was still hot on the bottom but not unpleasantly so. In fact it started to spread more warmth, curling inside her loins, melting her down below.

'Open your mouth, please.' He popped a tiny piece of rare steak on to her tongue. She began to chew. It was so tender, it practically melted inside her mouth. Meat had never tasted so good to her before.

'I want to see you,' she said suddenly. The game had gone on long enough. He had fed her to the edge of her desire, and now she wanted to see him.

'Whenever you want,' he said gently.

She pulled the blindfold off, blinking in the dimly lit room. Theo was there in front of her. Oh yes, he was the same as he had been the day before. Dark and feline, utterly irresistible.

He pinned her with his gaze, and it took her a couple of seconds to notice that he was naked as well.

'I want more,' she said, holding him with her eyes.

'There's plenty more steak.'

She reached down with her hand, placed it on his hard penis.

'That's not what I meant,' she said.

'What about dessert?' he asked her levelly. 'It's chocolate mousse.'

She arched her eyebrow at him, giving him a rare smile.

'Well I know what I can do with that. You're my dessert.'

That night was full of sensations for Valentina. The flavours, textures and smells of the food mixing with his scent and feel and taste. It was as if Theo was able to unfurl layer after layer of the passion that lay within her. Just when she thought she had peaked, he took her even higher.

The pattern was set for their affair. They would meet once, possibly twice a week, at a hotel, and indulge all night long. Sometimes they played games, like the time in the Savoia, and sometimes it was pure, straight-up raw sex. At first they used hotels in Milan, but after a couple of weeks they began to meet in different cities in northern Italy: Verona, Bologna, Turin, and of course Venice. Always they travelled separately and would meet at the appointed rendezvous. Somehow it made it more exciting, illicit almost, although neither of them was married or with anyone else. After about a month, Valentina began to take the initiative. She will never forget the time she sent Theo a message to meet her at a hotel in Bologna. She waited for him in the bar, still in her trench coat. It was pouring with rain outside. Theo came dashing into the bar, his hair laced with raindrops, his cheeks damp, his enthusiasm infectious. Her heart lifted just to see him. He sat down next to her at the bar, smiled at her slyly.

'Can I buy you a drink?' he asked formally.

This is how they would start, as if they were strangers once again. Meeting anonymously. Picking each other up.

Two glasses of prosecco later, Theo asked her if she wanted to take off her coat. Surely she was getting a little hot? She had been waiting for this moment. She spun around on her stool, and gave him a serious stare as she untied her belt and started to unbutton her coat.

'Are you sure you want me to do this here?' she asked him.

He looked at her in bemusement. She opened her mouth slightly, running her tongue along her bottom lip, while at the same time parting her legs, forcing her coat up her thighs so that he could see what she did or rather didn't have on. His eyes widened in surprise, and then darkened with desire.

'Why, Signorina Rosselli,' he whispered, his voice an octave lower. 'You are a shocking young woman.'

She swung off her seat and sashayed out of the bar, her coat half undone, not failing to turn a few heads in her wake. He followed her out into the foyer, and into the lift.

'What floor?' he asked, putting his hand over hers as she pressed the button, and bringing it to his lips.

'Four.'

He stripped her of her coat in the lift, delighted at her audacity, kissing her hard on the mouth before wrapping the coat around her again and literally dragging her to their room. There they made intoxicating love in the very spot they landed as they fell through the door.

This was how they continued for two months. The day he moved into her apartment started well on the office desk, but gradually the spontaneity waned. And curiously it was Valentina, rather than Theo, who sobered up first. She knew it was because of that telephone conversation with her mother, when Tina had claimed that neither of them could ever relate properly to one man. It had irritated Valentina to such an extent that she was trying hard to prove her mother wrong. So when Theo left one of his envelopes for her one morning after he had gone out, she didn't rip it open with glee as she had done before. Instead she read the contents calmly, tore up the card and instructions and rang him to tell him that now they were living together, there was no point to their secret trysts any more. They could go on a proper holiday that summer with the money they would save. She remembers the disappointment in Theo's voice.

'Are you sure that's what you want?' he asked her.

'Yes,' she replied emphatically. 'It was fun, but now we are living together, it's not appropriate.'

'I don't understand. Are we just roommates now? Do you not want to have sex any more?' he said in a low, anxious voice.

'No. I mean, of course I want to have sex with you. But . . . well . . . we are living together, and we have to be clear about things.'

She paused, and he didn't reply, so she continued in as light a tone as she could. 'I just think it's important that I don't think I own you . . . I mean, you're free to sleep with anyone else you want to . . .'

As she listened to herself, it was as if her mother was speaking. She was certain she had heard Tina use that very line to one of her many lovers.

Theo was silent for a moment.

'Valentina, let's talk about this when I get home.' His voice sounded tight, possibly angry.

She made sure she was out that evening with Antonella and Gaby, and by the time she got in, he was already in bed. Still awake and waiting for her. She didn't let him speak, putting her hand over his mouth as she made love to him. Neither of them ever brought the subject up again, and there were no more surprise envelopes delivered. Yet when she thinks back to that night, she has a vague memory that maybe, just maybe Theo did say something to her, after they had made love. She was drifting off, curled up within his arms, inhaling the sanctity of his scent, when she might have heard him whispering to her:

'I want what you want, Valentina.'

Did she dream it? She must have done, for he is almost as flighty as she is, disappearing on mysterious work trips and flirting easily with other women when they are out together. He never seems to mind any attention she might be receiving herself.

Have fun.

Maybe she should have continued to play those games with him. But she hasn't felt much like fun the past few weeks, despite her best efforts. In fact reading those two words, innocuous as they are, makes her uncomfortable. She is due to go on her first photographic assignment in Leonardo's club today. She wants to discuss her ideas for the shoot with Theo, and now he doesn't even know that she will be spending the evening in the company of sadomasochists.

It is one of the negatives from Theo's black book that has given her the idea for tonight's scenario. The image she was able to enlarge today was of a pair of naked breasts with a see-through lace scarf bound around them, almost flattening them, although she can make out the nipples emerging through the material. She had a memory then of a chest of old clothes her mother left behind in the attic. They belonged to Valentina's great-grandmother, and Valentina is sure she saw a similar lace scarf among them.

To her surprise, the chest isn't locked, even though she spent ages going through her bureau looking for the key. She opens the lid and sits back on her heels in delight. How could she have forgotten about this treasure trove of costumes? A powerful scent emerges from the chest. She recognises it but she can't identify it. It is a pungent aroma, like blooming roses. It must have been the perfume her great-grandmother once wore. She pulls out one delicate, exquisite garment after another: silk blouses, evening gowns of chiffon, velvet jackets and skirts, and a cloche hat in felt. There is even underwear, a pearly chemise and black silk stockings, along with frilly white garters. And there is a scarf. It's perfect. An absolute dead ringer for the one in the photograph.

Valentina dresses less severely tonight. She is nervous, no doubt about it. If only she had someone to come with her. But of course she can't tell a soul about what she is doing. She is not sure how some of her colleagues in the fashion world would react, although she suspects most of them would think it was fantastic. She likes to keep her creative work private. She puts on a little sixties suit that belonged to her mother. The skirt is very short, but then these ladies are going to be naked, so really she has no need to feel self-conscious. As she goes down in the lift in her apartment building, she wonders if she will see the man she saw yester-day, but as she steps outside her door, all is quiet on Via De Amicis.

The club feels different when she arrives this time. It is no longer empty. There are people now in those rooms, enacting their fantasies. Leonardo is nowhere to be seen, and she is greeted by a buxom blond woman clad in corset and suspenders.

'Oh you must be Valentina,' she says warmly. 'I'm Raquel.

You are very welcome.' She has a sweet, almost childish smile that looks incongruous with her corset outfit. 'The girls are waiting for you. They're very excited.'

Valentina catches her breath, tries to calm her beating heart and follows Raquel down the staircase. This is her last chance to back out. Once she goes into the Atlantis Room tonight, there will be no way she can return to her old way of looking at things. But she has no intention of going home. She is here now, and she always sees things through.

Raquel stands outside the wooden door, waiting for her.

'Ready?'

Valentina nods and walks into Atlantis.

Sitting on the daybed are two young women about the same age as her. Leonardo is right: they are both stunning. One has long curly red hair; the other short peroxide blond hair. Both girls are still dressed. The redhead is wearing a red dress to match her hair, stockings and high heels. The blonde is more casually dressed in a short blue dress with cap sleeves. Her legs are bare and she has no shoes on. They both look gorgeous. Their lips are moist and glossy, and their skin dewy in the fake sunlight streaming in from the skylight. Probably models, Valentina thinks, although she doesn't recognise either of them.

Raquel introduces the girls before departing, leaving Valentina alone with her subjects. She has set up shots so many times in her day job, yet for a minute her mind goes blank. Finally the redhead, Rosa, speaks.

'So what do you want us to do?' she asks, smiling at Valentina coyly.

'Well, I am a little new at all of this,' Valentina explains, not catching her eye.

'At photography?' asks Celia, the blonde.

'No, no, I'm a professional photographer.' She puts her bag down on the big black desk, opens it and takes out her camera, still unable to look either girl in the face. 'What I mean is, I don't really know what you do . . . I've never been into S and M . . .' She thinks it is best to be honest with the girls so that they don't make assumptions.

'For real?' Rosa says, and Valentina catches her exchanging looks with Celia. 'So why are you here?'

Valentina fiddles with the light meter. She feels gauche, and a little stupid.

'I'm interested in what you do . . . I want to understand.'

'Well the only way you will understand is by experiencing it.' Celia gives her a penetrating look, as if she can see her naked beneath her clothes.

Valentina ignores her, and turns to Rosa. She needs to remain businesslike, otherwise she is just going to look like a fool.

'Maybe you could start with what you were planning to do, and I have a few ideas with a prop I brought with me that we could possibly introduce at some stage. I might ask you to hold a pose, if that's okay?'

'Sure, no problem. Shall we start?' Rosa asks. Celia is still staring at Valentina, making her feel uncomfortable.

'Yes . . . do . . .' Valentina says, fumbling around with her camera, her heart in her mouth.

Protected by the camera, Valentina keeps her distance at first. The two women seem to go through a kind of mating ritual with each other, taking on roles. Surprisingly, Rosa appears more dominant, with Celia doing things to please her. Rosa sits on the desk, her legs apart, and Celia balances underneath her, pushing her head up beneath her dress so that she must be kissing her, although Valentina can't see her lips. Now Celia undresses for Rosa, as the redhead reclines on the daybed, watching her. She takes off her dress and stands on her toes for Rosa, her arms raised above her head.

Celia has peeled off her dress so naturally, without any kind of artifice, that Valentina finds she is not embarrassed at all. In fact she is almost enjoying this. The women are so focused on each other's pleasure. She sees no place for pain in this scenario.

A moment later, however, Rosa strides over to the desk and takes a chain from the bottom drawer. She binds Celia's hands to a beam above her head. What will happen now? Rosa stands behind Celia and begins to caress her between the legs. Valentina watches the expression on Celia's face as she responds to Rosa's touch. It is hard not to feel turned on as she watches Rosa fondling the other woman. She can't help wondering what a woman's lips and tongue might feel like on her own body. Celia goes up on her toes and raises her left leg in the air like a ballerina doing an arabesque, but to the side, and higher than ninety degrees. Rosa crouches and curls her arms around Celia's right thigh, and licks her between the legs. Valentina watches each minute detail of expression on Celia's face. At one moment she is the cool dancer; now the sensation of Rosa's lips passes through her body, so that Valentina can see the tension in her raised leg and pointed toes, she can see her teetering on the edge. Rosa knows just how long to stimulate her for before she pulls back and Celia drops back down on to the soles of her feet, breathless and potent with desire. Valentina takes a close-up of her face, her blue eyes electric and her expression open and yearning for Rosa, her mistress.

Rosa releases Celia from the beam and leads her to the daybed. Celia climbs on to the bed and allows Rosa to chain her wrists to the bedstead. She lies back with her legs open, waiting. Rosa takes off her red dress and her panties, although she keeps her stockings on, just like Valentina would. She walks back to the desk, shooting Valentina a provocative look, opens the top drawer and pulls out a large toy that looks to be a sort of vibrator. Valentina doesn't remember seeing it when she was here with Leonardo the day before.

Rosa curls up on the daybed with Celia. They kiss, and Rosa begins touching Celia again with her hands. Valentina watches her delicate fingers, the tiny half-moons of her pale nails, as she gently kneads Celia's skin. Slowly, slowly, Rosa circles her thumbs as she presses deeper into Celia, who yields herself completely in response to her mistress. Valentina moves closer and closer to the two women, certain that they are so lost in their ecstasy that they have forgotten she is there. She is a few inches from them now, taking a shot from behind Rosa of Celia, her eyes closed and lost in pleasure.

Rosa lies on her back now, so that the two women's legs are spread, the soles of their feet touching. She turns on the sex toy, and Valentina can see that it has two round massaging heads. It is some kind of twin clitoral massager. Rosa expertly fits the heads into herself and Celia, and Valentina sees Celia jolt with pleasure. Sounds begin to weave around Valentina, the noise of the toy mixing with Celia's high gasps and Rosa's low moaning. Valentina wonders which woman will come first, or will they orgasm together? Can she catch that on film . . . or is that too much of an invasion?

To Valentina's surprise, Rosa opens her eyes and looks at her. Her pupils are so dilated that they are pools of black desire. She switches off the toy, and Celia opens her eyes as well, as if stirring from a deep sleep. She looks at Valentina with the same expectant expression as her mistress. Valentina senses that they want her to do something with them. She pulls the lace scarf out of her pocket and approaches the two women. She takes hold of Rosa's hot hands and pulls her towards Celia. She unchains Celia's hands and without saying anything begins to wrap the scarf around their torsos so that they are brought together, their two pairs of breasts touching. Rosa looks up at her again, a question in her eyes, and

Valentina can feel Celia brushing the back of her bare leg with her hand. She steps back, a little unnerved, and starts snapping away, but the scarf has slipped and she has to retie it. She approaches the two girls again, and leans over, trying to tighten the lace scarf. They look like twins of passion. Young modern women bound by vintage lace. This will look so good in black and white, Valentina thinks, as she avoids looking at Rosa's beseeching eyes.

'You're so pretty, Valentina,' Rosa whispers. 'So gamine.'

Valentina looks at her, and at the same time she can feel Celia's hands tracing up her thighs. She freezes, unable to step away as the sensation of Celia's touch begins to affect her. Celia tiptoes her fingers all the way to the top of Valentina's legs, and pushes one of her hands underneath her panties. Valentina is trapped, unable to do anything, she is so rigid with anticipation. Why doesn't she push Celia's hand away?

'I think she wants to join us, Rosa,' Celia says.' I can feel it.'

The two girls wriggle out of Valentina's lace scarf, and make space for her between them.

'Come on,' Rosa cajoles her. 'Why not?' She takes a blindfold from behind one of the cushions on the daybed. 'If you prefer, you can wear this, and we will make your dreams come true.'

'No,' says Valentina, yet still she doesn't move. Celia's hand is massaging her gently, and she can feel herself beginning to throb inside, despite the fact that she has never wanted to make love to a woman before.

She looks at the two girls and everything is in soft focus, just like one of her dreams. She sees three spirits of sensuality weaving together like divine ether. And so Valentina steps forward. She cannot help herself.

$\mathscr{B}$elle

SIGNOR R. WRAPS BELLE'S LACE SCARF AROUND HER TORSO, pulling it tighter and tighter so that her breasts are almost flattened. It is a little itchy on her nipples, and Belle wishes she had suggested something else with which to bind her, but it is too late now. Signor R. has turned his back on her and picked up the bottle of oil on the dressing table. Belle reaches out for his trousers, which he left on the back of the chair, and pulls them on. The first time she played this game with Signor R., she was surprised at how much she enjoyed it. For once she was wearing the trousers. She was amazed at how different an item of clothing could make you feel. Certainly her client changed completely once he attired himself in his costume.

Signor R. is a wealthy and well-connected young banker in Venice. One can always hear him a mile off at social gatherings, his booming voice and rather uncouth manner. Yet he's not an unpleasant man. Belle knows that he has set up a philanthropic organisation to help the unfortunates of Venice. He has a heart, that is for sure. He is obviously desperately in love with his tiny little mouse of a wife, who is as shy as he is confident. You can't say a word to her but she blushes crimson. So it is quite clear to Belle that in his household Signor R. rules the roost, just like her own husband. However, unlike Signor Brzezinski, her banker friend has a need to reverse the roles sometimes. Something he could *never* ask his fragile little wife to do.

Signor R. swings around to reveal his transformation. Belle has to admit that he looks every inch her love slave. He has lathered his hairless, muscle-bound chest with one of the aromatic oils Belle purchased from the Abyssinian traders down at Ponte di Rialto. Signor R. has the most perfect physique, and as he stands before her, she takes in the symmetrical triangle of his bare chest, following the contours of his body across his firm stomach and down to his hips. He is wearing part of her Egyptian costume. Just the silk overskirt, which hangs low on his hips so that she can see his pelvic bones provocatively exposed. The silk skirt clings to his firm, powerful legs. The fine slinky cloth does nothing to conceal what lies beneath, and the sight of his erect penis pushing against his feminine attire only serves to make him even more manly.

It is quite specific what Signor R. wants to do. He doesn't want to look like or be a woman. He just wants a break from being an alpha male. He wants to be Belle's slave, stripped down and vulnerable in her most delicate skirts. It gives him pleasure, and why not, thinks Belle as she fastens his cufflinks on to the starched shirt she has now put on. She glances at herself in the mirror and is delighted by her reflection. With her black bob slicked back, she looks quite androgynous. It is a delicious sensation.

She walks over towards Signor R., feeling powerful and in control. She puts out her hand and massages his oily chest, watching his muscles ripple in response. She can see his erection pushing through the silk skirt, and she rubs it with her other hand, as Signor R. groans softly before speaking.

'What would you like me to do for you today, Belle?' His voice is unusually subdued, and husky with desire.

'I would like you to sit down on this chair.' Belle picks up a chair and places it in the centre of the room. 'And pull up your skirt so I can sit on top of you.'

'Can I please take off your trousers? Will you let me?'

She raises an eyebrow and stands over him, then nods sternly.

Signor R. leans forward eagerly and unfastens the buttons of her trousers. They slip off Belle and fall around her ankles. She steps out of them. Underneath she is completely naked. Signor R. admires her, twisting his fingers in her curly hair.

'Touch me,' she directs him, as she unbuttons her shirt. She imagines telling her husband to do this, and the thought of it makes her want to burst out laughing, which would be a disaster. She knows how upset Signor R. would be if she laughed at him.

Signor R. reaches forward with his fingers and begins to caress her. She feels so naughty and bold. It is wonderful to give orders for once. She stands over him as he buries his face in her and begins to lick. She pulls her nipples out through the gaps in her lace binding, licks her fingers and touches them herself, sighing with pleasure. She lifts his head up and away from her.

'You can stop doing that,' she directs him. 'I am going to sit on you now, and you are not to stop until I climax. Do you understand?'

'Yes, Belle,' he says humbly.

She takes his penis in both hands, hovering over him, then sits down on his lap, pushing him deep inside.

Oh, it feels so good.

She can feel herself quivering, his length reaching deep into her. She goes on to her tiptoes and rises, falls back down again. Signor R. groans, and closes his eyes.

'Come on, harder,' she says, her voice suddenly harsh, and she thinks that if she had a riding crop like her Russian, she would maybe use it now.

He lifts himself up against her and they are riding together, faster and faster, until she is climaxing gloriously without caring whether he is experiencing the same pleasure. Signor R. doesn't mind. Sometimes he climaxes and some days he doesn't. For him his visits are not about sexual gratification; they are more about escape. Today, however, he is with her all the way. As she collapses on top of him, cascading again and again, she hears him cry out and make one last dramatic thrust inside her.

* * *

After Signor R. leaves, Belle is still feeling rather manly. No doubt she will get a couple of slaps later for answering her husband back. But for now she has plenty of time to explore this sensation. And she feels like going out.

She flings open her wardrobe and flicks through her dresses, all the fantasies of her clients. Long, elegant evening gowns, along with her maid's outfit, her virginal nightdress, an array of corsets in different colours and textures, purses and stockings, boots, boas and feathers. At last she finds what she is looking for. She pulls it out and lays it on the bed. It is a simple sailor's outfit: flared white trousers, blue and white striped top, a red kerchief for round her neck, a long naval jacket, and a sailor's cap to top it off. Once dressed, she looks at herself in the mirror with satisfaction. With her breasts still bound, the hem of the jacket concealing her womanly bottom, and her long legs and slender frame, she could pass for a young sailor boy. All she has to do is tuck her black bob up into the hat and remove her lipstick.

She has never actually left her apartment in these clothes, but it has always been her fantasy to do so. Today she feels like being brave. With all the new arrivals in Venice, the city is buzzing with exotic and strange faces. She will fit in perfectly.

Belle strides along Fondamenta Nuove by the side of the lagoon, whistling as she goes. It is wonderful. For once in her life she has the freedom to walk down the street without men looking at her, measuring her up. Once she has reached the docked boats she can see from her apartment, she decides to dive into one of the local tavernas. She wants to have a drink amongst her sailor pals. Inside the crowded taverna she recognises a couple of faces, but of course they have no idea they are rubbing shoulders with Belle, the infamous Venetian courtesan. This amuses her no end.

The owner approaches her as she sits down at a small table in the corner.

'You look a bit young to be drinking hard liquor, son,' he says.

'And what business is it of yours?' Belle replies as gruffly as she can, putting some coins on the table and trying to hide her manicured hands in the process. 'Rum, please. Your finest.'

Belle knows that if she were a real sailor, she would knock her glass of rum back in one, but it is just too strong and she doesn't want to make a scene coughing and spluttering, so she leaves it sitting in front of her for ages, taking surreptitious sips when no one seems to be looking her way. Oh my, it makes her feel good. At first a burning sensation on her lips, but as it slides down her throat, it feels just wonderful, warming her belly. How good it is to be a man, she thinks, to enjoy such simple pleasures as choosing what you want to drink and when.

A crowd has gathered in the far corner of the taverna. Belle strains to make out what is going on, but it's impossible to see through the throng. She finishes her drink, and after having recovered from its powerful effects, she gets up and wanders over, pushing her way through a hubbub of sailors. Nobody minds. She is so small and lithe, they think she is a boy, and make way for her. Yet still she can't see what is going on. All she can hear is a voice. Perfect Italian, yet with a foreign twang to it.

'It seemed to be a hopeless situation, my friends,' she hears the voice say. 'Raoul and I were sure we were done for. However, luck was on our side. As we were being led away to certain death, some vicious bandits came tearing down the mountainside and attacked our guards. In the ensuing chaos Raoul and I were able to make our escape. Our hands still bound behind our backs, we ran through the rocky gorge towards the sea. Ah, we could not see the sea, but we could hear her, our darling saviour, slapping against the jagged rocks. I can tell you, it was hard work not falling down that treacherous gorge, with our hands bound, and beneath our bare feet scorpions and snakes snapping and hissing at us.

'Well, we made it to the shore, and were able to untie each other, rather tediously, which delayed our escape somewhat. Hunting around, we spied a small boat, a tiny rust-bucket in fact, but we were not fussy, my friends...' At this point everybody in the taverna laughs. 'We sprang into that boat and rowed away at double speed, and just in time, for we were not far out from shore when some of the bandits emerged on the beach, shaking the decapitated heads of our captors at us.'

Here there are a couple of gasps from the younger sailors in the crowd. 'Their message was quite clear. If our guards had not been such brutes, I would have felt sorry for them. As it was, I sent up a prayer, whatever good it may have done their departing souls.

'Off Raoul and I sailed upon the endless China seas. Ah, we suffered for days, my friends, and at times we wondered if it would not have been better to have had our heads cut off, now that our tongues were swollen and our need for water was so great. Hither and thither we drifted, our hope nearly crushed, until one day we saw another boat, and after that another, and another. We had arrived in Hong Kong. We emerged in the bustling port like two newborns screaming silently for nourishment, our throats so dry we couldn't speak. An old lady with a bucket of none too fresh water, I fear, ladled it into our parched mouths. Nothing tasted so sweet as that water in all my life.'

The gathering cheers, and congratulates the owner of the voice on his good luck. Belle cranes to see him, but the crowd is too dense. She pushes her way forward, and a large, burly docker in front of her finally lets her through. Sitting at the table in front of her, with a tankard of frothing beer, is the most devilish creature she has ever seen. She knows instinctively that it is the same tall, rangy sailor she noticed the other day as she walked home. Is it by the way he leans back on the bench, the sweep of his shoulders, or the curve of his chin? He has hair so black it makes hers look dirty brown, and his eyes are the full range of blue, the colours of all those oceans he has explored.

'Tell us another adventure, Santos!' someone yells out.

'I have no more to tell . . . that is my most recent adventure. However, my friends, here I am in Venice, the city of mystery and magic. Without fail some adventure must befall me here.'

And as he says these words his eyes alight on Belle. He looks her square in the face and a wicked grin spreads across his features. He knows, she thinks, panicking. He can see that I'm a woman.

'Oh yes,' he says. 'There are many secrets of Venice I would like to unveil.'

He is looking at her in such a way that her heart leaps into her breast, and she is more frightened than she has ever been in her life. She turns on her heel and flees the taverna, and doesn't stop running until she reaches her apartment door, where she stands for a second, her head leaning against its cool wood, slowing her breath. She tries to calm down, chiding herself for being so silly, yet she knows that what has just happened is not a trivial thing. For Belle has just laid eyes on her destiny.

$\mathcal{V}$alentina

VALENTINA IS IN THE DARK. SHE CANNOT SEE A THING. THE blindfold is made of dense black velvet, and not a chink of light penetrates. She is frightened and at the same time she is losing herself in the blissful sensations that are assaulting her body. One of the girls is teasing her with her tongue, while the other softly caresses her breasts. She feels a finger gently outlining her oval, and then pushing into its plushness. She gasps, all of her usual reserve abandoned. Rosa and Celia continue to play her. It seems they are masters of the art of bringing her close to the edge, and then pulling back, so that she is becoming more and more desperate for release. She imagines what kind of picture they must make. One she cannot photograph. Herself blindfolded and naked, her arms and legs bound to the bed with silk ties. The two young women entwined around her like Grecian nymphs. She is completely open to them, and she finds this risk, this trust in the unknown, enticing.

Everything is melting around her, and it feels as though the bed is rocking, as if it is a boat. Valentina begins to lose herself in fantasy. So this is why this room is called Atlantis, because she is being submerged into a lost place deep inside her. She imagines one of the girls untying her from the bedstead and the other pulling off her blindfold. She is throbbing still, burning to climax, but the girls are sitting back, smiling at her, their breasts pert and expectant, cross-legged in the lotus position. Rosa's red hair is flying in the breeze as the bed/boat bucks in the choppy sea. Valentina looks around in amazement. The blue-painted walls of the room have vanished, and instead they are in the middle of the ocean. She can see land in the distance, but it is far, far away.

'Where am I?' she asks.

'We are in your fantasy, Valentina,' says Celia, winking at her.

'Let's swim,' says Rosa, standing up in the rocking boat and gracefully diving overboard. Celia offers Valentina her hand.

'Come on,' she says.

Valentina lets her pull her up and the two naked girls dive into the ocean. Down and down they go, following Rosa's streaming red hair. The sensation of the cold seawater against her sensitised skin makes her feel weightless, as if she is letting the ocean bring her where it will, rather than the other way around. They dive fathoms deep, so deep Valentina wonders how they can breathe any more, but breathing she is, effort-lessly, as if she is a sea creature herself. They pass shoals of golden fish, which flutter through their legs, and long fronds of seaweed reach out and wrap around her before pulling away. A tiny seahorse rides in front of them, leading the way before disappearing into the night of the dark ocean. Finally Rosa stops by a mound of rocks on the seabed. Valentina sees a dark opening. Rosa beckons for them to enter the cave, but Valentina doesn't want to go in. She treads water, hesitating. Rosa swims up to her and takes her other hand.

Don't be afraid. We won't let go of you.

Valentina hears her voice inside her head. Hesitantly she lets the girls persuade her, holding each of them by the hand. Into the darkness they take her, so that all is hot and throbbing around her. What is in the cave with them? Will it hurt them? She senses a rush of water in front of her, like the jet of an underground spring. She feels a pair of lips pressed upon her own, and a wave of relief rushes through her. She recognises that kiss. It is Theo. He is here with her.

She is floating like a starfish in the sea, the two girls holding her arms out to her sides, and her feet pointed downwards as Theo kisses her. He puts his arms around her waist and pulls her to him so that their chests are touching. With the ease of a knowing lover he slips inside her, and she brings her legs up to wrap them around him. They are making love, the currents of the sea pulling them this way and that. She feels Rosa and Celia let go of her hands and disappear in the blackness. She wants to keep Theo inside her for all eternity. She doesn't want this feeling to stop.

* * *

Valentina wakes, her heart pounding. She opens her eyes. She is at home in her tossed bed. On her own. Yet her body is vibrating with emotions. The touch of Celia and Rosa on her skin is still present. She brings her hand up to her mouth in astonishment at herself. She really did do it. She let those two women make love to her last night. Immediately she wonders what Theo would make of it. She remembers her dream again. Was that her subconscious telling her it was okay with him? Or just wishful thinking?

The thought of Rosa and Celia bringing her into the sea cave, and the memory of Theo's touch, which felt so real, begins to turn her on. She puts her hand between her legs and gently rubs herself. She closes her eyes and imagines the sea cave again. Theo kissing her. Theo inside her. Her imagination begins to recede in time. They are climbing into the boat together, sailing back into the Atlantis Room. She lets Theo tie her to the bed and blindfold her. She wants to let him. She wants to show him she trusts him. And then she imagines Theo fucking her, hard, passionate, and she is climaxing, gasping and breathless, sprawled across the length of her bed.

An hour later Valentina is sitting demurely at her dining-room table in her dressing gown, a mug of tea in her hand. She is still reeling from her passionate adventure last night. Her hand is shaking as she brings the mug to her mouth and sips the hot liquid. She made love with not one, but *two* women. Does that mean she is gay? She knows instinctively she is not, for what unsettles her more is the power of her emotions in the dream, when she was with Theo. The force of her need for him. She tries to distract herself. She still hasn't solved the riddle of the negatives. The black photograph album is in front of her, and she begins attaching the pictures, one to a page. A bare back; a tied ankle; a gloved hand and arm with the pearls; a pair of lips; a downcast eye; an ear lobe with that ring in it. She has to work out what Theo is trying to tell her. Is he torturing her with these erotic images and his absence? Does he *want* her to be unfaithful? Yet he indicated that he wanted their relationship to be more committed. Isn't that what asking her to be his girlfriend means? She doesn't understand.

Valentina hasn't finished enlarging all the negatives from the book, and now she has to develop the film from last night. Her chest tightens with anticipation at the thought of the photographs. Will they be as sensual, as tasteful as she hopes, or will they be vulgar?

She hopes they will have a similar effect on the viewer as these old pictures have on her. Every single one is an erotic close-up of a woman's body; apart from the photograph of the ear lobe with the gold ring. She stares at this picture for a long time. She can see not just the ear with the earring but also the side of a cheek, and the end of a dark sideburn. She immediately thinks of Leonardo and his gold earring, and how it gives him the quality of some kind of pirate from the past. She has always thought that pirates are sexy.

She puts down the picture and looks at the remaining negatives. In the beginning she was desperate to enlarge them and find out what they were of, but now she wants to string it out. It is as if the images are entering her dream world and telling her a story. She is not sure whether it is about herself or the mystery woman in the pictures. But she feels there is a point to it, something to do with her and Theo.

Valentina gets up from the table and walks over to the window, looking out on to her street. She searches for a figure in the rain, wondering who the man was the other night. But the street is deserted apart from the odd car splashing past. She cannot remember such a wet, grey autumn before. If it were sunny, she wouldn't feel so low. She would be lying out in the park under a tree, reading a book and eating an apple. She would be watching her fellow Milanese, the stylish, the moody and the ambitious, as they rush on by. She feels that outsiders, especially other Italians, can be a little unfair on Milan. They see it as austere, businesslike and unfeeling, yet underneath this there is another city of magic and fantasy. Like the 1940s rationalist buildings hiding enchanted gardens from the sixteenth century or tiny medieval cloisters. She is defensive of her city because she knows how it feels to be misjudged. Often she has overheard others describe her as unfriendly, or standoffish. She knows it's because she never smiles. And she believes as well that some of these people are envious of her. They think her mother is cool, that she is the daughter of a celebrated sixties icon. If only they knew what it was really like for her.

Often Valentina is completely unaware of how the expression on her face puts people off her. She may well be smiling inside, but not many notice that. She is often told to cheer up despite the fact that she may be in an excellent mood. And that surprises her, how she might get a hostile reaction from someone, usually a girl, for some unknown offence. Of course she really doesn't care in the end what people think of her. She has Theo, and her close friends Antonella, Gaby, and Marco. And those two girls, Rosa and Celia. They liked her, didn't they?

Her phone rings and Valentina looks at the screen briefly before answering it. It's Mattia. She feels a jolt of worry; her brother rarely calls her.

'Hi, Mattia, is everything okay?'

'Yes, Valentina,' he says. 'Just wanted to update you on Mother.'

'Oh, right,' Valentina replies, trying to sound indifferent. She watches a sparrow sheltering on the windowsill of her apartment, while the rain gathers momentum outside. 'So what's up?'

'I just want to let you know that she's moved again.'

'Okay,' says Valentina. It's kind of her brother to let her know, but if her mother doesn't want to tell her where she is living now, why should she care?

'She's in America still.'

'Well, no surprises there. Do you see her?'

The little sparrow gives up and flies away, buffeted this way and that by the nasty wet wind.

'No, she's a long way from New York.' He pauses. 'Besides, you know how she feels about Debbie.'

'Oh yes.' Valentina had forgotten that. The big row at her brother's wedding all those years ago. She was only about twelve or thirteen at the time, so she never did quite work out what the problem was. Her mother just seemed to dislike her brother's fiancée intensely. Things have never been the same between mother and son since his wedding day. Mattia tried to patch things up, but neither of the women was willing to compromise.

Unlike Valentina, Mattia most definitely does not take after their mother in the slightest. He likes to keep things pleasant, and lives a safe, comfortable life with his wife and two children in New York. Valentina keeps meaning to visit, but in a way she is a little afraid. She doesn't really know her brother at all. What if it turns out that they hate each other? He is thirteen years older than her and had left for America by the time she was five. Shamefully, her only childhood emotion concerning her brother was jealousy. She couldn't help being envious when she looked through all the photographs of her mother, her father and Mattia together. She particularly remembers a series of pictures when they went on holiday in what was then Yugoslavia. There were so many photographs of six-year-old Mattia looking jolly by the sea, naked with his little fishing net, and hand in hand with her mother, who was wearing a tiny bikini. There were pictures of her father too, lying on the beach reading, his pipe in his mouth as always. She has no such happy family mementoes.

'So how are you?' her brother asks her.

'Good, you know, busy with work.'

'Great, and how's it going with Theo?'

How does he do that? Remember Theo's name? He has been married to Debbie for over fourteen years, and Valentina still manages to call her Libby sometimes.

'Good.'

'He seems like a nice guy,' Mattia says. 'You know, maybe he's the one.'

She doesn't reply, annoyed. How can Mattia comment on her boyfriend when he's never met him?

'Look, sorry, I can't stay on the phone too long, but I just want to tell you that Mum is living in Santa Fe, in New Mexico now. I'll send you her address if you want.'

'I don't want it, Mattia.'

'Oh, okay . . . Well, I have it if you need it.'

'Thanks.'

'She also posted me some old pictures of the family. Mostly photographs of her parents and herself as a child. Do you want any of them? I thought you might be interested, seeing as you and Theo are into collecting pictures.'

Again that familiarity. It annoys Valentina. Just because he is her brother, it doesn't mean he knows who she is.

'Just send me the ones you don't want,' she says brusquely.

'Right, well, okay, take care,' he says, suddenly whispering. 'Have to go.'

She realises that he must be calling her in the middle of the night, and perhaps without Debbie knowing. He is probably not allowed to make long-distance phone calls. How could her brother be so very different from her? She wouldn't even think of asking Theo's permission to do something like that. Besides, Theo wouldn't want her to. Yet her brother seems happy. He has managed to stay married for years, something her mother has not been able to do. Her mother always told her that Mattia took after her own mother, Maria, who was killed in a plane crash when Tina was only twenty-six. Her mother described Maria Rosselli as 'square', and claimed that she had always felt closer to her grandmother, who was a rather eccentric old lady. It is strange how people can inherit the characteristics of their ancestors, Valentina muses. She sincerely hopes that her mother's traits have skipped a generation.

Despite her offhand manner on the phone, she is in fact intrigued by the package her brother will be sending her. More photographs for her to investigate. She feels bad now that she snapped at him. He really does seem to care about her welfare, even though he has never actually spent much time with her. She really should try to get to know his family. Maybe one day she'll get her act together and go to New York. And then maybe, just maybe, she might head on to Santa Fe to see her mother. She bites her lip at the thought, drawing blood. No.

Why should she go to her? It's up to her mother to come back to Milan. It was she who abandoned Valentina when she was so heartbroken and alone. She put herself before her daughter, and really, Valentina wonders if she will ever be able to forgive her for that. It seems her brother is much more magnanimous, able to accept their mother despite her blatant rudeness to his wife and her lack of interest in her grandchildren.

Valentina turns away from the window and picks up her camera from where she left it when she got home last night. It's time to delve into her darkroom and develop the Atlantis Room pictures. This will be a test to see how far she can remain the observer in her erotic art, and how much she desires to be a part of it. She glances at her watch. She has more than eight hours before it's time to return to Leonardo's club. She has no idea what he has set up for her tonight. Part of her dreads it, and yet, if she is honest, another part of her is excited.

She hesitates, putting down the camera again. She should write Theo an email and tell him what she is involved in. Should she tell him about Rosa and Celia? No, she would rather do that in person. Besides, he hasn't told her anything about why he is away and what he is doing, so why should she fill him in on her news?

When she checks her inbox, there is an email from Theo already. She clicks on it, hopeful that he will explain to some small extent what his gift means. However, he has sent her only a bare few lines. They are frustratingly cryptic.

Dear Valentina, I am writing this in haste, and wish I could explain further. But for now my message is to trust no one if you are asked anything about me. I will explain when I get back. And my other message is, please, Valentina, try to have some fun. Theo x

What does he mean? Trust no one? Try to have some fun? Again, that word that is so incongruous with all of who she is. She is not a *fun* person! She has that feeling again, that he wants her to cheat. And yet he tells her to trust no one. Is he referring to himself in a roundabout way? Somehow she thinks not.

The apartment ticks in forbidding silence. She hears her neighbour in the flat above her thumping across his living-room floor and pulling up the blinds on his windows. She listens to the clock marking time on the wall, and the sound of a motorbike spluttering past in the rain. She looks at the painting on the wall facing her. It is one of Antonella's passionate compositions, layers of blue, from pale china to indigo, scraped away to reveal a wavering line of scarlet, as tactile as sticky fresh blood. The painting is called *Anticipation*. It matches her mood.

Valentina breathes in, and around her the apartment breathes out, but barely. It is as if she is holding her breath, waiting for something to happen. There is an electrical charge in the air, like the feeling before a storm. Valentina senses she is on the cusp of change. Whether it is for better or worse, she has no idea.

$\mathcal{B}$elle

THIS DAY SHE IS LOUISE. HER HUSBAND IS AT HOME, AND they have guests coming for dinner. Business associates of Signor Brzezinski, and their wives. Her cook, Renate, and Pina, the maid, have done all the shopping and preparation for tonight. She gives them free rein and couldn't care less what Renate puts on the table for dinner. All Louise has to do is look beautiful and be a good hostess. This she finds more challenging than anything. She would rather be Renate or Pina, behind the scenes in the kitchen, than centre stage in her husband's social scene. None of the women like her. She has heard their whispers about how standoffish she is, and why haven't they got children yet? Barren Brzezinska, that's what she heard one of the old cows call her last time they went out to dinner.

These women bore Louise so. All they want to talk about is their children, and if she tries to engage them in any kind of conversation that takes them beyond the domestic, they respond with hostile silence. Louise is ambivalent about having children. She certainly doesn't want one if it is going to turn her into one of these twittering fools. In any case, the likelihood of her having a child is pretty slim, since her husband has been trying to get her pregnant for years. There is no point in wishing for something she believes she will never have.

Her husband's male associates are nearly as bad as their wives. There are only a couple of them she likes: Varelli, because he seems less enthusiastic about Mussolini (and she suspects he has secret communist leanings); and Greenberg, because he is an American Jew and is the only one of the men who talks to her as an equal. She wonders how long those two will stay in Italy now Mussolini is getting into full swing. All the communists she used to know seem to be disappearing into thin air. She doesn't like this mood in Italy. All this talk of returning to the glory of Rome. Ancient Rome is not a society to be admired. It was far too brutal.

Yet of course there were all those orgies, she thinks, as she trims her fringe, snapping the scissors impatiently just above her eyebrows. The Romans seemed more open with their sexuality than Mussolini's Italy. She remembers hearing the story about the Princess Julia, daughter of Emperor Augustus, who disguised herself and worked as a prostitute in Rome. Louise is just like her, then. Leading a double life. She understands exactly why Julia would do it. The Roman princess was trapped in a loveless marriage as well.

Louise sighs with frustration. She puts down the scissors

and brushes out her hair, scowling at herself in the mirror. She is bored. She wishes she could escape and be Belle today. She feels like a caged bird. Maybe there is a way she can get out, just for an hour. That would be enough. All she wants to do is go to her apartment, have a cigarette and watch the gondolas gliding down the canal. Today she wants to be alone.

She glances at the little carriage clock on her dressing table. Her husband is having his afternoon nap. Sometimes he eats so much at lunchtime that he can sleep for two whole hours. She could be there and back in that time. He wouldn't know a thing.

Before she has a chance to change her mind, Louise ties a lace scarf around her neck, buttons on her boots, picks up her purse and skips out of her bedroom and down the staircase, pulling the heavy front door wide open with glee. She feels like a child released from her studies. The city is gleaming. How different Venice is when the sun shines. It becomes a metaphor – a fragile ring of joy that can sometimes surround the bereaved. Belle thinks of her mother, after her father died. The way her eyes shone when she told her daughter about the dreams she had of her dead husband and the messages he passed on to her. Or what he said to her the night he passed away.

I love you always.

Belle's mother grieved, but her grief was like the sun in Venice, an essentially melancholy city emblazoned with a sudden silvery burst of light. Such love her parents shared. It makes Belle clench her fists tight to think of it. Such selfish love.

She is not going to reminisce today. It is a sunny afternoon and she is free for an hour or two. What joy! She walks as fast as propriety will allow along the narrow streets and over the bridges. There are reflections everywhere, of the canal on the underside of bridges, and the sky in the water, and the water on the stone, and the people in the buildings. She makes her way through San Polo, crossing Ponte di Rialto and heading into Castello. She passes the hospital, and its marble façade is blindingly white, forcing her to close her eyes for a moment. When she opens them again, she sees him. The wolfish sailor. He is walking towards her across Campo San Giovanni e Paolo and she is not sure whether he notices her as well. Should she run into the church and hide from him? She watches him bending down and stroking a black cat, which rubs itself against his legs. She can't help thinking how she would like to be that cat, especially when she sees him lift the cat's chin with his hand, and stroke underneath it.

To feel those long fingers tickling her throat!

He straightens up and walks towards her. She is unable to move, forwards or backwards. He is an unforgettable figure, she thinks, attired in his sailor's white cap, long admiral's coat with waistcoat underneath, and white trousers. She takes a step forward, yet he makes no sign that he has seen her, and she suddenly feels overwhelmed with shyness. Usually she has no problem looking at men when she is Belle. She is adept at giving them the eye. Yet today she feels like a bashful young girl again. Just as the sailor passes by her, she gives him a quick sideways glance, but he is looking straight ahead. She walks along feeling a little disappointed, yet as she gets to the far corner of the campo, she turns around one last time and is surprised to see that he has done the same and is looking at her. Their eyes lock, and Louise feels the heat rising in her breast, up her neck, as she strives to remain calm and collected. He is the most beautiful man she has ever laid eyes on. She feels the same urge to flee that she felt the other day when she saw him in the taverna, and yet there is another part of her that can't walk out of this campo. As if his gaze has her trapped.

She circles the campo, peruses the window of a café, and he does the same in the opposite direction, staring up at the marble façade of the hospital before walking in a circle towards her. This time as they pass, he speaks.

'Have we not already met?'

She stops and looks up at him, pretending she has only just noticed him. Courage floods her as she is warmed by his admiring gaze. She gives him a rare smile.

'I thought sailors had more imagination than to come up with a line like that,' she replies teasingly.

'You are quite wrong.' He looks at her with a wicked gleam in his eyes. 'Sailors have no imagination at all. We have no need of it, since our fantasies are the true stories of all our adventures.'

She knows she shouldn't become Belle. She hasn't time. And yet she can't let this particular sailor walk away from her right now.

'I would love to hear about some of your adventures,' she suggests coyly.

'Certainly,' he complies, his smile wide. 'But only if you tell me some of yours.'

They walk out of the campo together, and Belle is now certain that she will not be home in time to wake her husband from his nap. Yet she doesn't care, despite the consequences.

'Let me introduce myself,' the sailor says. 'My name is Santos Devine. My father was a sailor from Cork in Ireland and my mother a dancer from Granada in Spain. However, I am from nowhere in particular. I have been sailing, or more accurately adventuring for twenty years.'

Belle looks at him in wonder. Is he a real man, or a figment of her imagination? She has never been so attracted to another person. She is magnetised by his tall, lean body, and his easy way of moving. He is as graceful as a dancer, a quality he must have inherited from his mother, and yet she senses his strength mixed with the ethereal, his Celtic heritage. His hair is as black as hers, and his face is a mixture of masculine rogue and feline beauty. Even his hands are beautiful as he takes hold of hers.

'And what is your name?'

'Belle,' she replies.

'Very appropriate. I don't think I have ever seen such a

beautiful woman in all the seven seas I have sailed.'

'I am sure you say that to the girls in every port,' Belle replies smartly, and Santos's eyes glint mischievously in response. He doesn't deny her accusation, and yet still he manages to charm her.

'Ah,' he says. 'But I cannot say that any girl has such hair as yours. So short and angular, the perfect frame for your delicious face, shiny and black like a blackbird's feathers.'

'I love the blackbird's song,' Belle says, holding him with her eyes. 'It is full of the joy of life.'

'Do you have blackbirds in Venice?'

'Occasionally, in the winter. But I remember them mostly from my childhood home.'

'Well I shall call you Belle Blackbird, then.'

As they walk through Venice, her home for so many years, it becomes another place altogether. In broad daylight they enter a part of the city where she is known, yet it matters to her not. She is seeing Venice through Santos's eyes as he tells her why he is in the city. He is currently trading, bringing silk from the East and exchanging it for Venetian glass. He tells her he has just sailed from China, and regales her with stories of Chinese warlords and banditry.

'But don't you ever get tired of moving around?' Belle asks him, fascinated. 'Wouldn't you like a home? A family?'

'I have never been interested in the things that most men are interested in,' Santos tells her. 'I have no desire to acquire great wealth or power. For with that comes bondage. I am seeking freedom for myself and others.' He looks at her searchingly, puts his arm around her waist and draws her to him. 'Particularly for women,' he says softly into her ear, and she can feel his lips brushing her neck as he speaks, sending a tremor through her body.

They walk together arm in arm across Piazza San Marco towards Canal Grande. Belle's world begins to tilt. As if she is losing a sense of perspective, as if she is standing on a shelf jutting out into the lagoon, and all these jewel-like buildings, the Basilica and the Doge's Palace, are a mirage on a marble raft floating on the pale green gloaming canal.

'Can I invite you for a cup of coffee perhaps?' Santos asks her. 'Although maybe you would prefer a glass of rum in my local taverna.'

He is grinning at her broadly. She looks at the deep cleft in his chin, and wants to push her finger into it. Her eyes lift to his, and she notices that they have changed colour. Now they are the colour of the canal, moonstone over green jade. She maintains her composure.

'A cup of coffee would be delightful,' she replies formally, but she can sense the heat in her glance as she looks at him.

He brings her to Caffe Florian. She knows it is a risk. This is where her husband often meets associates to discuss business and politics. But he is asleep, she reminds herself, safely snoring his head off at home, and it is siesta time. The square is quiet. Besides, she is not Louise for now. She is Belle. And Belle is as free as a bird.

It is such a fine day that they sit outside, the campanile and basilica behind her, so that all Belle can do is focus on Santos Devine, and his startling eyes.

'Where are you from, Belle?' Santos asks her, stirring his tiny cup of coffee with a small silver spoon, as daintily as if he were a duke.

'Why, I am from Venice,' she replies. 'I live here.'

'Ah yes, I know that . . . but you are not born Italian.' He puts his head on one side. 'Your Italian is very good, so I suppose you have lived in Italy for many years, yet I can tell it is not your mother tongue.'

She looks at him curiously. No one has shown much interest in where she is from in all her years in Venice. Not even the Russian.

'I am from Warsaw,' she says, casting her eyes downwards and stirring her own coffee.

'Ah, you are from the tragic kingdom of Poland,' he exclaims.

'It was not Poland when I was born. It was still part of the Empire.' She takes a sip of her coffee.' And why so tragic?'

'Poor Poland,' Santos says. 'Always stuck in the middle between two big brothers at loggerheads.'

'You mean Russia and Germany?'

'Indeed.' Santos nods, taking a sip of his coffee. 'So you and I are from very different places,' he continues. 'We are opposites in a way. I was born on the western edge of Europe. In my soul is the Atlantic, its big galloping waves, its freedom and abandon.'

'And what am I, then?'

'You are as deep as the thick soil of Poland, as secretive as her woods, and besieged on all sides. You are trapped, like Poland.'

She shakes her head, suddenly angry.

'No, I am not!' She smashes her cup down on her saucer, shattering it, so that what remains of her thick, dark espresso leaks on to the linen tablecloth. She brings her gloved hand to her mouth in shock. A waiter comes bustling over to clear up the mess, and she gushes apologies at him, while Santos remains silent, staring at her all the while. Despite her attraction, she wants to hate this man. He is condescending and intrusive. *Yet why do you want to hate him, Belle?* Louise asks. *Because he is right?*

Once the waiter has cleared up the mess, and replaced her coffee with a fresh one, Santos speaks.

'I am sorry if I have offended you, Belle.' He speaks to her in Polish. She is so surprised to hear her native tongue after all these years that she feels a lump of emotion forming in her throat.

'Have you been to Poland?' she asks, burning to know how he learnt to speak Polish.

'Why, yes,' he says, in Italian now. 'I had the misfortune to witness the retreat of the Imperial Russian Army in 1915, and their treatment of your countrymen and your land.'

Nineteen fifteen. The year Belle's father died. The year she got married.

'We had a lot of refugees in Warsaw,' she whispers. 'The Russians burnt everything in their wake as they retreated: the villages, the woods and the land. What they left behind them was uninhabitable.'

She sees herself reflected in the window of Caffe Florian. Who would have guessed that this sophisticated lady of Venice was once a tough little Polish girl? She was the only child of a Warsaw doctor, who adored his wife above everything. Her parents were so in love. She remembers their devotion to each other right up until the end.

Belle looks down and twists the wedding band around her finger. She is surprised to see it is still there. Usually she takes it off and leaves it at home when she becomes her alter ego, yet she was in a hurry today, to be out in the sun and feeling free. Now she realises that her freedom is a mere façade. Santos is right. She is like her home country. Bound in on all sides.

'Belle.' She looks up to see Santos gazing at her intently. He takes a handkerchief out of his breast pocket and hands it to her. She touches her cheek and realises that she is crying.

'Thank you,' she whispers, bringing the handkerchief to her face and smelling it – oh, the scent of it, spicy carnations, and peppermint – before dabbing her cheeks.

'I can see you have the sea in your soul,' Santos says, flashing his brilliant eyes at her. 'Let me set you free.'

She looks at him hopefully. Does he say this to all the unhappily married women he meets on his travels? It doesn't matter to her even if he does. She has already taken extreme steps to find some kind of release from her confined life. She doesn't care what Santos's motives might be; all she wants is for him to touch her. She is shaking with need as she clutches his handkerchief in her gloved hands.

They leave the café and walk arm in arm back across Piazza San Marco. It is getting late and she knows the hour of her husband's dinner party is fast approaching, and yet she wants so much to be with this sailor. His arm linked through hers feels so natural, not at all improper. He is enticingly close to her; the slight brush of his body against hers as they walk sets her heartbeat racing. They stop by the side of Canal Grande and stare at the boats drifting down its broad back. Belle looks at the colours of the buildings on the other side of the canal. They are the whole spectrum of her emotions in this moment as she stands next to the man of her dreams: the red of her passion, the cream of his artlessness, the burnt sienna of her spontaneity, the peach of the tenderness she wishes to share, and even the pale green of the melancholy shadowing their fate.

'What would you like to do now, Belle Blackbird?' asks Santos, putting his hands in his pockets and looking down at her. She almost feels as if he is putting the words into her head, as if he has cast a spell on her.

'I would like to take you home with me,' she says, not daring to look at him.

'Ah,' he says, turning her face to his, trailing a finger down the side of her cheek ever so gently and resting it on her lips. 'I think not today, my sweet little blackbird. I have a prior engagement, but I know we will meet again.'

Belle tries to hide her disappointment at his rejection. Despite herself, her eyes begin to water again, this time with shame.

He lifts her chin.

'Dear Belle, don't be sad. Have patience. Don't be too keen to fly so high too soon.'

He removes his finger from her lips, leans down and kisses her tenderly. She kisses him back hungrily, hoping he will change his mind, but after a few moments he pulls away, tapping her gently on the shoulder.

'I will find you, Belle,' he says, before stepping away. 'Trust me.'

She watches him disappear across Piazza San Marco. How can she be so disappointed at his rejection? Why does she care so much when she has only just met him?

He insulted you, Louise. He presumptuously told you that you are trapped. And he made you remember your past in Poland. He is a predator, hunting vulnerable married women. He is a bad man.

Yet as she turns and makes her way home, Louise knows that this isn't true. He said that he would find her. He told her to trust him, and for some wild reason she does. She can feel it. A little seed of hope planted in her heart, the roots pushing deep into her soul, keeping her resilient and uncaring when her husband takes a strap to her for being late.

*　*　*

She is another woman that evening. She makes small talk with her dinner guests, yet she doesn't hear her words; she just lets nonsense stream out of her mouth, and no one seems to notice. She eats her food, apparently delicious by her guests' accounts, but she neither tastes it nor notices what dishes are being put in front of her. She is trussed up in her formal gown, and yet she hardly feels her smarting red backside as she sits on her dining chair. All the while she holds Santos's damp handkerchief scrunched up tight in her fist. And later, as her husband makes his customary thrusts inside her in an effort to create an heir, she neither notices nor cares if or when he climaxes. After he has fallen asleep, she opens her palm, and uncurls Santos's handkerchief as if it is a water lily flowering upon the well of her want. She raises it to her face and inhales, closing her eyes and recalling Santos's face.

He spoke Polish to me.

This is how he won her heart. She is a woman in love, and everything around her is falling away and dying. It was all a terrible dream, her life as Signora Louise Brzezinska. She is waking up now. And she is Belle, waiting for Santos to come to her.

$\mathcal{V}$alentina

'YOU ARE LOOKING VERY VAMPISH, DARLING,' MARCO SAYS to Valentina as she joins her friends in Bar Magenta.

Gaby looks her up and down, giving her an appreciative smile.

'Wow, you really do look amazing, Valentina. I haven't seen you dress up like that for ages.'

'Yeah, not since Theo moved in with you,' Antonella joins in.

Valentina thinks about it. She hasn't consciously changed the way she dresses, but Antonella is right. She used to dress up a lot more before she met Theo. She has never been interested in looking like a femme fatale or a sex bomb. She doesn't have the figure for it, for a start. Her breasts are way too small, and she finds the idea of having anything done to change them repulsive. It makes her so sad when she sees those skinny models with their fake tits. To Valentina's eyes, they look like Barbie dolls, like a joke, all out of proportion.

And fake breasts don't feel so nice to touch either. That's what Theo told her.

Sometimes, however, Valentina likes to put on what she calls a sexy costume to create another persona. And tonight, seeing as she is visiting Leonardo's Velvet Underworld, she feels she needs to look a little more spiky than usual. That's why she dug out her mother's hot pants from the sixties. They fit her like a glove, an all-in-one black nylon suit, with a zip all the way down the front. She is wearing thigh-high black boots and a white belt around her waist to accentuate it.

'You are such a contradiction sometimes, Valentina,' Marco says as she sidles in next to him on the wooden bench. 'So shy and yet so way out . . . all at the same time.' He wags his finger at her, his eyes sparkling playfully.

'I like to maintain some mystery,' Valentina replies, keeping a straight face.

Marco kisses her cheek.

'What a marvellous woman you are, Valentina. If I were not the other way inclined . . . You could almost turn me, you know.'

'Why thank you, Marco, that is one of the nicest things you have ever said to me.' She kisses Marco back lightly on the lips. She feels so much better being in his company. No one understands her the way Marco does. They are so similar, both of them pedantic about their need to live their lives the way they wish, without censure or judgement. Both of them determined free spirits. She suspects it was Marco who was the most shocked (apart from her mother, of course) when Theo moved in with her. She could see it on his face, but unlike Gaby and Antonella he didn't question her decision, or ask her why. He just accepted it. His presence always makes Valentina feel relaxed and safe, as if nothing she can do or say will stop him loving her as his friend.

'Well I think you are even more mysterious than your famous mother,' says Gaby, giving her a sly grin. Gaby knows all about the clandestine, Valentina thinks sadly, as her friend gets up from her seat, and heads off towards the buffet.

Antonella leans across the table, grabbing Valentina's hands and hypnotising her with her false eyelashes and thick kohl.

'So where are you off to tonight, all dressed up like that? Is there a party somewhere? Can I come?'

Valentina extricates herself from her friend's grasp and takes a sip of her Negroni.

'No, there's no party, and you cannot come with me because it's a secret,' she says coolly, swirling the bittersweet Campari mixture around in her mouth.

Antonella huffs, crossing her arms so that her ample breasts spill over them. Valentina can't help wondering what kind of room Antonella would go into – Atlantis, the Underworld or the Dark Room? Probably all of them, one at a time, knowing Antonella.

'Come on, Valentina, you can tell us, we're your friends,' she whines, her eyes big and doleful.

Valentina shakes her head.

'Oh come *on*, Valentina. You're no fun at all!'

'Don't mind her,' says Marco, taking the olive out of his martini and nibbling it. 'She's been in a bad mood since her Spaniard went home.'

He turns to Antonella, who has put on a fake sulking face.

'Don't you know our dear Valentina by now? That's why she's such a good friend. Unlike *some* people, she knows how to keep a secret.'

'I didn't know I wasn't supposed to tell anyone about your man!' Antonella defends herself. 'How was I to know he wasn't out of the closet yet? It was so obvious he wasn't straight.'

Marco rolls his eyes.

'Maybe to you it was, since you are such a nymphomaniac!'

'Who's a nymphomaniac?' Gaby asks, returning to the table with several small plates of antipasta balanced in her hands and along her arms.

'Antonella, of course!' Marco exclaims, while Antonella gives him a shove from across the table. 'Hey, mind my drink!'

'Well, that's hardly news,' Gaby says settling down while they all dig into the food.

'Thanks very much!' says Antonella, munching grumpily on a roasted pepper, but her eyes are laughing and Valentina can tell that she is far from offended.

'Where's Theo?' Gaby asks suddenly, her expression expectant, a chip squeezed between her polished nails.

Valentina shrugs, trying to appear nonchalant.

'Away.'

'Where?'

'I've no idea,' she says, taking another swig of her drink. She catches Gaby and Antonella exchanging glances, as if they know something she doesn't. But of course they don't. They are her friends. They would tell her if they did, right?

'Reviewing another show, I expect,' Marco says kindly, squeezing her knee. 'Oh, you look so kinky, Valentina,' he adds. 'Theo *is* missing out!'

Valentina cycles to Leonardo's club this time. She must look strange in her outfit on a bicycle, but she doesn't care; she doesn't want to fork out on another taxi. She weaves through the traffic, the memory of Gaby and Antonella's exchanged look still in her head. Really, they have no right to be making assumptions. Antonella is completely wild. She is even worse than she used to be. Valentina has never known her to maintain a relationship for longer than three weeks. Gaby, on the other hand, is having a heart-wrenching affair with a married man. They should know by now who Valentina is. A woman who prides herself on her lack of dependency. And yet she *is* burning with curiosity. For some reason, this time she can't stop wondering where Theo is.

Maybe he is some kind of secret agent, she muses. No, that's a ridiculous idea: what secret agent writes about modern art and enjoys lazy Saturdays perusing antique shops along the Navigli canal? Or what if he is a crook of some sort? That's an even more stupid idea. Theo is the only person she knows who pays his parking tickets on time. Another possibility hits her. She remembers a Brazilian model telling her the story of her father, when they were stuck waiting for a storm to pass on a shoot in Cuba. Apparently he had two families, something she and her mother did not discover until the day of his funeral, when his other wife and children turned up to pay their respects. Theo could be living a double life. He could have a wife and children hidden away somewhere else. The idea of it makes Valentina sick. She is not possessive. She could even cope with the fact that he might have another girlfriend. But children . . . Somehow the thought of Theo having a baby with someone else upsets her. Why on earth should that be? As she brakes at the lights on Via Carducci, and a tram trundles past her, it dawns on Valentina that it is because it reminds her of Francesco and his wife. And his baby, a child now, that would always come before his affair with her. When the lights change, she whizzes down the wet street, a little shocked. That was nearly ten years ago, and still memories of it can hurt her.

When Valentina arrives, it is Leonardo, not Raquel, who greets her. Valentina finds herself feeling glad to see him; she can't think why.

'Good evening, Valentina,' he says. 'You are looking very nice.'

'So are you,' she replies smartly.

He is dressed more casually tonight, in a forest green shirt that brings out the hazel in his brown eyes, and figure-hugging blue jeans, slung low and provocatively on his hips. She can smell his Armani again, as it wafts across the hallway.

'So how did your pictures turn out from last night?' he asks her.

'Good,' she says, not looking him in the eye. 'I don't have them with me, though.'

Her series of shots of Rosa and Celia were a success, Valentina thought: really erotic and at the same time very beautiful. The lighting in the room was perfect. It was ironic that the reflections of light on the blue wall created dappled patterns upon the girls' skin, as if they were actually under-water, just like the name of the room – Atlantis – implied; just like her dream. The last shot was of the two of them, bound by the lace scarf, looking like vintage bondage twins. After that, there were no more pictures. After that, Valentina is not sure what happened . . .

'Well let me tell you about who you will be photographing tonight.' Leonardo scrutinises her, his eyes darkening. Maybe he knows? Did those girls tell him?

'Okay.' She nods, feeling unusually bashful as she fiddles with the strap of her camera bag.

'We have two friends of mine, Nicky and Anna. It is a bondage scenario. Anna is a dominatrix.'

He leads the way down the staircase, pausing outside the leather door of the Velvet Underworld.

'I thought it best that they already got started, so they are in character. You can just slip in and take some pictures. They know you are coming, but they are more comfortable if you don't interfere.'

'Oh, okay . . .' Does he know about her 'interference' with Rosa and Celia, then? Has she broken some kind of rule?

'Once you are introduced to the visible possibilities of such a scene, you can of course create your own scenario . . . maybe next time?'

He looks at her, his dark gaze penetrating her yet again.

'I can see by your outfit that you have a flair for the theatrical.'

His eyes travel the length of her, and she can't help imagining him unzipping her suit and pulling down her hot pants. She manages to show no emotion in her face, but she can feel her nipples hardening, and from the smile on his face he has seen them too, pushing against her thin nylon top. He pauses for a second, just long enough for her to wonder what could happen between them, before turning away, opening the door a crack and peeking into the room. He turns back and puts a finger to his lips, indicating for her to enter. She squeezes past him, aware of his strong thighs as her bare legs brush against him.

'Don't worry, Valentina,' he whispers. 'We don't go in for extreme torture here.'

She hesitates. What is the difference between normal torture and extreme torture? What is she going to witness in this room? Is it going to frighten her? Repulse her? Or, almost worse, is she going to get turned on by what she sees? It is too late to back out now. She can feel Leonardo urging her on. She will just have to cope with whatever is inside.

The Velvet Underworld appears bigger than last time. It is also darker. Most of the lights are on very low. The room is full of dark blood shadows. She lets her eyes adjust and fixes the settings on her camera, almost afraid to look past it at the two figures at the end of the room. A spotlight suddenly switches on, and illuminates the wooden cross she saw the other day. She sees a naked man strapped to it, his face concealed by a mask that leaves just a small opening for his mouth. In front of him, with her back to her, stands a very tall woman dressed in an incredible bondage costume. Her lower half is naked apart from some kind of armour strapped to the front of one leg. She wears a breastplate, which covers one side of her torso, and a belt around her waist that goes below her crotch to come up between her legs and sit on the small of her back in a small oval of leather. The cheeks of her bottom are bare. She has black hair that is tied high up on her head in a ponytail. She looks like some kind of futuristic fetish pirate queen. In her hand is a whip that she suddenly cracks against the floor, causing both Valentina and the naked man to flinch.

How to make this erotic? As far as Valentina is concerned, the scene looks corny. A stereotype of everything she has ever believed about S&M. Well, she is here now, witnessing these two people in their private fantasy. She should try her best to create something good. She slips around the woman, Anna, and crouches down between them, takes out her light meter. To her surprise, Anna looks directly at her. She has broad cheekbones and wide slanted eyes. She gives Valentina a Cheshire cat grin.

'Welcome, Valentina,' she says.

Valentina stares at her in shock. Didn't Leonardo say not to interfere with the subjects? How come Anna is acknowledging her?

Anna flicks her whip skilfully so that it flips gently across the skin of the man, Nicky.

'We have a guest.' She addresses him in an icy voice. 'She is here to witness your punishment, and your humiliation.'

Nicky says nothing in reply, but Valentina can't help noticing that he has an erection. She wonders whether Theo would find it erotic being tied up by this dominatrix.

Anna drops her whip on the floor and struts over to Nicky. She is holding something in her hand, but Valentina can't make out what it is. She bends down and licks Nicky's nipples, while stroking his penis. Then she takes two tiny pincers from her hand and attaches them to his nipples. Valentina sees Nicky wince.

'Today, Nicky, because we have a visitor, I am going to be very good to you,' says Anna, kneeling down and rubbing his penis against her one bare breast. Valentina watches as Anna puts Nicky's penis inside her mouth, stroking his balls with her other hand. She keeps snapping away. It's the only thing that stops her from fleeing from the room. She feels voyeuristic. Shouldn't this be private? But then Leonardo wanted her to record what really happens in his world. And it's not too bad, is it? He may be tied up, but Nicky is now being pleasured rather than hurt. Just as she is thinking this, however, just as she hears Nicky's breathing getting heavier with anticipation, Anna stops sucking him and pulls back. She wipes her mouth dramatically.

'Well now, that's enough of that,' she says, winking at Valentina. 'Remember you are my slave, Nicky, not the other way around.'

She picks up the whip again, and before Valentina has time to think, she suddenly lashes out and strikes Nicky. He emits a muffled scream. Oh, she's not so sure about this. Anna strikes Nicky again, very close to his penis. Valentina feels faint. How can he enjoy that? Yet to her surprise she can see that he is still stimulated. In fact she can hear him panting.

'That's right, take your punishment like a man,' growls Anna.

She strikes Nicky again, and Valentina can see red welts rising on his skin. No, she doesn't like this, not one bit. She picks up her camera and begins to back out of the room. Anna catches her, though, lunging at her with her free arm and digging her nails into her flesh.

'What's wrong?' she asks, a wicked gleam in her eyes. 'Too much for you?'

'No, it's just I think I have enough pictures . . . The lighting isn't great.'

Anna stares at her, and then laughs.

'I see,' she says. 'Who would you rather be, me or him?' She nods at Nicky, a gleeful look on her face.

Valentina doesn't answer, trying to pull away from the other woman.

'Oh yes, you have submissive written all over you. You don't like to see a man like this, do you? Well, my dear, it's more fucked up the other way around, don't you think?'

Valentina falls into the hallway, hugging her camera to her chest. She crouches down on the floor, trying to calm herself. She hates what she witnessed just now. It made her feel ill to see that woman hurting that man. Yet she knows in her heart that what Anna said to her is true. She brings her knees up to her chest, and breathes deeply. She is facing the door of the Dark Room. She stares at it intently. She can see her distorted reflection on its metal surface. She looks like a small child hiding from the big bad wolf. *What goes on in there?*

'Valentina, are you all right?' It is Leonardo. He is standing on the bottom stair, looking at her with a concerned expression on his face.

She pulls herself up, tries to compose herself.

'Yes, I'm fine. I just felt a little unwell. I needed some air.'

She knows her lies are transparent, yet to her surprise he doesn't mock her.

'I'm sorry,' he says, looking apologetic. 'Maybe it was a bit much for you?'

'Yes,' she replies honestly. 'I think so.'

He offers her his hand.

'Come on, have a drink. You'll feel better.'

She doesn't resist, letting him lead her upstairs into his sterile office. He opens a cabinet behind the desk and produces a bottle of red wine and two glasses.

'I've got a good bottle of Ripasso here,' he says smoothly. 'I've been looking for someone to share it with.'

Valentina puts her camera down on his desk and sits on the cream couch, still feeling a little foolish. She gratefully takes a glass and has a sip. The wine is rich and plummy. She feels a little better already. Leonardo circles the room, wine glass in hand, before sitting on his desk facing her. They don't speak for a few minutes.

'You look a little better now,' he says eventually. 'You were as white as a sheet.'

'Thank you for the wine,' she replies, taking another sip. 'Sorry,' she adds. 'I didn't realise I was such a lightweight.'

'I wouldn't say that. Not according to Rosa and Celia, anyway.'

Valentina feels herself colouring with embarrassment. Whatever happened to discretion? She wonders which of the two women spilled the beans.

Leonardo smiles at her, his eyes creased in amusement.

'Celia is an old friend,' he says in explanation, as if reading her thoughts. 'How did you find it?' he adds softly.

Valentina looks into his eyes and it dawns on her that he is not asking her out of prurience, but out of interest, as if he does actually care whether she enjoyed herself or not.

'It was fun,' she says, unwittingly echoing Theo's words from his email.

Leonardo raises an eyebrow as if expecting her to say more.

'It was very erotic,' she says slowly. 'And it took me some-where . . . inside myself . . .' She hesitates. 'It was confusing.'

'How so?' Leonardo asks, straining forward as if he wants to catch her every word.

'Well, I never expected to be so turned on by women. I mean, does that mean I am gay or bisexual now?'

Leonardo sighs, looking her straight in the eye.

'How I hate all this labelling. Hetereosexual. Homosexual. Bisexual. Asexual. Sadist. Masochist.' He lists them off on his fingers one by one, pausing for a moment. 'Narcissist . . .' The last word lingers nastily in the air between them.

He stands up again and goes to join her on the couch. He is so close to her now that she can see the dark hairs peeking out from the top of his dark green shirt.

'I believe that it is impossible to define a person's sexuality by a specific label. Our sexuality is multifaceted, constantly changing and evolving. It can be a source of great joy, and also a place where we re-enact our deepest fears.'

'So I am not anything, then? Just because I made love with two women' – saying it out loud seems even more fantastical to Valentina than the actual memory of it – 'it doesn't change me?'

'Well of course it changes you.' Leonardo leans forward and looks at her earnestly. She can feel his breath on her lips as he talks. 'Through sex we can actually purge ourselves. Become new again. Sex can be the purest, most innocent communication between two souls, and at the same time the darkest, most abusive interaction between two humans.'

He leans back, nursing his wine between his hands, his eyes shining so that Valentina thinks he looks like some kind of idealistic prophet, rather than the owner of a fetish club.

'At the end of the day, what we are trying to do here is learn about trust. My clients come here for so many different reasons. *Some* of them, Valentina, are in love with their spouses, yet they come here to have sex with strangers so that they can return to the marriage bed with new, liberated energy.'

'You don't really believe that, do you?' Valentina exclaims angrily. 'That's bullshit. You are just giving people an excuse to cheat on their partners.'

'What is the best kind of relationship, Valentina?' Leonardo asks, head cocked on one side. 'Isn't it best to be honest with yourself, and admit that no one owns anyone? What kills love is not infidelity, but jealousy.'

It occurs to her that Leonardo's words could be her own. Deep down she does agree with him. But she hates lies and deceit.

'I guess it's okay if both partners agree, but I don't think it's right if someone cheats behind the other person's back.'

'Of course not, Valentina. I believe in honesty as well.'

He gets up again to refill their wine glasses.

'So,' he says slowly, 'back to tonight. Did you manage to take any photographs of Anna and Nicky?'

She shakes her head apologetically.

'One or two . . . but I just found the whole thing . . .' She struggles to come up with the right word. She doesn't want to be judgemental. 'Not very sexy . . . I couldn't find the eroticism in the scene.'

'Obviously you are not a dominatrix. Sorry for the label.' He grins at her, and she relaxes slightly. He is not going to make her go back inside. Thank God. 'Otherwise you would have found what Anna was doing extremely sexy.'

'I am afraid I didn't, not at all. It's hard for me to create erotic pictures when—'

'You find the subject matter unattractive,' he interrupts, looking pensive now. 'I can absolutely understand that.'

Leonardo rings the top of his wine glass with his index fingertip. Valentina can't help looking at his long, elegant finger, wondering how it might feel on her skin. What is she thinking? This is a purely professional relationship. Is this what being parted from Theo is doing to her? Driving her crazy with frustration?

'Maybe I should explain what sadomasochism actually is? Would that help?'

Valentina nods, trying to banish all lustful thoughts from her head, which is hard given the subject matter.

'It's not as bad as you might think, being the dominant party. I do believe that if the dominants among us didn't find an outlet for their natural instincts in this contained environment, some of us could be aggressive, and abusive, in our everyday lives.' He pauses, looking at her intently. She can't help imagining Leonardo the dominant, angry, ripping his shirt off, devouring her right here on the cream couch . . . She blushes at the thought, and looks down into her wine glass. 'It's almost like a form of therapy, Valentina. And it is very honest and brave to admit to these instincts.'

She takes a sip of her wine, lifting her eyes to meet his gaze.

'But what about submissives? Isn't that a destructive emotion, particularly for women?' She drops her eyes, looking at him from beneath her eyelashes. Why on earth did she wear this provocative hot pants suit? It makes her feel so sexy.

'Not at all. Many women want to be submissive because in fact it appeals to their vanity. They are the centre of attention. It is quite egocentric, actually.' Leonardo speaks passionately. This is something he knows a lot about, Valentina thinks. She finds it attractive. The idea that he is some kind of sex teacher. 'When your dominator does things to you, it becomes purifying,' he continues. She raises her eyes, looking at him in surprise. 'Being a submissive is about trust. A submissive woman often taps into a hidden, secret side of herself.'

Valentina arches her eyebrows at him sceptically, yet she decides to say nothing.

'What attracts you, Valentina? To dominate or be submissive?'

She looks him square in the face.

'Neither.'

'Come now, Valentina. I have been honest with you. We are talking now about choice. Not having something forced upon you, but choosing to have things done to you, or choosing to do them to someone else with their consent.'

Valentina takes another sip of her red wine. Already the first glass has affected her, and maybe that's why she throws caution to the wind and decides to answer Leonardo honestly.

'I suppose I would choose submission,' she says, averting her eyes.

Leonardo is silent for a second.

'So,' he says eventually. In that one word she can hear that his voice has dropped an octave. 'I like to dominate. If you were to take pictures of me with, say, Celia, I think you would find that very erotic.'

She is not sure whether it is a question or a statement. She looks up at him, and he is staring at her with obsidian eyes, not a shard of brown left. She feels her stomach clench. She would much rather it were Theo sitting here suggesting this, and yet she can't help feeling incredibly attracted to Leonardo. There is a part of her that is craving for this man to touch her. He reminds her of Theo, with his easy sexual grace, and yet he is different. He doesn't want her to be his girlfriend, he doesn't want to possess one iota of her, and yet she can tell by the way he is looking at her that he wants to sleep with her. If she were to do something, she thinks, right now on this cream couch – let him unzip her hot pant suit and straddle her; let him have sex with her – would she tell Theo? Yes, of course she would; she would tell him so that he could see once and for all she was not relationship material.

'Let me think about it,' she says, trying to sound professional, indifferent, yet at the same time feeling her pulse speed up. Celia the submissive and Leonardo the dominator, together in the Velvet Underworld. And where would she fit in? A witness to their drama . . . or a participant?

It is a relief to be back outside, cycling through the night streets of Milan, listening to Lou Reed on her iPod. Part of her wishes she hadn't agreed to this photographic assignment. Has she bitten off more than she can chew? Yet another part of her is finding the whole experience revelatory. Her night-time fantasies now have the possibility of becoming real.

She listens to Lou Reed, encouraging her to walk on the wild side.

And what about Theo? If she were to take pictures of Leonardo and Celia together, would he judge her for it?

Because she knows deep down it wouldn't be just pictures she would be taking.

It is well after midnight by the time she gets home. She wheels her bike into the courtyard of her apartment block. She doesn't notice the figure leaning by her front door until she has her keys out.

'Signorina Rosselli?'

She starts with fright, immediately on the offensive, pushing her keys through her fingers ready to attack.

'Who are you?'

The man steps out of the shadows and the street lights illuminate his face. He looks to be in his late forties, with a head of thick curly grey hair, and a tired face. He is the same man who watched her take off in the taxi the other day.

'I am sorry to frighten you,' he says. 'My name is Inspector Garelli.' He shows her his badge. 'I know it's very late, Signorina Rosselli, but I need to ask you a couple of questions about your partner, Signor Theo Steen.'

'Is something wrong?'

'No, no . . . it's just routine,' he says. 'Can I come in?'

Valentina doesn't think twice. There is no way she is going to let this pushy police officer into her flat at this time of night.

'No, it's too late. I'm tired. Call me tomorrow.' She doesn't care if she sounds rude. Something tells her not to let this man into her apartment.

'Oh, okay.' He is surprised, yet he accepts what she is

saying. So he doesn't have a warrant. 'I just want to ask you where Signor Steen is.'

'I have no idea,' Valentina says sharply.

'Of course you do, Signorina Rosselli. What boyfriend goes off without telling his girlfriend where he is going?'

'He is *not* my boyfriend, Inspector Garelli,' Valentina snarls, before storming into her apartment and slamming the door in his face. She leans against the door, catching her breath. Inspector Garelli has made her mad. Her body is taut with frustration. Damn Theo. She doesn't want to be pulled into his private life. She doesn't want to care. She connects her iPod to the speakers, and turns Lou Reed on full blast. And she dances. One minute she is Celia, the submissive. The next she is Anna, the dominatrix. She becomes herself in love. And then she fights it and becomes herself against love. Hot as ice, and cold as fire.

$\mathcal{B}$elle

SHE WAITS A DAY, TWO DAYS, THREE, A WEEK. YET HER sailor doesn't come to her. She spends as much time as she can in her apartment, sitting on her tiny balcony watching the narrow canal below. A whistle, the splash of an oar in the water, a sailor's cap sends her heart into a spin, but it is never him. Santos Devine has disappeared into the twisting canals of Venice, obviously preoccupied with trading his silk or whatever other adventure he is busy with that is more interesting, more enticing than *her*. She tries her best not to care, to forget him. Yet it is impossible. Every night as she falls asleep she sees his roguish face. She knows that he is bad for her. Not considerate like the Doctor, big hearted like Igor or kind like Signor R. She knows that for Santos Devine she is probably just one more pretty girl in yet another port. Yet still she hopes that maybe he sees something in her that he has looked for all his life, like she sees in him.

She tries to distract herself with her clients, but it is not the same. She considers going to Ponte di Rialto again at night-time and picking up a stranger, maybe two, like the time with the Scottish captain and his Caribbean first mate. Yet when she sets off she is hunting for Santos's face among the men she meets, and when she makes do with someone else, it never ends to her satisfaction. She is left even more frustrated than before, wandering home wearily in the small hours and facing further anger from her husband. He tells her he cannot control her, and it is true. Up until now she always waited until he went away to undertake her secret adventures, but recently he is not travelling so much and she has to get out. He threatens her. Tells her he will lock her up. She screams back that he cannot cage her like a bird. As he lashes into her, her maid, Pina, stands by trembling in horror.

This morning she has enraged her husband yet again. She risked staying out all night, confident that he would have fallen into a whisky-induced slumber by midnight. As she creeps across the landing, her shoes in her hand, Signor Brzezinski comes up the stairs behind her, charging like an angry bull. He must have been sitting up waiting for her all night, for he is still in his dinner jacket and unshaven. She braces herself as he brings his hand up and slaps the top of her head, sending her flying. She cries out in pain. She scrambles to her feet, but he hits her again, this time punching her in the chest and winding her. She totters backwards and collapses again. He says nothing, just spits at her in disgust before storming into his bedroom.

She staggers to her feet and stumbles into her own room. There are tears in her eyes, but they are tears of frustration rather than pain. Yet she is relieved it is not worse this time. There is a gentle knock on her door, and her little maid enters. What is the child doing up at such an hour? Pina is fully dressed, although her hair is still unbraided and her eyes look heavy with sleep. When she sees her mistress, they begin to fill with tears as well.

'Oh please, madam,' Pina whimpers, as if she is the one who has been hit. 'Please don't anger him so.'

'He cannot keep me prisoner, Pina. I will die if I cannot get out. I will, you know!'

Pina makes her sit, rearranges her hair to hide the bruise beginning to blossom on the top of her forehead. And later that morning, while Signor Brzezinski is busy with his papers, she begs Louise not to leave the house.

'Tell him I have gone to visit the Countess,' Louise instructs her.

'He'll know that's not true. Please don't go, madam.'

Louise takes the girl's child-sized hand in hers.

'I have to, Pina. It is my only hope.'

And Belle hopes all the way to her apartment. Hopes she will see Santos Devine leaning against the wall by her front door, waiting for her. Yet each day she is disappointed, and she pays the price for her disobedience when she returns home, her pale skin mottled by bruises beneath her evening gown.

* * *

Today the Doctor is with her. She tries to enter into the spirit of things, but when he opens his bag and shows her his instruments, she doesn't feel scared or excited any more. In fact today she wants him to hurt her, *really* hurt her with one of those sharp tools. Maybe that will stop the pain that sears her heart ever since she met Santos.

'Now, Belle,' the Doctor begins kindly. 'I believe you have been feeling poorly of late.'

'Yes, I have, Doctor,' she says flatly.

'Well I am going to make you better. Please turn around.'

Instead of turning her back to him so that he can blindfold her and tie her to the bed, Belle gets up off the mattress. She drops her silk chemise so that she is naked apart from her stockings. She feels open and careless, as if she could walk the streets of Venice without a stitch on her, not caring who sees her or what they do to her. She walks over to the Doctor, and she can see him taking in her bruised body. She supposes he has never seen her this bad. His face pales, and he looks even sadder than normal. Belle bends down to pick up his doctor's bag. He looks at her, startled, unable to speak. She has broken the spell of his game. She puts the bag down on the bed and rummages inside it. She pulls out a pair of curve-ended scissors and hands them to him.

'Doctor, please, I want you to make me better,' she says, looking into his eyes with ferocious intensity.

The Doctor blinks behind his spectacles, the force of her gaze too much. His expression is puzzled. Eventually he regains his composure and assumes his character again.

'Yes, Belle, I will make you better,' he says, looking at the scissors in his hand.

She puts on the blindfold herself, and lies down on the bed for him. She waits for the feel of the sharp instrument on her skin.

'Please,' she begs. 'Make the pain go away.'

She senses the Doctor hovering over her.

'Belle,' he says. 'What's wrong?' And he sounds a little different, less steady.

'Doctor, please cut out my heart.' Her voice cracks.

She waits for the sensation of the metal piercing her skin, of the blood spilling out of her, and of the release she is hoping for. Instead the blindfold is pulled off and the Doctor sits down on the bed next her, the scissors no longer in his hand.

'Dear Belle, what is wrong?' he asks, stroking her hair ever so gently.

'Oh Doctor,' she cries out. 'I'm in love.' And she bursts into tears, burying her face in his bare chest.

The Doctor holds her in his arms, patting her back until her crying abates. She pulls away and looks up at his cloud-grey eyes, so like her dead father's.

'Oh Doctor, what am I to do?'

'Ah, poor, poor Belle. I am sorry to say that I have no cure for love.'

'Please, Doctor, tell me what to do.' She clings to him. 'I

am in love and yet he does not come. I have waited and waited for him.' She clasps her hands. 'I cannot bear it any longer. I shall throw myself in the canal. I cannot go home again without seeing him . . .'

'Now, now, Belle,' the Doctor says sagely, rubbing her back. 'Calm yourself, my dear. All is not lost.'

She looks at him hopefully.

'The only medicine I know for love is love itself. Why don't you go and find this man? You are Belle, famous courtesan of Venice! You cannot let love defeat you!' The Doctor proudly pats her bare bottom. 'I am sure you can seduce this man, especially if you love him.'

'But where will I find him?'

'Look and you shall find, my dear. Venice is small enough.'

She is so grateful for his encouraging words that she dries her eyes and embraces him. They are both naked, and yet it is the embrace of friendship.

'I am sorry, Doctor,' she says humbly, looking down. 'I have been selfish and spoilt your time today. Would you like to start again?'

'No, dear Belle. It is time I went.' He pats her head, and kisses the crown of it tenderly. 'You are very dear to me, you know.'

He stands up and takes his neatly folded shirt off his pile of clothes on the chair, begins to get dressed.

'You are a woman who deserves to be treasured. It pains me to see how carelessly your husband regards you.'

Belle looks down at her body and surveys the blue bruises on her thighs.

'I was defiant, I deserved it.'

'No wife deserves to be beaten,' the Doctor says sternly, lifting her chin and looking straight into her eyes.

She averts her gaze in shame. For it shames her to have the Doctor's pity. Why can't she be more tactful with her husband and avoid their violent confrontations? She believes she is a woman who should never have married. If only she had grown up in America, in a free-spirited modern family. She would have liked to be a dancer, maybe an actress in those movies she adores so much. Oh, if she could have danced the Charleston, kicked up her heels and had some fun. Her upbringing in Warsaw couldn't have been more different. There was no gaiety. And when the war came, there was too much death.

After the Doctor has gone, Belle sits on her bed thinking for a few minutes. The Doctor is right. She needs to find Santos. Is this a test he has set her? She doesn't know for sure. He told her he would set her free, but does she need to show him some faith first? She has waited too long for this moment to let it slip through her fingers. She can't let this man sail away. She flings open her wardrobe and takes out her sailor costume. It's time to become a boy again, and find the man who has stolen her heart.

Valentina

SHE IS WATCHING. HER CAMERA IS IN HER HANDS, protecting her like a shield, and yet she is not taking pictures. Celia is lying on her back on the four-poster bed in the Velvet Underworld, her arms above her head and tied to the bedstead, her eyes closed in ecstasy as Leonardo crouches over her like a lion, licking her and caressing her. Valentina raises the camera to her face and tries to concentrate on getting a good shot, but she can't focus. She is not sure what turns her on more, Celia in her wild abandon, or Leonardo as he pleasures her. Celia climaxes, and Leonardo sits back on his heels, gently stroking her before untying her from the bedstead. Celia sits up on the bed and smiles right at Valentina, like the cat that got the cream.

Leonardo turns to look at her as well.

'See how well I look after her if she obeys me,' he says to Valentina, his brown eyes warm and teasing. She is blushing deep down inside. Somehow watching Leonardo in this scenario rather than a complete stranger makes her feel more self-conscious. His body is different from Theo's. He is not as lean or tall, and yet he is all compact muscle and masculine power.

'Why don't you put down that silly old camera and join us?' Celia asks as she stretches her porcelain legs out in front of her. She looks flawless, Valentina thinks, so pure and fresh, like a lily. How she would like to smell her again, feel the texture of her incredibly soft lips on her skin.

Leonardo cocks his head on one side and smiles at her.

'Come, Valentina.' He offers her his hand. 'Don't be afraid. This is a gift for you.'

His words resonate within her and she thinks of Theo's gift. Those erotic photographs from so many years ago. Humans have always done this, she reasons, basked in the physical poetry of eroticism. How can something so pleasurable be wrong?

As if entranced, she puts the camera aside and walks over to the bed. She is naked already. Was she taking pictures with no clothes on? She climbs up on to the four-poster, which seems incredibly high, piled with mattress after mattress, like the bed in the story of the Princess and the Pea. The purple velvet curtains hang down around her as if she is on a stage and she, Leonardo and Celia are the principal actors.

'Lie down,' Leonardo commands, and she obeys him.

Celia crawls across the bed towards her. She leans over

Valentina and kisses her gently on the lips before sliding down her body so that Valentina can feel her breasts rubbing against hers. Lower she slides until she reaches Valentina's most private part. She puts her hand between Valentina's legs and pulls them apart, and before Valentina can think, she feels Celia's tongue right inside her. She gasps, with surprise, with pleasure. Leonardo is lying beside her. He cradles her head in one of his arms, and with the other hand he strokes her body, up and down, up and down, in rhythm with Celia's licks. Valentina is going deep down inside herself, to a sensation as luxurious and rich as the crushed velvet that surrounds her in this pulsing red room.

She hears the door open. Someone else has come in. She opens her eyes, and to her astonishment Theo is standing at the end of the bed, looking down at her.

'Theo!' she cries, trying to sit up, panicking, but to her astonishment he puts his finger to his lips as if to tell her to be quiet. He is actually smiling at her, and she realises that he likes this, to watch Celia and Leonardo giving her pleasure.

Theo undresses in front of her. She longs to touch him, and give him the pleasure she is receiving now. He climbs on to the bed and Valentina awaits him with anticipation. Celia's licks have become so deep, so intense that she is very close to the edge, and all she wants now is to feel her dear lover inside her. Theo puts his hands around Celia's waist and lifts her away from Valentina.

'Oh, Theo,' she whispers, burning with love and desire for

him. She is speaking in the throes of her passion. What is happening to her?

Celia is on her knees facing Valentina, Theo's hands still around her waist. Valentina gasps in shock as she watches Theo push inside the other girl. She stares at him in disbelief, and he looks at her magnanimously, smiling all the time. And suddenly, instead of being angry or hurt, she understands what Theo wants. She twists towards Leonardo, who with no prompting at all pulls her up from the bed so that she falls on her knees as well. She spreads her legs and pushes her backside up towards Leonardo, looking at Theo all the time as he slowly rocks in and out of Celia. And then she feels Leonardo's length inside her, and she sighs with satisfaction, holding Theo with her gaze all the while. It is incredibly intimate for her and her lover to be fucking other people while watching each other's pleasure. When they are together, just the two of them, she is almost lost from him sometimes, but now she watches him acutely as he gets closer and closer to climaxing. She pulls herself up and reaches her arms forward, and Theo does the same. They are holding hands over Celia's naked back, eyes locked, as they climax at the same time. And then they are falling back upon the bed, all four of them a tangle of limbs, and hot skin, and velvet. They are sinking into the bed, through its hundred mattresses and below into the plush carpet, through the floor, down, down into the red earth.

* * *

Valentina wakes tangled in her sheets. She flings them off. She is so hot, her body wet with perspiration. She swings her legs out of the bed, and holds her sides. Her body is still throbbing from the eroticism of what happened last night, her head aching with confusion. She doesn't understand. What was Theo doing there, in Leonardo's club? It really *was* him, wasn't it? Yet afterwards he left her without a word of explanation. She was so shaken by the experience that Leonardo called a taxi to take her home. He was so kind, making her sweet tea, stroking her hair and asking her if she was okay.

What was he doing here? she kept asking, but he avoided her question, instead instructing her to go straight to bed when she got home.

She expected Theo to be in the flat, waiting for her, ready to explain everything. She thought it would be like one of their passionate trysts when they arrived and departed separately to maintain the sexual suspense. And yet when she got home last night, the flat was empty, and it was clear that Theo had not been back since he left five days ago. It made no sense. Theo had asked her to be his girlfriend, and yet he fucked Celia right in front of her. Why isn't she outraged? Is it because she doesn't care enough?

She goes into the study and turns on her laptop to check her emails. She needs to hear from Theo. His phone is off and she is desperate to speak to him. She sent him a message last night asking him what the hell was going on, and where he was if he was back in Milan. She also told him that a police-man had called to speak to him. Was there something he was hiding from her? He had told her to trust no one; did that include the police?

She is relieved to see he has sent her a reply. Yet it is sparse and unsatisfactory.

Re: Policeman. Nothing to worry about but don't talk to him. It's to do with my family. Re: Last night. Did you have fun? Theo xx

She slams down the laptop lid, furious. What kind of game is he playing? How inadequate his words are. He pushed her into sleeping with another man last night. She squeezes her thighs tight as she remembers the sensation of Leonardo inside her. It was lovely, although not the same as Theo. He didn't fill her in the same way. And yet, she chews her lip, would she have slept with Leonardo anyway, even if Theo hadn't been there as well? She was on the verge of it, wasn't she? Before he came into the room. And what about Theo and Celia? Is he punishing her for not wanting to be his girlfriend? Well it won't work, she thinks stoutly. She doesn't do jealousy. She refuses to be pushed into it. The longer he stays away, the more likely she will be able to let him go in the end.

But she does have a problem. What if that policeman comes back? Is he going to tell her something awful about Theo? She tries not to worry. She *knows* Theo is not a bad person, even if he is playing games with her at the moment.

She weaves her way back out of the study. The room really

is a complete junkyard, she thinks, as she moves a stack of books to one side. She glances again at the new paintings on the wall, confused that he would choose to buy copies of pictures he doesn't like. Where does he get the money for all this art anyway?

Valentina stops in her tracks, a terrible thought occurring to her. What if . . . what if . . . he doesn't pay for them? She shakes her head, scrutinising the Watteau painting, and then the one next to it, the Dutch interior of the woman reading the letter. What if they *aren't* copies? No, Theo is not a thief. No way. It's a completely ridiculous idea. Although she can't help thinking of *The Thomas Crown Affair*, and how very like Thomas Crown Theo is. Suave. In control. Actually the idea of Theo being some kind of art thief is rather sexy, she muses, as she opens the curtains of her apartment and looks down at the dismal rain-streaked street. She scans it for the stranger with the camera, but she hasn't seen him since that first time. She must have been mistaken. He wasn't actually looking at *her*. He must be one of the new people living in her apartment block, or a visitor of one of her neighbours.

It's still pouring with rain. Valentina feels like hibernating. She is so exhausted and confused from last night that she wants to hide from the whole world today. She goes into the kitchen and looks in the fridge. There's not much in there – a couple of eggs and some overripe tomatoes – but she should eat something. She takes down the coffee pot and prepares some coffee. Just as it is gurgling with strong espresso, her phone rings. She picks it up and sees Gaby's name displayed on the screen.

'Valentina?'

'Gaby, are you okay?' She can hear immediately that something is wrong from the tone of her friend's voice.

'Oh Valentina, I broke up with Massimo.' Gaby is crying so much she can barely speak.

Valentina knew this day would come. Gaby's married lover always made it clear to her that he was never going to leave his wife. Valentina knew only too well how things would end. And yet when she saw them together, he and Gaby were so in love. It was bittersweet to see. It made her angry, almost unable to speak to Massimo, although she tried not to judge him.

'I'm so sorry, Gaby.'

'I ended it. I couldn't do it any more, Valentina. It hurts too much to be with him. To know I can never really have him.'

'Maybe he will leave his wife . . .'

'No, Valentina, he won't . . . you know that . . .'

Gaby sighs. Valentina cradles her phone between her shoulder and her ear, as she takes the coffee pot off the cooker and pours herself a neat black espresso.

'Do you want to come over?' she says. 'I'm not doing anything.' Maybe this is what she needs. If she could be distracted from her own confusing situation by Gaby's crisis, she might start to feel less worried about Theo.

'Would you mind, Valentina? I know you like your solitude, but I don't want to stay here. He might come over and I don't know if I have the will to resist him . . .'

'Sure, come on over. I've no plans.'

Valentina wonders fleetingly whether Leonardo is expecting her at his club again tonight. She needs a day off, especially after last night. She is not sure how she will face him next time she sees him.

'Can we watch Lulu in *Pandora's Box*?'

Valentina lets her face break into a wide smile, since there is no one here to see her. Gaby is almost as obsessed with Louise Brooks as she is.

'Don't you think that will make you even sadder?'

'I need a good cry, and it's the perfect film for my mood. Lulu is my heroine, Valentina. All she wants is to please men, and yet all they do is destroy her.'

A couple of hours later, Gaby and Valentina are curled up together on the couch, eating brioche filled with crema, which Gaby brought over, and watching Louise Brooks dancing.

'She is so beautiful,' sighs Gaby. 'There is something about her that is different from all the other movie stars.'

'She's uncompromising,' says Valentina, licking crema off her fingertips. 'And she has this spirit. It's intoxicating. That's why everyone wants a little part of her.'

'Lulu or Louise Brooks?' asks Gaby.

'Both. They are one and the same really, aren't they?'

The girls watch the film in silence for a few moments.

'Everyone goes on about Greta Garbo, and how mysterious and beautiful she was, but I think Louise Brooks was more of an enigma,' says Gaby, stuffing the last of her brioche into her mouth.

'You know that Louise Brooks claimed she and Greta Garbo slept together once?' Valentina stretches out on the couch, letting her tiptoes rest against Gaby's thigh.

'I didn't know Louise Brooks was gay.' Gaby looks at her in surprise.

'She wasn't. She was just curious.'

It's strange, Valentina thinks, that the only time she has ever really cried was when she saw *Pandora's Box* for the first time. The film still has a powerful effect on her, even though she's watched it countless times. To see this beautiful spirit misunderstood, mistreated and eventually destroyed.

After the movie, Valentina opens a bottle of red wine.

'Do you want to go out, Gaby, meet up with the others?'

Gaby shakes her head mournfully, and Valentina feels relieved. She knows that if she speaks to Marco she might very well break down and tell him everything. And she is not ready to confide in anyone about what happened last night. Not until she knows what she feels herself.

'No, I'm really tired tonight. Besides, we'll see them at Marco's party on Tuesday. Do you mind if I stay here?'

'Of course not.' Valentina pours them both a glass of red wine. 'You'll have to share my bed.'

'I'd like that, if it's okay. I feel safe here.'

Gaby hugs her, and although Valentina doesn't hug her back, it's nice to feel the warm appreciation of her old friend. Besides, she is glad she is not alone again tonight, with her head in such a mess. She is tired of waking up in that big empty bed.

She knows that Gaby will be all right eventually. She has never had a problem attracting men. She is traditionally pretty in a way Valentina will never be: petite, with long blond hair, clear skin and rosebud lips. Yet Valentina doesn't see the point of saying something encouraging, like *You're so attractive, you'll meet someone else, there are plenty more fish in the sea.* She knows what it feels like to lose your heart to a married man, and she has to let Gaby grieve. She is proud of her friend for being strong and ending what was ultimately a doomed relationship.

The two friends eat dinner together. Valentina realises it is the first proper meal she has eaten in days. She forgets to eat when she is on her own, a bad habit picked up from her mother, who never cooked for them. Tina Rosselli usually left Valentina to fend for herself in the kitchen, warning her daughter not to eat too much. If they had guests for dinner, however, it was quite the opposite. Her mother would cook way too much food, picking at her own meagre portion while watching her friends' every mouthful. How hard Valentina has fought against her mother's dysfunctional relationship with food. She tried her best to ignore her mother's instructions to cut back on carbohydrates as her bottom was getting too big, her daily comments on her weight loss or gain. Any normal mother would be worried if their daughter lost a dramatic amount of weight too quickly, but when Valentina lost her puppy fat, to such an extent that she turned from chubby child into skinny teenager practically overnight, her mother was delighted.

'Oh you look so lovely, darling,' she crooned. 'If you were a little taller, you could model.' She sighed then, patting her own flat stomach. 'You just don't know how lucky you are. It's so hard to keep the weight down once you've had children.'

The incongruity of her comment was sickening, her implication that because of Mattia and Valentina she had put on weight unfair. Over the years Valentina had noticed a pattern. If her mother was happy, which meant she had a lover, she would put on a little weight, look younger, prettier and generally more healthy. Even so, she would complain constantly that men made her fat, forcing her to go out for meals and drink too much wine. As soon as she was single again, she would go on a crash diet, her weight plummeting like a stone. She would be bad tempered and sometimes downright mean, monitoring everything Valentina ate. Usually Valentina celebrated the arrival of a new lover in her mother's life with a trip to the bakery.

Gaby's home life was the opposite of Valentina's. Sometimes Valentina could not help being a little envious of her friend, but usually she just loved to be included in her family gatherings. Gaby's mother is a curvaceous, cheerful lady, and like her, Gaby is an excellent cook. She always claims that cooking for others helps her when she is down, and tonight she has prepared her speciality: tortelli stuffed with pears and cheese, a divine combination.

'Shall we share another bottle of wine before we go to bed? Watch another Louise Brooks film?' suggests Valentina after they have washed up and put all the dishes away.

'Oh yes.' Gaby looks almost happy. 'Do you have *A Girl in Every Port*? I love it when she high-dives. It's such a sweet movie.'

'We can stream it off YouTube. I'll look it up. You go and get the wine. There's a bottle on the bookshelf in the study.'

'Wow,' Gaby comments as she comes back into the sitting room, bottle of red wine in hand. 'That's some art collection you've got in there.'

'Oh, they're just copies. All Theo's.'

Gaby looks thoughtful. She sits down in the armchair, nursing the bottle of wine between her hands.

'Did he tell you they were copies?'

'Well, no . . . why?'

Gaby is an art restorer. If anyone knows about authenticity, it's her. She puts the bottle down on the floor and gets up out of the chair. She says nothing, just takes Valentina's hand and drags her into the study.

'Look at this, Valentina, just look at it!'

Valentina looks again at the Dutch painting of the woman reading the letter in the window. It really is a pretty piece, a fine copy of a delicate masterpiece.

'I am currently restoring some Dutch interiors. In fact I am working on a painting by this very artist, Gabriel Metsu.' She taps the frame of the painting. 'I really am very certain that this is not a copy. And if it is, then the painter is as masterful as Metsu himself.'

The two girls stare at each, slowly comprehending the implications of the five paintings hanging on the wall.

'I am certain that the original was in a private collection in the United States. It's called *The Love Letter*.'

Valentina examines the painting. How can Gaby *really* know for sure that it is the original? She doesn't know what to say. It is just too shocking to consider that this painting hanging on her apartment wall might be worth millions.

'Why has Theo got these pictures?' Gaby whispers, even though there is no one in the flat to hear her. 'Is he a secret millionaire? Is he going round the world to art auctions or buying off private collectors?'

'I don't know, Gaby.'

Valentina thinks of Inspector Garelli. She feels a little sick. She pulls her friend out of the study and for the first time locks the door.

'Can we try to forget about it? I don't want to spend the evening imagining all sorts of crazy things.' She tries to pull herself together. 'I'll ask Theo when he comes back. I am sure there is a perfectly reasonable explanation. Besides, I really do think you are wrong. They *must* be copies.'

Gaby looks at her sceptically but says no more.

Later, as the two girls lie spooned together in her bed, Valentina finds she cannot sleep. The mystery surrounding Theo is plaguing her. She slips out of Gaby's arms and tiptoes into the study. She opens her iMac and googles Gabriel Metsu, *The Love Letter*. An image comes up, identical to the painting in the study. Underneath she reads, *Private Collection, New York, USA*. There is no mention of its theft or loss. So Gaby has to be wrong. Theo's picture is a copy. Yet for some reason she doesn't feel convinced. What are the chances of her best friend being an expert on Dutch seventeenth-century interiors? And a police officer nosing around asking her where Theo is?

She turns off her computer and picks up the old black photograph album. She puts it on her lap and flicks through the pages. Is this stolen as well? She can't help thinking how precious these images must be for whoever took them or had them taken. Yet surely both photographer and subject are dead by now? She looks at the last image she enlarged. It is the back of a woman's head and the top of her bare back. She has a black bob just like Louise Brooks; just like herself, Valentina thinks. She is tantalisingly close to seeing her face, yet she has only been provided with a tiny part of her profile. On her head is a sailor's hat. Obviously, not hers.

Valentina crawls back into bed as quietly as she can. Gaby stirs.

'V?' she whispers.

'Yes.' Valentina can see the whites of her friend's eyes in the darkness.

'I can't stop thinking about Louise Brooks and Greta Garbo.'

Valentina imagines the combination of Brooks and Garbo. Sleek black hair like lacquer and black eyes contrasting with soft fair hair and Sphinx-like grace, both of them so pale, both of them enigmas.

'Yes, it's rather a nice thought. Very aesthetic.'

Gaby laughs, and it pleases Valentina to hear her friend sounding lighter than she has all day long. She nestles back into the bed, and lets Gaby put her arms around her waist.

'Have you ever made love with a woman, Valentina?'

'Yes.'

She hears Gaby take a breath, feels her hands pressing into her waist.

'Really? What was it like?'

'Actually I slept with two women at the same time.'

'Two women . . . Oh my God, Valentina, you're so wild . . .'

Gaby squeezes her tight. It is so nice to be held. Valentina sighs sleepily.

'And it was very erotic.'

Gaby pushes her face against the back of Valentina's neck.

'Maybe we might sleep together one day,' she whispers.

'Maybe,' Valentina says. 'But not tonight. I don't want to be your rebound.'

Gaby kisses the back of Valentina's neck.

'You're too special for that, Valentina. You're like Lulu. Everyone wants a part of you.'

$\mathcal{B}$elle

BELLE IS LOST IN CANNAREGIO. IT IS A PART OF THE CITY she doesn't know well. She tries to follow her instincts, but it is impossible in Venice. The streets are a maze of twists and turns. She finds she ends up in the same piazza several times, although she took a different street out of it. It is early afternoon; her husband's after-lunch nap must be nearly over. Belle knows she will not manage to return home in time to avert his suspicions. Signor Brzezinski will not believe for a minute that she has been visiting the Countess, a woman he knows Belle despises. She has run out of excuses and lies. He will surely punish her. She is waiting for the day he throws her out on the street. She thinks that the only reason he hasn't yet done so is because he doesn't want any scandal surrounding him. *Why did his wife become a prostitute? Could he not satisfy her?*

Cannaregio is where the less wealthy of Venice live. She is glad she is in her disguise. She would not like to draw attention to herself. Hard-eyed men loiter in the alleys, smoking and looking shifty. Maybe this is a wild goose chase. She is not sure whether Santos's first mate was trying to trick her or not.

As soon as she had changed into her sailor boy's outfit, Belle went to the same taverna where she had seen Santos for the first time. But he wasn't there. She thought back to her night with the Scottish Captain and the Jamaican first mate and the boat she saw docked. She was almost sure it was Santos's, but she needed to check. She sat down at the same table she had sat at before and ordered a glass of rum to give her courage. When the owner returned with her drink, Belle asked him about Santos.

'Santos Devine!' the man exclaimed cheerfully, his eyes lighting up with affection, or was it admiration? 'Why, everyone knows which boat is his! It's the big white schooner, *The Queen Maeve*. Very smart it is. Must have money somewhere, that old devil.'

'*The Queen Maeve*,' Belle repeated, rolling the strange name around in her mouth.

'I believe,' said the innkeeper, 'it's the name of some old Irish queen. He told me his father had a boat called the same.'

Yes, of course, Belle thought. That is why he is so enticing, the two contrasting parts of himself – Irish sailor and Spanish dancer – creating a splendid contradiction of wildness and grace.

After knocking back her rum as fast as she could, Belle walked down to the boats, trying her best to swagger like all the other sailors. It was a funny way of walking, striding along as if you possessed the world. She found *The Queen Maeve* easily, and as she looked at the elegant white schooner, she knew she was right – it was the same boat she had been looking at all those nights ago. Was it Santos who had lit the lamp that evening, drawing her towards him even then?

She shifted nervously from foot to foot, not quite certain what to do now that she had found his boat. Should she go aboard uninvited?

'Are you looking for someone?'

She turned around. Behind her was an incredibly tall man. She barely reached his navel. He had on a long navy blazer, white trousers and a sailor's cap. His extremely long fingers delicately balanced a cigarette, which he puffed away on while surveying her through narrowed eyes.

'I'm looking for Santos Devine,' she said in as low a voice as she could manage.

The man rolled his eyes.

'Not another young dreamer wanting to have an adventure.' He tapped her on the shoulder, and he was so big and strong that she nearly toppled over. 'You look way too young to be thinking of going to sea. Go home to your mummy and grow up a little first.'

'You misunderstand me,' Belle said, trying to be as commanding and manly as possible. 'I am looking for Santos Devine . . . because I need to speak with him. I don't want to go to sea.'

The tall man narrowed his eyes further and looked at her suspiciously.

'I am Santos's first mate; you can tell me anything you want to tell him, and I will pass on a message.'

She could hardly tell this man the truth. How would he react if he knew she was a woman? Would he laugh at her and shoo her away?

'I have a message for him ... from my sister. It's of a personal nature ...'

Santos's first mate relaxed, and gave her a conspiratorial grin.

'Not another girl in love with Santos,' he exclaimed. 'I don't know how he manages to break so many hearts.'

At his words, Belle's own heart sank. This was a hopeless endeavour. To Santos she was just another pretty girl. Why was she making a fool of herself, hunting him down like this?

'All right,' said the tall man. 'You look harmless enough. He's in Cannaregio.' He gave her the name of a street Belle had never heard of. 'He is at the mask-maker's there, trading. Good luck to you and your sister.' He slapped Belle on the back so that she almost went flying off the pier and into the sea. 'And tell her if she has no luck with Santos, I make an excellent second best!'

He burst out laughing, and it sounded like a roll of thunder as he went up the gangway and on to Santos's pristine white boat.

So that is how she has ended up one hour later still searching Cannaregio for this tiny street. She passes the Jewish
ghetto again, and out of the corner of her eye she sees a narrow
dark alley she didn't notice the first time. She approaches it
and looks at the name of the street. That's it. She is here. She
enters the alley uncertainly. A black cat saunters in front of
her, and Belle follows it. The street seems to grow narrower
and darker as the daylight is squeezed out of it.

Suddenly she comes upon an opening by a narrow canal,
and there is a majestic crumbling Venetian house, shuttered
and empty looking, leaning on its side as if it might disintegrate
at any moment into the water. Attached to the moulting
plaster is a sign made of white china. *Laconi*, she reads. That
was the name Santos's first mate gave her. Belle licks her lips
nervously. This must be the mask-makers's. It occurs to her
that her intrusion might be unwelcome. Santos is after all in
the middle of transacting some kind of business. Well, she has
to go through with it now.

She knocks on the door. No answer. Maybe no one is
home. She knocks again more boldly, picking up the brass
knocker and dropping it from a height. She hears footsteps,
brisk and light, and the door swings open. To her surprise, a
woman stands on the threshold. She is older than Belle, but
still very beautiful, with eyes as black as apple pips and silky
olive skin. She is wearing a red petticoat, and is barefoot. Two
black cats are weaving in and out of her legs, purring, and she
holds another one in her hands, against her chest. She and the

cat look at Belle with indifference. The woman raises her eyebrows questioningly. Belle has lost the power of speech. She doesn't know what to say.

'I'm sorry, darling; you are way too young. Come back in another year,' the woman says, winking at her.

What kind of mask-maker is this? wonders Belle. She can see no evidence of a workshop in the dark hall behind the woman. With thumping heart she realises that perhaps Santos is not here to trade after all. She is just about to let the woman close the door in her face when courage seizes her.

'Santos Devine,' she croaks. 'I have a message for Santos Devine.'

She is almost hoping the woman will tell her he isn't there. That this is all some kind of bad joke. For how could Santos want to be with another woman, older and frankly more common than her, when he knows he could have Belle with one snap of his fingers?

The woman pushes her hip to one side, balancing the cat there, and flicks an auburn curl behind her ear.

'Yes, he's here. Who are you?'

'My name is . . . Louis,' she stutters. 'Can you tell him Louis Blackbird is here?'

She is so consumed with desperate longing that she doesn't care about the situation she finds herself in. The man she loves is sleeping with another prostitute. It doesn't matter to Belle. She still wants him.

The woman disappears down the dark corridor, and Belle

is left waiting with the cats. A second passes, two, and then a door at the end of the corridor swings open. Her chest tightens. There he is. The man she has craved these past two weeks. He is shirtless, but still wearing his white trousers and sailor's cap. He stands in the doorway, the light behind him so that his face is in shadow.

'Belle Blackbird?' he calls out. 'Is that you?'

She steps forward, scattering the cats.

'Yes.'

She can see his face now. It is perfectly symmetrical, with its heavy eyebrows and the cleft in his chin.

'What are you doing here?' he asks, sounding surprised.

The woman appears next to Santos. She drapes her arm around his neck possessively, and Santos does nothing to stop her.

'I came to find you,' says Belle in a small voice. She looks into his eyes, those amber and blue eyes promising all the sensual wealth she desires. They make her want to fall into his arms and push the other whore away.

'But why?' he asks. 'I told you that I would come and find you. One day.'

'I cannot wait any longer.' Her honest words sound clumsy now.

The other woman looks between Santos and Belle, uncomprehending.

'Well, Santos!' she laughs. 'I didn't know you were that way inclined.'

Santos grins, and tickles her under the chin.

'He's a girl, can't you see?'

The woman turns to stare at Belle.

'Oh yes, of course . . .' She smiles cruelly. 'But not much of a girl.' She addresses Belle coldly. 'Do you want Santos for yourself? Don't you know that he is just like a cat? You can't ask for his affection; you have to wait for him to deign to give it to you.'

Her voice sounds bitter, and Belle notices hurt in her eyes as she drops her arm from around Santos's torso. She wonders if this woman might be more than just another prostitute to Santos.

'I'll leave you to talk,' the woman says icily, disappearing into her room and clicking the door behind her. They are in near darkness, and all the while the other woman has been speaking Santos has not taken his eyes from Belle's. His gaze is so intense, she feels as if she is pinned to the wall by it.

'Belle,' he asks her gruffly, 'why did you come here? I didn't want you to see me here. I told you . . . when the time is right, I will come to you.'

'Why do *you* get to decide when it is the right time?' she cries.

She is suddenly so angry, consumed by the passion of her rage. She flies down the corridor towards him, raises her hand to hit him, but he catches it in his.

'You made me fall in love with you and then you left me stranded . . . hanging on for you. You're a monster . . .'

He flinches, and she thinks she sees him grow pale.

'We only spent an afternoon talking . . . Belle, you are married. I didn't think—'

'I am in love with you,' she wails, pulling herself away from him. 'Yet to you I am just another silly lovesick girl.'

She turns away from him, stumbling blindly out of the house and back down the narrow alley. He catches up with her.

'Belle, Belle.' He tries to take her arm, but she pulls away and storms on down the alley. He grabs her from behind, swinging her around, his strength taking her breath away. He presses her against the wall of the alley. It is siesta time and no one is around. She can feel his breath on her lips, so tantalisingly close.

'Shush,' he says, pushing her hair back into her cap. 'Your disguise is falling apart.' He gives her a smile, and it lightens her heart slightly. He cups his hands around her face.

'Dear Belle, you have to understand that I cannot give you what you want. I love all women, and no woman. Do you understand?'

She nods, a tear trickling down her cheek.

'Yet I find you hard to resist. Especially in your sailor's disguise.'

He leans down and kisses her tenderly, and she can taste the salt of her tears on their lips. She pulls away.

'I am a married woman *and* a prostitute, Santos. I am not an innocent child,' she tells him, letting her skin brush against the soft hair on his cheek. 'I don't want you to stay with me for ever. I just want you for now, until you have to leave again.'

'But is that enough for you?'

'Yes.'

As Belle says this, she knows she means it. Even if she has Santos for one night only, even if her love is unrequited, it is so much more than she has ever had before. And there is a part of her that hopes a little. Maybe he might come to love her too?

He sighs.

'All right, my little blackbird. I will meet you tomorrow, I promise. In the same piazza where we first met.'

She holds his hands tightly, her stomach filled with butterflies.

'Come with me now,' she begs. 'I am afraid I will lose you again.'

He shakes his head.

'No, I can't walk out on Lara. I am not a complete scoundrel. Although now that I have seen you, I think we will just be drinking tea and trying on masks!' He winks at her, and Belle feels herself relaxing a little. 'I made a promise to you,' he says. 'I will be there tomorrow, at three.'

He kisses her on the forehead, and spins her around, slapping her bottom lightly.

'Now run home, my little sailor boy, before I change my mind.'

She twists round and gives him a little smile. He comes up close and trails his finger over her lips. She licks his finger, holds him with her gaze.

'I think you are dangerous for me, Belle. And I know that I am bad for you.' He frowns. 'I am not sure—'

She interrupts him.

'It's too late. You promised!' she calls out triumphantly as she runs away before he can say another thing.

This time she flies through Cannaregio without taking one wrong turn. She is back in her apartment and changing into her Louise clothes before she knows it. She stands in front of her mirror, and pushes her hands between her legs, looks at her dilated pupils. She can feel her excitement. Tomorrow she will have him.

She trips back home with a lighter heart, ready to take another beating from her husband. Yet today she doesn't feel the strap against the back of her legs; instead she imagines it is the sea slapping against her as she swims with Santos by her side. In the distance she sees a tiny island: another, more enchanted Venice, a lovers' Venice, with castles in the sky.

*V*alentina

VALENTINA AND GABY ARE DANCING JUST LIKE LULU AND
her lesbian lover, Countess Geschwitz, on her wedding day in
Pandora's Box. Valentina, with her shiny black bob, is dressed
in white; Gaby, with her soft blond curls, wears black. The
two girls are spinning around and around the dance floor,
their bodies pressed against each other so that they can feel
each other's curves through the shifting silk of their flappers'
dresses. All the couples are looking at them, but they don't
care, their cheeks pressed together in unity.

The dancing crowd begins to dissipate and Gaby's lover
Massimo appears. He is wearing a dark suit and spats, and his
black hair is slicked back. He approaches the two of them and
taps Valentina on the back, trying to break them up so that he
can dance with Gaby. Gaby looks at Valentina, asking a silent
question, and Valentina automatically understands what she
wants. Gaby offers Valentina's hand to Massimo, then walks
away, disappearing into the soft contours of the dreamscape.

Valentina dances with Massimo. He smells of Gaby, and more of her love for him, as bitter and spoilt as burnt coffee. Gradually the other dancers disappear, so that it is just Massimo and Valentina dancing around and around the dance floor in black and white. No words pass between them, but Massimo bends down and sniffs her neck, and she knows that he can smell Gaby on her. The circle of their dance spreads so that they are brushing against the walls of the room as they pass by. They stop, and Massimo pushes her up against the wall. He peels off her dress and pulls down her pants. And as she looks at him, Massimo merges into an image of Francesco, her first and only married lover, and then back again into Massimo, her best friend's married lover. He tucks himself inside her within a heartbeat. There is no need to explain themselves, for it is quite clear that Valentina is a missive from her friend. Massimo pounds into her, and although it is not unpleasant, Valentina does not find it that erotic. Not until she looks over his shoulder and sees Theo sitting on a chair in the middle of the dance floor, one leg crossed over the other, watching her. She locks eyes with him, and his gaze is expressionless. Does he love her? she wonders. How can he watch her with another man and do nothing? And yet already he has . . . and she too has watched him with another. She flashes her eyes at him, as if to say, *See, I warned you. Don't try to fall in love with me. I will hurt you, and you will hurt me. All that we have will be worth nothing in the end.*

Massimo comes, calling out Gaby's name. He pulls away

from her, his face wet with the tears of remembrance. She pulls up her pants, but leaves her discarded dress on the ground like a phantom of her friend's lost relationship. And now she cannot help herself. She runs to Theo like a child to her father. She climbs on to his lap and puts her arms around his neck, linking her hands and nuzzling into him for comfort. He rocks her for a moment before standing up and carrying her. Her bare chest is pressed against the coarse material of his jacket. Its roughness soothes her, brings her back into her body. She closes her eyes.

I am so tired of being alone, so lonely without you.

When she opens her eyes again, he is carrying her down the hallway into their bedroom. And there is Gaby, sitting up in their bed, waiting for them. Theo puts Valentina down on the bed, and Gaby crawls over towards her. She peels Valentina's pants off her and holds them up to her face. Her eyes shine bright with grief, and Valentina can see that she smells her lost lover on a part of her dear friend. She takes Valentina's hand and squeezes it tight in a silent thank you.

And now Theo is in the bed with both of them, and Valentina doesn't mind at all. He comforts Gaby, stroking her steadily with his fingers so that Gaby closes her eyes and drifts away from them. And when he has made her friend climax, Theo turns his attention to Valentina. She climbs on top of him, and they make love like they have never done before, aware of how precious their fragile connection is. Valentina splinters into a thousand tiny shards, and in them all she sees the many hearts of her lover – his passion, his wisdom, his generosity, his desires, and yes, his devotion to her.

The light is enchanting on top of the Duomo. It is nearly midday, the sun creeping through the clouds, returning after days of rain. It might be cold up here, but Valentina doesn't mind that; she revels in the vision before her. The pale spiky spires of the Duomo, which look just like a princess's tower, glisten all around her. She knows that a lot of Milanese don't like the Duomo, but she has always loved climbing up on to the roof. Being like a bird and looking down on her bustling city with a rare detachment. This morning, though, she doesn't have time for such flights of fancy. She is on one of Marco's shoots for *Elle* magazine.

Marco is one of her few friends from the fashion scene in Milan. Their friendship blossomed on a shoot for *Vogue*, when they discovered they shared a passion for all things vintage, particularly the sixties. Today, though, it is all fairy-tale stuff. Marco tells Valentina that his theme is *You* shall *go to the ball, darling*. The two models are of Amazonian height, but are so pale and flimsy, Valentina fears they could be blown off the roof of the cathedral at any moment. They are both very young. One of them is from Latvia, and the other from the Ukraine.

They are just finishing the last shot of the morning when Valentina sees him out of the corner of her eye. She is sure of it. Marco is demanding her attention, touching up one of the girls, the poor thing quaking with cold in an insubstantial ivory silk dress. And yet Valentina ignores her friend for just one second and spins around. Yes, there he is, Inspector Garelli, pretending to be incredibly interested in one of the gargoyles. He is fooling no one, Valentina thinks, as she turns her attention back to the shoot.

Later that day she sees him again. She is with Antonella in La Rinascente, buying some underwear. Valentina is at the till, paying for a new pair of stockings and a little black corset with suspenders, when she sees him walking through the store, again studiously not looking at her.

She gives Antonella a hasty kiss goodbye, telling her that she forgot she had another appointment, and rushes down the escalator behind him. Two can play at this game, she thinks, annoyed that Garelli assumes she won't notice him. As she emerges from the department store, she sees him turn to the left, and she follows him as he walks alongside the Duomo. She really doesn't know why she is doing this. It is almost as if she is on automatic pilot, her curiosity fuelling her.

She follows him into the Galleria shopping arcade, for once not distracted by its art nouveau splendour, and just catches sight of him as he enters the Avatt Park Hotel. She glances at her watch. It is six thirty, and really she should go home and get ready for tonight. She has another session in Leonardo's club. Yet her curiosity is too much for her. She will just take a peek in the hotel, and double-check that it really is Inspector Garelli. Maybe she is mistaken?

She walks into the reception and looks around, but she can't see him anywhere. He appears to have vanished into thin air.

'Can I help you, Signorina Rosselli?'

She nearly jumps out of her skin, spinning around to come face to face with Garelli. He is standing right behind her, his stern grey eyes pinning her like a hawk's.

'I could ask you the same question,' she says angrily. 'Why have you been stalking me all day?'

She sees surprise register in his eyes.

'I think you must be mistaken,' he says calmly. 'However, since we have so fortunately bumped into each other, would you join me for an *aperitivo*?' He waves his hand towards the entrance to the bar.

Why not? thinks Valentina. Maybe he can help her find out what's going on with Theo. She still hasn't heard a word from him since her extraordinary experience at Leonardo's club on Saturday night.

They settle down at a small table in the centre of the bar. Valentina asks for a Bloody Mary, while Garelli orders a comparatively modest glass of white wine.

'I was wondering if you have heard from Signor Steen since I spoke to you on Friday?' the detective starts off.

Valentina is certainly not going to tell him about Saturday night, and what happened with Celia and Leonardo. She looks him square in the face.

'No. Have you?' she answers with hostility.

'Oh, I am sorry,' Garelli blusters. 'Did you break up? Am I touching a nerve?'

'No, we did not break up, Garelli.' He has annoyed her even more now. 'We just aren't joined at the hip.'

'Yes, I can see that,' he says, coughing pointedly, and Valentina wonders how many days he has been following her for. She imagines him inside the Velvet Underworld room at Leonardo's club and the thought amuses her. Maybe she could bring herself to take a whip to Garelli? She certainly doesn't like him.

'What's this all about?' she asks him directly. 'Has Theo done something wrong? Is he in trouble?'

'No, no,' Garelli replies meekly. 'I would just appreciate his help on a certain matter concerning the theft of six artworks.'

Valentina can feel her blood freezing in her veins, yet she manages not to react.

'What artworks?' she asks calmly, avoiding his eyes.

'A random selection of pieces, Signorina Rosselli, between which I can find no connection, apart from the fact that they are all European paintings and none of them was painted after 1930 or thereabouts. Some are more valuable than others. There is for instance a Dutch Master from the seventeenth century by an artist called Gabriel Metsu. Maybe you have heard of him?' He takes a sip of his wine. 'The first painting was taken from here in Milan. But the others were stolen abroad: one from New York, two from England, one from

France. The last painting to hypothetically go missing was taken from a private collection in the far north of Sweden, practically Babbo Natale's home.'

He took his snow boots and down jacket.

'What do you mean, hypothetically?'

'Well, it is rather strange,' Garelli tells her. 'The paintings are reported stolen, then less than twenty-four hours later the victims all change their minds. Say they want to withdraw their statements. In a couple of cases I followed it up. For instance, I travelled to London concerning one painting. The victim refused to show me the picture back *in situ*, even though they claimed that they were mistaken and it had not been stolen. I mean, Signorina Rosselli, how do you make a mistake like that?'

'What was the painting?' asks Valentina, trying to stay calm as she sips her Bloody Mary.

'It was by the French artist Watteau.'

Valentina drops her eyes, stares into the juicy scarlet of her drink. What *is* her lover involved in?

'But what has Theo got to do with all of this?' she asks, dreading the answer.

'I have a source,' Garelli says. 'It seems that your partner has happened to be in the vicinity of all these mistaken robberies. And since he is a celebrated art critic . . . someone who knows about these pieces . . . I felt bound to question him. It could all be a completely innocent coincidence, of course,' he adds lightly, hooking her with a sinister smile.

Valentina knocks back her drink.

'Well, it sounds very tenuous to me,' she says haughtily. 'I mean, paintings that are stolen and not stolen. There isn't even a crime. Maybe you shouldn't be wasting your time investigating Theo, and instead investigate all these victims of fake robberies.'

Garelli's eyes light up for an instant.

'Why, Signorina Rosselli, that is an excellent idea. Thank you for that tip.'

She gets up, not sure whether he is being facetious or not.

'I have to go,' she says brusquely.

She marches out of the Avatt Park Hotel, not sure whether it is Garelli or her lover she is angry at. What the hell is Theo involved in? This isn't their world. Robberies, conspiracies and the police. Or maybe it has always been Theo's and she just didn't know. She can't work it out. There is one thing she knows about Theo, and that is his sense of justice. He is a good man, not a thief. Why is he hiding all of this from her? Despite her best efforts, it makes her furious.

She is still a little angry when she arrives at Leonardo's club later that evening. One advantage is that her fury at Garelli, and Theo, helps her get over her nerves at seeing Leonardo again after their last intense encounter. After having dressed so carefully the last couple of times she came here, tonight she didn't think twice about putting on her new corset and stockings underneath a little black vintage dress. I don't care what anyone thinks of me, she says to herself as she storms through the door.

Leonardo is waiting for her in the reception. He is dressed simply in black jeans and a pristine white T-shirt. To her surprise, he is also wearing a pair of glasses, as he sits behind the desk in reception, reading a book.

'Oh, Valentina,' he says, looking up and taking off the glasses, smiling at her as if nothing extraordinary has happened between them at all.

Valentina wishes he would put the glasses back on. They take the edge off his Mediterranean stud look. He closes the book and she notices it is *Watt*, by Samuel Beckett. It is not the sort of book she imagines someone like Leonardo would be reading. She hardly took him for a fan of obscure literary works.

'I have been trying to call you, but your phone was switched off,' he says.

She pulls out her phone, registers two missed calls from Leonardo.

'Sorry, I didn't realise. I forgot to turn it on.'

Leonardo puts the book away in a drawer.

'First of all I wanted to check you were all right after the other night.'

She bites her lip.

'I'm fine,' she says sourly.

'And secondly, I know we were supposed to be doing another shoot today with Celia in the Velvet Underworld, but unfortunately she is sick, and I couldn't find another girl.'

'Oh.'

'You look very disappointed, Valentina.' Leonardo puts his head on one side and balances his glasses playfully between his fingertips.

'Not at all,' Valentina lies, wanting to appear indifferent. 'I just cancelled other plans.'

'I really am sorry. I will set it up again, unless . . .' She looks at him enquiringly. Please don't suggest watching another dominatrix session, she begs inside her head.

'I was actually thinking that for you to be able to take sensitive pictures of a submissive and her dominant . . . well, it would be good for you to try it on your own. I mean, the dynamic would be different if it were just you and me.'

Valentina feels a cold hand clasping her heart, a terror filling her belly.

'I'm not sure I am the submissive type.'

Leonardo smiles at her, his eyes dancing with amusement.

'I think you are,' he says. 'I can always recognise a born submissive when I see her. You know, it's not about being a doormat. It takes courage to be a submissive.'

Valentina says nothing for a minute. She watches Leonardo putting his glasses away, all the while wondering if *she* has the courage to do what he is asking. She takes a breath before speaking.

'Will Theo be there?' she asks quietly.

Leonardo looks up at her.

'Have you not spoken to him since Saturday?' he asks.

She shakes her head, her cheeks colouring.

'I don't understand what's going on,' she whispers hoarsely.

'I can't tell you what Theo wants, Valentina,' Leonardo says. 'You have to work that out for yourself.' He gives her a kind smile. 'But I can tell you that if you want to experience being a submissive, then it will be just you and me in the Velvet Underworld tonight.'

They stare at each other, the silence heavy between them. Even though she has already had sex with this man, the thought of Celia not being in the room with her makes his proposal all the more dangerous. There is no way she can do this. What about Theo? But then another voice starts up in her head. What *about* Theo, Valentina? He has abandoned you for a whole week now, with no explanation apart from an old photographic album full of erotica. To suddenly appear like that on Saturday night and fuck Celia in front of you! To wind you up like that. And what does he think those erotic pictures are doing to you alone in your bed every night?

'I live with Theo,' she says, not taking her eyes away from Leonardo's. 'He wants me to be his girlfriend.'

Leonardo blinks back at her.

'And I have a girlfriend too. Raquel. I think you met her. Unfortunately she is busy tonight, otherwise she could have taken Celia's place.'

The blonde in the corset is his girlfriend? She never imagined Leonardo in a relationship.

'This is a lifestyle choice, Valentina. It has nothing to do with issues of fidelity. You are choosing to experience something I believe you will find erotic. An experience you can use to enhance your sex life with Theo. Besides,' he adds, 'he need never know.'

He need never know. Yet she will know, always. She tries to reason with herself. If she does this, it will help her let go of Theo. She can prove to herself that she can't be the woman he wants her to be. It will save him from who she really is: a cold, heartless companion just like her mother.

'Okay,' she says, hardly believing her own voice. 'But I am a little frightened . . .'

Leonardo takes her hand in his, holds her warmly in his gaze.

'That's what makes it so erotic. You need to have a little fear, Valentina, otherwise it won't work.'

'What are you going to do to me?' she whispers.

He drops her hands, and she sees his eyes harden.

'I am going to take you to the part of yourself that is most hidden. First we will explore my version of the Velvet Underworld.'

Valentina shivers involuntarily, recalling the whips, and canes she saw hanging on the wall.

'And then, Valentina, I am going to take you into the Dark Room inside yourself.'

$\mathcal{B}$elle

HE LEANS HIS BACK AGAINST THE WALL OF HER BEDROOM, legs crossed, hands in his pockets, and watches her. His eyes are searing through her clothes as she begins to unbutton her jacket. Her hands shake with trepidation as she unties her scarf, drops her bag by the bed and bends down to unbutton her boots. He walks around her, to come up from behind. She can feel her skin prickling, reacting to his proximity. He lifts her hands into his, up over her head.

'Here, let me do that for you,' he says, kneeling down and unbuttoning her boots, delicately pulling them off her stockinged feet.

She places her hands on the top of his head, pushing her fingers through his thick mane of black hair. He looks up at her, and the concentration of their mutual gaze is something tangible, spreading thickly in the air, like honey on her tongue.

He stands up, towering over her, forcing her hands to

drop. He scoops her up and carries her over to the bed, laying her down carefully, as if she is made of glass. She lies there watching him. There is no need for her to seduce this man, or for him to seduce her. No effort is required. She can feel the charge between them, the current of their longing. He comes towards the bed, loosening his tie. He looks at her, lying in her silk chemise, as if he is looking at his heart's desire.

He leans down. With one hand he pulls her chemise up to her chest, and with the other hand he removes her underwear so that he is looking at her nakedness. She slips her arms out of the straps of her chemise so that now all she is wearing is her black stockings. She reaches up to him, and he bends over her and kisses her. Belle rarely kisses clients. But this man is no client. He is the possessor of her heart. A whisper of doubt occurs to her: maybe he thinks she is only a prostitute. She doesn't care. She has never been kissed so deeply and with such intensity. It is a kind of kissing that makes her want to give him every single drop of her essence. Their lips and their tongues are speaking to each other, with no words. Eventually he pulls away.

'Belle Blackbird,' he whispers. 'I would very much like to make love to you. Will you allow me?'

'Yes, Santos Devine. I will.'

He takes his clothes off and she admires his firm, lean body. This is a man who never rests, is always on the go. He doesn't have an inch of fat on him, unlike her sedentary husband. No, she will not think of Signor Brzezinski tonight. She knows she is sailing close to the wind. Risking scandal, losing everything, but it is worth it. To experience this intensity of passion, even if it is just this one time.

When Santos pushes into her, she cannot help but gasp in awe. Sex has never felt like this before. It has been pleasurable, exciting and erotic, but this feeling is all of those sensations and more. She is becoming a part of Santos. She can feel his pleasure, his ecstasy, which in turn deepens her own.

She has been found at last by this man. This transient Santos Devine, who she will probably never see again after tonight. He fits in her so perfectly. He moves at the same time as her; his spicy, salty scent is one she has always known; the feel of his skin, surprising soft, and the thickness of his black locks have lived inside her memory since the day she became a woman.

Santos and she are bonded. One minute he is on top of her, the next they roll over and she is on top of him. She feels him inside her, going deeper and deeper; she yearns for him to reach all the way into her soul and fill her up.

Take away my emptiness. Take away my loss.

And now something is happening to Belle. A sensation she has never felt before. She imagines the tip of him touching the tip of her, and she is hovering, like a sea swallow over the lagoon, wings flapping, faster and faster, beating inside. Oh, this feeling is impossible. So exquisite and yet so unbearable. She opens her eyes and looks at Santos. He is watching her as her guard drops. *Don't stop*, her eyes beg him. He puts his hands behind her back and lifts her up, so that she is above him, and he is still thrusting inside her. She gasps, as all self-control is washed away by the power of his touch. She flies. Santos has set her free.

After they climax, they lie side by side on her bed. Without saying a word, Santos picks up her hand and presses her palm to his lips. She turns to him and looks into his eyes. She can see all the places he has been within their golden blue, and she wishes she could be there too in his adventures. She leans forward and kisses his plush lips, which are as soft as baby's skin, incongruous for such a rugged man. She reaches up and twists the gold ring in his ear, moving her mouth to kiss him on his lobe. He pulls her to him and holds her tight against his naked body. She lifts her legs and wraps them around his waist, then reaches down and touches him. He is hard again. She knows he is. Caressing him until she feels he is full and ready, she guides him into her. Oh, she wants to make love to this man until they disintegrate. Until they are no more in the real world but become moths of desire fluttering around the light of her love. For she really has fallen in love for the first time in her life. Maybe it was even in that first moment of recognition when she passed by him in the piazza, but Belle knows that whatever happens to her now, Santos Devine will be the love of her life. And this night is filled with joy, as she forgets so completely about Signora Louise Brzezinska and her caged life, as she even forgets about Belle and her clients. She is the young Polish girl before her life in Venice, before she lost her country and her maidenhood. She is Louise in her innocence making love to her true love nine times in one night.

Valentina

HOW DO SHE AND LEONARDO START? HOW DO THEY GO from exchanging pleasantries to playing this very serious game of dominant and submissive?

It was so much easier with Theo. Their first language was with their bodies. It was so seamless, so very natural the way she and Theo came together. She didn't expect it to last, and yet the beginning of their affair flowed without effort. It was heady, and exciting, all those unexpected, anonymous appointments in the hotels. She had never felt so alive as those first few weeks with Theo.

Valentina takes a breath and tries to shove thoughts of the Theo she first met out of her head. Things changed, remember, when he moved in with her. Now he wants to possess her, just like her mother warned. He is playing mind games with her, getting some kind of revenge for her lack of commitment. She is not the girl Theo wants her to be. The kind of girl who is eager to meet the parents. With a sinking heart she realises she is just like her mother.

Leonardo pours them both a big glass of red wine, and Valentina wonders if he is nervous too. They are sitting in his office. He is at his desk, and she is opposite him. He hands her a piece of typed A4 paper.

'I just need you to sign this disclaimer,' he says. 'That you consent to whatever is going to happen tonight.'

She sits up with a jolt, her expression a question.

'A disclaimer?' she asks incredulously. 'But we've already had sex . . .'

He picks up a pen and sucks on the end of it, looking pensive.

'I am sorry to be so formal,' he says. 'It was remiss of me not to get you to sign it the other night . . . but then the whole point was that you had to act spontaneously.'

She frowns. He makes it sound as if she has been manipulated. She looks at his hands as he passes her the pen. Is she really going to submit herself to this man? Her hand shakes uncontrollably as she signs her name.

'I just want to reassure you,' Leonardo says matter-of-factly, as if he is outlining a normal event rather than a night of wild sex, 'that we practise safe sex here in my club. So you don't have to worry about that side of things.'

His baldness makes her blanch.

'It goes without saying that I will be using condoms if we do end up having intercourse, just like I did on Saturday.'

If? Haven't they just agreed that that's what they are going to do?

Leonardo has his glasses on, and as he speaks, Valentina can see herself reflected in them. She tries not to look at herself. She wants to be as far removed as she can be from what is about to happen. Is she really going to do this? Isn't it treachery? Only a week apart from Theo, and she is entering into a sexual liaison with another man, without his involvement or knowledge. She can't help it. She wants to understand another side of her sexuality. Ever since her night with Rosa and Celia, something has changed within her. She is not just curious to find out about sadomasochism; deep down inside her, she has this need, this longing to experience being dominated. It is hard to admit this truth about herself. Yet it is the truth. She needs to explore it outside the perimeters of her and Theo, with an expert so to speak, someone like Leonardo who knows what he is doing.

'So.' Leonardo has his elbows on his desk, his fingers knotted and his chin resting on them. 'Is there anything you want to ask me first?'

'When did you know that you were into . . . this?' she stumbles. 'I mean, how did you find out?'

'I have always known,' Leonardo says simply. 'Since I was a child. I was six, and playing with a girl a couple of years older than me. You know, according to Freud, all children have these sadomasochistic tendencies.'

'That's a very politically incorrect thing to say,' Valentina comments, feeling her hackles rise. *Keep children out of it.*

'I know.' Leonardo nods. 'But I think it is true. It doesn't mean that children aren't innocent or vulnerable.'

Valentina remembers something. She has tried to suppress it, but a vague, shadowy memory is emerging from her subconscious. A time when she was about eight years old. Something she saw. Her mother was such a free spirit that after Valentina's father left, she had a succession of boyfriends. There was always this atmosphere of new demonstrative love, until her mother blew her new man out. This one time Valentina saw something. A glimpse of her mother in her bedroom, tied to a chair. The image is quite clear. Her mother facing the back of the chair, wearing a bra and petticoat, her hands tied behind her back, her feet tied to the chair and her mouth gagged. Yet Valentina wasn't scared or horrified. In fact a few weeks later she played a game with one of the boys in her class in which she asked him to tie her to a chair and kiss her. The boy not only obliged but also pulled her skirt up over her head to look at her knickers.

So that was how this desire was planted inside her? It was from her mother. The other day Leonardo said that a submissive often had narcissistic tendencies. That would certainly describe her mother, and if she was honest, probably herself.

'You know,' Leonardo is saying to her, 'sadomasochism can be cathartic. The experience of being exposed and humiliated can actually be a way of reconnecting with a part of your personality you have put aside and repressed.'

Valentina licks her lips.

'I don't like pain,' she whispers.

'We'll see about that,' he says, polishing off his glass of wine. 'Okay.' He stands up, speaking briskly. 'Are you ready?'

Valentina follows him down the marble staircase. At the bottom he turns to her. Already she feels something different about him, as if he has almost grown a few inches taller.

'From here on in, you are subject to my will, Valentina. That means that you must do everything I tell you, exactly, and if not, there will be consequences. I will remind you one last time that if you want me to stop doing anything at all, you have to let me know. Is that clear? All you need say, loud and clear, is STOP. If you want me to tone it down a little, you can say PAUSE. Okay?'

Part of her wants to rebel, but another part of her is listening, silently in thrall.

'Yes.' Her voice is almost a whisper.

'I have decided that I would like you to submit to me first of all in the Velvet Underworld. I want you to go into the room and undress, so that you are in your underwear. I want you to kneel by the side of the bed, with your back to the door. When I come in, you are *not* to turn around and look at me. You must not look me in the face unless I tell you that you can. You must at all times keep your eyes averted. Is that clear?'

She nods. Her heart is beating furiously, and the palms of her hands are hot and sticky as she clenches her fists. Her logical brain is screaming at her to walk right out of here and never come back, but another part of her is pulsing with curiosity. She thought Leonardo was not her type, and yet what he is offering her attracts her. This experience of delving into a part of herself she has yet to explore. This venture into the unknown is exciting, and frankly sexy.

Leonardo turns on his heel and stalks off down the dark corridor. She is on her own. She unclenches her fists, and puts her hand on the door handle.

Inside the Velvet Underground, it feels like she has entered a warm, throbbing womb. The room no longer feels sinister, as it did when she was in here witnessing Anna the dominatrix and her slave Nicky. Nor does it seem as vast as last Saturday, when the four of them were on the bed. She looks around the room. What if Leonardo straps her to that cross thing and puts pincers on her nipples? She feels sick with fear. She tries to swallow it. Leonardo said that she can stop him at any time. He said that whatever she is subjected to is through her consent, and she has the choice to break the spell of their game. They are in this together. It is a kind of complicity. A trust of sorts.

How strange we humans are, Valentina thinks, as she unzips her little black dress and leaves it draped across the chair by the door. She wonders if he meant she should keep her stockings on and decides that they count as underwear. She pads over to the bed, and kneels down in her new black silk corset and black stockings. As she waits, she feels like a child kneeling by her bed about to say her prayers. An incongruous feeling. She begins to shiver, although the room isn't cold. She realises that she is terrified.

She hears the door open. Her instinct is to turn around and see who it is, although of course she knows it must be Leonardo. It takes all of her will not to look behind her. Leonardo does not even acknowledge her. She can see his dark figure walking around lighting candles in every corner and turning off the electric lights so that the room grows darker and more atmospheric, long shadows being thrown from some of the paraphernalia. Her knees are beginning to hurt, but she stays as still as possible. She certainly doesn't want to invite any punishment from her dominator. The suspense is almost unbearable, yet it is exciting her. What is he going to do to her? She is completely in his hands.

She senses that Leonardo is standing behind her, looking at her. Her breath quickens as she feels him standing over her.

'Stand up, Valentina,' he says.

She stands up shakily, her legs wobbly after kneeling for so long.

'Turn around,' he instructs her.

She turns, careful not to look him in the face. She can see his bare feet in front of her, and his muscular legs in tight black jeans. He has no top on. Above his chest she dare not look.

'You are not to move, not a muscle,' he says. 'Only I can touch you, not even yourself.'

He steps forward and drops the straps of her corset off each shoulder. Her conscience speaks urgently to her.

Valentina, you are letting this man who is not Theo undress you!

She shuts the voice out. It is too late now for morals.

He walks round and unclasps the back of her corset. Then he pulls it free from her body. She is naked, in her stockings, in front of Leonardo. She looks at his stomach, the circle of dark hair around his navel, and trailing up his chest. She is barely able to breathe.

He leans forward and puts his hand between her legs, and feels her with his fingers. She gasps, surprised by his sudden forwardness.

'Look at me.'

She tears her eyes away from the walnut floorboards and brings them up to Leonardo's face. His expression is not that of a lover; there is no awe or adoration. Instead he is looking at her as if she is a mirror of himself. She feels a well of intimacy between her and this man. A delicious complicity as they enter the private arena of their own erotic game. He pulls his fingers out of her, and hooks one on to the top of her stocking, dragging it down the length of her leg. He does the same with the other stocking. She has nothing to hide behind now, not even her signature black stockings and suspender belt. She is completely exposed. She knows that he knows by touching her that she is turned on. He knows that at this moment her pleasure is outweighing her fear.

'Get on the bed,' he orders her.

Valentina turns around and climbs on to the bed.

'On your hands and knees.'

Is Leonardo going to take her from behind, like Saturday yet minus Theo and Celia? Theo. The thought of him slays her heart, yet she can't stop now. And part of him is here with her. He is part of her sexual need.

She is on her hands and knees, waiting, her heart in her mouth. She hears Leonardo moving around, bringing candles closer to the bed, so that she can feel the heat of them all around her. She tries to see where he is in the mirrors that surround the bed, but it is too dark to make out anything distinctly, just lights flickering, and movement. She senses him getting on the bed behind her, and she notices he is still wearing his jeans as he rubs up against her. He ties a blindfold around her head so that she can't see anything at all, and then he pushes her nakedness against his denim-clad penis. She can feel its hard length against her soft flesh and it makes her feel so primal. She wants to scream at Leonardo, order him to make love to her, but of course she can't. She has to do whatever he wants her to do. The suppression of her initial instincts is extremely erotic, and her body is now singing with expectation.

'Go down on your elbows,' Leonardo tells her, 'and put your head between your hands. Now push your bottom in the air.'

She does as she is told. She feels extremely exposed now,

her backside sticking up like an animal asking to be fucked. Her field of vision is so black that her mind is putting pictures in her head. Leonardo naked behind her. Leonardo coming into her. Leonardo and her fucking. It is so bad, dirty, wrong, yet all she feels is him caressing her bottom, massaging it deeply and pulling his hands underneath her, touching her deep down inside of herself so that she is quivering with desire.

'Now I think you are ready,' he says coolly. 'I want you to keep very, very still, Valentina.'

She looks into the black material of her blindfold and she can see nothing. She holds her breath. What is he going to do? She flinches as she feels something hot against the skin of her bottom. Hot and liquid, very hot, and yet it is not burning her. She hears a crackle from the wick of one of the candles and she suddenly realises what Leonardo is doing. *Mio Dio*, he is pouring hot wax from one of the candles on to her backside! She is on the verge of screaming STOP or even PAUSE, yet she doesn't. If she tells him to stop now, then she will never know or understand his world. And with all her heart she wants to. Besides, it doesn't hurt that much. She thinks about all the times she has played with candles and wilfully trickled wax on to her fingers, only to pick it off a few minutes later. She always enjoyed that feeling of the hot wax as it stung her skin, and the cooling tightness of it on her hand.

She closes her eyes, even though she is wearing the blindfold anyway, and concentrates on the sensations of what Leonardo is doing. He seems to be trailing hot wax from the top of her bottom, over its curve and down towards her legs. He is getting gradually closer and closer to the most tender part of her. Her stomach clenches. Surely not? He wouldn't actually put wax there? But the sensation of this hot wax is surprisingly erotic. It stings her skin, trickles down her backside, to harden and tighten. She hears herself moan. It feels so strange. Here she is letting a man pour hot wax on to her bottom, and despite the discomfort, she is enjoying this subjugation.

The wax trickles closer and closer to the most hidden part of her. She can feel herself moistening with anticipation. A tiny dribble trickles between her legs but misses her. She is beside herself with anticipation, on the edge of fear and passion. He trails the wax again and again, and she feels it searing, layering and moulding to her skin. She can feel herself throbbing, pulsing spasms deep inside, and then to her utter shock she is climaxing. Leonardo has not even touched her with his mouth or fingers, let alone had sex with her, and yet she is having an orgasm. It is a different type of feeling from before: visceral, the utterance of her deepest need.

Leonardo stops pouring wax on her. Instead he reaches forward and presses his hot fingertip against her. She begins to climb again, and he pushes hard, circling his finger, pawing her, and she is climaxing once more, gasping as if she is drowning in her abandonment. He won't stop. Despite the fact that she feels as if she is going to disintegrate, he keeps on touching her with his hot waxy finger, making her come again and again. She cries out. *Please*. But he ignores her. For what is she begging? For him to stop, or continue? If she were not his submissive, would she push him away? His domination of her frees her from her own fears, for she is his and he will choose when to end her tortuous pleasure.

How many times does she climax? It feels like she will fall apart completely, unable to keep her body together, her essence shattered. Finally his finger stills and she collapses face forwards on the bed, her insides throbbing. She feels like she has torn away all the layers of herself in front of Leonardo, as if she is reborn. She lies on her face for a long time. The experience of what has just happened is so overwhelming that she can't speak, let alone move. She hears Leonardo walking across the room, opening a drawer and coming back to her. He covers her shoulders and back with a light woollen blanket, and then gently scrapes the hardened wax off her bottom, using cotton wool and cold cream. Slowly and methodically he scrapes and wipes, and it feels like a cleansing not just of her body, but of her soul. Finally he has finished. She lies on her side on the king-sized bed, the little blanket draped over her. She feels light headed and tired, as if her whole substance has become ether; as if she is just a shadow of her former self.

Leonardo pulls another blanket out from under the bed and covers her with it. He leans over her, tucking her in, and then he crouches down and pulls off her blindfold. She blinks in the red light of the room. The candles are all blown out now and the room is darker than ever.

'Well?' Leonardo asks her, head on one side, his eyes blacker than night.

She says just one word. It is not *humiliating*, *degrading*, *painful* or even *sexy*. The word she says to Leonardo is 'Sublime.'

He kisses her on the cheek, and they smile at each other. There it is again, this deep complicity, this equality. They are not in love. They are other people's lovers and yet they have shared this most private game. She should feel guilty, but she doesn't.

'Sleep now,' he says, tucking her hair behind her ear.

Valentina closes her eyes. She wants to take this feeling of sublimity with her into her dreams. She wants to bring it to Theo.

$\mathscr{B}$elle

DESPITE HER MOTHER'S DEVOUT CATHOLICISM, AND BEING
sent to a convent when she was twelve for her education, Belle
does not believe in God. Yet every morning she begins her day
in one of Venice's churches, usually the tiny marble Santa
Maria dei Miracoli near her apartment, or the more imposing
Santi Giovanni e Paolo. She doesn't know what else to do. She
wants God to grant her Santos Devine. Hasn't she paid her
penance by now? Fourteen years with a husband who loathes
her, her father dead, her mother insane, Poland lost, childless
and alone? Doesn't she deserve to be given the only thing she
has ever really wanted? The man she loves.

It is not too much to ask, and yet Belle knows it is the
world. Each moment she spends with Santos is divine, yet
tortuous. He warns her. Many times he suggests it best they
do not see each other again. He takes her hand in his, and
smiles at her wistfully.

'I don't want to break your heart,' he says.

And she wants to scream back at him, *And where is* your *heart? In what dark cave from the past have you hidden it?*

He tells her he cannot love only one woman. And yet the way he makes love to her, the way he says her name when he is deep inside her, the way he can sleep all afternoon in her arms . . . how can he not love her?

She hopes, and she prays, and she begs to be granted her heart's desire.

Often Santos arrives by the back entrance of her building, calling up to her from a boat. She leans over her little balcony and tosses down the symbol of their love, a white rose, which he catches and smells with gusto.

'Come down, my little Blackbird, come sail with me.'

She puts on her sailor boy's outfit, not bothering to strap down her breasts or hide her hair inside her cap, sometimes wearing a pair of black silk shorts rather than her white trousers. Santos loves her little shorts. They are so daring. He tells her his first mate had better watch out. And Belle fantasises about the possibility that she might one day accompany him on one of his sea adventures. She imagines herself as a swashbuckling pirate queen, and Santos as her dark captain.

Now Venice is no longer a prison for Belle. It becomes a city of sensuality for her and Santos. The constant murmur of the water lapping against the ancient stone is like the constant measure of her love for Santos. The scent of decay, crumbling plaster and sediment is like the smell of their sex, penetrating and ultimately tragic. Each time she crosses a high arched bridge, Belle wishes it could be a crossing from one man to the next. Yet those bridges never take her anywhere but around in circles, for difficult as it is to leave her husband, it seems it would be impossible for Santos to settle for her alone. The painful truth is that she is not enough for him, and yet he is all she has ever wanted.

Yet love is a generous soul, and Belle's love for Santos means she still gives all she can to him, knowing that in the end it will be washed away, like everything is in Venice.

This day, though, is a bright one for Belle. Her husband has gone away again, and she is free to abandon the whole day to Santos, her lover. She has given up her other clients. Suddenly no man's touch will do but his. She leans over her little balcony, dropping a white rose into her lover's boat. He plucks the petals, scattering them on the verdigris canal. He offers her his arms. She is down in a trice, clambering aboard his boat in her black silk shorts, little white blouse and sailor's cap. He rows her out into the middle of the lagoon, until they are just one tiny boat bobbing around on a vast expanse of opaque aqua. He feeds her strawberries, the juice of which stains her white blouse. Then they lie down in the rocking boat, and Santos makes love to her.

She watches the seagulls wheeling above her as she pulls her lover deep inside her. She wishes she could stain him with her love, just like the strawberry juice has stained her clothes. She wishes the power of their passion could somehow arouse his heart. Why does he not feel it? she wonders. Why can I not make him fall in love with me? Yet Santos remains enigmatic as ever. From one day to the next she does not know if he will come, and when he does turn up she lights a dozen candles in the church the next morning in gratitude.

This time it is night. They are sitting on her little balcony overlooking the dark lapping canal, the bleached buildings opposite silent like phantom sentinels of the city. It is a warm night, and Venice creaks with heat, the canal pungent with the flavours of the city. Santos is topless. She admires the fine curls of hair on his chest, the powerful delineation of his shoulders and arms. She is naked, apart from her dressing gown, which trails around them like a waterfall of blue silk. They have just made love. For Belle it has been the most intense and emotional lovemaking of her life. Her eyes are still moist from the tears she shed when she climaxed, and in that moment she saw a flicker of something in Santos's face. An emotion more than compassion for her heartache, and so much more than the light smile he usually bestows on her. He looked serious. And he looked right into her.

They sit in silence, watching the canal, until Santos turns to her.

'So you love me?' he says, looking at her with an expression at once old and young.

She frowns.

'I have loved you since the day I met you. But I have told you this countless times.'

He shrugs, trying to avoid her gaze.

'Many women have told me they loved me. But none of them actually did. They always wanted some part of me. Usually my free spirit.'

She takes his hand in hers, locks their fingers together and forces him to look at her.

'Santos, I don't want to take away your spirit. Why would I want to do that when it is precisely what I love the most about you?'

'Ah, Belle, what kind of love is it you feel? I was led to believe that if you are in love with someone, you wish to keep them with you until the day you die.'

She shakes her head passionately.

'If you love someone, you let them be who they want to be, Santos. That's why I love you, because you let me be who I want to be. How could I not do the same for you? I love you so much that I know that one day I will have to let you go.'

Her voice cracks. She drops his hand and brings her silk dressing gown up to her face, to bury her sorrow inside it.

Santos moves towards her. He puts his arms around her, her legs inside the V of his.

'Belle Blackbird, I may fly away one day, but I will come back to you.'

She looks up at him, her eyes glistening with new hope.

'You will?'

'How could I not, my sweet?'

He kisses her tenderly, and Belle feels almost delirious with joy. He said he would come back to her. One day. When that day might be, she neither knows nor cares. He has given her a reason to live.

They make love on her balcony, her sapphire dressing gown wrapped around them so that they are in a cocoon of passion. As Santos comes inside her, Belle watches the moonlight speckle the water like his seed drops speckled upon her flesh.

The next day it rains and Santos does not come. She waits by her window, sending wordless prayers to any God that might hear her. She pricks her fingers with one of their white roses, now yellow and crumbling, offering her blood in exchange for her wish. Yet the canal is empty, and the rain pelts down outside, splashing reflections across the sky. She waits for as long as she dares, and then she trails back to Louise's house, not heeding the downpour that drenches her, her heart filled with dread. Surely Santos wouldn't leave Venice without saying goodbye?

When she arrives at the Brzezinski house, she notices the lamp on in her husband's study, and fears he is back already. He wasn't due home until the following evening. She can't bear to face his questions tonight. The rain has stopped, so she goes round to the back entrance of the house, walking carefully along the stone ledge just over the canal. A bit of stone crumbles under her feet and she nearly topples into the water as she swings herself through the back door. She sneaks into the passageway, and up the stairs through the kitchen. She is shivering now with wet and cold. She has nearly made it to her bedroom when her husband appears on the landing as if out of nowhere.

'Where have you been?' he asks, a nasty grimace on his face.

'Walking.'

'What respectable woman of Venice goes walking around in the pouring rain on her own after dark? Just look at you!'

She glances down at her black velvet coat, which is stuck to her with rain. She sighs wearily. She is so tired of all this.

'Signor Brzezinski,' she addresses him. 'You must know by now that I am anything but a respectable woman.'

That is enough to set her husband off. He lashes out and slaps her hard across the neck and chest. She winces, but refuses to cry.

'Go ahead,' she taunts him. 'Hit me again. You think you are such a big man, but you're a joke. Everyone is laughing at you, because your wife is a WHORE!'

The words are out of her mouth before she can stop them. Her husband grabs her by her fringe and pulls her into her bedroom, slamming the door behind him. His anger is so intense he can't speak to her, but he can hit her. He knocks her back on the bed, and pulls the belt out of his trousers. She sees the metal buckle sparkling in the dusky light. And then down it comes, again and again. So hard he hits her this night that by the time he is finished with her, her whole body is shattered. Yet she doesn't care. She is happy to pay this price if she can have Santos.

Afterwards, when he has finished beating her, he screams into her face.

'You shall give me a child, you barren bitch. Or I will kill you.'

He storms out of the room to go down to dinner, stuff his anger with beef and cream.

Louise is beyond food. She lies for an hour on her bed, unable to move. She is unable even to take her wet garments off, although she knows she should to avoid a chill. Eventually the door of her room opens. He is back, Louise thinks, to finish me off. Yet it is not Signor Brzezinski but Pina who appears, her face rigid with horror when she sees her mistress. She says nothing – she has no need to – before scurrying out of the room. A few moments later she returns with a bowl of warm water, some oils and cloths. She peels Louise's wet garments off her, and gently cleans the blood off her bruised legs. She speaks in her Sicilian dialect words of tenderness that Louise finds hard to understand, but her tone soothes her, and although the girl is more than ten years younger than her, she feels as if she is caring for her like a mother might. She is not sure, for she knows her own mother never did such a thing for her.

Pina does her best to help her mistress, applying poultices of aromatic herbs against Louise's stinging skin, but her mistress's body is racked with pain. All Louise wants is to be held in Santos's arms. What if that never happens again? The thought of Santos sailing far away from her in his white schooner is worse than the pain from the lashes her husband has just given her. She would rather die than never see him again.

$\mathcal{V}$alentina

SHE SITS UP IN THE FOUR-POSTER BED LIKE A FAIRY-TALE princess awoken from a hundred-year slumber. Her eyelids are heavy, and the dark air sparkles around her as if it is filled with fireflies. The drapes are closed around her and it feels as if she is on a velvet island. She draws them back, and the waves of the Velvet Underworld surge around her. She gets out of bed, unsteadily, as if she might be swallowed up by the plush carpet beneath her bare feet. She looks around for her clothes, but her stockings and corset have disappeared and her dress is no longer on the chair. She doesn't care for her clothes now anyway. After her experience with Leonardo, she feels her most natural naked, pure and clean. She opens the leather door, and steps out into the dark hallway. The building seems to hum around her. She stands in the hall, shivering, staring at the cold, hard metal door of the Dark Room.

I am going to take you into the Dark Room inside yourself.

Leonardo's words echo inside her head. She walks

unsteadily towards the door, her heart in her mouth. Can she do it? Is she brave enough to go into the Dark Room? It is just a room, she tells herself. Four walls. A floor and a ceiling.

Nothing *really* bad could happen in there, could it? Like rape . . . or murder?

Although she knows there are some who get their kicks from taking extreme physical risks, she doesn't think Leonardo would let that happen. She hardly knows the man and yet she trusts him. Even so, one of her mother's sayings pops up in her head.

Eroticism is assenting to life even in death.

Georges Bataille wrote that. Her mother was always quoting him. She hailed him as a ground-breaking philosopher on sex. Valentina thought his ideas were rather sick. How can death be sexy?

She takes a breath and puts the palms of her hands against the door. It is so cold that it burns her, like ice. Yet she doesn't remove her hands, and instead leans into the door, putting her head against it and listening. She can hear nothing. Just the rushed beat of her own heart. She looks down at the handle. It is a round metal doorknob, its soft contours in contrast to the hard steel door. Slowly she drags her hand down the length of the door and puts her hand on the knob. She twists, yet the door doesn't yield. It is locked.

'Valentina?'

She turns to see Leonardo standing behind her. He is fully clothed again, and on his arm is draped a white towelling dressing gown. She is suddenly aware of her nakedness. She blushes, feeling like a naughty child caught stealing from the candy jar.

'I wanted to look inside,' she says.

He raises his eyebrows.

'It's locked,' he says.

'I know.'

For a moment neither of them moves. She can see him thinking, as if he is trying to decide something. Finally he takes a step towards her.

'You must be cold,' he says, wrapping the dressing gown around her shoulders. She slips her arms inside it, and he ties it tightly round her waist. It is incredibly soft and snug, and smells of lavender.

'You've been out for quite a while,' he tells her, taking her hand in his and leading her down to the end of the hall. Here there is another door. It is painted the same colour as the walls of the hallway, probably the reason why she never noticed it before.

'I thought you might like to take a bath,' he says, opening the door and ushering her into one of the most luxurious bathrooms she has ever seen. It is decorated in the style of a hammam, with mosaic floors, burning incense and candles flickering all around its circumference. She can hear Egyptian music playing softly in the background. There is a large circular bath in the centre, filled with fragrant water bubbling with little jets. She can see the steam rising off it, and she is overcome with a desire to sink her tired body into it. Yet what about their agreement?

'The Dark Room,' she whispers. 'I thought I was going to go inside it.'

Leonardo looks pensive for a moment. He leans down and tucks her hair behind both her ears.

'I am not sure you would be up for that tonight, Valentina. You look exhausted.'

She cannot help but feel relief sweeping through her. She feels turned inside out by her hot-wax experience. He is right. She is not sure she could take any more erotic discoveries tonight. She feels weak, and insubstantial. Her head is in a fog.

'There is no rush,' he says, smiling slowly. 'Believe me, I *will* take you inside the Dark Room. Next time . . .'

Her breath quickens with the thought of it. Part of her wants to question him: what will he do to her there? Yet part of her doesn't want to know. Besides, she is sure he wouldn't tell her anyway.

'Will you take a bath with me?' she asks suddenly, surprised at her offer. She thinks of Theo. How he often gets into the bath, tucking her between his legs as he washes her breasts, her stomach, all of her. Leonardo smiles at her benignly, like the teacher he is.

'No, Valentina,' he says. 'I think you need to be alone.'

She submerges herself under the aromatic water, and stares open eyed at the ceiling of the hammam through the dusky, dappled light. A memory comes to her unwanted, and she imagines herself within it again. She is in their bath in the flat. Theo is leaning over her, reaching for her hands and pulling her up so that she emerges spluttering and naked in his arms. He grabs a towel and wraps her in it. She feels swaddled, trapped, yet safe in his embrace. It was only six weeks ago, less even, and yet this memory feels like it comes from a faraway place in time. She struggles to forget it. Yet it is still so close to her. She can smell her own body on that day. Its failing, and its loss.

'What happened?' he is asking her. 'Why is the water full of blood? Are you hurt?'

She squeezes her eyes tight, pushes her chin into his chest, her mouth a rigid line of non-communication.

'Speak to me,' he cajoles her. 'Valentina, please . . . what has happened?'

But she can't. It hurts too much. She wriggles to free herself from his embrace. She wants to run away from him into the bedroom, to lock the door and wait for him to go away. Yet even if he goes, Theo always comes back.

'Oh Valentina.' She hears his shocked whisper as he registers the reason for the blood. 'Why didn't you tell me?'

So many reasons why. She didn't want the baby . . . she did want the baby. She didn't want to love Theo. She did. She didn't want him to be trapped with her. It was too humiliating a thought. She wanted to face it on her own. And yet she didn't. She wanted it all to go away . . . and now it had, and for some reason she wished it were not so. She had been unable to answer him.

And now, as Valentina bathes in the cleansing waters of the hammam pool, she looks down at her belly. In there . . . in there was Theo's child.

She places her hands just below and on either side of her belly button and presses down gently. She wished their baby away. That's what she did. She felt it fluttering inside her, and she panicked, not at the idea of having a child, but at the commitment it would mean between her and Theo. She prayed for that baby to go. She asked it to leave, and it did. She gives a little gasp of grief, yet still she bites the tears back. She sinks back under the warm water, pulsing with tiny jets, and twists her body around and around so that she is in a whirlpool of sensation. She shouldn't be maudlin and dwell on such things. Logically she knows that the miscarriage was a blessing. And yet she will never forget the look on Theo's face as he tried to comfort her. It was the look of love. He was feeling her pain, for her. How it terrified her. Far worse than indifference, or kindly concern even.

She emerges from the water again, shakes her head, spraying droplets of water around her. Stop thinking about it, Valentina, she commands. You live a certain kind of life, with no room for babies. Look where you are now. In a sex club, for God's sake. You are *not* mother material.

$\mathcal{B}$elle

DESPITE HER HARSH BEATING, LOUISE WAKES EARLY THE
next morning. The sun is only just nudging above the horizon,
and her room is full of gloaming shadows. Her sleep has been
besieged by uneasy dreams of Warsaw in her youth. The night
her father died, and the torture of getting her mother to leave
him. Begging her to come with her and Signor Brezinski, to
Venice, where she would be safe. Her mother was so frightened. She remembers her fear, her constant shaking, which
intensified every time she or Signor Brzezinski tried to reassure
her.

Louise drags herself out of these dark dreams. They give
her a strange taste in her mouth, and an uneasy feeling, as if
she is a player in a drama she doesn't know the story of. When
she sits up stiffly in bed, she is surprised to see Pina, still in her
uniform, asleep on the chair beside her. What could the girl
still be doing in here?

'Pina,' she whispers, but the child is in a deep sleep. Louise looks at her face in repose, free from fear or worry. She looks like an angel. And then it hits her. She *is* an angel. This girl she has barely considered before is asleep on the chair next to her bed because she is protecting her. A woman nearly twice her age.

'Pina.' She leans over and shakes her gently by the arm. Pina wakes with a jolt. She looks confused for a moment, and then embarrassed when she realises where she is.

'Oh, madam, I'm sorry . . .' she stutters, her cheeks flaming red.

Louise clasps the girl's hands.

'No need to be sorry, Pina. No need.'

'How are you feeling, madam?' asks the girl, her bright cheeks beginning to calm down.

'Sore.'

Louise takes a breath, pulls back the covers and swings her legs out of the bed. She gasps with pain as she stands up. She is not sure where it hurts the most. Her ribs, or her legs, or her head. There is a deep throbbing in the small of her back, where Signor Brzezinski punched her. Stupid man, she thinks. If he wants a baby so badly, why is he damaging its potential bearer?

'Madam, I think you should get back into bed. I will bring you more poultices to take the pain away.' Pina's eyes are wide with concern.

'I have to go, Pina.' It is hard even to talk, and each word is forced out of her stiff mouth. The bastard slapped her on the chin as well.

Pina opens her mouth, dumbfounded, and Louise waits for her protest. Then the girl snaps her mouth shut again. Her next words surprise Louise greatly.

'You must love him very much,' she whispers.

Louise turns to Pina, leans on her shoulder and takes another breath.

'I do, my dear. Will you help me?'

It takes them a while to dress Louise, so slowly, so painfully. By the time she is hobbling through the narrow alleyways of Venice, the sun has risen, yet it is still early enough for it to be safe for her to leave the house. It was Pina who came up with the idea of pretending to be Louise and getting into her bed, in the unlikely event of her husband looking in on her. Usually after beating her so severely he avoids facing her, and the marks he has made on her, for at least a day or two. Louise is sure he will not want to look at her for several days at least this time. It makes her pleased to think of her lowly maid fast asleep in her silk sheets, tasting a little luxury for once.

She pulls her cloche hat as low as possible over her forehead. Her husband forgot to be careful last night, and despite Pina doing her best with make-up, Louise has a black eye. She has decided she will wait for Santos for one hour, and if he has not come by then, she will disguise herself as a sailor boy and look for him down by the boats. If his schooner is gone . . . well then she doesn't know what she will do.

She sits in her apartment, waiting. She is in the old rocking chair by the bed, a blanket wrapped around her. She is still shivering from the beating she took, and feels as if the dampness from the rain yesterday has taken a hold in her bones. She closes her eyes and begins to drift, the sound of the lapping water like a lullaby. She imagines Pina singing to her, the only other soul apart from Santos who seems to have a care for her heart.

'Belle . . . Belle . . .' She hears his voice first, whispering. It is him, and yet he sounds different. Shocked.

'Oh Belle.'

She opens her eyes, the lids heavy, and her vision is blurred for a few seconds. In the fog of her room she begins to make out Santos crouched down in front her. A look on his face she has never seen before. No more gaiety. Just horror.

'My darling girl!' he exclaims.

What's wrong? she thinks. Why is he looking at me like this?

And she realises. He has never seen me beaten so badly, she thinks, her head pounding dully. This is the first time since she met Santos that Signor Brzezinski has laid into her with such force. She had always been able to explain away the other minor bruises. She didn't want Santos to know about Louise. But how will she explain all this? She wasn't thinking this morning about how Santos might respond to her beating; she just wanted to see him.

Santos pulls back her blanket and looks at her. He puts his hand to her bruised eye, and she flinches when he touches her.

'Who did this to you?' he asks, his voice hoarse with anger.

She is unable to lie to him.

'Who do you think?' The words stumble out of her slowly, stuck inside her stiff mouth.

He comprehends, and his face clouds with anger.

'Show me,' he commands.

'No,' she says, weakly, 'I don't want to.'

'Show me what he did to you because of me.'

His voice is harsh. It almost frightens her. She rises slowly from her chair, unfastens her dress and lets it fall to the ground. She is so sore, she can hardly lift her arms to take off her chemise.

'I can't . . .' she whimpers.

He leans over her, and lifts the chemise up over her head.

She stands before him, a blackbird with broken wings. She looks into his face and sees anguish in his eyes. He falls on his knees in front of her and buries his head in her stomach.

'Forgive me,' he mumbles into her soft belly.

'It's not your fault,' she whispers, pushing her fingers through his hair, gripping his soft curls.

He pulls away and looks up at her. His eyes are blazing.

'I will kill him,' he hisses.

Fear shoots through her. She has no doubt that Santos would be true to his word, but she cannot let him go near Signor Brzezinski. She cannot risk her lover being hurt, or arrested for murder . . . executed. The thought makes her sick.

Signor Brzezinski has tainted everything in her life so far. She cannot let him destroy Santos.

'No,' she begs, stroking Santos's hair. 'No, my love, please don't . . .'

'I cannot promise you that,' Santos says sternly, standing up and circling her within his arms. 'He is a monster to beat a woman. How can you expect me not to want to right this wrong?'

'No, no.' Louise can feel the edge of hysteria mounting within her. She cannot put Santos in danger . . . and what about her mother? If Santos didn't kill Signor Brzezinski but maimed him, she knows exactly how her husband would make her pay. He would ensure that her mother *never* gets to leave Poveglia. He would allow that cruel doctor to do a lobotomy on her. He has threatened as much before. For Signor Brzezinski is the one who committed her mother. He has all the power.

The fear builds inside her, and now, held in her lover's arms, the shock from her beating begins to hit her. Last night she thought Signor Brzezinski might kill her. She thought she was never going to see Santos again. She begins to shake uncontrollably, tears falling down her cheeks, running into her mouth.

'Please, Santos.' She is sobbing. 'Please don't go near him.'

'Ludwika,' he says gently in Polish. 'I won't ever let him touch you again.'

Always Santos has called her Belle. To hear him speak the

name her parents christened her, to hear the Polish words roll out of his mouth makes her feel as if she is being carried on a wave, away from reality and into the land of her heart. She is shedding the skin of her other self, showing him who she really is. She collapses into Santos's arms, and cries from deep down inside her belly, bringing up the grief of all these years. Her father dying. Her mother going insane. Her loveless wedding that felt like a funeral. The loneliness of her marriage. Her husband becoming a monster. Santos holds her in his arms, stroking her hair, letting her saturate his shirt with tears.

'Ludwika, my beautiful Ludwika . . .' Again and again he chants it. Gradually her tears subside. Santos bends down and scoops her up in his arms. He carries her to the bed and lays her down. He smoothes her black bob with his hands, and she feels comforted by his touch. He lies on the bed next to her, takes his damp shirt off so that he is only in his trousers. He strokes her naked battered body, and she has never seen him so serious, so subdued. He begins to kiss her. Every mark her husband made upon her body, Santos kisses. He kisses her bruised eye and her sore chin. He kisses bruises blooming on her chest and breasts, the burn on her wrist where Signor Brzezinski twisted it. He rolls her over and kisses all the way down her spine, to the point where her husband punched her. He rolls her back over and kisses her swollen legs. He crawls back up her body and kisses her belly, where the pain throbs deepest. Although he doesn't say a word, Louise can feel his love upon her skin. It is the most healing balm of all. With each kiss her physical pain recedes, and her heart expands.

'Make love to me,' she whispers, looking into his jewel eyes.

He frowns.

'Are you sure, my little blackbird. I don't want to hurt you.'

She shakes her heavy head at him.

'You could never hurt me, Santos,' she says.

He hovers over her, studying her face with concern.

'This has happened to you because of me. I am not worth it,' he says, stroking her cheek gently. 'I cannot stay here with you for ever, Ludwika. I cannot give a woman like you what she needs.'

She takes his hand in hers, and lays it on her breast. Her nipples harden beneath his touch.

'Yes you can,' she says hoarsely.

It is the trust he sees in her eyes that finally turns the key to his heart. He sees that she would die for him, and he feels in awe. He wants to worship this woman who risks all for him.

He bends down and kisses her softly on the lips. Louise loosens her hold on his hands and closes her sore eyes. She feels him trailing his hands lightly down her body, and cupping her sex within his palm.

'Oh please, Santos, make me better,' she whispers. 'Make love to me.'

He kisses her again in reply, and tenderly pushes her legs

apart, bringing his fingers back inside her and caressing her deep within. She is melting, all pain transformed into passion. Her raw emotion courses through her body, so that each time he tips her with his finger, the sensation becomes more and more intense.

She cries out his name. *Santos*. And in reply he enters her gently, pushing his way deep inside her. She opens her eyes, trembling with desire and emotion, and looks into the face of her lover. He is gazing at her in a way he has never looked at her before. It is as if her vulnerability has made Santos vulnerable, for his eyes are laced with tears as he climbs deeper and deeper inside her. There is no need for any more words. They are in complete harmony. He feels her pain, and she feels his passion. Together they climax in perfect unity, the love between them overflowing like a flood of emotion submerging them.

Valentina

SHE TURNS ON THE LIGHT BOX IN HER STUDIO IN THE apartment. White light blasts upwards, splashing on to the walls and ceilings of the room, leaving the corners untouched, the doorway to her own little darkroom bathed in shadows. She wants to know what this negative is of, yet she doesn't feel like setting up her darkroom and enlarging it yet. She is going to cheat and take a look using her light box and special zoom-type loupe.

She takes the negative out of the plastic cover and slides it on to her enormous light box, which is in fact a converted counter top. She picks up her loupe and bends down, resting it against the image and pressing her eye into the piece.

What she sees makes her hold her breath for a second. This isn't mildly erotic like the other photographs; this is full-on erotica. It must be rare, she thinks, to have a picture like this from the twenties. It must be worth a fortune. Is that why Theo gave them to her?

She stares at the negative and its contours seep into her subconscious. It looks so much like an image from one of her dreams.

This picture is different from all the others. It is the same model, she imagines, but instead of a close-up, she gets to see her whole body. It looks to have been taken outside, as the woman is lying on her front on brilliant white stone or marble, obviously in the full blaze of sunlight. It appears almost as white as her own light box. This dazzling background sets off the tonal contrasts on the woman's naked body. Her legs are apart, and bent upwards at the knee. She is wearing a pair of black button boots. Her torso is twisted around, as is her head, and she is wearing a white Venetian mask which completely obscures her facial features, apart from her mouth, which is parted slightly as if in anticipation. She has a dark helmet bob, the signature hairstyle of the twenties. All of these elements of the model – her parted legs, her twisted back and head – are moving towards one central focus in the picture. Her right arm is reaching back towards her bottom, creating an angular line as her elbow bends. She has pushed her hand between her bottom cheeks, parting them slightly, her fingers spread. Her middle finger is pushed right down and is pulling up the most private part of herself. She is offering herself to the viewer.

Look at me, how open I am for you, waiting to feel you inside.

The blinding white light beneath her body has leached to

the area between her legs, so that is edged in white. It reminds Valentina of a halo, and gives the image an almost spiritual quality, incongruously. It is also intensely erotic. Valentina bites her lip. She just loves this image. It is beautiful, stylish and sexy. It is everything she wants to bring into her own erotic photography. She imagines enlarging it until it is really big, framing it and putting it on their bedroom wall. What would Theo think of that?

She is jolted out of her reverie by a loud crash. She opens the door of her studio and listens. She can hear noises coming from the kitchen. She runs down the hall, and flings open the door to see a blackbird frantically flapping around. How did it get in here? The window is closed. She stands rooted to the spot for a moment, watching the blackbird seeking a way out. It swoops towards the sink, its wings slapping against the draining board, and takes off again, skimming over her head. She can feel the panic of this little bird. She can't bear to see it trapped, and frightened.

She runs over to the window and opens it, hoping the bird will fly out of its own accord. Yet it seems possessed, unable to find its way. It continues to fly around the room, knocking into the saucepans hanging down from the rack and the jars of spices on the windowsill.

Come on, little blackbird, out you go!

Finally the bird lands on top of the fridge, blinking at Valentina with its tiny jet-black eyes. She waits by the window, waves to the bird. She is not sure if it senses her, but suddenly it launches itself across the room and just like that is out of the window. In the end so easily; no need for its fear.

Valentina closes the window quickly. She sits down at the kitchen table and chews her bottom lip, thinking about the bird. Is that good or bad luck to have a blackbird in your kitchen?

She spreads her hands on the surface of the wooden table and takes a deep breath. Last night. She finds it hard to believe it really happened. But it did. She puts her hands on her backside. It feels a little sore, but not painful. She gets up and goes into the bedroom, stands with her back to her mirror, twisting around to look at her bottom. Remarkably, it is blemish-free. Not one little burn or redness from her experience with Leonardo.

She feels different today. All of these erotic investigations are having a profound effect on her. She is realising that sex can never just be casual, even if it is free spirited. She thought that she could remain an observer, like a true photographer, but there is something within her that cannot resist participating. She thinks of Theo's emails: *Have fun*, as if he is encouraging her. He was there in Leonardo's club the other night, with her and Leonardo and Celia. He is part of it all. She thought that by doing what she did with Leonardo last night she could break free from Theo and let him go, but instead it makes her want him more. She can't understand the logic of her need. But it is there, primal and urgent, heating her blood. And why oh why has he disappeared again? He was there one moment, gone the next. He didn't even talk to her. Is he trying to prove a point? It is all very convoluted and confusing . . . just like Theo himself, she supposes.

A possibility occurs to her for the first time. Maybe she could try to be his girlfriend, like he asked. Maybe she can take the risk and trust him.

If only he would come back. She has had enough of waiting for him. Okay, she thinks as she picks up her phone and scrolls down to his number, you win, Theo. Yet the phone rings out; it doesn't even go to voicemail. She flings it down on the bed in frustration.

Her doorbell buzzes. She goes into the hall and picks up her intercom.

'Package for Signorina Rosselli.'

It is from Mattia. Her mother's pictures that he said he would send her. Although the package looks a little large to be just photographs. She tears open the wrapping to find two bundles. One is an old cardboard folder decorated with the winged lion of Venice. She opens it up, and a sheaf of photographs flutter to the floor. Some of them are recent. Of Valentina when she was growing up. A serious, heavy-browed, plump little girl, with her signature black bob even then. She cannot bear to look at the ones when she was a teenager, she was so pitifully thin. How could her mother have let that happen to her? And then there is a stack of really old photographs. Not of her mother, but of her grandmother, Maria, when she was a little girl. Maria was a smiling child, and obviously adored by her own mother. Picture after picture of Valentina's grandmother and great-grandmother hand in hand in front of the grand old palazzos of Venice, or her grandmother on her own mother's lap in a gondola, the misty black and white landscape of the Adriatic lagoon bleaching into a nothing sky. There are no photographs of her grandmother's father, or any siblings, and Valentina has a distant memory of being told that her grandmother's father died when she was a baby, and that she was an only child.

There are two pictures that intrigue Valentina in particular. One is of her great-grandmother dressed in a sailor's outfit, looking thoroughly modern in her flared white trousers, an admiral's jacket and sailor's cap. She isn't smiling; in fact her expression is ferocious. Most remarkable of all is her hairstyle. A sleek black helmet bob, just like Louise Brooks; in fact very similar to the model in the erotic negative Valentina was just looking at. Very close in style to her own hair, although her bob is slightly longer, and more feathery. Finally, to her surprise, Valentina finds a picture of herself as a baby, on the lap of her great-grandmother. She can recognize it as the same woman, because although she is obviously very old, she has the same powerful gaze as in the other pictures of her, and of course there is the bobbed hair, now as white as snow. Valentina trails her finger over the image. She wishes she had known her great-grandmother when she was young and living in Venice. She has a feeling about her, as if they might have understood each other better than herself and her mother.

Valentina turns to the second bundle Mattia has sent. It is much larger, and to her delight it is full of vintage clothes. She pulls out item after item. Some of them look very rare. Are these from her mother as well? She guesses by the style of them that they could have been her great-grandmother's clothes. She feels a thrill of excitement. They are all absolutely exquisite. She hunts around for a card or note of explanation from her brother, but she can find nothing. She thinks of her friend Marco, and his obsession with all things vintage. He will go crazy when he sees this hoard. There is a very short maid's uniform, a divine Egyptian costume, a tailored pinstripe suit that is too small to be for a man, a trilby, a cloche hat, a short black ballerina dress with a stiff tutu, all sorts of ancient corsets, suspender belts and feathers. She pulls out a pair of black silk shorts and a sleeveless white silk blouse, a little discoloured but wearable, and a black silk scarf tied in a floppy bow. There is a long string of pearls that Valentina can't believe her mother would give her. Surely they are worth something? But the real thrill is when she finds the sailor's outfit from the photograph she just looked at, along with the hat. Here is the evidence that these are her great-grandmother's party costumes when she lived in Venice.

Valentina tries on some of the costumes. Everything fits her perfectly, as if they were tailored for her. She could actually wear some of these clothes out. She remembers that today is Tuesday, and Marco's party is later. She should wear one of the outfits. The more flamboyant the better. That will please her friend.

So she won't be going into the Dark Room tonight at least. Her heart skips a beat. Is she disappointed, or relieved? She really isn't sure. She opens the French windows and steps out on to her tiny balcony, her dressing gown slung loosely over one of the old corsets. Now that the rain has gone, it is warm for October. Maybe she could show a little flesh later. She surveys the street. She notices one of those tiny Smart cars parked opposite her apartment, with a tall man sitting inside it, his head almost crushed against its roof. Really not the car for a man with such a build, she thinks. She wonders who he is waiting for. Which of her neighbours is dating a Smart car man? It is hardly romantic to have to sit behind your boyfriend while he drives, as if you are in the cockpit of a plane. But then it could be slightly sexy, she muses, if you could reach around the front seat and caress him as he drove. He could feel you, but he wouldn't see you.

Just as she is thinking this, the man turns and looks up at her. To her surprise, he picks a camera up off his lap and directs it at her. Did he just take a picture of her?

She steps back inside the room and closes the French windows. She is furious. How dare some stranger take pictures of her? She realises now that he must be the same man she saw in the garden last week. She pulls on a pair of jeans and a T-shirt, not caring about a bra or panties she is in such a hurry. She doesn't even have the patience to wait for the lift, and runs down the three flights of stairs to street level in her bare feet. She storms out of her apartment building, but despite the fact that she is so quick, the Smart car and its occupant is gone. She thinks about ringing the police, but what could she tell them? She *thinks* a strange man in a Smart car took a picture of her? It sounds stupid, and really she doesn't want to focus any attention on herself after Inspector Garelli's interrogation about Theo and the pictures.

Back in her apartment, she dresses for Marco's party. She is going to cycle to his flat, and it's warm enough to wear the black silk shorts, with the little white blouse tucked into them and the bow tied loosely around the collar. When she looks in the mirror, it occurs to her that she looks very like Louise Brooks in her famous sailor outfit. She opens up her laptop and searches for an image of Louise. Sure enough, there she is, looking just like Valentina looks tonight. Louise Brooks was a rebel, and her free spirit cost her dear – a Hollywood career. Yet Valentina admires her greatly. She was an advocate for sexual liberation for women in the twenties and thirties. Yet still, nearly ninety years later, women are dealing with much the same prejudices. Valentina wonders if that is why her mother sometimes appears so hard. She was supposed to be living the ideal relationship in the sixties with Valentina's father, the perfect balance of freedom and possession. Yet something went wrong. Did her father begin to judge her mother? Was he not the liberated man he claimed to be? She has no idea. It is the one subject her mother refuses to discuss. This infuriates Valentina. The man may have walked out on her mother, but he is still her father. He walked out on her and Mattia too. Shouldn't they know whether he is dead or alive, at least? But Mattia claims he doesn't care, and something always stops Valentina from looking for him herself. Fear, she supposes. Of getting hurt.

By the time she arrives at Marco's party, it is in full swing.

'Valentina!' he cries when he sees her, his eyes flashing from too much wine already. 'You look amazing. Where did you get that outfit? It looks vintage.'

'It *is* vintage,' Valentina tells him, as he hooks his arm through hers and brings her into the sitting room. 'I got a package of old clothes belonging to my great-grandmother today.'

'*Dio mio!*' Marco looks like he is about to pass out with excitement. 'When can I come over?'

Valentina balances her glass of red wine in one hand and a cigarette in the other. She doesn't smoke often, but sometimes she enjoys the luxury of a cigarette with a drink. Marco's sitting room is thick with smoke. She is disappointed to see that he has invited some of the dope crowd. She has never understood the attraction that most of her contemporaries in Milan have for marijuana. Many of them grow their own, and approach its cultivation as a fine art. She finds smoking it okay, yet she feels she doesn't need it to get out of her body, if that is why they are doing it in the first place. Drugs in general don't interest her, since her dreams are psychedelic enough. She doesn't judge anyone if they want to take drugs, but if everyone is smoking dope, she finds that the party becomes a bit boring too early on, and conversation is certainly limited.

She walks through the lounging smokers; a few of them call out to her, offering her a spliff, but she politely shakes her head and makes for Marco's terrace. Where has he gone? She wants to tell him all about her great-grandmother's costumes. Maybe he could come over tomorrow and they could dress up together. Maybe she could talk to him about Theo. Out of all her friends, he is the most likely to understand how she feels. She might even tell him about the Dark Room. She wonders if he knows what it is.

She pulls back the sliding door into Marco's tiny back yard. It is good to breathe in some oxygen after the smoky confines of his apartment. She steps outside to finish off her cigarette, balancing her glass of wine on top of an empty plant container.

'Do you have a light?'

What a corny line, Valentina thinks as she turns around. The man in front of her looks vaguely familiar. She has obviously met him at one of Marco's parties before.

'Sure.' She takes her lighter out of her shorts pocket, and steps forward to light his cigarette. He cups his hand around hers, although there is no breeze. She hesitates, looking him in the eyes before she pulls back. She notices how long his eyelashes are, like a woman's, although the rest of his face is angular and rugged, and he is very tall with a broad build. She can tell by the way he looks at her that he isn't gay.

'I like your outfit,' the man says, looking her up and down.

Valentina instinctively pulls down the tiny black shorts, which have ridden up her thighs. She supposes she does look a little provocative, but then this is one of Marco's parties. Everyone dresses up, although this man looks quite ordinary in his blue and white shirt and blue jeans.

'So how do you know Marco?' she says, ignoring his comment.

'Oh, you know, from round about,' he says vaguely, puffing away on his cigarette.

'Do you work in the fashion trade?' she asks him.

He laughs shortly.

'Do I look like I work in fashion?'

'No,' she says, stubbing out her cigarette, suddenly annoyed. She picks up her glass of wine and makes to pass him, but the man blocks her way back into the apartment.

'Excuse me,' she says, trying to push past him. He doesn't move quickly enough for her, and Valentina gives him a shove, in the process of which she spills her red wine, fortunately not on her great-grandmother's silk blouse, but all over the man's shirt.

'Oh,' she says, a little embarrassed. 'I am sorry, but you didn't get out of my way.'

'I didn't realise you were in such a hurry to get away from me.'

'I wasn't . . . I was just cold . . . Look, do you want to take it off? I could get some salt from the kitchen and we could try to remove the wine with it.'

The man smiles at her, although it is not an altogether friendly smile.

'Sure,' he says, unbuttoning his shirt and peeling it off. He has very pale skin, nearly as pale as hers. It is free from any body hair whatsoever, yet his chest is broad and manly. He hands her the shirt.

'Why don't you soak it in the bath?' he says, his eyes narrowed.

She has a sudden image of herself in a bath, immersed in steaming water, and this man looking at her naked.

'Okay, I'll go and do that,' she says, making to walk past him again.

'Can you answer a question first?' he asks, catching hold of her arm.

She pushes his hand away.

'What?' she asks sharply, although her instinct is to tell him to go to hell.

'What boyfriend goes off and leaves his girlfriend all alone for one whole week, with no explanation at all?'

She stiffens, and looks directly into this man's face. Who is he? Is he something to do with Garelli?

'That is none of your business.'

He takes a step towards her, until he is so close that she can feel the naked skin of his chest brushing against her breasts through her silk blouse.

'Oh but it is, Valentina.'

How does he know her name, let alone the fact that she doesn't know where Theo is? She feels a cold prickle of fear down her spine. He is so close to her that she can smell him, an intoxicating scent of male sexuality. Despite his rudeness and her fear, this man is turning her on slightly. He leans down so that his lips are almost brushing hers.

'He has abandoned you to me, Valentina. I can't help wondering why.'

'Who are you?' she whispers back, feeling his long lashes brushing against her cheeks like butterfly wings.

'I am real, Valentina, that is all you need to know.'

He puts his arm around her waist, and pulls her to him with such force, she almost falls down. He kisses her so violently that he bites her bottom lip, and she can taste blood. It takes all her strength to pull away from him. She slaps him roundly on the face, but he just grins at her, not in the least unnerved. Speechless, and before he can touch her again, she runs back into Marco's apartment, past all the slouching smokers and up the stairs, into his bathroom. She locks the door, and stands with her back against it, breathing heavily. She walks over to the mirror and looks in it, sees the blood on her lip, and her flushed cheeks. She doesn't look like Valentina. She looks in disarray. It is only then that she realises she is still holding his stained shirt. She holds it up and smells it. The scent is so powerful it makes her feel sick. She throws it across the bathroom, and turns on the cold tap, splashing water on her face as if she needs to sober up. But it is not too much wine Valentina has had.

She wants to stay in the bathroom all night, hiding, but she is forced to come out by a stoned friend of Marco's banging on the door and begging her to let him in before he has an accident. Warily she comes back down the stairs and surveys the sitting room. Even more people have arrived and some are dancing in couples to Fats Waller on the stereo. She sees Marco dancing with a beautiful young man Valentina knows he has had a crush on for ages, and despite the fact that she is dying to ask him who the strange man is, she knows it wouldn't be fair to disturb him now. She hunts around for the stranger. She is going to shove his dirty shirt back in his face, and demand an explanation for his behaviour. But she can't see him anywhere. He is no longer out on the terrace, or in the kitchen, where both Antonella and Gaby are ensconced, munching through a bowl of crisps.

'Did you see a blond man? Tall, with no shirt on?' Valentina asks them.

Gaby stares at her with big black eyes, and Valentina can tell she is stoned, which means she is also mute. Grass, however, has the opposite effect on Antonella.

'Sorry, did you say a man with no shirt on? What did you

do to his shirt, Valentina?' Antonella laughs. 'You are a naughty girl, ravishing some stranger while your man is out of town.'

'Yes, well did you see him?'

'No, no, I wish I had, I would certainly have had some of that,' she says, stuffing a fistful of crisps into her mouth.

Valentina pours herself another glass of wine. It's no good asking those two anything; they are both off their faces. She downs her wine in one and decides to go home. She is no longer in a party mood.

Valentina cycles through the Saturday night throng of Milan. The city is bursting with energy, music pounding from the clubs, students spilling out on to the streets of Bocconi as she cycles through. Every now and again she hears the scream of police sirens as they fly by. There is plenty of traffic on the road home, but that doesn't stop Valentina from noticing the ridiculous little Smart car trailing her. In an instant it is clear to her. The man at Marco's party is the same man in the Smart car. But who is he? And what does he want with her?

ℬelle

SANTOS BRINGS HER A GIFT. IT IS NOT A RING OR ANY OTHER type of jewellery. Not clothes or flowers. Nor is it an exotic article from one of his travels. It is a little black box, with a lid.

'Open it,' he tells her.

She lifts the lid and gets the most delightful surprise. A soft black bellows springs up, with two delicate lenses on the end of it, one large and one small. Underneath the large lens are the letters *Kodak*.

'A camera!' she exclaims. Despite the fact that she didn't know it, this is a gift she really wants. 'It's so beautiful,' she says, fingering the art deco springs.

She hands it back to Santos as if it is the most precious jewel she has ever seen.

'Show me how it works,' she demands.

At first they take pictures of Venice. They take the camera and a small light meter with them in Santos's dinghy, and Belle

315

follows his instructions as Santos rows her around the city. She photographs the gondolas and their candy-striped mooring poles; she photographs the old churches and the decaying palazzos.

The following day she brings the film to the pharmacy, almost shaking with anticipation. The first series of pictures are a disaster, much to her disappointment, but gradually she finds her feet. Santos tells her she has a talent for taking pictures. Sometimes she has no need for the light meter. She knows by instinct how long to leave her finger pressed down.

For Belle, these photographs are more than mementoes of Venice, or memories of her limited time with Santos. They are *him*. Since he won't let her take a picture directly of his face, each piece of Venice is a part of Santos. The Campanile his pride and strength, the horses on the façade of the Basilica his wildness, the sky reflected in the canal the tranquillity of the refuge he gives her, the pigeons taking flight in St Mark's Square his spirit.

Belle does not know this, but Santos stays longer with her than he has stayed with any woman. For once, luck is on their side. The day after his brutal attack, Signor Brzezinski disappeared on business without a word. She has no idea where he is, and she doesn't care. His absence gives her and Santos precious time, so that her lover is able to stay with her until her bruises yellow and begin to fade. He stays with her because despite his experience, and the many lovers he has had, he has never expressed himself so completely as through his lovemaking with Belle. And he loves her most when she is preoccupied with her camera, lost from him fleetingly since she is so immersed in her picture-taking. It gives him a taste of how much he will miss her when he leaves.

This day is a bright Venetian morning. The sky is the colour of angels' eyes, reflected in the water outside Belle's apartment. They open her shutters and French windows wide, and the sunshine pours into her bedroom, drowning them in its splendour as they make love. Belle feels the heat of the sun on her back as she sits on top of Santos, and he raises his knees, pushing the small of her back so that she falls on to his chest. He is slipping his fingers through her short silky hair, and pulling her face down so that their lips meet. Belle closes her eyes and feels him deep inside her, tipping her in her most vulnerable and most joyous place. She loves him so much she would let him take her heart out with a spoon. As long as she has him, she can endure the violence of her husband. She tries to banish the thought that her husband will return one day. And soon Santos will be leaving. Can she make him stay? Despite her deep love for him, Santos would not be Santos if he settled down. It would change their love. She supposes they are destined to be star-crossed lovers, and that all the agonies she will have to face once he is gone will be worth it for these rare days of ecstasy.

Afterwards she lies in the crook of his arm, watching the curtains flutter in the breeze. She hears the song of a blackbird.

She has an urge to see it, and gets out of bed to stand by the window, the light muslin curtain fluttering around her naked body. She feels Santos's eyes upon her, but she doesn't cover herself.

'Stay quite still,' he demands.

She hears a click, and turns in surprise to see Santos sitting on the bed with the camera in his hands. Her eyes widen into a question.

'I don't think there is enough light for that to come out,' she tells him.

'But I would like to take some pictures of you,' he says. 'So that I can have them with me when I go.'

When I go. She feels the dread of his departure as a dull ache inside her heart.

'What kind of pictures?' she asks him.

He rests the camera on his naked lap.

'Special ones. So that I can look at your beauty, and imagine that you are with me.'

To remind you to return to me one day.

She wonders if Santos asks all his lovers for pictures. Somehow she knows not. He is a man of the moment, moving on to new futures, never looking back. Can she, Belle, make him look back for her? Can she speak to him through her body so that it is more than a shell, but an articulation of her love?

'My darling Belle, will you pose for me?'

She smiles, just for him. A crooked, mischievous smile. She

knows that he wants to take pictures of her naked.

'Well, they will have to be taken outside,' she tells him. 'We need more light. Where exactly do you suggest I pose? In the middle of Piazza san Marco without a stitch on?'

He laughs, then comes over to her and pulls the fluttering curtain away from her body. He traces her with his finger, from the tip of her head all the way down to her belly button.

'How about the roof?'

'Isn't that a little dangerous?'

'Not for an experienced cat burglar like myself, and his nimble accomplice. Besides, I do believe there is a rooftop terrace on the building next door.'

It doesn't take much to convince Belle. Wearing just her silk dressing gown and her black button boots, she lets Santos pull her up on to the roof of her building. They sit for a moment on the terracotta slates, looking at the skyline of Venice.

'Sometimes this city feels like a father to me,' she whispers.

'In what way?' asks Santos, tucking a stray hair behind her ear.

'It has such spirit in the face of adversity. It protects its inhabitants, despite the fact that its very foundations are merely sticks stuck in the sand at the bottom of the lagoon.'

'And what about Warsaw?'

She shakes her head.

'I never felt safe in Warsaw, not how I do in Venice.'

He looks at her, surprised.

'But your husband . . . how can you feel safe with him?'

'Santos, don't talk to me about him, please.'

He takes her chin and swivels her head. He forces her to look at him, and she notices how dark his eyes have become, like the night sky despite the brightness of the day. He is wearing just his trousers, and his chest is bare.

'He must never hit you again.'

She reaches out and puts her hand against his heart, pushes her fingers into his chest hair. 'Please, Santos . . .'

He puts his hand over hers, squeezes it.

'Why don't you leave him, my love?'

She tears her hand away from his, and grips it with her own. She looks out across the skyline of Venice. She wants to tell him about the promise she made to her father. Yet she is too ashamed. And would Santos even understand? He has never let any soul tie him to one place, not even her.

'I can't.' She turns away from him and starts to crawl along the roof. 'I don't want to talk about him.'

Inside her heart another voice is screaming.

Oh but you can leave, Belle. You have paid your dues . . . Go with Santos, run away with him. You cannot help your mother now. It is too late for her.

She tries to silence this voice, yet hope has sprung within her. Maybe Santos will take her with him.

They scramble down the side of the roof, and along the edge of the next one, dropping on to a tiny terrace belonging to one of Belle's neighbours, who it appears is not at home. The freshly whitewashed terrace is sparkling in the sunlight.

At one end is a line of washing strung between the two walls. At the other are baskets full of red carnations, white roses and myrtle bushes. Belle walks over to the wall and looks out across the city. The aroma from the flora encircles her with a slight spiciness, sweetness and tangy herbal scents; all the contradictions of her sensations when she is with Santos. She lets her dressing gown drop, and feels the sun's light warming her skin. She remembers how she felt all those nights she waited for Santos to come to her. She crosses her arms in front of her breasts and hugs her sides, dropping her head so that she is looking down. Santos takes off his sailor's cap and positions it on her head, before stepping back. She hears the camera clicking and then Santos comes over, whipping the hat off her head and dropping to his knees behind her before kissing one of the cheeks of her bottom.

He gets up and spins her around so that she is facing him. As trusting as a bird in the palm of his hand. He has the camera right in front of her face and he takes a picture of her downcast eye. He kisses her closed eyelid. She opens her eyes and sees him pull her lipstick out of his pocket.

'Pout for me, Belle.'

He smiles at her, and as she pushes her lips forward, he applies crimson lipstick to them, before taking another photograph. He kisses her lips, and she can feel her nipples erect, her body softening, craving him. She wants him to make love to her on this roof terrace. She doesn't care who sees them. She finds it so erotic to be objectified by him like this.

'Make love to me,' she whispers.

Santos shakes his head, his jewel eyes gleaming at her wickedly. He hasn't finished taking pictures. He pulls a lace scarf from the washing line and binds it around her breasts. He takes a picture, and kisses her nipples, which have pushed through the fabric. And so the game continues. He puts her in position, takes a photograph, and she begs for him to make love to her, yet all he will give her is a kiss on whatever part of her anatomy he has photographed. He unwinds the scarf, takes a jug of rainwater from the terrace and tips it over her naked breasts, before taking a picture. He kisses her wet breasts, and Belle wonders if that image will look like her spent tears upon her naked flesh, the sunshine sparkling through the drops of water like shards of broken heart-ache.

Now he makes her lie down on the blinding white stone of the terrace. It is hot from the sun, and warms her naked skin. He takes a picture of her lying on her side, with her back to him. Now she lies on her back and he takes a picture of her stomach and navel with one of the white roses upon it, petals scattered. He pauses for a moment, and she sees him picking up a sack he slung on his back before they left her bedroom.

'What's in there?' she asks.

He smiles enigmatically at her, opening the sack and pulling out a Venetian mask. He hands it to her.

'It is one of Lara's masks,' he says.

She stiffens at the mention of her rival's name.

'I don't want it if she made it,' she says, trying to hand it back to him.

He looks amused.

'But she made it for you, Belle.'

Belle frowns.

'Why would she make me a mask?'

'Because she is my *friend*, not my lover. She is one of my oldest friends here. I always stay with her when I come to Venice.'

'Oh,' says Belle, fingering the mask. She remembers the red-haired woman and her hostility towards her. 'It didn't look like that to me, Santos. I think she is in love with you.'

Santo shakes his head.

'Maybe,' he sighs. 'But she understands how I am. That is why she made you this. It is a token of her respect. You should not reject it, Belle.'

Belle looks at the mask. She has to admit she has never seen anything so finely crafted. It is light as a feather in her hands. Its surface looks like porcelain, covered in tiny black lines, the eye holes delineated with long black lashes. It is decorated around the edges with swirling gold patterns filled in with the palest lilac, white and black spirals, petals, curves and dots. In the centre of the mask, between the eyes, is set a crystal, from which plumes a peacock's feather.

'Put it on,' Santos commands.

She holds it to her face, and he ties it snugly at the back of her head.

'Now,' he whispers into her ear, 'you really are free, my blackbird. You can do whatever you wish.'

Her anonymity makes her bolder. She sits with her back against the terrace wall, facing Santos. He picks up the camera again and waits for her. She raises her knees, slowly moves her legs apart to reveal herself. He pauses, looks at her with interest.

'Tease me, Belle,' he says.

Instinctively she brings her right arm down between her legs, pushing her fist against the white stone, grinding her flesh into it, so that her knuckles are grazed. She wonders if the most private part of herself will be visible in the picture. The thought thrills her. She feels it igniting the expression in her eyes behind the mask, so that she challenges the camera with her gaze.

You are all to me.

Santos takes his picture.

'Again,' he says. 'Tease me again, Belle.'

She flips over on to her stomach on the hot stone, so that she is facing the wall. She spreads her legs again and bends her knees, twisting her neck and head around to look at Santos, bringing her right arm behind her and touching herself with her hand. She pushes her index finger into her soft self, and makes a tiny gasp. Click. Santos has caught it. She pushes herself again with her finger, and she can hear Santos's breath quicken. He puts the camera aside and crawls towards her across the hot terrace.

'That is a very provocative pose,' he says, leaning over her, kissing her neck.

'I thought that was what you wanted,' she replies, twisting her head around further so that she finds his lips, silencing him.

He peels his trousers off, lies on top of her. She feels the length of him in the small of her back. She wants to offer herself up completely to him. She puts both her hands behind her back and guides him into her. She doesn't care about the hot stone rubbing her stomach and breasts, or the glare of the sun emblazoning them; all she wants is to feel Santos inside her. If they could take a picture of this, how she would treasure it. The moment he comes inside her, when she can feel him at his most vulnerable and yielding. All hers.

Afterwards they lie side by side, hand in hand, staring at the gulls circling in the blue sky. Her heart is flying with them, dancing in the sky above. This is her and Santos's Venice, a paradise of passion. Despite her abusive marriage, she feels free inside her heart because of the love she has for this man, lying beside her on the hot stone.

'I love you, Santos.' She leans up on her elbow and looks down at her lover, trying to imprint the image of his face inside her memory.

The silence hangs between them. What she wants now is for him to say those words to her. She waits, yet Santos remains silent, looking up at her with an unfathomable expression.

The tension is unbearable. She turns away from him, and

sees her little bellows camera, sitting where he left it on the terrace. She leans over and picks it up, and without looking through the lens hastily turns around and takes a picture of Santos.

'Oh no you don't,' he says, grabbing it off her. 'Pictures of me are not allowed.'

'Well that's probably of your ear anyway. I didn't even have a chance to see what I was taking a picture of.'

Santos sits up and closes the camera, clicking the lid shut.

'I'll take this with me tomorrow,' he says, pulling on his trousers. 'I'll try to find a discreet pharmacy where I can get the film developed.'

She sniffs at him in mock disdain.

'If you get those pictures developed in Venice, *everyone* will know about them.'

Santos never takes the film to be developed. It is something Belle does later, when she has finally built up the courage to do so. This day will be the last she ever spends with the love of her life. It is a golden fragment of her existence that she peruses time and time again in years to come. As if this white terrace in the sun is a promised land she has lost the way to. For this last day is an erotic memory made poignant by loss. Each time she relives it, she is fortified and has no need for another man. She will wait for Santos to return. And buried deep within her womb, unbeknownst to them, is the token of their love.

This faith in Santos is what saves Belle, for when she leaves her apartment today, she will face the hardest trials of her life. And always when she remembers her walk home from Belle's apartment to Louise's house, from joy to pain, she remembers the seagulls screaming.

$\mathcal{V}$alentina

SHE IS SWIMMING WITH THEO. IT IS THE SUMMER JUST past, and they are in Sardinia. She swims behind him, watching the light dancing on water, its blue as brilliant as his eyes when he turns to her. The sun has turned him as brown as a native of the island; it looks incongruous when he speaks with his American accent. They wade out of the water, pick their way across razor-sharp rocks and lie down on the sand to dry off. There is no one else on this strip of beach, the rocks putting off any others. Theo and Valentina have it to themselves. They could make love. They did so just the day before, under the sun, with the steady crash of the waves urging them on. Yet today the two lovers lie side by side, naked as the day they were born, holding hands, wordless and staring at the unblemished sky. Valentina realises she wants to hold the purity of this moment for ever. The simple pleasure of being in the present, feeling her fingers curled inside Theo's warm hand, of connecting her life to his, of not worrying about tomorrow.

Yet Theo sits up and pulls his hand away from hers. She feels a little grief at losing his touch, and yet she doesn't reach out for his hand again. She has too much pride. He picks up his snorkel.

'I'm going back in,' he says.

'Don't go out too far,' she warns him.

He cocks his head on one side, smiles at her.

'Are you worried about me?' Always there is this game between them. Theo trying to pull her out, make her admit she cares more than she says she does.

She shakes her head, trying to feign indifference.

'I just don't want to have to go in and rescue you. That's all.'

She watches him saunter off towards the waves admiring his tall, lean figure, and wonders what he sees in her. She looks at him for a while, flipping under the water and up again, but the sun is so bright it hurts her eyes, and she finds she has to close them. The heat of the late afternoon seeps into her bones, and she imagines herself sinking into the warm sand beneath her, drifting away under the shade of their parasol.

When she wakes, it is cooler. She shivers and opens her eyes. There are clouds now in the sky, and the sun is sliding behind one of them. She sits up and looks out to sea. It has turned from serene blue to stormy grey. She has no idea how long she has been asleep. She stands up and walks towards the water. There is no sign of Theo. She glances back at the beach, but his towel is exactly where he left it next to hers. She steps into the sea, letting the water lap her ankles, and peers towards the horizon. All she can see are the buffeting waves, and blankness. No Theo. She turns and looks behind her at the beach again, but it is definitely empty. Where is he? She tries to remain calm, but there is a voice in her head berating her.

Why did you let yourself fall asleep? You should have watched him.

He is not as strong a swimmer as her. She has been warned of rip currents off this beach. Why did she let him go in alone? She begins wading out to sea, looking into the clear blue water, but of course it is a ridiculous thing to do. If he is gone, he is gone. Fear strikes her heart, panic fills her mouth. She can't lose him, not him as well.

'Valentina!'

She spins around. There, standing on the beach, a net full of shells in one hand, is Theo. He is waving to her with his free hand. The relief rushes through her, so that she feels her legs almost buckle. In the same moment, anger courses through her, as she launches herself through the offending waves back to shore.

She runs towards him across the beach, and half of her wants to hurl herself into his arms and cling to him. He is waving to her, smiling innocently, unaware of her terror. She strides towards him, and instead of embracing him, she swings her arm through the air and slaps him across the face with all her force. He steps back in shock, slowly raises his hand to his cheek.

'Where did you go?' she screams, unwanted tears sprouting in her eyes. She is so angry with him for making her lose her cool. She tries to calm down, but she can't.

'I just climbed over those rocks to some pools.' He waves his arm behind him and lifts the net. 'I was collecting some pretty shells for you.'

She grabs the net and smashes it against the rock.

'You should have told me where you were. I thought you had drowned,' she continues to yell.

'You were sleeping, I didn't want to disturb you,' he says carefully, looking at her as if she is a wild animal he has to tame.

'Well you should have woken me up,' she shouts at him. She is shaking with the force of her emotions, and it makes her even more enraged.

She has to get away from him now. She has to be on her own. She turns to walk back to the towels, but he grabs her by the arm, forces her to turn around and look into his piercing gaze.

'Valentina,' he says gently. 'It's okay.'

'No it's not.' She pulls away from him, swallowing down her tears. She stomps back to her stuff on the beach and hastily packs it up. She is shocked. She hit him. And instead of getting angry with her, he looked at her so tenderly. He looked at her with love. It frightens her more than anything.

As they pick their way across the rocks, back towards the car, she hears a distant roll of thunder, and sees a flash of lightning far out to sea. That night, as the rain pounds upon the roof of their little seaside villa, Theo makes love to her with such passion it takes her breath away. She is beginning to unravel, and as she tries to gather herself up, he is undoing her all over again.

She hears that thunder again as she lies in her bed in Milan. She packed away her incomprehensible behaviour that day in a box inside her head. When they returned from their trip to Sardinia, it was never mentioned again. She has never wanted to revisit it. She is ashamed of her hysterical outburst. Now, weeks later, she is lying in bed on her own, remembering her terror at the thought that he might have drowned. She turns on her side, squeezes her eyes shut and tries to go back to sleep, yet the thunder is still drumming in her head. In fact the thunder isn't in her head at all. It is a real noise. And it is not thunder. She rolls on to her back, opens her eyes and listens carefully. There it is again. A heavy, dragging sound, as if someone is moving furniture in the flat. She feels her breath quicken. Is there someone in her apartment? No, she is just imagining it. Yet there is the sound again, followed by a click, as if someone has opened a door. She holds her breath. What should she do? Should she get out of bed and investigate? Or should she ring the police? Her phone is in the kitchen, so she is trapped if there is someone in the apartment.

She sits up in bed, listens intently. She can't hear anything now. She must have been mistaken. If there was a noise, it was probably her neighbour banging around upstairs. She is just about to get out of bed and check the apartment when she hears someone outside her bedroom door. She is sure of it. Shuffling footsteps. She flops back down on the bed and closes her eyes. She tries to make sleep-breathing noises, steady, deep breaths. She imagines the intruder opening the door, shining a light on her face. But is he really there? She is too afraid to open her eyes and look. She lies like this for several moments, tight with anticipation, her ears straining for sound. Gradually she begins to relax. She can hear nothing, and when she opens her eyes she can see there is no one in her bedroom. She sits up again, and listens. The apartment is completely silent, except for the tick of the clock in the hall.

She gets out of her bed, and instinctively tiptoes across her bedroom, just in case. She peeks around the corner of her door. The apartment is silent and full of shadows. The light she left on in the kitchen when she went to bed is still on, casting a glow across the hall. There is no one here. She slides down the marble-floored hall and into the kitchen. All is as she left it. She checks her bag. Her cards and cash are untouched. Her computer is still sitting on the table. There is no sign of disturbance. And yet there is this smell in the air. Something feels different. She checks the other rooms in the apartment and everything looks normal. The last room she checks is Theo's study. As far as she can see, nothing has been taken. The same paintings are on the wall. *The Love Letter* by Metsu is facing her, and next to it the Watteau. Everything is exactly how it was this morning. Isn't it? Yet once more she smells something, a strong, cloying scent like overripe plums. And there is something amiss in this room. She just can't put her finger on it. There is no sign of a break-in, no smashed windows or splintered doors, yet she feels a little on edge. She doesn't want to be on her own.

She wanders back into the kitchen to make herself a cup of camomile tea to try to calm her nerves. It's three in the morning, and she's not going to sleep now. She needs to talk to someone. She tries Theo, but of course he doesn't answer. She feels a twinge of hurt. What could he be doing that would stop him from answering her call? He would know it must be important for her to ring him at this time. She considers trying one of her friends, but Antonella and Gaby were so stoned just a few hours ago that she imagines they are fast asleep by now and no good to her. She doesn't want to disturb Marco in case he is having a night of passion with that guy at the party. And if not, he would just get hysterical and insist she take a taxi over to his place. That is something she doesn't want to do. There is only one other person Valentina is sure will be up at three in the morning. In any case, after their last encounter, she considers they are sort of friends now.

'Valentina?'

'Leonardo, sorry to ring you at this hour.'

'Is something wrong?'

She circles the kitchen, chewing her lip.

'I think someone might have broken into my apartment.'

'Are you okay, Valentina? Did you ring the police?'

'Well I'm not really sure someone did . . .' She pauses. 'I heard noises, but nothing has been taken.'

'You probably just had a bad dream. Are you sure you're okay?'

'Yes, I'm fine . . . just a bit spooked, you know. I needed to talk to someone, and you're the only person I know who would be awake.'

'What about Theo?'

She sighs.

'He's unavailable.'

There is an awkward pause. Valentina presses the phone tight against her ear.

'Would you like me to come over?' Leonardo asks.

Valentina promises herself that if she says yes, nothing will happen. She really doesn't want to go back to bed alone. She just needs some company.

'Yes,' she says, before she has a chance to change her mind. 'Just for a little while . . . if it's okay with Raquel.'

'Raquel is away,' Leonardo tells her. 'Give me your address and I'll take a taxi.'

Valentina supposes she should put on some clothes. Her great-grandmother's vintage wardrobe is still strewn on the couch where she left it earlier today. She slips on a silk chemise and a pair of silk pyjama bottoms underneath a blue silk kimono, which she belts around the waist. It is completely over the top, and yet Valentina feels better, as if she is in some kind of costume.

Leonardo arrives armed with a bottle of red wine.

'So,' he asks, 'is it night-time or morning for you? I've just finished work, so I could do with a drink. How about you?'

'Wine too, thanks,' Valentina says, tipping her mug of camomile tea into the sink. She opens the dresser and takes out two wine glasses.

They sit at opposite ends of the kitchen table.

'So what were you doing tonight?' asks Valentina, trying to break through her shyness. 'Being dominant? Pouring hot wax on to some unsuspecting girl's backside?'

Leonardo puts on a mock frown.

'You know I can't tell you that, Valentina,' he says, wagging his finger at her. 'If I broke my clients' confidence, my credibility would be ruined.'

She sighs and sits back in her chair, takes a big slurp of wine. She feels so much better now, having Leonardo here with her.

'So did you see anyone in your flat?' Leonardo asks her.

She shakes her head.

'No. I heard noises, as if someone was dragging furniture, and then I thought they were outside my bedroom door.'

She thinks about telling Leonardo about the man at Marco's party, and that maybe he broke in, but it all seems bit preposterous now she is sitting opposite him at her kitchen table. And yet that smell . . . She can still sense it lingering in the air of her apartment. It was the same smell as that man's shirt at the party.

'But they didn't come into your bedroom? You didn't actually see someone?'

'No, I thought he stood in my bedroom doorway and shone a light on me, but my eyes were closed and maybe I imagined the whole thing.'

'Were you scared?' Leonardo leans forward across the table, picks up her limp hand and squeezes it.

'Yes,' she whispers.

He takes his hand away, and dips his finger in his wine, licking it, looking at her the whole time.

'Were you turned on?'

'No! Of course not!' Yet she cannot look him in the eye. How does this man know these things about her?

They sit in silence for a few moments. Valentina shifts in her chair. She can feel her silk clothing sliding all over her body, her skin prickling with anticipation. Isn't it a sick thing to feel turned on by the idea of a stranger attacking you in your bed? And yet Leonardo is right. The idea of it is erotic to her.

'So, Valentina,' Leonardo finally asks. 'Do you want to play a game?'

It starts like something she played as a child with friends from school. A kind of hide and seek, but in the dark and with a torch. Leonardo has turned all the lights off in the apartment, and it is still dark outside. Only a small amount of light from the street manages to leach through the slats of the blinds, so that she can see his shadowy outline in the blackened room, just like the intruder in her imagination. He is standing in the doorway, swinging the torch rhythmically from side to side, like a searchlight. The idea is that she has to get to the other side of the bedroom without being caught in the beam. If he does catch her, she has to remove an item of clothing. She has already lost her dressing gown and pyjama bottoms. She only has her chemise left, and she is not sure what happens to her after she has lost that.

She creeps out from behind her dressing table and crawls along the marble floor. She is making for the doorway, hoping she can slip through behind him, but she knows he senses she is there, and the beam of the torch is moving irrevocably towards her. She holds her breath, tries to quieten her excitement. She realises she is having fun. She is nearly there. How much she wants to fool Leonardo, but just as she is about to slip past him, the full force of the torchlight is shone on her face and she is momentarily blinded.

'Miss Valentina.' She hears his taunting voice. 'You are caught! Take off your top.'

She obeys, pulling her silk chemise over her head and dropping it on the rug. Now she is completely naked, in the full beam of his torch. She tries to see him, but it is impossible. She is in the spotlight, trapped.

'You are now my prisoner,' Leonardo tells her. 'You must do exactly as I say.'

She should stop the game now, Valentina thinks, remembering the promise she made to herself when she invited Leonardo over. And yet she doesn't want to. It doesn't feel like she is doing something wrong, even though she is naked in front of this man. She can't understand why it feels all right to be doing this; all she knows is that she is excited. She doesn't know what he might do to her, but she wants to find out. She wants to submit to whatever Leonardo tells her to do.

'Lie down,' he orders. Still in the torchlight, she lies on the rug on her back.

'Raise your knees and open your legs.'

She does as she is told, feeling wicked and incredibly turned on.

He is illuminating me with his torch. He is looking right into me.

'Touch yourself,' he says. 'Show me how much you want me.'

She pushes her right hand between her legs and begins to caress herself with her finger. She opens her legs wider and closes her eyes. She feels exposed, and primal. She opens her mouth, licks her lips with her tongue.

'What do you want, Valentina?' Leonardo says.

She submerges herself in her fantasy.

'I want to be fucked,' she whispers.

She opens her eyes to realise that the flashlight has been

turned off and the room is completely dark again. She sees Leonardo's sturdy shadow coming towards her. Her heart begins to pound faster. She should stop him, yet she feels so primed for sex, aroused by Leonardo's masterful persona. She wants to be in his power.

Leonardo leans over her, takes her hand from between her legs and pulls her up on to her knees so that she is facing him. He is still dressed, and she clings on to the waistband of his jeans, desperately feeling his hardness against her cheek.

'Unbutton my jeans,' he orders, and he no longer sounds like the Leonardo she knows, but another man. Hard and unforgiving.

She quickly does what he has told her, and pulls his jeans down his hips to the floor. He kicks them off.

'Take off my shorts.'

She pulls down his shorts, and he springs free, his erect penis brushing against her cheeks, making her breath quicken.

'Pleasure me,' he growls.

She licks the whole length of him with her tongue, and then pivots it around the top of his penis. She can feel him stirring, responding to her touch. She takes his length out of her mouth and strokes him with her hand, squeezing him tightly before pushing him back inside her mouth again. Leonardo bends down and brings his hand between her legs, touching her with his fingers.

'Valentina, you are so plush, so ready for me,' he whispers. 'You are like velvet.'

He brings his hands up, licks his fingers and places them spread upon her shoulders. He steps back so that his penis is pulled out of her mouth and goes down on his knees opposite her. They look into each other's faces. He smiles. For a moment he is the Leonardo she knows again.

'Okay?' he asks her softly.

'Very,' she whispers back.

His eyes darken, and he squeezes her nipples tightly between his fingers, causing her to melt further.

'Turn around,' he says, his voice reverting to its earlier hardness.

She turns, and he puts a hand on the small of her back, pushing her down on to all fours. He puts his arm between her legs so that his hand is on her stomach and drags it down her belly, across her pelvis, through her pubic hair and under, slowly, slowly, enticing her with his fingers.

'What do you want, Valentina?' he asks her again.

'I want you to fuck me!' she hisses.

Leonardo pushes inside her, and she gasps with shock. He pounds into her again and again, and she is panting with excitement and fright, her fingers digging into the thick pile rug. This is pure sex. No love attached, just the complicity of Valentina and Leonardo's friendship. It is what she needs right now. He thrusts in and out of her with such force. She can feel his hairy chest against her back, and she imagines his dark skin aflame with desire, glowing as if it is on fire from within. She is so close now. Leonardo cries out, coming inside her with one final thrust. It is too soon for her. She tries to hold him still inside her, pushes back against him, but he withdraws.

She bends over, stares into the patterns of the rug, aware of Leonardo beside her, taking off the condom, pulling on his shorts. She is taut with frustrated desire, and another emotion, rocketing through her. Anger. It is so intense, she cannot move. She is furious. Not with Leonardo, or even herself, but with Theo. She realises that no matter how many men she sleeps with, no one will do but him. How did she let this happen to her? In the very moment she has realised that Theo is right, that they do have something special together, she has destroyed it. What boyfriend will ever understand what she has been doing with Leonardo?

'Valentina . . . Valentina . . .'

She feels someone shaking her, pulling her out of her sleep.

'Valentina, wake up, you're having a nightmare.'

She opens her eyes. Leonardo is leaning over her, his brown eyes filled with concern.

She breathes out slowly, takes in the scene. She is lying in her bed, Leonardo next to her. It is day. And she can tell by the way sunlight fills the whole room that it is late.

'Are you okay?' he asks.

She nods, although she is still a little shaken by her nightmare.

'Do you want to tell me about your dream?'

She sighs.

'Not really. I'd rather try to forget about it.' Underwater. Darkness. Sinking. Suffocating.

She sits up in bed, wipes the sleep from her eyes and looks at her bedfellow properly. She begins to register what happened the night before.

'I can't believe we did what we did last night . . .' she begins to say.

'Did you enjoy it?' Leonardo asks, head cocked to one side. 'Did you have fun?' Is it her imagination, or has he just laid particular emphasis on the word *fun*?

'Of course I enjoyed it!'

She throws a pillow at him playfully. He laughs for a moment, then throws the pillow back.

'I wasn't too sure,' he says. 'You seemed a bit upset afterwards.'

'I'm just confused . . .' She pauses. 'About Theo. And what about Raquel?'

'Don't be,' Leonardo says. 'Raquel and I have an open relationship. She was with someone else last night as well.'

Valentina's eyes widen in shock. So there are some people who really can do this and still stay together.

'As for Theo, trust me, all will be clear after you go inside the Dark Room tonight.'

The way he speaks, it's as if he knows something she doesn't.

'What are you hiding from me, Leonardo?' She pokes him with her finger.

He gives her a honeyed smile.

'Patience, Valentina.' And the way he says it reminds her of Theo. Now her anger at her lover has dissipated and she is filled with concern. Has she ruined any future she and Theo might have, by sleeping with Leonardo? Should she hide it from him? And yet she can't regret last night. That's the odd thing.

'I would like you to do something for me, Valentina,' Leonardo says.

She looks at him questioningly.

'In order for me to ensure that the Dark Room fulfils your needs to perfection, I want you to tell me about your most erotic fantasy.'

He looks at her intently, and she can feel her cheeks colouring as if he can read her mind.

'Do you think you can do that, Valentina?' He sidles over to her side of the bed.

'I don't know,' she mumbles. 'I'm not sure I know what it is.'

'I could help you think of something,' he says, stroking the top of her thighs underneath the covers. Her body immediately responds to his touch. She is still left wanting from last night.

'Okay . . .' she whispers.

'Close your eyes,' he instructs her, and she does what he asks, so that all her senses are focused on his touch. She feels his finger pushing against her clitoris, gently rubbing it.

'Go into your fantasy, Valentina.' His voice purrs. 'Take me to your deepest, darkest desire.'

As Leonardo's fingertips bring her closer and closer to the edge, in Valentina's mind is illuminated an image. Her ultimate fantasy. Hesitantly she relays her vision to Leonardo.

When she has finished, the image is replaced by another scene. One she doesn't share with him. In it she returns to her bedroom at night. Theo is there, torch in hand, and he is gloriously naked. He drops the torch so that it is spinning on the floor, projecting light around the walls of the room like a disco ball. He lifts her up with both hands, up so high that the top of her head is brushing against the chandelier, making the glass tinkle and projecting even more reflections, like raindrops cascading all around them in their bedroom. He brings her down again and she puts her legs around his waist, guiding him into her. One thrust and she is open wide, the frustrations of this week melting away as if a door has been opened in the small of her back and a flood of emotion is pouring out. And so Valentina comes again and again, the magic of Leonardo's touch transporting her into the arms of her lover, Theo.

$\mathcal{B}$elle

SIGNOR BRZEZINSKI IS BACK. BELLE HAS NOT SEEN HIM, BUT she heard him last night, stomping around the house, and shouting at Renate in the kitchen that his meat was not cooked right. He is biding his time, she thinks, but it will not be long before he hits her again. She can't risk it, not because she is frightened of him, but because she needs to protect Santos. She knows her lover will be true to his word if he sees one more bruise upon her skin.

I will run away, Belle vows when she wakes the next morning. She has a delicious fantasy of herself and Santos far, far away from Venice. She is wrapped in furs, crunching in the snow, Santos at her side, the steam from their breath mingled as they look up at the bright domes and spires of St Basil's Cathedral in Moscow. Clutched in the palm of her hand, inside her coat pocket, is the Romanov emerald that they have retrieved from a communist stronghold. Or they are some-where tropical, sailing on his white schooner and stopping off in Cuba, where they spend the night dancing and gambling with shady characters, only to escape with all the winnings. Yes, luck would be on their side, for surely when two people are meant to be together, they will be granted a greater measure of good fortune.

The door opens and Pina enters with her breakfast tray. Belle sits up in bed, patting the pillows behind her and feeling more positive than she has in ages. It is time to break her promise. What kind of promise is it anyway when it is demanded from you by your father on his deathbed? That is bribery, Belle reasons. It is time to live for herself and no longer feel responsible for her mother.

She looks down at her breakfast on the tray on her lap. Milky tea in the bone-china cup from Vienna, two neat triangles of toast and a softly boiled egg in a silver eggcup. She knocks the lid off the egg with her teaspoon. Just looking at the yolk turns her stomach. She hastily shoves the tray aside and gets out of bed.

'Madam? Are you all right?' Pina is at the windows, drawing back the curtains.

Belle nods, unable to speak as she rushes into her bathroom. She barely makes it to the toilet before she throws up.

As she sits on her haunches by the toilet bowl, Pina hesitantly enters the bathroom.

'Madam, are you ill?'

'I don't know, Pina. I was feeling fine a minute ago. It was the egg. It's made me rather queasy.'

She puts her hands on the cool black and white tiles of her bathroom floor and then up to her forehead, but she doesn't have a temperature.

'You should get back into bed. Rest.'

Belle stands up shakily, leans over the sink and looks at her pale face.

'No. I have to go out.'

She locks eyes with Pina in the mirror. The younger girl blushes scarlet. She knows my secret, Belle thinks. I don't know this girl at all, yet I would trust her with my life.

'Tell me, Pina,' Belle says as she starts to apply her make-up. 'Do you miss your home in Sicily?'

The girl nods, her eyes doleful, her mouth drawn in a sad line.

'I remember when you sang to me in your dialect. It was quite beautiful.' Belle leans forwards and starts shaping her eyebrows. She still feels a little sick, but she is not going to let it stop her from seeing Santos today. 'So are your parents in Sicily still?'

'My mother is dead, madam, and my father has a new wife and family.'

'Oh, I am sorry, Pina.' So that is why the girl is always here, never home for holidays and no visits from relatives.

She pauses, and looks at Pina. She is so young, she thinks. Nearly the same age as Belle herself was when she first got married.

'You are so pretty, Pina, you must have many admirers.'

Pina blushes an even deeper shade of red. She casts her eyes down to the floor.

'I really don't care for any of them,' she says.

'Then don't be persuaded to marry,' says Belle firmly. 'Enjoy your freedom while you can.' As she says these words, she wonders what kind of freedom Pina might actually have. Certainly not as much as her.

'I am not able to choose my own husband anyway.'

Belle turns around and scrutinises Pina's face. And she sees, under all the shy softness, an anger burning inside the young Sicilian girl.

'Why not? Your father seems not to bother with you any more. This is 1929, Pina, not the eighteenth century.'

'There is an agreement between my father and Signor Brzezinski.'

Belle frowns. What does the girl mean?

'What kind of arrangement?'

'Signor Brzezinski is to select my husband,' says the girl, barely audible.

'Why does he get to choose your husband, Pina?'

Pina looks distressed. She clasps her hands, and tears spring into her eyes.

'I shouldn't say.'

Belle thinks. What kind of power could Signor Brzezinski hold over another man?

'It's to do with money, isn't it, Pina?'

The girl nods, her voice barely raised above a whisper.

'My father had to give me as a maid to Signor Brzezinski in payment for his debts to him. It was agreed that when I was seventeen, Signor Brzezinski would arrange my marriage to his own advantage.'

The young girl's voice is shaking with emotion. Belle sits down on the stool in the bathroom, her eyebrow brush still in her hand. The shock of what she has just heard registers slowly. Her husband is no better than a pimp. What other young women has he controlled over the years? She looks at the maid, a thought suddenly occurring to her.

'And how old are you now, Pina?' she asks.

'I was seventeen last week.'

Belle looks into Pina's tearful eyes and she sees herself, the little Polish girl, and the last conversation she had with her dying father. An unpleasant thought occurs to her. What exactly did her father say to her? She dredges back the words.

'It is a good marriage, Ludwika. He is a rich man and can provide well for you and your mother. He has contacts with the Germans. He can get you both out of Warsaw.'

How she begged her father.

'I don't want to go, Tata. I want to stay here with you. Please.'

Her father raised his hand weakly, his eyes filled with tears.

'It is my dying wish, my daughter. You must promise me you will marry this man, and look after your mother.'

'No, Tata, I can't. I don't love him . . .'

'He will save your lives, Ludwika. You must do it.'

She was sobbing, clinging on to her father's hand. He didn't look like himself any more. He was a shadow of his former self. Where was her big strong father, who could knock down any man? She looked across the bed at her mother, but she was so beside herself with grief that she didn't even see her daughter.

'Alexsy,' she was whispering. 'Alexsy, don't leave me . . .'

'Promise me,' her father hissed with his dying breath, and she did it. She looked straight into his eyes and said yes, she would marry Signor Brzezinski. She has never really understood why her father demanded such a thing of her, until now. Suddenly the reason is as clear as day. She was bounty as well. She knows her father had money problems, for after he died it materialised that he had not a penny left to his name. So she was the return on an unpaid debt. She feels sick again at the thought of it. How could her father, and her mother, have done that to her? Their betrayal cuts through her, makes her heart so heavy she feels like crying, and yet she can't, not in front of this poor Sicilian girl.

Now her decision is irrefutable. Today she will cut the ghosts of her parents free. It is too late for her mother anyway. She knows in her heart that she is never coming back. The last time she saw her she was lost, for ever relegated to that place of no return. Signor Brzezinski cannot hurt her now. Belle takes a deep breath and turns back to the mirror, lifts her chin to her reflection.

'You must run away, Pina,' she says to the reflection of the red-eyed girl. 'I will give you money.'

Pina is shaking her head.

'No, I cannot leave you,' she says.

Belle raises her eyebrows and stares at the girl for a moment.

'Well if that is the case, my dear, then we must escape together.'

'But what about my father, and his family? He is indebted to Signor Brzezinski. What will happen to them if I run away?'

Belle spins around on her stool, leans forward and takes the girl's hands in hers.

'You must not worry about them, Pina,' she says harshly. 'Your father has given you up to Signor Brzezinski. You must think of yourself now. You owe your father nothing.'

She feels the expression in the girl's eyes lighten, as if for the first time she has been given a little hope.

'But where will we go?' she asks.

'I don't know,' says Belle, her eyes flashing with excitement. 'All I can tell you is that we will be sailing out across the lagoon and never coming back.'

As she speaks, Belle hears the door of her bedroom banging open. The two women exchange glances. There is no one else in the household who would make such an entrance.

'Louise!'

It is Signor Brzezinski. Not even nine in the morning and he is angry, Belle thinks wearily. How will I avoid being hit? she muses.

'Stay here,' she whispers to Pina, putting her finger to her lips. Today she must placate her husband if it is to be the day of their great escape.

Belle emerges from the bathroom, still not fully made up. Her husband is dressed in one of his smart business suits. His thinning grey hair is slicked back, and his large pale forehead shines like the top of her boiled egg.

'Is something the matter, sir?' she asks politely.

'I have heard reports,' he says.

She raises her eyebrows.

'You mean rumours, sir? You should not trust gossip.'

Signor Brzezinski takes a step towards her and grabs the wrist of her right hand, squeezing tightly. She tries not to react, although he is hurting her.

'I have received an eyewitness account that you were seen on a rooftop in Venice, naked, and with a strange man.'

She laughs with false jollity.

'Oh really, Signor Brzezinski,' she says. 'Why on earth would I do something like that? I would have to be mad!'

He shoves his face into hers. His eyes are black slits.

'Yes, that's what I thought, my dear. But you see, this is a very reliable witness. It was reported to me that not only were you naked on this rooftop, but you were also fornicating in broad daylight with a common sailor.'

She holds his gaze and stares back at him, brazen in her denial.

'I may have misbehaved in the past, sir, but you have

taught me well not to disobey you. I can assure you that I would have to be crazy to attempt to do such a thing and invite your wrath yet again.'

She manages to pull her arm away, and rubs it in an effort to hide the mark.

'What woman does a thing like that?' she says. 'Not even a prostitute.'

'A woman like you, Louise. A foul, sinful creature,' her husband hisses through his teeth. 'If I had known you would be so much trouble . . . If I had known you would be a useless wife, not even able to give me a child, I would have made a different choice.'

He grabs her by the arm again, and pulls her close to him. She can see the perspiration on his forehead, smell his disgusting breath.

'I needn't have married you, for I had your mother anyway.'

His words are worse than a punch to the stomach. Belle wants to double over, but as she writhes away from him, he grabs her other wrist so that he is so close to her, she can see the blood in his eyes.

'You want to know what drove your mother mad? It was me, Louise. She made your father sacrifice you to me. I never wanted *you*.'

'You're a liar,' she whispers.

He drops her arms and steps back, looking pleased with himself.

'What I wanted was quite simple, really. Your father owed

me money. I desired his wife. Conveniently, he was dying. I told him that I would take his wife as mine, in payment for his debt.'

The room begins to spin. She mustn't faint, she has to stay upright.

'Oh, but your parents were so *in love*,' he says nastily. 'They loved each other more than they loved you, Louise, because your father convinced me to marry you instead of your mother.'

He begins to laugh.

'The stupid man! Do you think I would let any woman turn me down? Why do you think I brought her all the way from Warsaw to Venice after your father died? As far as I was concerned, I was getting two for the price of one. Your mother did for me until . . .'

A shadow crosses his face, and for a moment Signor Brzezinski doesn't look too pleased with himself. She sees him collecting himself, his eyes hardening again.

'Until she got sick, and then . . . when I was forced to place her on Poveglia, well then it was your turn, Louise.'

She looks at the dark, damaged soul of her husband, and she knows that what he says is true.

'No!' she says through clenched teeth.

'You are not normal,' he continues, spitting at her in anger. 'You can't give me a child, and you behave like some kind of depraved creature, fucking the whole of Venice right in front of my eyes. In my opinion you are insane, just like your mother, and it is time for you to join her.'

He surges forward and grabs her in a headlock, but Belle's rage is so great that she strains forward and bites his neck. He cries out, stepping back, and she can see her teeth marks and blood springing through the punctured skin.

'Oh, wonderful.' Signor Brzezinski laughs. 'More evidence of your insanity. I think it will be easy enough to obtain an annulment, don't you? Then I can find myself a new, clean bride, and I won't have to put up with a dirty whore any more.'

He pushes her back on to the bed, so that she falls upon it, the tray of her breakfast things scattering on the floor. He slaps her face, and she is kicking back. He is not sending her to that island of terror so that she becomes like her mother, hearing the screams of ghosts from the time of the plague. All those poor people dragged out there to rot. She will not be left to wander along its beach layered with the ash of their burnt bones. She remembers meeting her mother's doctor, a chilling figure, who, despite Signor Brzezinski's assurances that he was a leader in his field, Belle was convinced was some kind of sadist. He performed lobotomies, for God's sake. No, she is not going to Poveglia. She would rather die here on this bed now than let that happen. She doesn't care about her promise to her father any more. She is not going to look after her mother, for her mother never looked after her.

She kicks Signor Brzezinski between the legs, and he doubles over in shock. She jumps up off the bed and makes for the door, but then she remembers Pina, in the bathroom, and hesitates. Her chance is lost. Signor Brzezinski grabs her from behind and spins her across the room. She stumbles, falling and landing backwards on the carpet. He is standing over her, his foot raised above her stomach.

'I am going to crush you, Louise, obliterate your useless womb,' he snarls.

He looks like a demon, Belle thinks. She closes her eyes and waits for pain. In the middle of her fear she feels a second of grief for the darkness that is her husband. How did he become like this?

'Stop!'

She hears Pina screaming. She opens her eyes and sees her maid pulling at Signor Brzezinski's arms. Her husband is so surprised he momentarily calms down and puts his foot back down on the floor. Pina continues to pull at him desperately.

'She's with child!' she screams.

Signor Brzezinski teeters back as if he has been drinking, and looks at Belle lying on the ground in front of him.

'Is this true?'

She is about to say *Of course not*. She can't think why Pina is telling Signor Brzezinski that she is pregnant. She is Barren Brzezinska. And then a thought occurs to her. It is not her, but *him*. He is the Barren Brzezinski. And she remembers that time with Santos after Signor Brzezinski beat her, when they were not so careful. Since then she has not bled. She brings her hand to her stomach protectively. Of course, that was why she was sick, and that was how Pina knew. She looks at Pina in awe. At the girl's flushed cheeks, and the terrified look in her eyes, like a lamb about to be slaughtered. She is so brave to come between Belle and her husband.

'Yes, I am with child,' she whispers.

'Well,' he says darkly, 'I am sure it is not mine.'

'But no one will know . . .' whispers Pina.

So courageous, Belle thinks. This girl is my protector.

Signor Brzezinski looks at Pina and considers her.

'So this is my heir?' he asks the young Sicilian. 'Some sailor's bastard child?'

Belle sits up, pulls the hair away from her face.

'Yes,' she challenges him, and he turns to look at her. *And you will never set eyes on this baby. We are leaving Venice.*

'Your condition has saved you from Poveglia, Louise, for the time being,' he says gruffly. 'I need this child to be mine. Finally you will give me an heir . . . even if it is not my own flesh and blood . . . but you must be punished for this. Severely.'

She sees the cold flint settle in his eyes, and before she can think, he has grabbed Pina by the arm and pushed her up against the wall. The girl screams, and Belle leaps to her feet and runs over to her brute of a husband, clawing at his back. He is too strong for her and knocks her aside. He swings his arm wide and punches Pina in the belly. The girl doubles over in agony.

'You bastard!' Belle screams.

Signor Brzezinski backs away from Pina, who flops on to the floor. Belle rushes over to her and protects the girl within her arms. The child is shaking uncontrollably. Belle has never felt such a killing rage for her husband.

'You leave her alone,' she hisses.

'I can see that there is a fondness between mistress and maid,' he replies, such venom in his voice. 'So, my dear, if I have any reason to believe that you are not performing your duties as a respectable wife with child, it will be Pina who will have to take your punishment.'

He walks over to the two women.

'And I won't just be hitting her either.'

He shoves his hand between Pina's legs, and the girl winces in pain and fright. Belle pushes his hand away.

'I will tie you to a chair, Louise, and make you watch me take this girl's maidenhead. You will be responsible for her ruin.'

Pina is quaking in Belle's arms. She pulls the girl closer, feeling her frantic heartbeat against her chest.

'If you touch a hair on this girl's head, I will kill you,' she hisses at her husband.

He steps back and laughs at her. He is the picture of masculine mirth, hands on his hips as if he doesn't have a care in the world. Her threat is preposterous to him.

'Excuse me, ladies, I must away, for I have important business to attend to.'

As he strides out of the room, Belle has a vision of herself grabbing the candlestick on her dressing table and driving it through the back of his head.

Stay calm, she tells herself. Run away.

She turns to Pina, lifts the sobbing girl's chin.

'Are you all right?'

The maid nods, still unable to speak. Belle pulls her to her feet.

'As soon as he has left the house, we have to go.'

'But where will we go?'

Belle rushes to the wardrobe and pulls out a carpet bag.

'Trust me, Pina. I know someone who will help us.'

'But I can't go with you! My family . . .'

'You have to. Signor Brzezinski will hurt you if you don't. Your family hasn't protected you. You owe them nothing.'

'But what if he catches us?' She hears the terrified tremor in the young girl's voice.

'He won't. I promise.'

Belle has made one more promise to decide another person's fate. Yet she is confident that soon she and Pina will be safe.

We are escaping, Pina, the baby and I.

Santos will save them. How can he not?

$\mathcal{V}$alentina

VALENTINA ENTERS THE DARK ROOM. IT IS SO BLACK INSIDE that when she raises her hand she cannot see it in front of her face. It is cooler in here than the Velvet Underworld, and she can feel her naked skin goosepimpling with the chill and anticipation. She has no idea how large the room is. Or if there is anyone else in here with her yet. She walks blindly forward in her high-heeled boots, afraid she will stumble. There is a sound in the room. A deep bass throb like a heartbeat inside her head. It is as if the room, though dressed like death, is in fact alive around her.

Suddenly there is a click, and a blaze of white light. In the centre of the black room is a huge light box, made out of a table. Just like her one at home but even larger. Beside the box stands Leonardo, naked apart from a Venetian mask with a fantastic black plume in its centre, and a pair of black leather gloves, exactly as she described it to him. She walks towards him and her legs are shaking. Why is she so frightened? This is *her* fantasy. Her secret desire, kept safe inside the Dark Room for no one else to find. She is even anonymous herself, the mask she is wearing concealing her identity as well.

She approaches the light box and stands facing it. She recalls the erotic negative she was looking at this morning. This is the beginning of her fantasy. To re-enact the image that Theo gave her.

Leonardo silently offers her his hand, and she climbs on to the light box. She feels the heat of the bulbs beneath the glass, and the blinding light makes her look up, yet she can see nothing and no one else in the Dark Room. She cannot even see the way out. She takes a deep breath, and lies down on her front. She imagines how she might look, her body emblazoned by the floodlights. She is completely naked apart from her boots and the mask on her face. She parts her legs and bends her knees upwards, kicking her high heels out to the side provocatively. She lifts her bottom and exposes herself, feeling a delicious thread of seductivity coursing through her body. She twists herself around and places her hands between her buttocks, then spreads her fingers and pushes her index finger into herself, lifting her backside so that she is showing herself off. She feels wanton, and bold. Leonardo stands behind her, watching, his mask concealing his reaction. She looks at him, and opens her mouth, trails her tongue along her bottom lip.

He comes right up to the edge of the table, so that the light illuminates him from below and gives his masked face an otherworldly aspect.

'What is your desire, Valentina?' He speaks in his dominant's voice.

'To please you,' she whispers, pushing her finger further inside herself, and raising her bottom so that she is offering herself to him.

He lifts her hand from her bottom and brings it around and above her head. On either corner of the light box table are leather restraints. He slips her hands through the restraints and buckles them tightly. She feels her nipples hardening with anticipation, her breath shallow. He trails his leather finger down her spine, all the way to the curve of her bottom, and down. She gasps as the cold leather touches her inside. He removes his hand quickly and she is throbbing now, desperate to feel his touch once again. He pulls her booted legs further apart, bringing them down so that she is lying spread-eagled on the light box. He belts her ankles to either corner of the table.

He strokes her legs with his gloved hands, massaging her flesh with the leather, going higher and higher up her thighs. Now his hands are above her backside, pawing and massaging her cheeks. The sensation of the supple leather against her pliant skin becomes more and more intense. Suddenly he stops massaging her. One hand is pushing down on the small of her back, and the next thing she feels his gloved palm smacking her buttock. She gasps from shock, fear, excitement. He spanks her again. The leather stings against her skin, sending her mind into a delirium. He spanks her one more time, and this time it resonates deep within her, vibrating through her body, stimulating her deep inside.

Oh yes, this is just like her fantasy, but so much more.

Four. Five. Six smacks and Leonardo stops. She is quivering inside, her passion screaming at him to touch her again. He walks around the table to the top of the light box. She looks at him from beneath her mask. They are two players in her erotic drama. Exposed, and yet protected. She watches him pull each glove off, slowly, finger by finger, and then he removes the plume from the top of his mask with a flourish, dragging the fine black feather between his fingers. She licks her lips, holding her breath with anticipation. In silence he walks around behind her again, trailing the tip of the feather all the way down her back, drawing circles on her skin so that she is imagining them as tattoos of her yearning, imprinted upon her. The signs of what she craves.

Leonardo's feather has now reached her backside, and he is tipping it under her, teasing her clitoris with it. It is light, caressing her delicately after the severity of the leather smacked against her skin. The contrast warms her blood, makes her soften further inside. He circles the feather, and at the same time she feels his fingers pushing inside her. Not one, but two fingers, up, up deep inside, making her quiver and tremble with want.

'Oh please,' she stutters, breaking her silence.

Leonardo pulls his fingers out, and gradually slows the action of the feather upon her clitoris.

'I believe you are ready now, Valentina,' he says. 'For your surprise.'

She tenses slightly. What surprise?

'Isn't this what you really want?'

As he speaks, she hears a match strike, and sees it flare in the expanse of the dark room. There is someone else in here. She sees the tiny flame light a candle, and a pair of hands lift it. The throbbing music in the room builds until it is consuming her body with anticipation. The beat is no longer outside of her but inside, making her heart race. As the candle approaches her, she sees a masked face above it, the light from the flame colouring it gold, in all this black and white. There is another man in the Dark Room with her and Leonardo, watching her on the light box, illuminated and submitting. She is their object, to be looked at, admired and adored.

Yet she cannot control the fear that courses through her body. She is completely in their power, tied to the light box. She could tell Leonardo to stop – he promised her that she could call a halt to her Dark Room experience at any stage – yet maybe he will ignore her and carry on. There is always the chance that he is not who she thinks he is. Maybe he is as dark as the room itself, and cannot be trusted. Maybe something terrible is about to happen to her.

As if he reads her thoughts, Leonardo strokes her hair gently, as though he is soothing a spooked horse.

'Don't be frightened, Valentina. I *know* this is what you want.'

The figure with the candle approaches her. She squeezes her eyes tight, her mouth suddenly dry. What will Leonardo and his companion do to her? He says that he knows this is what she wants, but she is not sure herself what she wants now. Does Leonardo believe she wants to be really hurt? How much more submission, pain would she be able to take? What is her limit?

As she lies there, conflicted, not knowing whether to bail out of the Dark Room, she feels herself pulsing deep down inside. Her fear is turning her on. She squeezes her eyes tighter still and starts as she feels a hand upon hers. It is warm and gentle. It is not a cruel hand. It is stroking each one of her fingers, and unbuckling the restraint around her wrist. She opens her eyes, and looks up at the second masked man. She cannot see Leonardo in the Dark Room any more. It is just her and the stranger. He moves around her, slowly unfastening the restraints on the light box. There is something in the way he moves that looks familiar to her. She strains to see him more clearly, but she is blinded by the glare from the light box.

Finally she is freed. She brings her legs together and kneels up. The masked stranger stands in front of her. She watches him, unsure what to do. He cocks his head to one side, as if asking a silent question, and in that exaggerated movement she suddenly sees who he is.

'Theo!' she gasps, crawling towards him across the light box. 'Theo, is that you?'

The man doesn't answer. She reaches for his mask to pull it back, but he catches her hands in his, holding her back. Then he leans down and kisses her. Oh yes, it is her lover, no doubt. She recognises his full kiss, the tenderness of it. Oh, how she has missed his touch. She pulls her mouth away from his.

'Theo,' she says. 'What's happening? Why are you here?'

Instead of responding, Theo raises his finger to his lips.

'Shush,' is all he says.

She feels a spark of anger. Why is he playing this game with her?

'Theo, answer me,' she demands.

But he shakes his head, and again puts his finger to his lips, and it occurs to her that this is what she does to him every time they make love. She won't let him speak. For the first time she realises how frustrating that must be for him, not to be able to share his thoughts and emotions with her.

The light box flickers as Theo reaches over and lifts her off it, then turns it off altogether. How safe she feels in her lover's arms, although it is now pitch black inside the Dark Room. She knows not where he has brought her inside the room, but when he puts her down it is on something soft, a bed of some sort, covered in velvet and silk. The throbbing bass is ebbing away, and all she can hear now are the sultry tones of ambient music from the East. The room fills with the fragrance of frankincense, adding to the mood. Her body is still open from Leonardo's games with her. Now that her fear is gone, she feels as languid as a cat, and liquid as syrup. She doesn't care any more why Theo is here, or what he thinks of her and Leonardo. He must be complicit, if he is in the Dark Room and part of her fantasy.

She lies back upon the bed, pulling Theo down on top of her. He takes their masks off, yet she can see nothing. And because they are blind and mute, the sensual music filling their ears, all sensation is focused on the interaction of their bodies. How right and true he smells within her arms. She buries her head in his neck and inhales. She realises how much she has missed him. They kiss deeper and deeper and she tastes his sweetness. No man could taste as good. She wraps her arms around him tight, never wanting to let him go, as he pushes inside her. She groans in satisfaction. Oh, how she was made for this man. He fills her so completely. He is perfection. They rock slowly together at first, and then gradually he builds up speed. All of Leonardo's teasing has made her sensitised to her lover's touch. She feels each push, the tip of him penetrating right into the very heart of her. Leonardo is right, this is her ultimate fantasy. To have her lover with her, here in the Dark Room. To show him her love. Although he cannot see or hear it, surely he can feel it. He brings her with him, higher and higher. His silence turns her on all the more, and she is spiralling in his passion, at one with him as they climax together.

They lie entwined in each other's arms. She is so tired, more tired than she has been in her whole life. She lies with her head upon his chest, comforted by the beat of his heart lulling her to sleep.

When she wakes, she is still in the Dark Room, but now it is full of candles, their flames flickering, illuminating the dimensions of the room. She can see it is a vast space. All black. Yet soft. Brushed velvet on the walls, thick-pile black carpet, black silk and velvet cushions. The light box has disappeared. She looks around for Theo, but he is gone. She feels a tear inside her heart.

'Theo!' she calls out in distress.

The door opens, yet it is not Theo who enters, but Leonardo. He is without his mask now, and wearing a silk dressing gown tied loosely around his waist. He is carrying a large bowl in his arms. Steam rises from it, and she can smell ylang ylang and jasmine as he approaches her. It is such a familiar scent.

'Where's Theo?' she asks, sitting up.

He sets the bowl of water at her feet, and produces a stack of miniature towels from beside her black bed.

'Relax, Valentina,' he replies enigmatically, smoothing back her hair tenderly. He dips one of the towels in the scented water, wrings it out.

'Close your eyes.'

Instinctively she obeys him. He places the scented towel on her face, and the effect is instantaneous. Immediately it soothes her. She realises that her body is sore, turned inside out by her

369

adventures in the Dark Room. She hears him dip another towel in the water, and bring it out. A steaming towel is placed upon her chest, and another upon her stomach. She lies back, swooning as if he has drugged her. It is only when he places a scented towel between her thighs and another one upon her pelvis that she remembers. He knows. Theo must have told him.

'Oh,' she murmurs, so softly it is almost inaudible.

As Leonardo bathes her with the fragrant towels, she remembers her lover doing the very same thing to her the night she miscarried. He carried her naked blood-streaked body out of the bathroom, into their bedroom, and placed her on the bed. And as she lay there, motionless, in shock, he bathed her with towels soaked in steaming water scented with ylang ylang and jasmine oils. He tried his best to heal her, and most astonishing of all, she let him. For the first twenty-four hours after the miscarriage, she surrendered herself to Theo. She let him care for her. All this time she had thought it was his sexy, mysterious persona that had attracted her to him, made her not want to let him go, yet it was his tenderness that made all the difference. As he bathed her, and afterwards when he held her in his arms and she said not a word, his compassion healed her. It was when Theo comforted her in a way her parents never had that Valentina fell for him. She has been trying to deny her feelings ever since, pushing Theo away bit by bit.

With shame she remembers how she shut him out when

she went to the hospital the next day. Theo had insisted she should go to check everything was all right. He had booked her an appointment, and said he would go with her. Her natural instinct to be independent took over, however, and while he was out lecturing, she rang the hospital and changed her appointment. By the time he came home to pick her up and drive her there, she had already been. Groggy and tactless on painkillers, she told him that there was no need for him to feel sorry for her any more. She had been all cleaned out and would be ready and up for action again in a few days.

The look on his face comes back to haunt her. He looked so horrified by her words, so devastated and hurt, but she turned away from him, locking herself in her studio and sleeping on her couch for the next couple of nights. How could she have been so cruel? Why didn't he leave her then, when she showed him just what sort of a bitch she really is?

Because he loves you, Valentina.

Can he really? Is this why all this is happening with the book of erotic photographs, Leonardo and the Dark Room? What is Theo trying to tell her? She wishes so much that he was still here so that she could interrogate him, but her lover has disappeared again, and now she is just going to have to trust him.

Belle

SHE SCOURS THE QUAYS, WHILE PINA STANDS UNDERNEATH a stone archway, gripping their big carpet bag and shivering. It can't be. She is sure this is where Santos had his schooner moored, and yet she can't see it. She paces up and down alongside the choppy lagoon, uncomprehending. She cannot believe he would leave without saying goodbye. So where is he?

It begins to rain. A raw wind sweeps in across the lagoon, and in a matter of minutes the two women are soaked.

'Come on.' She takes Pina by the elbow, and they scurry along the cobbled Fondamenta Nuove. Maybe he has moved his boat, she thinks desperately. Maybe he is waiting for her at the apartment as usual.

The water of the lagoon is getting wilder by the minute. It splashes over the stone steps into their pathway, wetting their feet. They cross a bridge, and the wind is so fierce that Belle has to push against it with all her strength. She can hear Pina breathless beside her. They turn down Fondamenta dei Mendicanti by the side of the hospital. They are out of the wind now, but the rain continues to lash into them. They run for shelter. Belle leads Pina across the campo and down the tiny alleyway to her apartment. She takes the key from her purse and unlocks the front door, and the two of them stumble into the dark stairwell, drenched and shivering. She leads Pina up the staircase, and unlocks the door to her apartment.

It is how she left it yesterday. The bed is still unmade. She looks at the swirl of sheets and imagines the imprint of her and Santos within them. There are two empty wine glasses by the bed, the dregs of a bottle of Amarone beside them. She goes over to the dressing table and takes one of the white roses out of the vase, bringing it up to her face and inhaling. Only yesterday her lover was scattering rose petals on her naked body.

'Where are we?'

Pina is still standing shyly in the doorway. The rain drips off her face, and her meagre clothes are wet through.

'We are in my hideaway, Pina,' Belle tells her, walking to the window and looking out over the canal, hoping to see a boat approaching, her lover within it. But the canal is empty.

'You own this?'

'I rent it,' says Belle, turning around. 'Here I am no longer Signora Louise Brzezinska. Here I am Belle.'

Pina's mouth drops open.

'Belle . . . the courtesan?'

'Who else, my dear?' She opens her wardrobe wide and shows Pina her costumes.

Pina looks at her mistress in awe.

'You are Belle of Venice. Really?'

'Yes, one and the same.'

Pina drops down on the bed, all the time staring at Belle as if she is looking at a mythical creature.

Belle smiles.

'Is it really that hard to believe, my dear?'

The girl shakes her head, seemingly coming to her senses.

'No, no . . .' She pauses, colour returning to her cheeks, her eyes lighting up. 'I think it is wonderful!' She brings a hand to her mouth to stifle a giggle. 'Oh, if Signor Brzezinski knew!'

'It is my way of getting my life back,' Belle says, and her maid nods, as if she understands.

'I think we should get out of our wet clothes, don't you?' Belle says briskly, suddenly aware that they are both drenched to the skin. 'Pick anything you want.'

Pina approaches the wardrobe hesitantly. She tentatively fingers the hem of one of Belle's silk dresses.

'I couldn't . . .'

'You have to, Pina. You will catch cold if you don't get changed.'

The maid reluctantly sifts through the clothes. She pauses when she sees her old uniform's transformation.

'You can try it on if you want,' Belle offers, but the girl shakes her head, her cheeks blushing scarlet.

'I don't know what to put on,' she says. 'All of it is too good for me.'

'Nonsense,' says Belle. 'Besides, you are just wearing something until your own clothes dry.'

'You choose for me.'

Belle dives into the wardrobe. She knows already what she is going to wear. She is anxious to get changed and get out again. Her eyes light upon her black ballerina dress. She pulls it out and hands it to Pina.

'I think you will look quite adorable in this,' she says to the girl.

Pina looks at the dress in admiration.

'It's so fine,' she says, taking it with shaking hands.

Belle watches Pina peeling off her wet clothes as demurely as possible. She herself has tugged off everything without a care for modesty. They are both women, after all. When Pina turns around to take the dress, Belle can't help admiring her body.

'Why, Pina, you really are beautiful,' she tells her. Her Sicilian maid has an hourglass figure, something she never really noticed before. She has lusciously smooth brown skin, ample breasts with dark nipples, and jet black curls of pubic hair shaped in a perfect heart between her legs.

Pina looks at the floor with embarrassment, hastily pulling on the skimpy ballerina dress. It fits her perfectly, and is so short that her shapely legs are on display as well. What a shame, Belle thinks, that this girl is wasted as a servant. She is so exquisite, she should be a dancer or an actress. To think her wretched father sold her to Signor Brzezinski. Just like her own father. The thought angers her. Men can be foul.

As she is thinking this, Pina has been standing in front of the mirror, looking at herself in Belle's costume. Belle sees her own naked reflection behind her, and she catches Pina's eye in the mirror. There is something in the way Pina looks at her. It reminds her of someone but she can't think who. It is a look of fondness, protective even. Why would her maid have such feelings for her?

'I think *you* are beautiful, madam,' Pina whispers.

Belle considers Pina's gentle offering. How sweet a love could be between two women. If only she felt the same, and yet she is crazy to find Santos. She needs her man, and only he will do.

'Thank you, Pina,' she says, reaching past her into the wardrobe and pulling out her sailor boy's costume.

The women's bare legs brush each other, and Belle can feel Pina's reaction to her touch. Spontaneously she feels moved, and she turns, kissing the girl on the lips. She closes her eyes, and it is as if she is giving herself the kiss of life, bringing back the little princess she once was, when she lived in Warsaw, before her marriage and the rape of innocence.

'Sweet Pina,' she says, pulling away. 'I will look after you. There is no need to worry, believe me.'

Pina looks at her with serious brown eyes.

'I believe you,' she says.

Belle pulls on her white sailor's trousers. She has to find Santos. They can't go back to Signor Brzezinski. She wishes they could stay here, but it would only be a matter of a few days before her husband found them. They need to get out of Venice for ever.

'I am going to find my friend,' Belle tells Pina. 'I will be as quick as I can. Wait here for me.'

The taverna is empty, apart from a couple of sailors up at the wooden counter. Belle swaggers over to them, trying to remember to keep her sailor's cap low over her forehead. She was hasty in her preparations and is not sure whether she took all her make-up off.

'Hello there, young man,' the innkeeper addresses her. 'What can I get you?'

Belle orders brandy and downs it immediately. It settles her still queasy stomach, and warms her after her run through the rain.

'I'm looking for Santos Devine,' she says. 'Have you any idea of his whereabouts?'

'I have no idea where he is now. All I can tell you is that he is no longer in Venice.'

No! She wants to cry out, shake this innkeeper by the shoulders, beg him to tell her that it's not true, but she has to be a man in her sailor disguise. She has to hide her emotions. Even so, she feels as if she has taken a punch to the stomach, and she almost keels over in shock.

'Hey, what's wrong with you?' one of the sailors asks.

She grips the wooden counter for support, draws herself up again.

'Are you sure he's gone?' she asks the innkeeper.

'Oh aye, I saw it with my own eyes. He was told to leave by the authorities. It seems that he stole something off some important businessman here in Venice.'

'A Pole,' one of the sailors adds. Belle doesn't need him to tell her his name. So Signor Brzezinski knows who her lover is and has had him banished from Venice. She feels a lick of fury inside her belly.

'I think they knew that there was no truth to the accusations, otherwise they would have arrested him, but in any case they told him to get out of Venice. For a while at least.'

These are the words Belle needs to hear. *For a while at least*. Oh, she knows her love won't abandon her for ever. He will come back. And what news she will have to tell him. She is going to have their child.

Yet what is she to do in the meantime? The idea of going back to Signor Brzezinski's house makes her feel sick, but with Pina in tow, it appears it is their only option.

When she returns to the apartment, Pina is asleep on top of the bed. She is still wearing Belle's black ballerina dress and looks like a black swan, her arm flung over her head and her skirt ruffled up on the white sheets.

Poor child, Belle thinks. Why did I involve her in all of this?

And then she remembers that it wasn't her who involved Pina. It was Signor Brzezinski. In all their years of marriage, she has never been able to call him by his Christian name.

She walks over to the French windows and looks down at the green canal. So Santos is gone. The fact of it is beginning to sink in. She crosses her arms and hugs herself, as if she wishes to keep warm their love inside her. Only yesterday, this view from her room seemed full of the poetry of love. The unblemished blue sky was a symbol of the perfection of their coupling, the faded grandeur of the Venetian palazzos across the canal the deep heritage of their love, the constant lap of the canal the rhythm of their union, again and again and again. Just one day later and everything she sees is changed. The sky is banked with dark, unloving clouds, weeping openly, the palazzos are not grand but falling down, forgotten, abandoned, and the canal hides its depths from her, reflecting back her yearning, slapping her in the face as if she has been dunked in icy water.

She closes her eyes, tries to summon a memory of him, yet already he is vanishing from her grasp. She can just see him, a dot on the horizon, riding the waves of the Adriatic Sea in his ghost boat, his statuesque first mate by his side like a macabre keeper. Could he not have waited for her? Maybe he knew her story all along and thought she would not leave Venice because of her mother's residence on Poveglia. But her father put her mother before her, and now it is her turn. She would choose Santos over her mother, if she had the chance. She brings her hand to her belly. And what about this little life inside her? Would she choose Santos over her child? A child with his thick black hair and blue jewel eyes.

He is gone. She steps back from the window and sinks to the floor. Now she can cry, her hope trailing out of the window like a banner of loss. She tries to cling on to the innkeeper's words. *For a while at least.* He has to return. He told her he would, didn't he? And yet there is something deep down inside her that tells her otherwise. She begins to sob, for it is too much to consider the torment of her pregnancy without Santos. Signor Brzezinski will steal his child. Claim the baby for his own. What kind of father will he be? Will he beat Santos's child like he beats her, like he beat Pina this morning? Why of course he will.

If only she were a man. The frustration of it makes her clench her fists, grit her teeth through her salty tears. She would kill Signor Brzezinski if she could.

As she feels herself disintegrating, falling apart on the floor of her apartment, a tiny hand is placed gently upon her shoulder.

She turns, and through her veil of tears she sees Pina, bending down and taking her by the hands. She leads her to the bed and makes her sit upon it. Wordlessly her young maid tenderly wipes away her tears, kissing her again and again on the mouth. Belle shakes her head. Her misery is so great, no one can make her feel better, no one but Santos. And yet Pina persists. She unbuttons Belle's damp admiral's coat, and takes off her sailor's cap. She pushes her fingertips through her mistress's wet hair, and blows it with her breath. In the ballerina dress she looks even more of an angel, as she undoes Belle's wet clothes and peels them off her. She makes Belle lie down on the bed, and she strokes her to warm her chilled skin. She strokes her face so that Belle is lulled and closes her eyes. She strokes her neck and her shoulders; each one of Belle's fingers she brings to her mouth and kisses. She strokes Belle's belly, and its hidden treasure, her breasts, which are beginning to blossom in early pregnancy, teasing each nipple gently between her fingers. She strokes Belle's legs and feet, working her fingers through the toes. And she strokes Belle between her legs, so very delicately, her gentle fingertips gradually replaced by her soft tongue.

Belle sighs. It is a sigh of ages; so old it began in her sixteenth year, and ends in this moment of comfort with Pina. She lets this young woman do this to her, because these physical sensations are the only things that keep her alive. She is not able to feel it, yet she is aware of Pina's devotion, and she lets her layer her with her love, as if it is a soothing balm to her heart.

'Louis Blackbird! Louis Blackbird!'

Belle wakes.

'Louis Blackbird!'

Is she dreaming? She is held within the embrace of the sleeping Pina. She carefully lifts the girl's arms off her chest.

She can hear the slap of water against the side of a boat, right outside her window. And a voice.

'Louis Blackbird!'

It is not a man's voice, and yet she knows its owner brings a missive from Santos. She gets out of bed, grabs her blue silk dressing gown and goes out on to her balcony.

It has stopped raining now, although it is still overcast and the canal is full of grey shadows. Below her is a gondola, with a woman sitting in it. She is wearing a long scarlet dress and is barefoot, yet she wraps an elaborate black cape around her, and wears a plain white Venetian mask upon her face. Despite her disguise, Belle recognises her hair, long tresses of auburn curls that cascade down her shoulders. It is Lara, the mask-maker.

'Lara,' she calls down. 'Lara, please, where has Santos gone?'

But Lara raises her masked face to her and shakes her head as if to silence her. She stands up in the gondola, and Belle can see that her hands are cupped around something. When she opens them, a blackbird emerges from her hands, flying up into the air above the canal. Belle can see something attached to the bird's legs. Her heart fills with panic. Blackbirds are wild. How can she get it to come to her? And yet it is as if the blackbird senses her desperation, for it flies right towards her and lands on the railing of the balcony, blinking its knowing eyes at her.

Belle reaches out tentatively with the palm of her hand,

and the bird struts on to it. She can see clearly now that there is a little velvet pouch tied to one of its legs. With shaking fingers she unties it, and takes it into her free hand. Then she raises her palm to the sky and lets the bird fly free. By the time she looks back down at the canal, there is no sign of Lara or her gondola. Did she imagine it? Yet she has the tiny pouch between her fingers. She goes back inside her apartment, and unties it.

Inside is a tiny gold ring. Not a ring for her finger. Oh no, this is Santos's gold earring. To see it between her fingers, to remember the last time she touched it, as she cradled his face in her hands when he came inside her, is almost too much to bear. She holds her breath. It is a miracle to have this gift.

There is something else in the pouch. A tiny scrap of paper. She pulls it out and marvels at her lover's miniature writing. She realises she has never seen anything he has written before. She reads the minuscule script. She reads it again; and again. She cannot believe what he is telling her to do.

Valentina

THE ENVELOPE WAS IN HER POSTBOX, ALTHOUGH IT IS NOT stamped or postmarked. She recognises the handwriting instantly. She rips it open, not even waiting until she goes back up to the flat. A train ticket falls out into her hands. It is a first-class ticket from Milano Centrale to Venezia Santa Lucia. It is dated for today, and the departure time is in two hours. Has Theo lost his mind? What is he playing at, putting a train ticket in her postbox with no word of explanation? She could be on a shoot today, or busy with something else. He has given her only a couple of hours to get ready, and get to the train station in time.

After last night, in the Dark Room, she thought he would be at home when she got back. She was ready then to confess her feelings for him. To tell him that she saw now the depth of his love for her. What he was willing to do for her. She was going to say sorry. But he never came back, and as the hours ticked by, her remorse turned to anger. She spent a sleepless night tossing and turning, and now she is tired and emotional. He is manipulating her, that's what he is doing. And this train ticket is just another piece of evidence to prove it. Well, she is not going. That will show him.

She rides up to her floor in the lift, chewing her lip, indecision beginning to flood her. But what will happen if she does go? As the lift jolts to a stop and she pulls back the bars, a thought occurs to her. He is playing a game with her. Like the album of erotic negatives from the past. Like before they were living together, when they used to meet in secret locations as if they were anonymous lovers. How she enjoyed that. Maybe all Theo wants is for her to have some fun.

Okay, she thinks grudgingly as she goes back into her apartment. She'll go. It's just lucky she's not working today.

Her two sides are in conflict – her soft self, her heart; and her protective self, her reason – and because of this, she selects one of her great-grandmother's more ambiguous costumes to wear. It is the tiny pinstriped suit and trilby hat, with a delicate silk camisole and feminine French knickers underneath. She decides against flat brogues, and goes for a pair of high-heeled lace-up shoes, to give her a little extra height. She feels more confident now, like an androgynous gangster.

She picks up the black album that Theo gave her, and flicks through it. She has now developed all the negatives. The last four prints were the most beautiful. There is the one she had already viewed as a negative that inspired her fantasy of wearing the mask and showing herself off. There is a close-up of a naked breast sprayed with drops of water, and another of the stomach of the model from just below her breasts to just above her pubic bone, scattered with what look like white rose petals. The last one is the most seductive. The print is of a young woman sitting with her back to some kind of wall. She is naked, apart from a white Venetian mask on her face, obscuring her identity. She has what seems to be a short black bob, as was the style of the era. So it is the same woman from the light box picture, as Valentina thinks of it. Her knees are bent and her legs are apart in a comely V. She is leaning forward, and has thrust one arm through her open legs, her hand clenched into a fist, so that she is concealing her private parts. Although it is impossible to make out her expression behind her mask, Valentina can see that her lips are parted and her body language is a fiery flirtation. *Come and get me if you dare.* She just loves it.

She slips the album into her black briefcase. She is bringing it with her. She wants to know where Theo got these negatives, and if he knows who the woman is. More than anything, she wants to know why he gave them to her. It feels as if these pictures set the whole ball rolling, pulling her into a deeply erotic world culminating in Leonardo's club and the Dark Room.

She is just on her way out of the door when she hears her phone beeping inside her jacket pocket. She pulls it out.

Bring the Metsu painting with you.

Just one line. No *How are you? Are you all right?* or *Love you*. Not even a smiley face. She is furious and texts back instantly.

Where are you? What's going on?

But Theo doesn't reply. What a frustrating man. On top of everything, he now wants her to walk out of the flat with a priceless painting under her arm, if it really is an original as Gaby claimed. She is sure Garelli or one of his cronies has been watching the apartment the last couple of days. Moreover, there is also the blond man who accosted her at Marco's party. She hasn't seen him or his Smart car since Tuesday night, but instinct tells her she hasn't seen the last of him. There is something about him that frightens her.

She glances at her watch. She has very little time to get to the station. What should she do? She rushes back into the study and considers the painting still hanging on the wall. It is quite small, she supposes. She hasn't time to debate the wisdom of bringing it; she doesn't want to miss her train. She grabs the picture off the wall and hunts around for something to put it in. There is no time to pack it properly. She sees her great-grandmother's lace scarf abandoned on the chair, and she picks it up and wraps it around the picture. Not great, but better than nothing. She shoves the lace-bound painting in her black briefcase and runs out the door.

As Valentina weaves her way through the crowds in Stazione Centrale, feeling diminutive in the classical sweep of the grand hall, she can't help thinking she is being followed. She spins around and sees him straight away. Garelli, at a newsstand, trying to look engrossed in a magazine. Really, he is a useless detective, she thinks. Even so, his presence worries her. She could be walking around with a stolen painting in her brief-case. If he catches her, arrests her, she will look very guilty indeed. Moreover, she doesn't want him trailing her all the way to Venice and finding Theo. In fact Theo could be right here as well, in the train station, running for the same train. She looks around, but the station is thronging with crowds and she can't see him anywhere.

She glances at the clock. She has about three minutes before the train leaves. She has to get rid of Garelli. She walks away from the platforms and back out into the main hall of the station. Out of the corner of her eye she can see Garelli following her. She goes down the walkway to the lower floor, and makes towards the metro, before darting into the bookshop. He has probably seen her go inside, but if she is quick she can trick him. She runs through the bookshop and up the stairs inside the shop, to come back outside to the main hall of the station again. Just one minute now before her train leaves. She runs through the crowds to Platform 13. She sees the guard about to blow his whistle and she waves at him. Oh, the value of being a pretty woman in Italy! The guard opens the door of the train for her just in time.

'*Grazie!*' She blows him a kiss, making sure to give him a flash of her camisole.

'*Prego, signorina!*'

She looks triumphantly out of the window of the train to see Garelli running down the platform, too late to get on.

He knows she is on this train, but he doesn't know where she is getting off. It could be Brescia, Verona or Padova, rather than Venice. At least she has bought some time. She tries to push from her mind the worry that her lover has done something really wrong. Is she going to lose him anyway into the arms of the law, and for a long, long time? She tries not to think past today, as she checks her train ticket and walks down the corridor hunting for her compartment.

Valentina takes off her trilby hat and puts it in the luggage rack above her. Since its contents are so precious, rather than putting her briefcase up there, she tucks it in between herself and the window of the train. She is sitting in a compartment all on her own. She waits, expectantly. Any minute now, she thinks, Theo is going to enter the compartment. Yet as the train speeds away from Milan and the miles lengthen, it becomes apparent that Theo is not on the train with her. What will happen when she gets to Venice; where should she go? He will be at the station to meet her, she reassures herself. And if not, she'll call him.

She leans back and takes out the novel she is currently reading, *Jezebel* by Irène Némirovsky. She can't help comparing the main character with her own mother. The beautiful, irresistible temptress Gladys Eysenach is a woman whose vanity comes before her own child. A woman who is terrified of looking old, and will even commit murder to conceal her age. No, even her mother isn't *that* bad. Despite Némirovsky's lyrical prose, as soon as Valentina has read a few lines, her eyelids begin to drop. Last night she didn't sleep at all, and she is exhausted from the drama of the Dark Room. She still doesn't quite understand why Theo was part of it. How could he be happy about Leonardo touching her? Her relationship with Leonardo is how she thought her and Theo's should have been: platonic, yet sexual. Are they friends who fuck? No, the dynamic is different. Leonardo is more like her teacher, a guide of sorts. She knows that most people would judge her for sleeping with another man, yet Theo is obviously different. When he first moved in, he said that they did not have to be monogamous. She agreed, yet she asked him never to tell her about other women he might be with. It is best to focus on what we have together, she thinks as she nods off, rather than all of the circumstances around us. Her last thought as she drifts off to sleep is of Theo's lips, soft, plush, opening up her heart in the Dark Room.

She is kissing him. She can taste him. She feels his hands upon her shoulders, the brush of his stubble against her cheek. She opens her eyes, and Theo is right there in front of her.

'Oh, Theo!' she cries. 'You're here!'

He smiles, and his eyes crease.

'Yes, I'm here,' he says, and she can see that he is looking a little tense, on edge. 'You brought the painting?'

'Yes, but why . . . I mean . . . what's going on?'

'Keep it safe, will you?' he asks. 'Until we get to Venice.'

'Okay.' She pulls him towards her. 'Why are you doing all of this? The old photos . . . the club . . . the Dark Room?'

He looks at her questioningly.

'Haven't you worked it out yet, Valentina?'

'But . . .'

He silences her with a kiss.

'Time for words later,' he whispers. 'There is something I've always wanted to do on a train.'

She can't help it. She is grinning at him. Oh, it is so good to see him, to feel him again.

'Really, Signor Steen? And what would that be?'

He sits down next to her on the seat, and leans over, pushing her jacket off her shoulders so that it slips off to reveal her silk camisole.

'Do you know what I want?' He puts his hands on either side of her face, and forces her to look at him. She can see his pupils dilated to black, his chiselled cheeks and strong chin. 'I want you, Valentina.'

Her breath quickens. Is Theo serious? Does he actually want to make love on this train? What if someone comes into the compartment or sees them?

Theo unbuttons his shirt and drops it on to the floor. He takes her limp hand and pushes it through his chest hair. Her hand cups around his heart. She feels its frantic beat, and she looks into his eyes. She wants this too, she realises. She wants this moment of pure primal need with her lover, this spontaneity of passion that keeps love alive, just like when they first met.

'I want you too, Theo,' she whispers.

He stands up and undoes his jeans, pulls them down. He is wearing no underwear. His penis is erect, so beautiful, her darling Theo. She reaches out to touch it.

'I am all yours, Valentina.'

She looks at him, a question forming in her head.

Am I really? But where do you go?

'You are my all,' he says, taking her hands in his and pulling her up to face him.

It is as if she is in a trance. She undoes her trousers and slides them off her body. Now she is only in her silk underwear. She stands up to face her man, and he pulls down the straps of her camisole, stroking her breasts and erect nipples as it slithers off her over her bottom and legs. He puts his hands either side of her hips and pulls down her French knickers. As she steps out of them, she feels his hand stroking between her legs.

'Oh yes, you want me, don't you, Valentina?' he says, and she looks into his blue eyes, hypnotised.

'Turn around,' he tells her.

Valentina turns to face the window of the compartment. The train is speeding through the Italian landscape, and she can feel it rocking beneath her feet.

'Lean forward and put your hands on the window.' She does as he tells her, and she can feel him spreading her legs. He is stroking her, widening her with his fingers, preparing her. The next moment he pushes up into her. He is so big that she feels as if he has reached her navel. She squeezes his penis tight as the train rocks beneath them, pushing them towards and away from each other.

'I am going to fuck you now, Valentina, like you want me to.'

He is breaking their golden rule. Talking during sex. And yet his dirty words turn her on. She feels herself clenching him tight, sending vibrations through her body.

He withdraws slowly, so that she is almost bereft with need, and then suddenly slams into her. She gasps, pressing her hands against the window. A thought comes into her head: what if they get to a station or go through a town? People will see them. But she doesn't care. She wants Theo to bring her so outside herself that she is a screaming dervish, all her wild elements dancing gleefully inside this train compartment, celebrating her abandon. She pushes her bottom up against him, and he slams into her again, gradually building up speed. He is touching her so deeply, right down inside the heart of her sex. She clenches her teeth, pulling her dark self outside of her and looking it full in the face.

'Fuck me!' she hisses urgently. 'Fuck me!'

The train picks up speed and so do they. It is as if they are all part of the same mechanism, rocking, fucking, moving forwards. She is gloriously close to release, and as she comes, she feels her palpations having an effect on her lover's cock as he climaxes inside her. Her hands slip off the window of the compartment and she loses her balance. They collapse on the floor, still joined together. He lies on top of her, and despite his size, she is comfortable. She closes her eyes, feeling as if she is liquid, so light now that the dark part of her has gone. She sinks into the floor of the compartment, drips down underneath the train and showers the rails with her essence. It litters the tracks like pearls among the gravel.

They lie like this for a few moments, Theo kissing the back of her neck. She shifts under his weight, and she feels him lifting himself off her, pulling her up and back into his arms, cradling her naked in the first-class compartment.

'*Mio Dio*, I can't believe we just did that,' she whispers.

Theo stands up, pulling her with him.

'We'd better get dressed.' He winks at her. 'Better not push our luck.'

He looks himself again, Valentina thinks. And she realises that he hasn't seemed quite so happy since before the time of the miscarriage.

'Theo?' she says, pulling on her trousers over her silk underwear. 'What is going on with this painting?' She taps the black briefcase. 'Is it stolen?'

He sits down next to her, chews his lip.

'That's a difficult question to answer.'

'How so? Either you stole it, or you didn't.'

She can't really believe she is seriously asking her lover this question. How could Theo Steen, critic and art historian, with his privileged and very civilised upbringing in New York, be an art thief?

'Well,' he says slowly, holding her with his magnetic eyes. 'I did steal this painting, you could say, but you could also say that it is not actually a stolen painting, not any more.'

She gasps. This is a nightmare.

'Oh my God, Theo. Who *are* you?'

She stares at his familiar face. She doesn't know this man at all, does she? And yet she feels she does. She cannot believe that he is a criminal.

'What will we do?' she says in a horrified whisper.

He clasps her hands.

'Trust me, darling.'

She shakes her head.

'You have to trust me.' He glances at his watch. 'I can't explain everything now, but I promise you I will later.'

He stands up, smoothes down his crumpled shirt.

'What are you doing?'

'I have to get off the train at Verona. I'm picking up a car there.'

'But why?'

'It's better if we travel separately. You stay on the train, with the picture, and I'll see you in Venice.'

She folds her arms and glares at him.

'Why can't I go with you?'

The train begins to slow down as it pulls into Verona station. She feels seized with an unaccountable panic. She doesn't want Theo to go. He has to stay with her. And yet she doesn't want to show him the rawness of her need. Stay calm, Valentina, she lectures herself. Keep your distance until you know what's going on.

'What if I get caught with the picture on me?' she snaps. 'Have you thought of that, Mr Art Thief?'

He stops in the compartment doorway, all tousled hair and devilish blue eyes, and laughs. He actually laughs.

'I promise you, Valentina, that if you get caught with that painting, you will not get into any trouble.'

He has made her cross again. Why does she keep swinging between rage and desire when it comes to Theo? The train pulls out of Verona, and she peers out of the compartment window, but Theo seems to have disappeared into thin air. She sighs. Well, he told her he would explain everything later. She just has to be a little patient. But she wants to know *now*. She is too agitated to read her book. She sits back in her seat and crosses her legs. That's when she sees the envelope on the floor of the compartment. Right in front of her eyes. When did he put that there?

She bends down and picks it up, rips it open.

Hotel Danieli. Bar. 20.00.

She chews her lip, smiling slightly to herself. Another secret tryst. At last she will get to keep Theo in her arms all night. It has only been eight days since they were last together in their apartment, and yet it feels so much longer to her. She is glad she brought one of her great-grandmother's silk evening dresses, rolled up in her case. She wants to look bewitching tonight.

There is a sudden jolt as the train screeches to a halt. They are not in a station but somewhere in the countryside, not far from Venice Mestre she reckons. She yawns, slips her feet out of her shoes and sits cross-legged on the seat. The door of the compartment slides open, and as she looks up, she feels the blood drain from her face. Standing in the doorway is the blond man from Marco's party. It is irrational, and yet her fear takes over. She grabs her briefcase and jumps up from her seat. Without bothering to put her shoes back on, she pushes past him and runs down the corridor to the exit doors. She presses the open button, and since the train is stationary the door slides open. She steps down on to one of the metal steps and leans out of the train, holding on to the handrail. She looks up the track, and then twists around and looks the other way, but she can't work out where they are. Even so, isn't it better to get off the train and call Theo? She has no shoes on, but he can pick her up wherever she is.

She is just about to jump off the train when she feels a hand on top of hers, prising her fingers off the handrail and gripping her around the wrist. She twists round to see her blond nemesis.

'Hey!' She tries to swing at him with her other arm and the

case, but she has hardly any balance at all.

He is holding her hand in his now, and if she lets go of him she will fall hard on to the track. She hears a whistle blow, and the train begins to move. She has to jump now, before it speeds up. She twists and turns, trying to break free, but he is gripping her around the wrist so firmly it is impossible. And now the train is going faster and faster, and she is frightened. It is too late to get off. What if he drops her? She could die. She grips the briefcase and swings her free arm in an effort to propel herself back into the train, but she doesn't have the strength.

He drags her inside just before the door shuts automatically, and she slams into his chest, breathless with fear and anger. He lets go of her wrist and she pulls back from him.

'What do you think you're doing?' she yells.

'Saving your life, Valentina,' he says, head on one side, looking amused.

She is not so sure about that.

'Who the hell are you?' she says, getting straight to the point.

The man leans back against the toilet door, crosses his arms. He is wearing a blue T-shirt that matches his eyes, and dark jeans. She notices the blond hairs on his pale arms, whiter than the hair on his head. He doesn't look the least bit Italian and yet his accent is perfect.

'I'm a colleague of Theo's,' he says. 'Has he never told you about me?'

'At the university?' It is hard to believe this muscle-bound thug is some kind of academic.

'No, no,' he says. 'An entrepreneurial colleague . . . Well, I suppose we are more competitors than colleagues.'

The man smiles at her. He runs his tongue over his teeth, which stick out ever so slightly, as if to suggest a kiss.

'Why are you following me?' she snaps.

He raises his eyebrows, and doesn't answer her.

'If you don't stop following me, I'm going to call the police,' she threatens him.

'Go ahead,' he says lightly. 'Although I don't think your boyfriend will thank you for it.'

Valentina takes a breath. Is this man a policeman as well? But he knows Theo. He said they were colleagues . . . or competitors.

'Who *are* you?' she asks again.

'I really don't think that is important right now,' he says. 'I am sure Theo will fill you in when you see him again.' He gives a short laugh. 'He is not as clever as he thinks. I *knew* he didn't have the painting. I guessed you had it all along.' He taps her briefcase, and she feels herself tensing, digging her nails into the leather handle.

'Is it in there, Valentina?' he says. 'Be a good girl now and give it to me, nice and quiet.'

The train shunts sideways, and they both lose their balance slightly. The blond man staggers backwards and slams against the toilet door, which opens, causing him to fall inside.

Valentina takes her chance. She turns and runs away from him, along the empty first-class corridor. She sees her compartment, darts inside and grabs her shoes and trilby hat before shooting off again and into second class. To her relief, the carriage is packed with tourists. She spies a spare seat by the window, surrounded by a group of young Americans with backpacks. That's what she needs. Safety in numbers. She squeezes into the seat and sits back, gripping the bag, shoes and hat to her chest. The girl opposite her looks at her curiously and smiles at her.

To Valentina's surprise, the blond man hasn't followed her, but she knows he is there, lurking in first class, waiting to catch her once they get to Venice. She pulls her mobile phone out of her pocket to call Theo, but to her horror the battery is flat.

She is shivering with terror, yet she realises that it is not for herself but for her lover.

Oh Theo, what have you done?

$\mathcal{B}$elle

SANTOS HAS TOLD HER TO RETURN tO SIGNOR BRZEZINSKI'S house. She cannot understand it. She hoped he might have some kind of plan. A way she could escape Venice and meet him somewhere. Or even that he might suggest she transform completely into Belle, although Signor Brzezinski would surely put a stop to that now she is pregnant. Yet Santos doesn't know she is carrying his child.

She reads his note again.

Go home, my little blackbird. I promise you that after today, Signora Louise Brzezinska's ordeal will be over.

Could he not have given her a few more words? A promise that he will return? Yet Belle knows that Santos makes no oath he cannot keep, and he has promised her that her life as Signora Brzezinska will be over after today. What can he mean? He must be far away by now. He cannot return, for he will surely be thrown in jail if he does. And imprisonment for Santos is worse than death.

* * *

Belle does not know it yet, but there is something apocalyptic about this day. Although it is only eight hours since she left her husband's house, his world has turned on its axis. For today is 29 October 1929. It is a day that will ruin many men.

Santos Devine predicted it, for although he lives like a gypsy he is not penniless and has often speculated on the New York stock exchange himself. He first noticed trouble months ago, problems with stocks and shares in the spring and whisperings from business forecasters that others chose to ignore. He could see it all about to happen, the great crash. And so he made it part of his revenge. He has never forgotten the bruised body of his lover, and he swore he would avenge her suffering. He would find a way of taking from Signor Brzezinski whatever would hurt him the most. His money.

In fact Signor Brzezinski's accusations against Santos Devine were not completely unwarranted. He *had* stolen something from him, if under a legitimate guise. For the past three weeks Santos Devine has posed as an American stockbroker looking for an elite group of European businessmen to invest in the thriving American stock market and make their fortunes. The truth is, there was no such group. Just Signor Brzezinski. And Santos Devine – or as Signor Brzezinski knew him, Mr Frederick Harvey of Brooklyn, New York-persuaded that greedy man to invest *all* of his money in American stocks and shares.

Thus at the precise moment Belle and Pina are reluctantly making their way back home, trailing along the tiny alleyways of Venice, tearful and forlorn, silent in dread, Signor Brzezinski is discovering the full extent of his ruin, thanks to the financial advice of said Frederick Harvey.

Does Signor Brzezinski have a heart? Once maybe. Yet consider the young man who watched his father, mother and sister bayoneted to death by invading Germans, while hiding under the staircase whimpering in fear. Either he died with his family that day, or he survived by hardening his heart to his shame and ensuring he was never weak again. And consider the young man in love with a woman, Magda Zielinska, who rejected him for the love of another. He had to have his revenge. And so he enslaved Magda's husband to him through his debts. He hoped to buy her from him, yet his plan backfired. He did not expect his rival to give him his daughter rather than his wife. Alexsy Dudek was just as bad as he, and yet *she* loved him. Even after his death, Magda loved her husband still. It enflamed Signor Brzezinski with rage, so much so that he was determined to have her no matter what. That was why he brought Magda Dudek to Venice along with Louise. At his first opportunity he took her. Yet it was so unsatisfactory, such an anticlimax. Magda lay back without a fight and looked at him with dead eyes, whispering her husband's name again and again.

Alexsy Alexsy Alexsy.

He kept trying to wake her up. Make her want him as much as he desired her. She was like a drug that never eased his pain. Again and again he made love to her, and yet Magda made no response to him, either in hatred or pleasure. In the end it became more satisfying to beat her daughter, force himself upon her, for at least she fought back, at least he got a reaction from her.

He told Louise that he had driven her mother mad. Yet now he sees clearly that it was not his fault. It was Magda's own guilt that stripped her of her senses. She had let her husband sell their daughter to protect herself. She was worse than Alexsy Dudek. She deserved her exile. Signor Brzezinski offered her the whole world, and she thought herself too good for him.

Since he sent Magda away to that island asylum, all Signor Brzezinski has wanted is a child. To be a better man for. And even that has been denied him, for despite the fact that his wife, as sinful as her mother, is pregnant, the child is not his. He knows this child will become another reminder of his failing every day. So what tiny piece of heart Signor Brzezinski has left is torn in half on this day, just like his money as it crashes on the floor of the American stock exchange. Within an hour he is a pauper. He can no more face the mocking laughter of his hateful wife than the pity of his business associates. If he has no money, then he has no power, and therefore he is nothing. He may as well be dead.

Signor Brzezinski stands on his wife's balcony. It seems fitting to end it here. He has no gun, but he has a large slab of Venetian brick, and some rope. He is glad for once that he cannot swim. He ties the brick around his foot, knotting the rope again and again, and drags himself over to the edge of the parapet. He thinks to cross himself first, for maybe there is mercy after death.

The last thing Signor Brzezinski sees as he plunges feet first into the canal is a blackbird circling above his head. He thinks how loudly it sings for such a small creature. It is like a fanfare for his entrance into death. Ludwika will be happy, he thinks, that I am gone. And as his lungs fill with water, Signor Brzezinski's heart finally heals, for his final thought is: *I am glad of that.*

Valentina

HER HEART LIFTS AS SOON AS SHE EXITS SANTA LUCIA train station. She has hidden herself amongst the pack of American tourists, who are only too happy to take her with them, after her offer of showing them a good hotel. They walk down the steps towards the canal and the landing stages for the vaporetti. She looks around her. She cannot see Theo anywhere, and yet she feels safer than she did on the train. Her disturbing encounter with the blond man and the feeling of despair it gave her begins to fade away as Venice starts to work its magic. She feels a mixture of joy and excitement well up inside her as she queues to buy her vaporetto ticket. Always this happens to her in Venice. This overwhelming sense of belonging, and something more, as if she has lived here before and been so very happy in this place. Everything is familiar to her. The elegant yet decaying palazzos, the milky green canal, the smell of its age-old saltiness, the tiny alleyways, the jewel-like bridges, and this sense of togetherness with other people, even if they are visitors just like her. Despite this city having been described as a floating museum, to Valentina it is anything but that. It helps her believe in another world beyond the physical, a place of spirit and passion.

In only a couple of hours, Valentina will see Theo again. Apart from finally finding out what is going on with the stolen painting, she is tingling with anticipation at the thought of their reunion in the Hotel Danieli. I will tell him that I can do it, she thinks. I will tell him I want to be his girlfriend. *I will tell him I love him.*

Valentina ushers her American companions on to Vaporetto 5.2 to Fondamenta Nuove. She is taking them to the hotel she and Theo stayed in last time they were here, on one of their erotic encounters before he moved in.

Locanda La Corte is tucked away down a tiny alley. Although it is so close to all the hustle and bustle of Venice, it feels like an oasis of calm in the middle of the city, with its intimate Venetian garden and the meditative lap of the canal backing on to it. Despite the chatter of her companions, who are a group of students from New York University taking in the sights of Europe, Valentina feels a sense of peace, a detachment as they walk across the square in front of the ornate marble façade of the hospital and the imposing gothic Santi Giovanni e Paolo. She feels as if she is another woman. Although she has only stayed in this hotel once, it is as if she knows her way by heart. Down the tiny Calle Bressana, the sunlight gradually squeezed out as she follows its path, to come out by the hotel, a bridge and the quiet backwaters of the canal.

She helps the Americans get booked in, and then says her goodbyes. They entreat her to come out for dinner with them later, but she explains that she is meeting someone. They part on the landing as she unlocks her bedroom door, slipping inside with relief. Her room is furnished simply with a large double bed, and French windows opening above the canal, while another window looks out over the alleyway. Valentina kicks off her shoes and lies down on the bed. She glances at her watch. She has a couple of hours before meeting Theo. She wonders where the blond man is now. She was careful when they were getting on the vaporetto and was sure he didn't follow her group on board. Surely he has no idea where she is now? Yet Venice is small. It is only a matter of time before he finds her.

She sits in the bar of the opulent Hotel Danieli, sipping a glass of red wine. It is just eight o'clock. She has the black briefcase leaning against her armchair, the Metsu painting within it, and she is watching the entrance like a hawk. *Where is her man?* She is beside herself with anticipation. She is not a demonstrative person, and yet she believes she might very well throw herself into his arms when she sees him. Despite the fact that she prides herself on her independence, she has to admit that she has missed him so much her heart is sore. The few fleeting times she has been with him have just fuelled her passion, making her want him all the more.

It is now five minutes past eight, and there is still no sign of her lover. She watches an old lady walk into the bar and survey the room. She is tall and elegant, although obviously very frail. To her surprise, the old lady's eyes come to rest upon her, and now she is walking over to her table.

'Signorina Rosselli?'

Valentina frowns.

'Yes.'

The old lady offers her a gloved hand.

'My name is Gertrude Kinder. I believe you have something for me.' And much to Valentina's bemusement, the old lady lowers herself into the armchair next to her.

'I am terribly sorry,' Valentina tells her, 'but I don't know who you are, or what you are talking about.'

Gertrude Kinder gives her a piercing look behind her glasses.

'The painting,' she says, as if Valentina is an imbecile. 'Signor Steen said you would have it with you.'

'The painting . . .' Valentina repeats, a little stunned.

'Yes,' the old lady says with the irritation of the wealthy and powerful. 'My painting. *The Love Letter* by Gabriel Metsu. Don't you have it with you? Signor Steen told me I could collect it from you tonight.'

Valentina stares at the old lady. She can almost feel the painting burning through the black briefcase next to her legs. What the hell is Theo playing at? Why didn't he tell her about this woman? Should she give her the painting? Who *is* she?

'Theo . . . I mean Signor Steen gave me no instructions to give you a painting. He just told me to meet him here. He didn't mention you.'

'I asked him not to mention me. I don't want any trails . . .'

Valentina looks at Gertrude Kinder in puzzlement. Is this frail octogenarian a crooked art dealer? It seems highly unlikely.

'And he is supposed to be here as well,' says the old lady, looking around and wringing her hands. 'I don't want to stay long. I just want to collect the painting and go.'

A waiter comes over to their table, but Gertrude Kinder waves him away.

'Is it in there?' she says, pointing to Valentina's briefcase. 'Can you please give it to me so I can go?'

'I'm sorry,' Valentina says. 'I can't do that, not until I check with Theo.'

She takes out her phone, which she managed to charge in the hotel, and dials his number, all the while looking at Gertrude, who is staring hungrily at the briefcase. Of course Theo doesn't answer.

'Why don't you have a drink while we wait for him?' suggests Valentina.

Gertrude looks at her as if she is crazy.

'No time,' she croaks, adding, 'you don't know, do you?'

'Don't know what?'

'Who I am? What the painting is?'

'No, I'm sorry.' Valentina holds Gertrude's gaze.

'It's *my* painting,' the old lady says passionately. 'Well, it was my husband's. It was taken from us. I thought we would never get it back, but your Signor Steen has helped me.'

'But if it was taken from you, why didn't you go to the police?'

Gertrude Kinder's face twists into an expression of utter disdain.

'I am talking about the Second World War, my dear. I am talking about the Nazi plundering of art belonging to Jewish families.'

At last Valentina is beginning to understand. A wave of relief floods her. She knew it, Theo is a good man. He is helping this old Jewish lady retrieve something stolen from her family during the Second World War. Yet it still doesn't make sense.

'I thought that all the Nazi plunder had been returned. Didn't they find out who all the dealers were? Couldn't you have gone through official procedures?'

Why go to the bother of stealing something when it can be reclaimed legally, Theo?

Gertrude Kinder is getting agitated.

'I don't have time to explain all of that now, dear. Please, I have to go before he comes.'

'Before who comes? Theo?'

'No, no, I wish he *was* here. I would feel a little safer. No, the other one. The one who wants the money . . .'

Valentina is becoming more confused by the minute. The

old lady puts her hand on top of hers. It is as cold as stone, yet her eyes are bright and gleaming.

'Please, dear, let me have it.'

There is something in the old lady's expression that makes Valentina trust her. She can see the history in her face. The suffering and the loss. She unzips the case and hands over the picture, still wrapped in its scarf.

'Oh, what's this?' says Gertrude Kinder, starting to unwind the lace. 'Do you want it back?'

Valentina thinks about her great-grandmother and what she would want her to do with the scarf.

'No, you keep it. To protect the painting,' she offers.

Gertrude Kinder hugs the picture to her chest as if she is being reunited with a long-lost child.

'Thank you, my dear. You have no idea how much this means to me. And please thank Signor Steen with all my heart. Tell him all is forgiven.'

The old lady gets shakily to her feet. Valentina wonders whether she should offer to accompany her. She really does seem frightened and frail. Yet she doesn't want to miss Theo if he turns up.

'Would you like me to take you home?' she asks.

'Oh no, it's fine. My assistant is waiting for me outside in a water taxi. He will help me.'

It is only after Gertrude Kinder has disappeared that it dawns on Valentina what she has just done. *I have given a priceless*

painting away to a total stranger on the strength of instinct.
And what did the old lady mean when she told her to tell Theo
that all was forgiven?

It is now nearly nine o'clock and her disappointment is
beginning to turn to anger. She has had enough. If Theo
doesn't turn up in the next ten minutes, that's it, she promises
herself. She is sick of his games. In the Dark Room she thought
she loved him, on the train she wanted to hold on to him for
ever, and yet now she is beginning to hate him. He is controlling, manipulative and disrespectful of her feelings . . . She
could go on. She orders another glass of red wine and kicks
off her shoes. She doesn't care that she is in the grandest hotel
in Venice.

Just as she has almost given up hope, the last person she
wants to see comes sauntering into the bar. Garelli. He has
found her. His eyes roam the room and his face lights up in
triumph when they settle on her.

'Well good evening, Signorina Rosselli, fancy meeting you
here,' he says, approaching her.

'Fancy,' she replies sarcastically.

'And would you be waiting for a certain Signor Theo Steen,
by any chance?'

'That is absolutely none of your business.'

'Is it now?'

Garelli sits down in the wing-backed leather chair not long
vacated by Gertrude Kinder. He waves a waiter over.

'I wouldn't bother to order a drink on my account,'

Valentina says, pushing her feet back into her shoes. 'I was just leaving.'

'Oh that is such a shame,' Garelli says evenly. 'Seeing as I came to thank you for helping me uncover the mystery behind all those stolen pictures.' He looks at her with dancing eyes, knowing full well that she can't resist.

'Well I guess I can spare you a few minutes,' she says gruffly, letting him order her another glass of wine. Really she needs to eat soon, otherwise all this drink will go to her head.

'You see, Signorina Rosselli, I couldn't stop thinking about what you said when we met before.' Garelli leans back in his seat and knots his fingers.

'What did I say?' Valentina frowns in confusion.

Garelli rests his chin on the bridge of his fingers and sits forward, staring at her intently.

'You suggested I investigate the victims of these false crimes rather than your Signor Steen. And you were quite right. The answer to why each of these people would change their mind and claim their painting wasn't stolen when it most clearly *was* came down to the provenance of the art.'

Nazi plunder, Valentina thinks. Just like Gertrude Kinder's lost painting.

'I know what you are thinking, Signorina Rosselli,' Garelli says. 'However, when I did investigate the provenance of each of these paintings, I could not see any connection to known Nazi art dealers at any stage. This I have to admit had me puzzled.'

'And if it was Nazi loot, the art would have been legitimately returned to the rightful owner in any case,' Valentina tells him haughtily.

'Yes, quite right,' Garelli says, sitting back again. 'However, in times of war, amid all the loss of life and suffering, there is much confusion. People can get mixed up over right and wrong. The fate of paintings, no matter how valuable, somehow fades in comparison to the fate of a whole country and its people.'

He says nothing for a moment, watching her reaction. Valentina frowns in puzzlement. What kind of riddle is this man presenting her with?

'As you say, paintings that have been recorded as plundered by the Nazis are hunted down and returned through legal channels, but there were many paintings and other artworks that were lost, that slipped through the net so to speak,' Garelli says, sweeping his arms dramatically. 'Some were taken by Allied soldiers when they uncovered the Nazi plunder hidden in mine shafts and caves in the mountains; some were found by others and passed through dozen of hands. It would take a skilled and persistent art detective to trace these paintings and retrieve them. It would take a special kind of person.'

Like Theo, Valentina thinks. The first word she would use to describe him is *tenacious*. Look how he is with her. Even after months of her swearing that she could never fall in love with him, he still hasn't given up.

'Often it is impossible to prove who is the rightful owner

of a work,' Garelli continues. 'It would appear that *a person* might take desperate measures and steal them.'

Their eyes lock, and Valentina knows that Garelli is referring to Theo. What will happen now when her boyfriend walks into the Danieli? Will Garelli arrest him? Will Theo run away and the policeman give chase, or worse still pull out a gun? She tries to stay calm, reminding herself of the facts. After all, officially there has been no crime committed.

'But I don't understand,' she challenges Garelli. 'Why do the victims change their minds and say that a theft hasn't been committed after all?'

'Shame, Miss Garelli. I can only think that these people didn't know the true provenance of the pictures hanging on their walls. Maybe they wouldn't have given them up easily – I mean, most of the pictures are worth millions – but once they were gone, they might have been persuaded by the thief to keep it quiet.'

'Persuaded in what way?'

'Told that he had evidence of the true owners; that they would be subjected to a lengthy and humiliating legal battle. I know for a fact that two of these so-called victims were Allied war heroes from the Second World War. I mean, imagine the shame for those men, to own Nazi plunder.'

It is an intriguing theory, and yet something doesn't sound right to Valentina.

After a slug of his white wine, Garelli ploughs on with his explanation.

'I do believe that what happened was that *someone* stole the pictures, and once the victim was informed that their painting was originally owned by a Holocaust survivor, well of course they retracted their statement of theft.'

'But what would be the motive for the thief?' Valentina asks. Was Theo that much of a philanthropist? That he would risk life and limb to return pictures to little old ladies like Gertrude Kinder?

'That's what I don't understand either,' Garelli says, scratching his head. 'And that's why I am here, with you, waiting for the same person.'

Neither of them speaks for a moment, as they eye each other up.

'He's not coming, you know,' Valentina says eventually.

'I know.' Garelli nods towards her briefcase. 'However, would you mind if I took a look inside your bag?'

Valentina glances at her briefcase, empty now apart from the erotic photograph album.

'Sure, why not?' She smiles to herself, looking forward to witnessing Garelli's reaction to the pictures.

And now she is walking home alone through the narrow streets of Venice in her great-grandmother's silk evening gown, her emotions in tumult. She is angry, disappointed and hurt, yet at the same time she is proud of Theo for what he has done, confused as well, and a little in awe. Her Theo. Her intellectual and not very practical boyfriend (he can barely hang a rack of shelves) is an undercover art detective, roaming the world for plundered art, *stealing it* and returning it to its rightful owners. She still doesn't understand why he doesn't work in conjunction with the police, or why Gertrude Kinder told her that all was forgiven. And who was that old lady so frightened of? Hardly Garelli.

Valentina enjoyed Garelli's initial embarrassment at the erotic photograph album, but in fact it was the policeman who gave her a shock with something he said as he was leaving. It was mentioned so casually, as if it was something someone might say to her any day. Yet no one ever had, her whole life.

'Goodbye, Valentina. It's been a pleasure. You know, your father would be proud of you.'

He was on his way out of the bar of the Danieli as he said it. She stood up suddenly, swaying slightly from all the red wine she had drunk.

'Do you know my father?' she called after him.

'Yes,' said Garelli, smiling smugly in amusement. 'Of course I do.' And before she had a chance to question him further, he had walked away.

Garelli knows her father. Of course he does. Her head is aching with all the information she has had to take in over the last couple of hours. This tease of information about her father is the last straw. Having avoided the policeman, she now wants to interrogate him about her father. Who is he? Where is he? How could he forget all about her? It is a moonless night, and the sky is as black as her humour. Still no Theo. She wants him now. She needs him to take away the pain in her heart.

The streets are deserted. It is always this way in Venice at night. The tourists go home, and it appears that the majority of the city's residents are ghosts. She wanders along by the canal, trying not to get lost. She hears footsteps behind her, but when she turns she can see no one. A church bell strikes midnight, and a black cat runs across her path. She has luck on her side tonight, then, although it doesn't feel like it. Her thoughts drift back to Gertrude Kinder. She didn't tell Valentina what had happened to her husband, but she guesses he must have died in the Holocaust. She finds it hard to think about that time in history. It is incomprehensible to her, the possibility of such darkness in the human soul.

What was it that Leonardo said to her about sado-masochism? That in fact by acting out these instincts in the bedroom, some people manage to avoid sadistic behaviour in the real world. Is that true? Or is sadomasochism a perversion that contributes towards humanity's cruelty to each other? She wants to believe Leonardo. There are enough things to feel guilty about in this world without including pleasure.

Again she hears the footsteps, and yet still when she turns she can see no one behind her. She speeds up. Yes, Gertrude Kinder really was scared. She wanted to leave before *he* came. Who was *he*? Not Garelli, she is sure. And not Theo, of course. She thinks of the blond stranger on the train. He said he was

Theo's rival. Is that who Gertrude Kinder was so frightened of?

She speeds up as she hears the footsteps getting closer and closer. She is nearly back at Locanda La Corte. She dashes over the last bridge, and across the square, literally flying down the alley to charge breathless through the hotel doors, much to the consternation of the concierge.

Once she is safely inside her room, she turns out the lights, pulls back the curtains and looks down into the alleyway. She can see him there, standing with his back against the wall, his cigarette glowing in the dark, his eyes hooked on her like a cat's. He is waiting for her.

$\mathscr{B}$elle

AS BELLE PUSHES OPEN THE FRONT DOOR OF SIGNOR Brzezinski's house, and she and Pina shuffle in, filled with dread, the scene that greets her is the last she expected to see.

The hall is full of people. Associates of her husband, their wives, the staff, including Renate, a cloth clutched to her breast, her face as white as a sheet. Strangers as well, police. They are all staring at her, suddenly silent amid the commotion. And in among these voyeurs, looking at her as if she is the main attraction, is a friendly face. Her very own Doctor. He moves quickly through the crowd, his face creased with concern.

'My dear Signora Brzezinska,' he says. 'Please come with me.'

She grabs Pina's hand instinctively.

'What is it? What's wrong?' Her heart is in her mouth. Oh Santos, what have you done? For she knows that all these people, the police, the Doctor means only one thing. Someone has died.

'The maid can stay here,' the Doctor says gently. 'But please follow me, my dear.'

'No, Pina must come with me.' Belle squeezes Pina's hand tightly in her own. She mustn't let her out of her sight. Just in case.

'Very well,' he says.

She and Pina follow the Doctor up the staircase, the eyes of these people who loathe her upon her back. She feels like it is she who is the murderer. Her bedroom is as she left it only this morning. The wardrobe wide open, her clothes strewn across the floor, her jewellery box empty. And the balcony door is wide open. The Doctor looks at her, and she knows he has figured out that she ran away.

'I think you should sit down, Signora Brzezinska,' he says softly. Yet she cannot sit. She is all agitation.

'Tell me,' she demands. 'What has happened?'

'It's your husband . . .'

'Is he dead?'

'Yes.' He doesn't say he regrets it, or that he is sorry. Why would he? He has seen what her husband did to her.

Pina gives a little cry, and Belle steps back in shock. She feels as if the wind has been knocked out of her. She is free at last. And yet at what cost?

'How . . . how . . .' she stutters, almost unable to speak. Oh, if her darling Santos has returned to Venice and killed her husband, what is she to do? If he is arrested, charged with murder, sentenced to death, she would want to kill herself as well, and yet she cannot because of the baby.

'Louise,' the Doctor says, taking her hand in his, 'I am afraid your husband took his own life.'

Pina gasps, bringing her hands to her mouth.

'What?' Louise is speechless. It is the last thing she expected him to say. 'But Santos Devine . . . what about Santos?'

The Doctor looks puzzled.

'Who?'

Relief floods her. Signor Brzezinski has killed himself. It is nothing to do with Santos, and yet why would her husband, so determined, such a survivor, want to kill himself?

'I don't understand. Why would he do such a thing?' She is calm now that she knows Santos is all right. She sits down on the bed, puts her hands in her lap and looks up at the kind Doctor, waiting for him to speak.

'Louise, something rather dramatic has happened in the world.'

'Oh?'

'Yes . . .' The Doctor pauses, licks his lips, hesitating before he speaks. 'There was a big crash on the American stock market. Within a few hours, shares that were worth millions the day before became worthless.'

Belle looks at him uncomprehending.

'What has that got to do with Signor Brzezinski?'

'I am afraid that he invested all his money in American shares.'

'He did?'

'Apparently he was taken in by a con artist by the name of Frederick Harvey who persuaded him to invest all his money on the American stock market.'

So someone got the better of her greedy husband, eventually. She can't help thinking this nasty thought, despite the fact that the man is dead.

'It is a very odd thing,' the Doctor says, looking at Belle quizzically. 'Because this Frederick Harvey only conned your husband. He didn't pick on any other businessman in the whole city. And nor did he make any money out of it himself. It seems quite bizarre.'

Santos.

Belle knows in an instant what her lover has done. He fulfilled his promise by killing her husband, but in a very clever way. She clasps her hands and tries to drop her head, careful not to show the Doctor her true emotions. She senses Pina sitting down beside her, taking her hands in hers.

'It's all right now,' whispers the maid. 'We're safe.'

Belle looks up at the Doctor again. Her eyes are shining with tears. She knows they are not tears of grief, but of relief. Just as Santos told her in his note, her ordeal is over.

'Tell me, Doctor, how did my husband kill himself?'

The Doctor winces.

'Are you sure you want to know such details quite yet?'

'Yes,' she commands him. 'Tell me, please.'

The Doctor walks over to the balcony door, takes the handle in his hand and swings it open, as if showing her Signor Brzezinski's way out of their world.

'He attached a brick to his leg and threw himself from your balcony.'

'He cannot swim,' she whispers, looking out at the grey skies of Venice.

'Indeed,' says the Doctor.

Signor Brzezinski's downfall becomes the talk of Venice. Once the full extent of his financial ruin is revealed, no one questions the motive for his suicide. Belle tries to find a place of compassion for him in her heart. Yet she finds it impossible to say even one prayer for him. Instead she gives the task over to Pina, who despite the fact that Signor Brzezinski threatened to rape her seems more able to forgive than Belle.

What would she do without Pina? Not one week after the death of her husband, the bailiffs arrive, removing the very carpet from underneath their feet. The servants and all her so-called friends desert her, and it is just she and Pina left to be thrown out of the house. Fortunately she still has the apartment, and a little money from the kind Doctor to cover the rent. She sells all her jewellery, but her husband was never lavish with his gifts and the money doesn't last long. If it were not for Pina, they would have starved. Belle keeps suggesting that she take up her work again as a prostitute, although surprisingly she has no taste for it now. Yet Pina will not allow it. She insists that now Belle is pregnant, she needs to focus on looking after herself in preparation for the arrival of the baby. She assures Belle that there must be another, more respectable way to make a living, and in the meantime she charms the stallholders down at Ponte di Rialto to supply them with spoilt food they cannot sell.

It is the pictures that give Pina the idea for their future. She is reorganising the cupboards in the tiny apartment when she comes across a stack of photographs of Venice that Belle took with Santos.

'Where did you get these?' she asks, fanning the photographs in her hand.

Belle looks at the pictures, and she feels a lead weight pulling at her heart. Oh, she remembers that day. The joy of Santos rowing her down the canal, the excitement of taking the photographs, and the pleasure she succumbed to after Santos rowed them out into the middle of the lagoon.

'I took them,' she says, not expanding on the other details.

'You did?' Pina asks, surprised. 'Why, they're really good. Do you have a camera?'

Belle opens the drawer in the tiny bedside cabinet and takes out the little bellows camera.

'Santos gave it to me,' she says, handing it to Pina.

Whenever Santos's name is mentioned, Pina's shoulders

stiffen into a rigid line, and her face takes on a serious expression. Belle knows that Pina believes he has abandoned her, leaving her pregnant and destitute, yet Belle herself believes otherwise. He will come as soon as he can. Now that Signor Brzezinski is dead, nothing can stand in their way. It is true she is surprised that it has taken him so long, but maybe he hasn't heard the news yet. Who will tell him that she is now free?

She tried to find Lara, but when she returned to the mask-maker's house in Cannaregio, she found it abandoned. A neighbour told her that the red-headed courtesan had disappeared, leaving behind no information on where she might have gone. For a second Belle was seized by a pang of jealousy. Was it possible that Lara knew where Santos was? Had she gone to join him? And yet when she brought to mind their last tender lovemaking, she was certain in her heart that Santos was hers. She just had to be patient. He could be waiting for all the gossip about the blackguard Mr Frederick Harvey to die down.

Pina opens the lid of the camera and the little bellows lens springs up.

'You know,' she says, 'why don't we try to make money taking pictures?'

Belle returns her thoughts to the present, and their urgent need to survive.

'Don't you need a better camera for that? A studio, and lighting?'

And yet for the first time since she was thrown out of her husband's house, she begins to feel a little hope. What if they can do something with the camera?

'I am talking about snapshot pictures of visitors to Venice. Out and about in the city,' Pina says, her dark eyes flashing with inspiration. 'We approach tourists, take their pictures, and once we have got them developed, drop them off at their hotels over the next couple of days.'

Belle leans forward, and grasps Pina's hands in hers.

'That is an excellent idea, my dearest Pina, for it is quite new and different from the formal portraits most people have taken. I think it might just take off.'

Blackbird Photographers Esq., Calle Bressana, Castello, Venice is born. This is how Pina and Belle make their living. They become infamous characters of Venice, and many of their tourist customers request photographs taken *with* them as well as on their own. The two friends dress up to go out and about looking for customers, Belle in one of her fancy silk dresses, Louise Brooks bob and furs, Pina preferring to wear a miniature pinstriped suit Belle has had specially tailored for her.

Each day as Belle takes her pictures on the streets of Venice, she is also looking for Santos. Hoping, praying she will find him again. She plasters a smile on her face, a welcome to their customers, and yet inside she is clinging to her faith. When will he come?

*V*alentina

SHE CAN'T BREATHE. HER MOUTH IS GAGGED AND HE IS pushing her under the water. She kicks against him, but the water is as thick as treacle, pulling her down. She can feel her strength ebbing. He drags her up, and her nostrils flare as she tries to take in more air. Her eyes beg for mercy, yet the blond stranger is possessed. He looks at her without recognition, his eyes blank, his mouth set in a grimace. He dunks her back into the water, as if he is drowning a kitten. She twists and turns, flailing with her arms, trying to push up against the pressure of his hand that keeps her down. Water floods in through the gag in her mouth. She can taste it, the sea. It is pulling her down to its bed, and she can feel it in her body, her eventual submission as her limbs relax and she falls back into the depths.

She takes a deep gulp, dragging the fresh air deep into her lungs.

'Valentina?'

She sits up in her bed in the Locanda La Corte, her eyes wide open. She is alive. It was a dream, just a bad dream.

'Valentina?'

Yet the voice is real enough. She looks into the blackness of the room, and she can see a figure sitting on a chair by the window. It is her lover's voice she hears, she is sure.

'Theo?' she whispers tentatively.

The figure gets up and walks towards the bed, leaning over and turning on the bedside lamp. Oh thank God it *is* him. Her heart lurches with relief and yet at the same time she still feels a shard of anger that his very absence makes her feel so weak and lonely.

'Where were you?' she hisses. 'You left me sitting in the Hotel Danieli for over two hours.'

He sits down on the bed next to her, pushes the hair off her forehead and flattens it down again gently.

'I'm sorry, darling,' he says. 'There was nothing I could do about it. That detective was hanging around and I didn't want to run into him.'

She pushes herself up against the headboard of the bed, taking herself away from his touch, and gives him a hard stare.

'Theo, you have to tell me what the hell is going on right now. There was this old lady and I gave her the Metsu painting . . . and then Garelli came in and told me that it's Nazi plunder . . . and then . . .' She stutters, the image of her dream returning, the blond stranger trying to drown her. 'There's this horrible man who keeps following me, and I think he wants to hurt me . . .'

To her surprise, a grin spreads across Theo's face.

'You mean Glen? I would hardly call him a threat!' he guffaws.

Valentina is incensed.

'I don't know what his name is, but he's a nasty piece of work. He was on the train after you got off. He tried to push me off it.'

Theo frowns, the smile wiped off his face.

'Are you sure? I mean, I don't like Glen, and I don't approve of some of his methods, but I don't actually think he is a killer, Valentina.'

She crosses her arms.

'Well I *think* he tried to push me off,' she says. Yet when she really thinks about it, maybe he was actually trying to pull her into the train. She was so frightened, she can't remember clearly now.

'Anyway,' she says, 'he followed me home from the Danieli, and he was outside the window, staring up at me.'

'I know, he's still there,' Theo says evenly.

'What!' She jumps out of bed and storms across the room, pulling back the curtain to take a look.

'Er, Valentina, maybe you want to put something on. Glen might get the wrong idea.'

She throws the curtain back down, and picks up her great-grandmother's silk evening gown, slipping it on again.

'That's a beautiful dress,' Theo remarks.

She ignores him, more concerned with her stalker. She goes back to the curtain, pulls it ajar slightly, and there is the blond man, Glen, still waiting for her. She drops the curtain and turns around.

'What's he doing there, Theo?' she asks. 'Why is he following me?'

Theo pats the bed.

'Come here,' he says, beseeching her with his wide blue eyes. She can't help but feel drawn to him, despite her anger.

She sits back down on the bed, glowering at him.

'I think you owe me an explanation,' she says.

'Okay, darling, but come right over here, will you?'

She lets him pull her to him. She slides down him, with her back to his chest, as he puts his arm around her shoulder and picks up her other hand in his.

'Let's start with Glen, shall we?' he begins. 'I expect Garelli filled you in on the background to my work.'

She snorts with sarcasm. She can't help it.

'I would hardly call stealing paintings a proper job.'

He laces his fingers through hers.

'Come now,' he says. 'Don't you know me by now?'

'I know that you steal art that's Nazi plunder and give it back to the original owners, but I don't understand why you don't work alongside the authorities.'

'Because it takes too long,' Theo says simply, sighing. 'Look, I'll explain why I do what I do in a moment. Firstly I want to tell you about Glen.'

'Who *is* he?' she asks.

'Does he frighten you?'

'Yes.' She is done pretending she is tough. Let Theo know how shaken she is by that man's presence.

He tucks her in even tighter under his arm.

'I'm sorry, honey. I didn't think he would try to get at you. I'll talk to him tomorrow, tell him to lay off or else . . .'

Can she hear a trace of humour in his voice? It is unaccountable.

'Can't you tell him to go away *now*?' she says crossly. 'I mean, he is right outside.'

Theo squeezes her hand in his.

'I can't do that because of Mrs Kinder. I have to give her a chance to leave Venice without Glen confronting her. It's better he is here, outside our hotel window, rather than bothering her.'

She twists around and looks at him questioningly.

'Glen does much the same as I do,' Theo explains. 'He hunts down paintings lost or stolen during the Second World War, and returns them to their owners. However, unlike me, Glen demands a big fat fee for his endeavours. And the original owners of these paintings are usually so frail and old by now that he is able to bully them into giving him way too much money.'

So that was why Mrs Kinder was so frightened.

'Originally Gertrude Kinder hired Glen to find her painting. She agreed to give him one million dollars for the job.'

Valentina gasps in shock. No wonder the man is so persistent.

'It just so happened that the Metsu was one of *my* paintings. So I took it first,' he says simply.

'But Theo,' she exclaims,' you are breaking the law. You can't just break into someone's house and steal something, even if it belonged to someone else before.'

'I always explain,' he says, lifting their knotted hands and raising them to his lips, so that he kisses the back of her hand. 'Afterwards, of course. I made the mistake of asking nicely once, and when I returned to collect it, the painting had magically been moved to another location. So I realised that stealth was the only way.'

'But why? I just don't understand why you would put yourself in such danger, and for what? If you are returning all these paintings to the original owners and not getting a cent for it, well, why do you do it?'

He drops their hands and extricates his fingers from hers, wrapping his arms tightly around her waist as if he is afraid she might run away.

'It's for my grandfather.'

She twists around again, trying to catch his eye.

'Your grandfather? I didn't even know you had a grandfather!'

He strokes her hair, then leans down and kisses her forehead, looking at her sadly.

'Well, you have never been that interested in my family, but if you had been, you would remember that my grandparents live in Amsterdam still. They have lived there all their lives.'

'Are they Jewish?' Valentina whispers, suddenly ashamed that she doesn't know even this about Theo's family.

'No, they're not Jewish,' Theo says stoically, pausing. 'My grandfather worked for one of the most famous art dealers in Europe in the thirties. *He* happened to be Jewish. His name was Albert Goldstein and he had an impressive collection of Dutch Masters and rococo art, as well as more modern works. When the war began, before Holland was actually invaded by the Nazis, several Jewish families decided to leave, and they deposited their art with Mr Goldstein, in the belief that they would be able to return to collect it one day. But of course the Germans invaded and poor Mr Goldstein had to flee. He entrusted this collection to my grandfather. It was his job to protect all this art.'

'So what happened?'

Theo sighs, and she can feel the heaviness of his heart as he tells her the secrets of his family.

'My grandfather was persuaded by the Hermann Göring Division to sell the entire collection to him for a ridiculously small amount of money, a fraction of what it was worth. My grandfather never forgave himself. He felt he had betrayed Mr Goldstein and his Jewish friends.'

'I am sure he had no choice, Theo,' Valentina says, touching his arm gently. Theo gazes down at her. In his eyes she can see what kind of a man he is, one who would risk his freedom for the honour of his kin.

'Of course he had no choice,' he says, his voice heavy. 'He knew what would happen to his family if he refused to sell, and yet he still considered that he had let his employer down. He has spent most of his life trying to track down this art and return it to its rightful owners. My father used to help him, but now he's too old, so I've sort of taken over. It's a very difficult business, Valentina. There is no one database of plundered art in the world. It can take a long time to find something.'

'I still don't understand why you don't just go to the police with the relevant information so that the pictures can be returned legally.'

Theo shakes his head.

'My grandfather used to try to do that. But do you know how many years it can take to get things returned? The worst thing is if the picture is in a state collection. You can forget it then, especially if it is in Russia. Breaking into someone's house is one thing, but an art gallery, no way. Even so, it might take years and years to retrieve artworks from private collections.' Theo pulls her closer to him. 'It was destroying my grandfather to fight legal battle after legal battle, and finally win, only to find that the original owner of the picture had died waiting. And now, you see, my grandfather is dying too . . .' Theo pauses, his voice almost a whisper now.

'You never told me.' She twists round to look up at him again.

He looks at her, and his gaze is so piercing she has to turn away. He doesn't need to say anything; she knows what he is thinking. He never told her because he knew she wouldn't want to know.

'I wanted to finish his life's work, so to speak,' he starts to say. 'There are only a few paintings left to return . . . I felt compelled to do it.' He pauses, squeezing her hand again. 'I'm sorry I never told you before, Valentina. I wanted to confide in you.'

'Why didn't you? You know I can keep a secret,' she says passionately.

'Because I needed to know how you feel about me, so I could trust you . . . and you kept telling me how our relationship is casual. Besides, I thought you might run for the hills if you really knew what I did for a living.'

Valentina puts her hands over his and holds them tight.

'Theo Steen, lost art investigator. Sounds good,' she declares, trying to lighten the mood.

'So you're not shocked?'

'Of course I'm shocked.' She slaps his arm gently. 'You're not the man I thought you were.'

'Is that a good or a bad thing?'

She looks up at him again, cocks her head on one side and smiles her crooked smile.

'I'm not sure yet,' she says, poking her finger at his face. 'In any case, I think I've heard enough for now,' she says, snuggling into him. 'The time for words is over.'

She lifts his arms and turns around on her knees. She leans down and kisses him on the lips, lingering, inhaling his familiar scent. It is good to be in his arms again.

'Valentina?' Theo says softly. 'Do you mind if we just go to sleep?'

'Really?' She looks up at him in surprise.

'I'm so tired; actually, I'm exhausted. I just want to hold you in my arms and fall asleep.'

'Sure, honey.' The endearment slips out, and Theo raises his eyebrow, a slow smile spreading across his face.

'Honey?'

She blushes furiously.

'Slip of the tongue.'

'If you say so, honey,' he drawls, but he looks pleased.

She takes off her dress and slips under the covers. Theo undresses, switches off the light, and gets in next to her. They lie side by side, naked, neither of them speaking for a moment. She absorbs everything Theo has told her. It seems so fantastical, and yet at the same time quite ordinary as well. He is just trying to help some old people get their stuff back. He is trying to help his grandfather make his peace before he dies.

'Come here,' he whispers into the darkness. She slides over in the bed and lets him hold her in his arms. They lie on their sides, and he is spooning her. She can feel his heartbeat on her back, his breath upon her neck. Theo is here at last with her. Tomorrow they will talk about them. She will find out why he gave her the erotic pictures, what he was doing at the club with Leonardo, and why he was in the Dark Room. She thinks she knows why, but she needs to hear him say it for sure. Yet for now she ceases to worry. She lets herself succumb to the sanctity of falling asleep within her lover's arms. And finally she exits the Dark Room of her solitude, for she believes at last she has come to understand what love is.

$\mathscr{B}$elle

SHE CALLS THE BABY MAEVE MARIA MAGDA, TO BE KNOWN as Maria. Maeve after the Irish queen, the namesake of Santos's boat; Maria after Pina's late mother; and Magda after her own mother, forgiven now she is dead.

Magda Dudek dies exactly one month before the baby is born, to the day. The first Belle knows of it is a letter forwarded to her apartment from the new owners of her old home. It is on the official headed paper of the Poveglia Sanatorium, regreting to inform her that Mrs Magda Dudek died whilst in surgery from a heart attack. They're vague about what the surgery was for, but Belle suspects the doctor was doing some kind of horrific lobotomy in an effort to restore her mother's sanity. She feels a moment of remorse, pushing her hands on her dome of a belly, sensing the life within her.

After Signor Brzezinski died, should she have gone and rescued her mother? It was her intention. And yet the weeks passed and she was preoccupied with survival, and with her pregnancy. Maybe her mother didn't deserve to be rescued. She had betrayed her; let her be married to that brute. She *must* have known what kind of man Signor Brzezinski was. Magda Dudek failed to protect her own child; Belle swears she will never put herself before Maria in the same way. And yet despite knowing all of this, she cannot help but mourn her mother, for she loved her, of course.

As Belle is in the throes of childbirth, she hears her mother's voice one last time.

Ludwika, Ludwika, where is my little girl?

And she knows in a moment of lucidity that her mother regretted her actions, so much so that maybe that was what drove her mad in the end. As she pushes her daughter out into the world, she asks her mother to protect the baby. It will make up for everything. And as the years pass, Belle has a feeling that her mother is indeed Maria's guardian angel, for her daughter grows up to be blessed with the same pretty features as Magda Dudek that drove her husband, and Signor Brzezinski, so wild. In fact she is even more striking, for she has inherited her father's exotic blue eyes as well.

The years spin by, and still Belle doesn't give up hope that Santos will return one day. He promised her. She imagines him returning, and his joy when he discovers he has a child. And such a sweet, easy little girl, a lover of the sea and a dancer, just like her father. By the time Maria is four, she is so well behaved that she accompanies her mother and Auntie Pina on their photograph-taking excursions, tripping along behind them like a little fairy in a tiny ballerina dress, or a miniature clown in a harlequin costume with a jester's mask. She has no father with her, but that doesn't matter, for the whole of Venice is Maria's family. She knows every gondolier, every artisan and stallholder. They all keep a watchful eye on the little girl with the beautiful eyes. Everyone knows who her real father is, for Santos Devine is a legend in Venice. And just like Belle, the city waits for him to return.

Yet he never comes. The years turn and turn as Belle holds on. Despite the comfort Pina offers her, for her friend is deeply in love with her, Belle will not take it, not even a kiss. It is not fair to Pina to lead her on, for she is saving herself for Santos. Often at night she pushes his gold earring on to each finger one by one, trying to warm the cold metal with her hope, yet still it feels like a dead man's ring. She strives to keep her faith in him, as the cracks in her heart multiply.

It is three days before Maria's eighth birthday when Belle's long vigil finally comes to an end. She is smothered with a heavy cold, and Pina insists she stay in bed while she and Maria go out and ply their trade. Her friend and daughter clatter out of the apartment, Pina dressed in Belle's sailor boy outfit, and an adaptation of the black ballerina's dress for Maria's tiny frame.

Belle is listless. She cannot rest, and yet she is too ill to get out of bed. As she tosses and turns, she hears birdsong coming from the window. She recognises the flute notes instantly. She sits up in bed and there is her little blackbird. She has not seen him since the day Lara brought him to her all those years ago. She listens to his song, and it is as if she can hear her lover's words beneath it.

Here I am. Here I am.

The blackbird flies away into the ethereal mists of Venice, and in his place stands Santos Devine. She cries out to him, in joy, in fear. He looks exactly how he did when she last saw him. His prowess, his power, his passion all perfectly combined. He walks towards her, across the shadowy room.

'Santos? Is that really you?'

Her lover doesn't speak, but still he comes towards her. She sits up in bed and holds out her arms to him. They embrace, her heart raw with the pain of the missing years.

'Santos,' she whispers, as she inhales his scent. She could never forget his sweet perfume. 'Where have you been?'

Santos doesn't reply. Instead he lifts her face to his and kisses her. She feels his love within their kiss, the burning power of it.

'I have been waiting for you, my love,' she whispers. 'I knew you would return to me.'

Still he doesn't speak, and yet the expression in his eyes tells her all she needs to know. He loves her.

Santos kisses each part of her, waking up her body, so long asleep, so long untouched. She curls around him, pressing into him, feeling their limbs entwine so that they become one beautiful, sublime pulsing heart. He pushes inside her, and she opens her mouth and releases all the anguish of her long wait for this moment. Their eyes lock as they rock together on the bed. She looks love full in the face, commits to memory every curl of his hair, every freckle upon his skin, each crease around his eyes, that divine cleft in his chin. This is the mountain she has had to climb, yet she never gave up, and now she has her reward. In her head she composes a poem, just like Veronica Franco would.

All my life I have lived for this summit of bliss, when the love of my life tells me he loves me.

I will write these words down, Belle thinks, so that I never forget the eternity of our love. She closes her eyes and loses herself to their passion.

As she and Santos climax in perfect, shimmering symmetry, she feels the rain of feathers upon her body, the slip and slide of his soul as it retreats back into the hazy land he now inhabits.

'No!' she cries. 'My love, don't leave me again.'

Yet when she opens her eyes, her arms are empty. She hugs herself, bereft with the knowledge of where her Santos is gone. It can be the only reason he has never come back for her. And now she realises that she knew it all along. Her love is gone, the air still spinning with black feathers like dying moths as the light fades from her heart. Beside her on the pillow is the blackbird, a bead of blood upon its yellow beak. She knows with certainty that her lover is dead. She does not know where or how, but Santos *is* dead, for this is how he finally came back to her and made love to her as she always dreamed he would.

That night, while Maria sleeps beside her, Belle slides over into the middle of the bed next to her daughter, and pulls back the covers on the other side for Pina. It has taken her eight years to accept the woman who loves her best, yet at last she lets her in.

Valentina

VALENTINA SITS OUTSIDE CAFFE FLORIAN WATCHING THE
dirty pigeons of Venice scavenge off the tourists in Piazza San
Marco. She is sipping her cappuccino, slowly whiling away
the day and waiting for Theo. He rose early this morning,
before she woke, leaving a note on the bedside table explaining
that he had gone to talk to this Glen character. He wrote that
he would meet her here at Caffe Florian at midday.

Theo insists that Glen is not dangerous, but Valentina has
a gut feeling about that man. She twists her napkin through
her fingers. She hopes everything is okay. Despite the fact that
she spent the night in Theo's arms, she is still anxious. Now
she knows all about the art thievery, she is not so sure in
the cold light of day what she actually thinks about it all.
If she and Theo are to become a proper item, that will be
her life as well. She wishes he had talked to her about it
before. In fact the whole of this week he has denied her any
kind of communication or explanation about anything. He

has still left her hanging this morning.

He is trying to possess you, Valentina. She hears her mother's warning yet again. *He is controlling you by not talking to you.*

Is her mother right? Valentina chews her lip. Is Theo hoping to gain some sort of power over her? So that she is weak and needy, compliant? She thinks of everything that has happened this week. The mystery of the erotic photographs, the scenarios in the Atlantis Room, the Velvet Underworld and the Dark Room. Even being here in Venice. In every instance she has surrendered control over her own life. She has been silenced through his lack of communication. And yet as she sits in the Venetian sunshine, drinking her coffee, an uncomfortable prickle of memory comes to the surface. It is a rainy afternoon in Milan, herself and Theo sitting at the kitchen table, the food in front of them untouched. It is one week since she lost the baby, and still she is refusing to talk to him.

Don't shut me out. Tell me how you feel.

Yet she couldn't tell him, because she didn't want him to know the truth, that she had wanted his baby. She didn't want him to think she was weak, or dependent. That is not who Valentina is.

Do you not want me to go away?

He asked her that question more than once. In fact every time he went away after she lost the baby. She had forgotten that. And what did she do? That day she pushed her chair back and walked out of the room, sweeping his questions away.

I don't care what you do.

That was what she told him. She drops her head, the sudden illumination of this memory too much for her. Something else occurs to her. Is it possible that she has hurt Theo? Has she been so busy trying to protect her own heart that she forgot he has feelings too? She struggles to understand. She finds it so hard sometimes to consider the feelings of men. She has always experienced the opposite, the male preoccupation with lack of commitment. And yet Theo is different. He asked her to be his girlfriend.

She pushes her hands into the deep pockets of her suit jacket, and from one of them she pulls out a card. She looks at it in surprise. It is from Mattia, her brother. He must have put it in the pocket of the jacket when he posted the package of clothes to her. What a strange thing to do? And how odd that she never noticed it before.

Dear Valentina,

Mother also gave me these costumes of our great-grandmother, Belle Louise Brzezinska. They date from the late 1920s and could be quite valuable, though I don't think you will sell them, will you? Mother said she had a feeling that you might have a use for them. I hope you enjoy the photographs. I should have given them all to Theo when he came by, but he only took the book of negatives. Mother told me that they are pictures of the very same great-grandmother. I would love to see copies of the enlargements once you have a chance to make them. Please give Theo my best regards. He's a good guy, Valentina.

Love, Mattia

Valentina reads the card again in disbelief. Theo went to visit her brother in America and he *never* told her! Why on earth would he do that?

And the negatives! Of course, why didn't she notice it before? She has been wearing the answer to the mystery almost every day. The lace scarf, the string of pearls, the sailor's cap.

She has them all.

She opens her bag, and pulls out the black album. She flicks through the prints yet again. So this is Belle Louise Brzezinska, her great-grandmother. And it is most certainly not the version of her great-grandmother she has always believed true: the devoted wife of a Venetian entrepreneur, the widowed mother living a life of seclusion in her home in Castello. This is another story. It is the secret life of her great-grandmother. Valentina examines the erotic beauty of the close-ups in the book. She can see the artist's eye in the composition of each picture. The play with the textures of the model's body, the white skin and dark hair, and the stunning effect of suggestion within each image: a finger upon a lip, a downcast eye, a naked back, the naked breast and the draped pearls in a gloved hand. There is the enticing picture of her staring into the camera, Venetian mask concealing her identity, her arm between her legs, her open mouth seducing the photographer.

Was he the owner of the gold earring?

She knows instinctively that the man wearing the earring is most certainly not her great-grandmother's husband, the seemingly conservative and uptight Signor Brezezinski. She flicks through the album again and again, hypnotised by the passion of the images she sees. What is Theo trying to tell her? She would not let him speak, so is he finding a different way of communicating with her?

Does he know how comforted the book makes her feel? She has never felt such a bond with anyone else in her family before. She never knew her grandparents, or her father, of course. Her brother has always been a distant presence. And her mother . . . well, she was too intense a force in her young life, so that Valentina has had to emotionally banish her. But this Belle feels like a kindred spirit. Valentina wonders if there is such a thing as genetic memory, and whether she could let her great-grandmother live her life of passion again through her. The thought amuses her, and makes her do a rare thing. She laughs. It is a small burst, almost under her breath, but nevertheless it is still laughter. So this is what Theo has done for her. He has made her realise that she is not alone.

'Valentina, you're laughing, and in broad daylight too!'

She looks up, and there, standing in front of her, is Theo,

smiling at her warmly. She was so engrossed in the book she didn't even see him approaching the café. The sun is in her eyes, and she squints up at him, the brilliance of the basilica behind him. Theo Steen, her errant lover. There is his tall frame, dark looks and gentle demeanour so missed from her life these past ten days. She feels a rush of emotion. She wants to fling herself into his arms. Tell him how much she missed him. And yet she can't do it. Even as she looks at him, her heart about to burst inside her, she starts to react as always, pulling down the shutters, trying to lock them tight. Instead of falling into his arms, she converts her emotion into anger.

'Theo, where have you been? You're nearly an hour late,' she spits at him, her laughter gone.

'I'm sorry, darling,' he says, looking as if she has slapped him, holding back from her. Why can't he lean down and hug her? 'But it took longer than I thought to talk some reason into Glen.'

She calms down slightly.

'Is everything okay? Is he going to leave us alone?'

He sits down at her table, so close to her and yet so far. She is craving to touch him. She looks at his hand, his long, elegant fingers as he waves over a waiter and orders a coffee for himself, and another one for her.

'I hope so.'

She can't help feeling a little alarmed.

'Don't you think we should report him to the police? Garelli?'

'What for? He hasn't actually done anything wrong, and in fact it could do me more harm than good if he decided to work with the police.'

He finally picks up her hand and squeezes it.

'Don't worry, my love. Everything will be okay.'

Why do people say that to each other, Valentina thinks crossly, when it is impossible to know?

She taps the black photograph album on her lap, deciding to change the subject.

'So,' she says. 'Are you going to tell me what all this is about?'

The light comes back into his eyes as he takes the album off her lap and starts to flick through it.

'You enlarged them all,' he says, delighted. 'God, they're gorgeous.'

He pauses on the light box image, Valentina's Dark Room fantasy.

'This looks familiar,' he says under his breath, looking up at her slyly.

'You were watching me the whole time?' she whispers.

'Of course I was watching you. Wasn't that what it was all about?'

They stare at each other, eyes locked, and she can feel her heartbeat quicken.

'I don't really know what it's all been about,' she says quietly. 'Why didn't you tell me where you got the album of negatives from when you gave it to me? Why didn't you tell me they are pictures of my great-grandmother and a family heirloom? I thought it was stolen, like the paintings . . .'

'I wanted you to discover for yourself, negative by negative. I thought it would be fun.'

There is that dreadful word again, reminding her of English tea parties and jolly hockey sticks.

'Fun?' she hisses, anger heating her blood again. 'You went behind my back and visited my brother in New York. Why did you go and see him? Why didn't you tell me?'

'I knew that if I told you I wanted to see Mattia, you would tell me not to go,' he says matter-of-factly.

She bites her lip. He is right. She would have ordered him to stay away.

'Valentina,' he says softly. 'You changed.'

She looks up at him, uncomprehending. What does he mean?

'As soon as I moved into the apartment, it was as if you froze up. You were so contrary. One minute you wanted to make love, and the next you would be angry with me for no apparent reason.'

'But you are just as contrary,' she defends herself, not willing to admit he is right. 'With your secret art thievery, disappearing for days without telling me where you are, and sneaking off to see my brother.'

'That's different. I have always been consistent in my feelings for you.' He pauses. 'Right from the beginning, from the first night we met.'

She can't help but snort derisively.

'That's ridiculous, Theo. How could you know how you felt the night you first met me? You didn't *know* me at all. We didn't even speak.'

He cocks his head at her and smiles, although his eyes look sad.

'Maybe you are right, Valentina, for since the moment I moved in, you haven't stopped reminding me that there is no way you can ever fall in love with me.' He pauses, takes a sip of his espresso. 'I was going to leave, after we came back from Sardinia, but then you had the miscarriage, and . . . well, I couldn't go.'

The hurt in his eyes angers her. He has no right to make her feel so guilty.

'I didn't want your pity,' she snaps at him. 'How dare you stay with me because you felt sorry for me?'

'Oh no, Valentina, you don't understand me.' He looks her in the eyes, and her anger begins to ebb. 'I really wanted to try to find a way to make things work. It was so amazing when we first got together and I wanted to bring that life back into our relationship. That's why I went to see Mattia. I wanted to find out more about you.'

'Why didn't you just ask me?'

'Because you wouldn't talk to me. Not about anything important, at least.'

She looks down at the table, her empty coffee cup. She is beginning to understand Theo's motives, and yet she is not sure how it makes her feel. She is still angry with him, for nosing into her life, going to see Mattia, and yet he has always had strong feelings for her, right from the very first night. Is that possible? Or is he deluded?

'But why did you take the album from Mattia?' she says, skirting around the issue.

'He offered it to me. Said you could enlarge the negatives in your darkroom. And when I got it back here, and looked at the negatives on your light box, I had an idea. I thought this could be a very Valentina way of reaching you. If I could bring you on a journey through the pictures, you might hear my message. I thought it might be easier than trying to make you listen to my words.'

'And what is the message?' she asks him, stunned by the lengths this man will go to reach her.

'Have you not worked it out yet?'

He catches her with his gaze. She remembers now how she often thought his icy blue eyes intimidating, but now they look so pure and clear, and her anger dissipates. She is suddenly ashamed of herself . . . her lack of trust, her non-communication, shutting him out . . .

'It's erotica from the twenties, so I guess it shows that my great-grandmother was quite a free spirit?'

She looks at the book still on his lap, unable to bear his gaze any longer.

'And it's quite incredible the connection I feel with her.'

Theo puts his hand on hers and she feels a charge through

her body. As if he has turned a light on in her heart. If they were not in Piazza San Marco in the middle of the day, she would jump on top of him, right now.

'That's what I thought,' he says. 'When I looked at the negatives I could see they were really erotic. And I remembered those pictures you took in Venice, and I thought, here is a way I can speak to you. If you can see the connection between yourself and this amazing lady from the past, your own ancestor, Valentina, maybe you will hear my message.'

Of course, these pictures are more than just images from the past. They are a part of *her* history. They are a part of who she is.

'So?' Theo asks again, suddenly leaning forward and cradling her chin within the palm of his hand, tipping it towards him, looking into her eyes again.

He is forcing me to show him my heart, she thinks, desperately trying to remain in control.

'What did the book tell you?' he asks, his voice low and husky.

She pulls her head away, confused and strangely nervous.

'It's very sexy?'

He frowns. She knows her answer is lame.

'Is that all?'

She stares at him, holds his gaze. Her mouth has suddenly gone dry, and she licks her lips.

'What do you want me to say?'

He looks a little disappointed. He brings her hands to his

lips and kisses them. She feels herself stir, and she looks with longing at his lips. How she wants to feel those lips upon her body. She has such an ache inside her, such a yearning for her lover.

'Theo,' she whispers. 'Let's go back to Locanda La Corte.'

As soon as the hotel room door clicks behind them, they fall into each other's arms. They embrace, kissing deeply, all the while walking as one, slowly towards the bed. It hits the back of her knees and she drops down on to it. She pulls off her jacket, and he undoes her trousers. She hastily undoes his jeans, and within seconds they have stripped each other of their clothes. They pause, connecting once again with each other's naked body. She strokes the tiny scar upon his chest; he caresses her hard nipples, and brings his lips down to kiss them, pausing in between to speak.

'Did you miss me last week?' he asks, with such feeling it almost stings her. *Yes, yes, yes*, she chants inside her head. Yet she resists the temptation to let him know.

'Why did you stay away for so long?' she counters, finding it hard to conceal the hurt in her voice.

'I was there all the time, Valentina,' he says in a low voice, and she looks at him intently. Yes, of course he was. Yet her thoughts are fading away as her body takes over. She wants to give Theo so much pleasure that he will never abandon her again. She has never felt such an intense physical union with any other man. She feels as if she will never have her fill of him. She begins to crawl down his body, kissing his arms, his chest and nipples, his legs, slowly approaching his penis. She pushes him inside her mouth, and it feels so good to taste him again. Theo is touching her, but he spins her around now and she knows what he wants to do. She stiffens for a second. Will she let him? She let Rosa and Celia kiss her there. Why not a man . . . why not her lover, Theo?

'Will I?' he whispers. She pulls back from his penis, hesitates before speaking.

'Okay.'

She tries to concentrate on adoring Theo's penis, licking him, caressing him with her tongue, pleasuring him all the way to the edge, and yet at the same time she feels herself slowly losing control. His tongue is flicking inside her, making the tension of her passion fade, until she feels it transform into a river of want flowing into him. She is letting their essence unite.

And now she imagines they are not just on any bed in a hotel in Venice, but on their marriage bed. They are making love as if for the first time, the scent of wild roses mingling with the pure tang of their arousal. This day she is free, for the moment Theo said *I do*, her fear disappeared, and the knot of their love tightened around her heart. She imagines a glittering day in Venice, sunlight streaming through the open window, holding up her hand, and a gold band upon her finger, shining with promise.

They are falling, cascading together, as tender on each

other's naked bodies as soft rain on a summer's day. She is stunned by the release she feels. She has never felt this way before. *I love you*. The words are so crystal clear inside her head she is not sure whether she has actually spoken them out loud. Yet her lover is silent, caressing her, holding her within his arms, unaware of her silent declaration.

Gradually they untwine from each other's bodies and sit back against the bedstead. Theo puts his arm around her shoulders. She would like to stay like this forever, in the comfort of stillness after such passion, listening to the sounds of Venice: the clatter of footsteps outside and the voices of Italians and tourists all mixed up, the lap of the canal, and the odd motorboat buzzing past, a clock striking two, and the ghosts of past lovers whispering through the windowpanes. Yet Theo stirs, breaking through the surface of their silence.

'Have you considered my question, Valentina?'

'What question?' she asks lightly, stroking his bare shoulders and inhaling his longed-for scent.

He drops his arm from around her shoulders and turns to her, looking at her earnestly.

'The one I asked you ten days ago, when I had to go away.'

She shakes her head, trying to look as if she has forgotten, as if it's not important now.

'I want you to be my girlfriend,' Theo says, stroking her hair. 'Can you trust me now? Do you think you can love me?'

Again inside her heart she hears a tiny voice, *oh yes, yes, yes*. A voice long silenced, put out in the cold when she was young and forgotten about. She wants to let it speak. Only this morning she decided she would tell him she loved him. While they were making love, the words sang out within her body. Yet now Valentina cannot bring this voice past the lump in her throat. She cannot open her lips and give Theo what he wants. To hear her say it.

'Valentina,' says Theo, giving her a blinding look, 'I love you. From the moment I saw you on the metro, I have loved you . . .'

She sits back against the pillows as if he has hit her, forcing him to drop his hand from her hair.

'No, it's not possible. Don't say that,' she whispers hoarsely, trying to fight back the tears.

'I love you,' he repeats, transfixing her with the passion of his gaze. 'I know you don't think you are worth it, but you are. Can't you see what all this is about?'

She shakes her head, unable to speak.

'The night I met you, I fell in love with you because you are such a free spirit. Finally I had met someone who didn't want to possess me, or control me. You let me be free, Valentina. And I loved you for it.'

She looks at him in awe, beginning to comprehend.

'Do you remember how it was? When we used to play games with each other, meet up in hotels, make love? It was erotic, so thrilling, it heated my love.'

'Of course,' she whispers hoarsely. 'But you can't do things like that for ever. It's not normal.'

'Why not? Who says that fifteen years from now, we couldn't be doing exactly the same thing? Playing our game of secret lovers?'

He sighs.

'I fell in love with that Valentina. Free spirited yet shy; liberated yet elegant; passionate yet never cheap. I never wanted her to change.'

She looks at him questioningly.

'But you did, honey. As soon as I moved in with you, you shut yourself away from me. You suppressed that girl. Why?'

His words pierce her heart, and she looks up at him, her eyes loaded with unspilt tears.

'I don't want to become my mother.' Her voice cracks.

'I don't know what you mean, but then why would I?' He sounds bitter all of a sudden. 'You have refused to tell me anything about her. Everything I know about your mother is from a conversation I had with Mattia.' His voice softens. 'I hear she is a difficult woman.'

'Very,' Valentina says tightly. 'I think she drove my father away. She was so obsessed with her freedom, with never being tied down. She treated her lovers very badly.' She pauses, taking a breath. 'I asked you to move in with me because I was afraid I was going to turn into her.'

'Not because you wanted me to move in?'

She shakes her head dolefully.

'Not then, no. But now I do want to live with you.' She

turns to look at him, hoping he can see the truth of her statement in her expression.

'What's changed?' he asks her.

'This week. Before you went away, I thought I had to suppress who I really was to make it work. It was driving me crazy. Deep down I knew I was like my mother really. And it made me angry not to be able to be myself.'

Theo picks up her hand and holds it in his.

'That's all I have wanted, for you to be yourself. But you wouldn't talk to me, tell me what was wrong.'

She twists round to look at him, plants a kiss upon his shoulder.

'I'm sorry. I promise I'll try harder.'

Theo smiles at her sadly.

'I want it to be effortless for you. I want you to understand that my love is unconditional. That is what the erotic album meant, Valentina. Those pictures were taken by your great-grandmother's lover, and even back then you can see how that man worships her free spirit. I wanted to show you that you are like her, and there is no shame in that.'

'Is that why you were in the club; is that why all those things happened there?'

'Yes,' he says. 'Leonardo is an old friend of mine. I asked him to help me.'

She raises her eyebrows at him. She can hardly believe what he is saying.

'And you didn't mind that we had sex?' she asks him

incredulously. 'Or that I slept with those two women, Rosa and Celia, or that I was Leonardo's submissive? You didn't mind what I did in the Dark Room?'

'No,' he says. 'In fact I was there most of the time, watching.' He takes a deep breath. 'It was very erotic, Valentina, watching you open yourself up, really seeing your pure heart, your liberated spirit . . .'

'But I didn't do things just in Leonardo's club.' She ploughs on. She has to tell him everything now, make him see how bad she is. 'He came to the apartment and we had sex there,' she says brutally.

'Yes, I know,' he says calmly. 'I was there that night too.'

So that was who she heard banging around the apartment. There was no intruder.

'Remember I had sex with Celia, right in front of you,' he continues. 'How did that make you feel?'

She thinks back to the memory of her and Theo in bed with Celia and Leonardo.

'It was strange,' she says slowly. 'It made me feel so close to you.'

He smiles at her triumphantly.

'So you see, Valentina, there are no hard and fast rules. You are a free spirit and I love you for it. I don't want you to change.'

She looks at him in awe.

'You are such a strange man,' she says. 'I can't believe you are real.'

'For us to work,' he continues, 'I need to know you trust me. We have to be completely open with each other. But if you cannot . . .'

He trails off and looks away from her. She stares at the back of his head in surprise. What kind of man is this? The type who shows her so much of his heart? Who risks all?

The silence hangs between them, heavy and loaded. She knows he is waiting for her to say those words. She wants to say them. She does love him, and yet she can't speak. It hurts her so much to let go of her old ways. They make her feel safe. She is happy to make love to Theo for the rest of her life, but she can't tell him she loves him. She wants to stay outside the Dark Room of love, because to her love is dark. It is full of the danger of being hurt, rejected, humiliated, exposed and weak.

She hears him sigh, and it almost kills her. She is hurting him, yet she can't say those words to reassure him. He gets out of bed, and she looks at his naked back as he walks over to the chair and picks up his jeans, pulls them on.

'I can't do this any more,' he says finally, turning around as he buttons his shirt and searching her face desperately for the answer he wants.

'But Theo, we can go back to how things were before you moved in. We can be secret lovers again, can't we?'

'It's not just about sex for me, Valentina,' Theo says, pulling on his jacket.

'Please come back to bed.' She gives him her little half-smile, trying to lighten the mood. If she can just make love to him again, and afterwards tell him she loves him . . .

'No,' Theo says emphatically. 'I want us to have something more.'

He buckles his belt roughly, and she thinks he is angry. Finally she has made Theo mad.

'That is what all this week was about, for God's sake!' he says with exasperation. 'I wanted to show you that I know who you are. All your fears. All your fantasies. I wanted you to know that you are the bravest girl I know and yet you are afraid of the one thing in life that brings the greatest joy. Love.'

'And the greatest pain,' Valentina adds darkly.

Theo looks at her sadly. He walks over to the bed and traces her face with his finger.

'I know,' he says wearily. 'You have always said this. And yet I hoped with me it would be different.'

He takes his hand away, and the magic of his touch still taunts her. He walks towards the door.

'I'm sorry, Valentina, but this is it.'

'Theo, come on, wait . . . don't be so dramatic . . .'

But her words are inadequate.

'It's over,' he says.

She knows she should run to him, tell him her true feelings, and yet instead of doing this, anger flashes through her.

'Go on then, leave.' Her voice sounds unnaturally hard. It shocks her.

He turns and looks at her with such pity, it makes her squirm on the bed, yet still she doesn't back down. She glares back at him hotly. What does she care? He is just like her mother, making demands of her. How dare he? Yet deep down she knows she is being a fool, she needs to stop him. She takes a breath, tries to calm down. She closes her eyes and concentrates. She clutches at the words. They are so close to being spoken. She can say it. *She can*.

'Theo . . . I . . .' she begins, but when she opens her eyes, he is gone. He has left her in mid-sentence.

She sits on the bed, stunned. Surely he will come back? Yet the minutes tick by, and Theo doesn't return. He *will* come back. Of course he will. This is another stupid game.

She circles the room, clutching her hands, anxiety prickling her heart. She picks up the black album and begins to flick through it again to distract herself. She remembers his expression of disappointment when he asked her what she thought of it.

She looks again at the images of Belle Louise Brzezinska, her body language and how she expresses herself to the anonymous photographer, her lover. It occurs to her that she has misunderstood her great-grandmother's gestures. Yes, her body is charged with desire, but it is not just for sex. It is for love. And as Valentina leafs through the book, she realises that it is not just a book of erotic photography, it is a book of love and how it should be. Of how the giving and receiving of sensual pleasure tightens the knot of love, not loosens it. Now she understands what Theo is trying to tell her. The most intense form of eroticism is the eroticism of love. He wants her to have it all.

As he kept saying, he is not trying to trap her; he is trying to set her free.

I love you.

She whispers the words in the empty gloom of the hotel bedroom in Venice. But it is too late. Theo has not heard them, and she knows that he has walked away for good. He gave her enough chances. She has lost him because she cannot tell him she loves him, and he wants nothing less. She has to let him go.

Valentina slips on her silk camisole and French knickers, and opens the blinds. She looks down at the green canal, as murky as her mixed emotions. She feels terrible. She wants to lie down on the tiled floor of the room and let the world go on without her.

She wanders back into the bedroom and picks up the old photograph album again. She prays for guidance as she flicks through the pages, her grief blurring her vision so that the images become a mess of black and white. And in the dark silence of her heartache, she begins to rip the back cover. She wants to destroy this book, and all that it represents. Yet as she tears away at the black paper, she sees writing underneath, faint pencilled calligraphy. It must have been written by her great-grandmother.

All my life I have lived for this summit of bliss, when I tell the love of my life that I love him.

The realisation hits her like a punch to the stomach.

Valentina catches her breath, hugs herself in pain. Theo is the love of her life. She knows that now. She turns to the mirror and looks at her reflection. In her eyes she sees another woman, and her power speaks to her. The image flickers for just one second, like a projection from a magic lantern. Valentina is Louise, and Louise is her. What would her ancestor do?

She knows, of course. She would not give up. She would get Theo back.

As Venice casts its magic all around her, Louise Brzezinska takes Valentina by the hand and spins her.

Wake up, Valentina, wake up.

Faster and faster she spins her as her hurt, her sorrow, her anger and fear fly out of her. Away and across the cerulean lagoon like a big black bird.

And so Valentina's great-grandmother takes her out of the Dark Room of her past, towards hope. And beyond that to love.

$\mathcal{A}$cknowledgements

Thank you to Vicki Satlow for bringing me into the world of Valentina and taking such a massive leap of faith with me. Thank you to Marianne Gunn O'Connor for her belief, trust and vision, and to both Vicki and Marianne for their unerring dedication and work as agents *and* inspiring women.

Thank you to Antonio Crepas and his family for entrusting me with Valentina, and honouring me with the opportunity of bringing Guido Crepax's iconic character alive within the pages of this book.

Thank you to my editor, Leah Woodburn, whose inspired and insightful work has brought this book alive. Thank you also to Veronique Norton, Lynsey Sutherland, Kim Hardie, Emily Kitchin and to all the team at Headline, particularly Imogen Taylor. Thank you to Emma Herdman at Waterstones for her enthusiasm.

Thank you to those in Milan who made my time there so welcoming and helped me with research: Angela, Agata and

Roberto, Giancarlo, Daniela, and Giulio. Thank you to Carol and Michel for helping me with my Polish research, to Monica for her support and to Kate for her valuable feedback, as always.

Thank you to my friends in Bergen who have supported me so well: Nina, Ila, Tracey, Hege, Anne, Synnøve, Louise, Ane, Elisa and Charlotte.

Thank you to my brother Fintan and his wife Eimear, and to all my friends and family in Ireland, England and all over the world.

And my biggest thanks go to my darlings: Barry, Corey and Helena, with all my love.

Have you been seduced by Valentina?
Her story continues in the second addictive book
in the Valentina series,

Valentina on the Edge

Coming soon from Headline

Meet the original Valentina . . .

The character of Valentina in Evie Blake's novel is inspired by the iconic character created in the '60s by the celebrated Italian illustrator, and master of the comic art form, GUIDO CREPAX (1933–2003).

Crepax's *Valentina* graphic novels became noted for their psychedelic, dreamlike storylines which involved a strong dose of eroticism. Travelling round Europe on her photography projects, Valentina would live out exciting and often glamorous, dangerous and erotic situations among the artistic elite of the '60s.

Edgy, sophisticated, independent and always in the right place at the right time, Valentina fast became a symbol of a free-spirited era, and has remained a cult figure in Crepax's native Italy and among art aficionados the world over.